Praise for *The Space Be...*

"*The Space Between Sisters* explores the complex relationship between sisters, their differences, their mirrored histories, their love and support of one another. This triumphant story had me reading until the wee hours of the morning."

—Debbie Macomber, #1 *New York Times* bestselling author

"The perfect book to bring on summer vacation, this stay-up-all-night novel . . . is one that readers will love. With well-developed characters who captivate and a deeply emotional subplot . . . this novel is one to add to your collection for keeps."

—*RT Book Reviews* (4 ½ Stars)

Praise for the Works of Mary McNear

"A great, emotional read for every woman who must face the past before moving forward."

—Sherryl Woods, #1 *New York Times* bestselling author

"Butternut Lake is so beautifully rendered, you'll wish it was real."

—Susan Wiggs, #1 *New York Times* bestselling author

"A delicious setting and a heroine to cheer for . . . my favorite kind of book."

—Susan Elizabeth Phillips, *New York Times* bestselling author

"This charming debut should attract fans of Susan Wiggs and Luanne Rice."

—*Booklist*

"Well-written with realistic characters . . . this novel is one that you will find yourself wanting to finish in one sitting. . . . Readers who enjoy this story will rejoice at the thought of more novels in the future set in this charming little town."

—*San Francisco Book Review*

Praise for *Moonlight on Butternut Lake*

"McNear skillfully shows the strength and encouragement a woman needs to draw upon in order to leave her abuser. . . . This solid story will find an audience among readers who enjoy novels involving social issues."

—*Library Journal*

"*Moonlight on Butternut Lake* by Mary McNear is the next entry in the bestselling and emotionally rich Butternut Lake series, and it's a nuanced story of healing and second chances. . . . Suffused with all the magic of firefly-lit summer nights. . . . "

—*BookPage*

"Mary McNear has been on my author radar since the very first book in this series. She knows how to engage the reader right from the very first page and gets you right into the characters' lives. She makes them seem like they are your old friends. . . . "

—Susan Dyer, Fresh Fiction

"I know that not everyone can find their way to Minnesota to a cabin on the lake, however, opening up this book can be the next best thing."

—Book Journey

"[A]n exceptional and highly recommended addition to personal reading lists. . . . "

—*Midwest Book Review*

Praise for *Up at Butternut Lake*

"The first in a homey, feel-good series, McNear's small-town tale offers lakeside views and likable characters. . . . McNear has admirably crafted people worth following."

—*Kirkus Reviews*

"[A] heartwarming love story."

—*Woman'sDay*, Best Book Club Pick

"*Up at Butternut Lake* is charming and uplifting. . . . Readers will likely cherish and appreciate this romantic and refreshing debut."

—*RT Book Reviews* (4 Stars)

"McNear's charmingly light *Up at Butternut Lake* gives voice to this enduring Midwestern fantasy in easy-to-swallow prose. It would have been simple for McNear to tie up every plot line with a neat bow, but her writing proves more complex than mere vacation fluff. Still, if you're packing your lakeside tote and hefting the canoe to the top of your vehicle, you might want to take along *Up at Butternut Lake*. The North Woods won't be the same without some heartfelt reading to go along with the smell of a campfire and toasting marshmallows."

—*Star Tribune* (Minneapolis)

The Space Between Sisters

By Mary McNear

The Space Between Sisters
Moonlight on Butternut Lake
Butternut Summer
Up at Butternut Lake
Butternut Lake: The Night Before Christmas (novella)

The Space Between Sisters

A Butternut Lake Novel

Mary McNear

WILLIAM MORROW
An Imprint of HarperCollins*Publishers*

P.S.™ is a trademark of HarperCollins Publishers.

THE SPACE BETWEEN SISTERS. Copyright © 2016 by Mary McNear. All rights reserved. Printed in the United States of America. No part of this book may be used or reproduced in any manner whatsoever without written permission except in the case of brief quotations embodied in critical articles and reviews. For information address HarperCollins Publishers, 195 Broadway, New York, NY 10007.

HarperCollins books may be purchased for educational, business, or sales promotional use. For information please e-mail the Special Markets Department at SPsales@harpercollins.com.

FIRST EDITION

Designed by Diahann Sturge

Library of Congress Cataloging-in-Publication Data has been applied for.

ISBN 978-0-06-239935-9

16 17 18 19 20 OV/RRD 10 9 8 7 6 5 4 3 2 1

For Susie, Alex, and Amanda.
Sisters extraordinaire.

CHAPTER 1

When they turned onto Butternut Lake Drive that night, Poppy rolled down her window. She watched as the car's headlights glided over birch, pine, and spruce trees, and, after a bend in the road, she saw a deer standing, motionless and alert, in a clearing. Soon after that, a little cloud of white moths fluttered across the windshield. She could smell, too, something she could never quite define—some mixture of the air, the trees, and the lake. *Butternut Lake. This place is beautiful, even in the dark,* she thought. She hadn't been up here for almost thirteen years, but she still felt as though she knew it by heart.

"What did you say your sister's name is?" Everett asked, fiddling with the radio.

"Win. Her name is Win," she said. She twisted around in the front passenger seat and reached into the backseat where her cat, Sasquatch, was riding in his pet carrier. She unlatched the door of the carrier and slipped a hand inside. "Poor thing," she said, softly, stroking his fur. "You've been cooped up for too long."

"Win?" Everett repeated, glancing over at her. "That's an unusual name."

"Short for Winona," Poppy explained, feeling the gentle vibration of Sasquatch's purr for a moment before easing her hand out of the carrier and latching the door shut again.

"Isn't there supposed to be a lake somewhere?" Everett asked, taking the car into a steep turn. "Or is 'Butternut Lake Drive' a misnomer?"

"No, there *is* a lake, through those trees," Poppy said, pointing to their left. "But you can't see it. There's no moon tonight."

"No kidding," Everett said. "The only thing that's missing is the fog."

"The fog?"

Everett nodded, steering into another turn. "If there were fog, it'd be exactly like a scene out of a horror movie. You know the one. A college coed and her boyfriend are driving down a desolate country road at night, and the fog is closing in around them, and then, suddenly, somebody appears on the road, right in front of their car, and—"

"Okay, that's enough," Poppy said. "We are *not* in that movie. I'm not a college coed—and that phrase, by the way, is totally outdated—" *And you're not my boyfriend,* she almost said. "Besides, this is not a desolate country road," she continued. "Trust me. Butternut Lake is a very well populated summer community. There are *tons* of cabins in these woods."

"I'll take your word for it. Four and a half hours ago, I didn't even know Butternut Lake existed."

"Well, now you know," Poppy said flippantly. And then she felt guilty. She hadn't been very good company on this drive. Everett, after all, was doing her a favor. "I haven't been much of a tour guide, have I?" she asked him now.

"It's fine." He shrugged.

"The town of Butternut, Minnesota, which we drove through

ten minutes ago," she began, in her best imitation of a tour guide's voice, "has a population of twelve hundred. It has numerous local businesses, including Pearl's, a world-class coffee shop, Johnson's Hardware, where my grandfather indulged his inner carpenter, and the Butternut Variety Store, where my sister and I once accumulated the largest collection of glass animals east of the Mississippi. Butternut Lake, approximately twelve miles in length, is one of the deepest, cleanest lakes in Minnesota and is a popular vacation destination for people from the Twin Cities, who come here to fish, canoe, kayak, water ski, and, sometimes, just to wiggle their toes in the water. Any questions?" she asked brightly.

"Yeah," Everett asked, gesturing at a seemingly deserted stretch of road. "Where are all those tourists now?"

"They're here. Look, there's a driveway," Poppy said. "And there's a cabin at the end of it, too. You can see its lights through the trees."

"All right," Everett said. "But if my car breaks down, I'm not knocking on that door. I've seen that movie, too. We spend the night there, and when we wake up in the morning, we discover that our kidneys have been harvested."

"Ugh," Poppy said, wincing. "I had no idea you were so dark, Everett."

"No?" he said, with a trace of a smile. "It's amazing how much you can learn about someone on a two-hundred-and-forty-mile drive."

"That's true," Poppy mused. "So, what have you learned about me?" she asked. She wasn't being flirtatious. She was just curious.

"I've learned . . ." He looked over at her, speculatively. "I've learned that you think corn nuts are revolting."

"That's because they *are* revolting."

"Corn nuts," Everett said, concentrating on another turn, "are the ultimate road trip food."

"Not even close," Poppy said. "Because that would obviously be Red Vines."

"Yeah, I don't think so," Everett said. "I mean, they have, like, zero nutritional value, unless you count whatever's in the red dye, and—"

"Oh, my God, look," Poppy said, excitedly, of the driveway they were passing. Beside it a large sign with a wintery pinecone painted on it spelled out WHITE PINES.

"What's that?" Everett asked.

"It's a resort, and it means that we are now exactly three miles away from my grandparents' cabin. I mean, my *sister's* cabin," she amended, feeling that familiar jab of resentment she felt whenever she was reminded of the fact that this beloved piece of family real estate had been passed down to Win, and only Win, three years ago. This resentment was part of the reason that Poppy had avoided coming to Butternut Lake since Win had moved here year-round a couple of years ago. But if there was any comfort to be found in Win being the one to own the cabin, it was in knowing that she would never sell it; it meant as much to her as it did to Poppy.

Poppy and Win had spent all of their childhood summers here until Poppy was sixteen and Win was fifteen (they were thirteen months apart), and Poppy, who was just shy of thirty, could still remember every detail of the cabin. It stood on a small bluff, just above Butternut Lake, and its dark brown clapboard exterior was brightened by cheerful window boxes that overflowed with geraniums. And the homey touches continued inside: colorful rag rugs, knotted pine furniture, red-checked slipcovers on sofas and chairs. The living room, everyone's favorite room, was as comfortable as an old shoe, with its fieldstone fireplace, and its old record player and collection of albums (some of which dated back to the 1950s). In one corner, there was a slightly wobbly card table for playing gin rummy, and on the shelf next to the table, a collection of hand-painted duck decoys. Mounted on the wall above the mantelpiece was the prized three-foot walleyed pike that had *not* gotten away from their grandfather. The living room windows looked out on a flagstone patio, their grandmother's begonia garden, and a slope of mossy lawn leading down to the lake. And the kitchen . . . Poppy remembered it as though it existed in a perpetual summer morning: the lemon yellow cupboards, the row of shiny copper pans hanging on the wall, and the turquoise gas stove, a monument to 1950s chic.

"Do you think you should give your sister a call now?" Everett asked, interrupting her reverie.

"Why?"

"To tell her that we're almost there."

"Oh," Poppy said, momentarily at a loss. And then she tossed her long blond hair. "No. I'm not going to tell her," she said. "I thought we'd surprise her."

Everett stole a quick look at her. "But . . . she knows we're coming, right?"

"Not exactly," Poppy said, feeling a first twinge of nervousness.

Everett was quiet. Then he asked, "Does your sister like surprises?"

"Not really," Poppy said, and there it was again, that nervousness. She tamped it down, firmly, and said, "But what are sisters for if they can't just . . . drop in on each other?"

" 'Drop in'?" Everett said, after another pause. "It looks like

you've got a lot of your stuff with you, though, Poppy. Isn't it more
like, 'move in'?"

Poppy ignored this question. *Harder* to ignore were her suitcases, wedged in the trunk of Everett's car, or her boxes, stacked
on the backseat beside Sasquatch's pet carrier. And it wasn't just
a lot of her stuff, as Everett had pointed out. It was *all* of her stuff.
Though, truth be told, that wasn't saying much. It had taken her
less than an hour to pack everything up. Traveling light was a
recurring theme with Poppy, and a necessary one, too, since her
peripatetic lifestyle was the norm.

"Sisters don't have to call ahead. They're there for each other,"
Poppy said now, though she was annoyed by the defensiveness
she heard in her own voice.

"But do you think *your* sister—Win—will be home right now?
It's ten o'clock on a Saturday night."

"Oh, she'll be home. If I know her, she's probably . . . alpha-
betizing her spice rack," Poppy said, "or color coding her sock
drawer." As soon as she said this, though, she felt disloyal. "Actually, she's a sweetheart," she said, turning to Everett. "And I don't
blame her, at all, for being a little . . . neurotic or controlling, or
whatever she is. I told you about what happened to her, didn't I?"
And Poppy pictured Win as she'd been the last time she'd seen
her, her dark blond hair pulled back in a ponytail and her girl
next door approachableness only slightly tempered by the wistful
expression on her face.

"Yeah, you told me what happened to her," Everett said. It was
quiet in the car again as he negotiated another sharp turn, and
as Poppy watched the car's lights skim over an entrance to an old
logging road. She smiled. She and Win had driven down that
road as teenagers, looking for bears at dusk.

"All right," she said, after a few more minutes, "we're getting close. After this next curve, it's the first driveway on the left." And, suddenly hungry, she added, "Here's hoping Win's got some leftovers from dinner."

"Yeah, and here's hoping she's in a good mood," Everett added wryly.

CHAPTER 2

Win, it turned out, *was* in a good mood, or at least in what passed for a good mood in her life these days. After dinner—a sesame shrimp and noodles dish whose recipe she'd found in a cooking magazine's "gourmet dinners for one" column—she'd emptied out her kitchen's utensil drawers and begun rearranging their contents. Not that they *needed* rearranging; they'd been rearranged less than two weeks before. But Win found this particular organizing project so satisfying that tonight, after she'd washed the dishes and wiped down the countertops and swept the kitchen floor, she'd thought, *Oh, what the hell,* and dumped all four utensil drawers out onto the kitchen table and gotten started on them. Now, an hour later, with just one utensil—a cherry pitter—left, she was still so absorbed in this project that she didn't even hear a car pull up outside.

Where to put the cherry pitter, she wondered, picking it up and studying it critically. For the most part, she had a simple classification system. The more a utensil was used, the higher a drawer it went into. So a whisk, or a vegetable peeler, or a garlic press, for instance, went into the top drawer, while a fish scaler, or a canning funnel, or an olive stuffer went into the bottom drawer. Utensils that fell somewhere in between went into one of the two middle drawers. But the cherry pitter was a special case. Before tonight, it had been in the third drawer, with, among other things, a citrus zester, a nutmeg grinder, and a gravy separator, but now, with cherry season upon them, Win wondered if it should be promoted, at least temporarily, to the second drawer, where it would take its place alongside utensils like a cheese grater, a marinade brush, and a ladle.

Yes, it should go in the second drawer, Win decided, but she hesitated for a moment and, in that moment, she heard car doors slamming outside. Startled, she glanced at the kitchen clock. It was a little after ten. The only person she knew who'd stop by at this hour was her friend Mary Jane, and even Mary Jane wouldn't do this without calling her first. She knew how much Win hated surprises.

She put the cherry pitter down and left the kitchen, feeling the little tremor of unease she imagined was familiar to any woman who lived alone in a rural area. But by the time she got to the front door, she could hear laughter and voices, and one of those voices was as intimately familiar to her as any voice on earth.

"Poppy?" she said, swinging the door open before her sister could knock on it.

"Win!" her sister said, pulling her into a hug. "I told you she'd be home," she said, looking over her shoulder at the man who was with her. Win hugged Poppy back, a little distractedly.

"I can't believe you're here. Is everything okay?" she asked.

"Yes, everything's okay," Poppy said, letting go of her. "Well, I mean, it's not *perfect*. More about that later," she said, with a roll of her eyes. "But I thought it was high time I visited you here. You've only asked me to come about a million times."

"I know I have," Win said. *But a little advance notice would have been nice,* she thought.

"Um, are you going to invite us in, or are we going to stand out here all night?" Poppy asked, cocking an eyebrow.

"Oh, of course, come in," Win said, gesturing them inside, but she was still flustered. "When did you decide to drive up?" she asked, closing the door and following them into the living room.

"Oh, it was spur of the moment," Poppy said.

"But, Pops, I talked to you a couple days ago," Win pointed out.

"It was spur of the moment *since then,*" Poppy said. She stretched her arms over her head and arched her back. "It is *so* good to be out of that car." She sighed. "We only stopped once. I think we set a record or something. Everett is an excellent driver," she added, glancing at her companion.

"Are you going to introduce us?" Win asked.

"Oh, my God," Poppy said, slapping her forehead. "I am *so* rude. Everett, this is my sister, Win Robbins, and Win, this is Everett, Everett . . ." Her voice trailed off.

"Everett West," he finished for her, stepping forward and holding his hand out to Win.

"Hi Everett," she said, shaking his hand and giving Poppy a look that she hoped said, *Who is this guy?* But no explanation was forthcoming.

Instead Poppy was taking in the living room as though she was seeing it for the first time.

"Look at this place," she said softly. "It's *exactly* the same as I remember it." She walked over to a bookshelf and took down a duck decoy, turning it over in her hands. "I'm so glad you didn't change anything."

"Well, you know me, I'm not great with change," Win said,

shooting a glance at Everett. "Um, Poppy, can I see you in the kitchen?" she asked, pointedly.

"Okay. We'll be right back, Everett," Poppy said, following Win through the kitchen's swinging door.

But as soon as it shut behind them Win turned to her. "Pops, what's going on?"

"Nothing," she said, mystified.

"I mean, who's the guy?"

"That's Everett. Everett West."

Win rolled her eyes. "No, I mean, are you dating him?"

"What? *No*," Poppy said. "He's a friend. Well, an *acquaintance*, anyway. We both get our coffee at the same place every morning. You know, that little hole in the wall near my apartment? I took you there when you came to visit at Christmas."

"So, you hang out together there?" Win said, still trying to clarify their relationship.

"Not *hang out*, exactly, but we've stood in line together a couple of times."

Win's eyes widened. "And that's the extent of your relationship?"

"More or less."

"And other than his first name, and where he gets his coffee, do you know anything else about him?"

"Well, those things and . . . oh, *and* he's a techie," Poppy said, proud to have remembered this much about him.

But Win shook her head in disbelief. "Poppy, am I the only one seeing a problem here? You drive up with someone you barely know, and then you invite him into my cabin. I mean, for all you know, he's a serial killer," she hissed.

"Oh, for God's sakes," Poppy said, "Everett is *not* a serial killer.

He's a *web designer*. And trust me, I have excellent radar when it comes to men. He is *not* dangerous. I would think even *you* could see that, Win."

And Win, irritated by the implication of Poppy's "even you," had to admit, to herself anyway, that Everett didn't seem very dangerous. He reminded her, in fact, of a type that was popular now on television and in movies; the smart but accessible guy who worked in the lab on a police procedural, or the soft-spoken but humorous sidekick to the male lead in a romantic comedy. *Geeky-cute,* she decided. And there was something about his eyes, too, that was appealing, the way they drooped down, just a tiny bit, at the corners, making him look just a little bit sleepy.

"Is he tired?" Win asked suddenly, glancing in the direction of the living room. "Everett, I mean. Is he tired from the drive? Or do his eyes always look like that?"

"Like what?" Poppy asked, perplexed at the direction the conversation had taken.

"You know, his eyes look kind of sleepy."

Poppy shook her head. "I don't know what you're talking about. I've never noticed his eyes before. But I'm assuming this means it's okay for him to be here now."

"It's okay," Win said.

"And it's okay for me to stay here?" Poppy asked.

"*Yes*. You're always welcome here, you know that," Win said, but this was followed by an awkward pause. Win knew without having to be told that Poppy believed the cabin should belong to both of them. "But what's, uh, what's Everett going to do to-night?" she asked, returning to the matter at hand.

"Oh," Poppy said, her blue eyes widening with surprise. "I don't know. I hadn't really thought about it. Drive back to the city, I guess."

"At this time of night? He won't get back until . . . two o'clock in the morning."

"Maybe he can get a motel room," Poppy suggested.

"Are you going to pay for it?"

"No. He's a big boy. He can pay for it himself."

"Poppy, that's not the point," Win said, shaking her head.

"What is the point?"

"The point is that he drove four and a half hours to get you here," Win said, with forced patience. "You can't just say 'good night' and push him out the door."

Now it was Poppy's turn to look incredulous. "Win, two minutes ago you were afraid he was a serial killer, and now you're worried I'll hurt his feelings? And, just for the record, he didn't do me *that* much of a favor. When I bumped into him this morning at that coffeehouse, and I asked him if he could drive me up here today, he said yes right away. He said he loved coming to this part of the state. You know, the north woods and all."

"Oh, that must be it, Poppy. He's here for the flora and fauna," Win said, amused in spite of herself. "He couldn't possibly be interested in a gorgeous girl like you." But Poppy—whose official position on her beauty was to refuse to acknowledge it—shrugged this off.

"Besides," she said to Win, "his cousin has a cabin an hour north of here, on Birch Lake. Starting next week, Everett's going to be able to use it. He wants to get into the habit of doing this drive."

"All right. Whatever," Win said, shifting gears. "Why don't you two bring your stuff in from the car? You can have our old room," she said, of the guest room she and Poppy had shared during summer vacations as children, "and Everett can have the couch, if he doesn't mind."

"He doesn't mind," Poppy said, confidently.

"Good," Win said, warming now to the idea of having guests. "We can all have a late breakfast together tomorrow morning— I'll make French toast—and after that, you'll have time for a swim before you head back to the city. Unless you want to leave *really* early Monday morning to get back in time for work."

"Yeah, about that . . ." Poppy said. "Um, I've been meaning to talk to you about the whole work thing."

Win frowned. She didn't like the way that sounded. "What happened to your job, Pops?"

"What happened to it is that I don't have it anymore."

"You were . . . fired?"

"No," Poppy said, offended. "I quit."

"Pops," Win groaned. "Why?"

"Because it was *so* unbelievably boring. I mean, have you ever been a receptionist before?" She pantomimed wearing a head-set. "Hello, Johnson, Lewis, Lester and Grouper, how may I help you? I did that two hundred and fifty times a day. Can you imagine? Plus, one of the partners, Grouper"—she paused here to shudder—"was really starting to creep me out."

Win took a deep breath. *Do not freak out,* she counseled herself. *Stay calm. You can't kill Poppy. Not with someone else in the next room.* She exhaled, slowly. "Just out of curiosity," she asked, "did you find another job before you quit this one?"

To Poppy's credit, she answered this question with admirable directness. "No, I didn't. And there's something else, too."

"What's that?" Win asked, a little weakly.

"I'm subletting my apartment."

"Why?"

"Because I can't afford it, Win. No job, no paycheck. No pay-check, no money for rent. No money for rent, no apartment."

Win rubbed her temples. "No, I see the connection," she said. "But you're not . . . you're not moving in with that guy you told me about, are you?"

"*Patrick?*" Poppy said. "God no. No, he kept telling me he wanted to take our relationship to 'the next level' and I kept thinking, 'Look, I don't know what's on that level, but I am *not* going to go there with you.' So, yeah, he's kind of out of the picture now."

"Okay, but . . ." And Win paused here, not really wanting to know the answer to this next question. "Where are you going to live now?"

"Here?" Poppy asked, hopefully.

"Poppy," Win said, shaking her head. "Do you remember the last time we—"

"Look, I know what you're going to say. And I get it. I do. Before you say it, though, I want to ask you one question. One simple question."

There was more massaging of temples from Win. But Poppy, undiscouraged, pressed on. "What day is today?"

"That's your question?"

"Yes."

"It's Saturday."

"No, what day of the *month* is it."

Win sighed. "It's the twenty-first."

"It's *June* twenty-first," Poppy said, significantly. "Think about it, Win."

"It's . . . the first day of summer?"

"*Yes,*" Poppy said triumphantly. "*Yes, yes, yes.* It's the first day of summer, and here I am. Here *we* are. At the cabin. At *your* cabin," she added, quickly, "but still, the cabin where we spent every summer of our childhoods. Don't you get it, Win?"

"Not really."

"*This is it, Win*. This is our chance to have another summer together, on this lake, at this cabin, for the first time in thirteen years. I mean, I'm between jobs, and you're on vacation, and—"

"I wouldn't call it a *vacation*—" Win interposed. She was a social studies teacher at the middle school in Butternut and she used summer break to plan for the year ahead.

"All right, fine, you're on a *working* vacation. The point is, you're still going to have some free time, and now, you're going to have it with me," Poppy said, giving Win her most charming smile. "It'll be fun. We'll go canoeing, and we'll go on picnics, and we'll go raspberry picking. And skinny-dipping. There's no age limit for that, is there? And that goes for making s'mores, too. Oh, and playing Monopoly. We can do that, and maybe, *maybe*, if you're really nice, I'll even let you have the thimble this time," she said, of the Monopoly game piece they had battled over as children. "And Win, seriously, when was the last time we watched *13 Going on 30*?" she asked of their favorite chick flick.

Win chewed on her lower lip. "I don't know," she said. Because while she and Poppy had had fun together over the years, they'd had other things, too: hurtful words, screaming matches, slamming doors. And the six months they'd shared an apartment during Win's last year of college came to mind now. Poppy had left a trail of wet towels, unwashed dishes, and unpaid bills in her wake—unpaid bills that, in the end, Win had paid for her. And she was always avoiding some lovelorn suitor, and worse, always carrying that godforsaken cat around with her.

"Look, I really need this," Poppy said, with an urgency that surprised Win. "I need a change. I need to figure things out. And, for some reason, I feel like . . . like this is the place I'm supposed to be right now," she said, looking around the kitchen.

"Right here, with you, on Butternut Lake." She smiled at Win, a little tremulously.

"Oh, Pops, then of course you can stay," Win said, with a rush of emotion.

"Yay!" Poppy said, grabbing her and twirling her round. "You won't regret it. I promise."

But as they were spinning around, something caught Poppy's eye, and she stopped, mid-spin, and pointed at the cherry pitter, still sitting on the kitchen table. "Winona Robbins," she said, with mock seriousness, "were you rearranging your kitchen drawers tonight?"

"No," Win lied.

"No? Then where are the cherries?"

Win didn't answer.

Poppy walked nonchalantly over to the kitchen table and picked up the cherry pitter. "So you don't mind if I just put this . . . in here?" she asked, opening the top drawer.

"Go right ahead," Win said, and she couldn't help but smile. No one had ever been able to tease her the way Poppy did.

"Or what about . . . this drawer?" Poppy asked, opening up the bottom drawer. "Can I put it in here?" She dangled it over the drawer.

Win started laughing. She couldn't help it. This was the best thing about Poppy. This was what made everything else about her worth putting up with. She could always be counted on to make Win laugh. Laugh at life, yes, but even more importantly, laugh at herself. And suddenly, it seemed ridiculous to her that this was how she'd spent her night, at home, alone, rearranging her already perfectly arranged kitchen drawers.

"I missed you, Pops," she said, through her laughter.

"I missed you, too," Poppy said, giving Win a hug.

Win hugged her back, hard. "And you're right. We *will* have fun this summer. Stay, Pops. Stay as long as you want." This would be good for Poppy, Win thought, but it would be good for her, too. Because for every night Win made a gourmet dinner for one, there was a night she ate a bowl of cereal leaning against the kitchen counter. And for every night she curled up on the couch after dinner to read an edifying novel, there was a night she ended up on her bed, tearfully perusing old photo albums until she fell asleep, in a soggy heap, on top of the covers.

"We should let Mom and Dad know I'm here," Poppy said, giving Win one final squeeze before she let go of her. "They'll be happy we're together."

"*Oh,* I got a postcard from Dad," Win said. She plucked it out of a basket on the kitchen counter and handed it to Poppy. Their father, who was divorced from their mother, was a part-time carpenter, a part-time musician, and a full-time drinker who spent most of his time ricocheting around the country, going wherever his work or his drinking took him.

"He sent me the same one," Poppy said, studying the postcard. She flipped it over and read it. "Same wording, too." She glanced over at Win. "Where, exactly, is Shelby, Montana?"

Win shrugged. "Do you really think he's found a regular gig playing in a bar there?" she asked Poppy, a little skeptically.

"I think . . ." said Poppy, putting the postcard down. "I think that he's probably got a regular gig sleeping with the woman who owns the bar. And I think she'll probably keep him around until she gets tired of him. Or until he drinks her out of Jack Daniel's."

"One or the other," Win agreed, wishing Poppy wasn't right, but knowing that, in all but the details, she probably was.

"I got a phone call from Mom, though," Poppy said, with artificial brightness. Their mother, like their father, could never be accused of being an overinvolved parent. But unlike their father, she was not a drinker. She was instead, as she'd explained to her daughters many times before, on a lifelong journey of self-realization, a journey that had not often included, when Poppy and Win were growing up, such mundane things as attending their orchestra performances, or school plays, or parent teacher conferences. Now she and her most recent boyfriend were living in a trailer outside Sedona, Arizona, and she was trying to get her new crystal business off the ground. "Apparently, selling dream catcher jars is much more competitive than she realized," Poppy explained. "I guess Sedona's a crowded market."

The two of them shared a look that spoke volumes about their respective relationships with their mother, and then Win remembered something. "Poppy, what about your friend?" she whispered. "We've just left him sitting out there this whole time."

"Oh, Everett hasn't just been sitting out there," Poppy said. "He's been getting his ax out of his trunk so he can . . ." She used her hand to make a hacking motion at her neck.

"Very funny," Win said, and pushing through the kitchen's swinging door she found Everett sitting, ax-less, on the living room couch.

"Hey," he said, standing up. "I hope you don't mind . . ."

"That you sat on my couch? No. I hope you don't mind that you'll be *sleeping* on it tonight," Win said. There was a third bedroom at the cabin, one that their grandfather had turned into a study many years before, but Win knew, from experience, that the fold-out couch in it was almost comically painful to sleep on. Everett would do much better to bed down in the living room for the night. "Really, you're welcome to stay," she said, gesturing at the overstuffed couch. "Unless you decide to drive back, and I think it's a little late for that, don't you?"

"Probably," Everett agreed. "Especially since I don't know these roads that well." He pushed his light brown hair out of his light brown eyes. He looked both shy and sleepy at the same time.

And Win, who soon discovered that Poppy and Everett hadn't had dinner yet, started to make it for them while they unloaded the car. When the grilled cheese sandwiches were browning in the pan and the tomato soup was bubbling in the pot, she stuck her head out the kitchen door to check on their progress. Everett was carrying one of Poppy's suitcases into the cabin, and looking at it, Win cringed reflexively. It was overpacked, bulging at the sides, and something—a bathrobe, she thought—was trailing out of it. Soon, she knew, that bathrobe would be flung, carelessly, over a piece of her furniture, most likely the living room couch. But just then, Win saw what Poppy was carrying into the cabin, and her jaw dropped.

"Poppy, you *didn't* bring him. You know I'm allergic to him," she said, pointing at Sasquatch's pet carrier.

"Of course I bought him," Poppy said, mystified. "What else was I supposed to do with him?"

"Leave him with a friend?"

"Win, I can't leave him with someone else. You know that," Poppy said, looking wounded.

But Win was already heading back into the kitchen, and already convinced her eyes felt itchy.

CHAPTER 3

W in, I don't need this many towels," Poppy protested, as her sister filled her arms with towels from the cabin's linen closet later that night. "*Nobody* needs this many towels."

"You never know," Win said, adding another bath towel, hand towel and washcloth to the stack. She was in full bed-and-breakfast mode now, Poppy saw, and she made a mental note to suggest this career to Win if her teaching job ever fell through.

"Now, what else do you need?" Win asked.

"*Nothing* else. And stop treating me like I'm a guest. I'm your sister, remember?"

"I remember," Win said, giving the towels Poppy was holding a final pat and closing the closet door. "But what about your friend Everett?" she asked, lowering her voice, because they were in the hallway and Everett was no more than ten yards away from them, hunkered down on the living room couch she and Win had just made up for him. "Do you think he needs anything else?"

"You mean other than the thirty-six towels you've already given him?" Poppy asked.

Win nodded.

"No, Win," Poppy whispered. "We've already fed him *and* given him a place to sleep. He's a man. He's not that complicated. He doesn't need anything else."

"All right, well, then what about your feline friend?" Win asked, with what was probably an unconscious wrinkling of her nose.

"Sasquatch? Come see," Poppy said, leading her down the hallway to the open door to the guest room, where the cat in question could be seen lounging, luxuriously, on one of the twin beds. "Sasquatch," Poppy announced, "has got the world by the tail."

"It certainly looks that way," Win said, with a little sigh, and Poppy wondered, for the thousandth time, how her sister could be so immune to Sasquatch's insouciant charm. But, alas, she was. Now, for instance, Win starting clearing her throat, and when Poppy asked her what was wrong she said, "Nothing. It just . . ." She rubbed her neck. "It just feels a little scratchy, that's all."

"Are you going to be okay?" Poppy asked, with what she hoped was the appropriate amount of concern. Privately, she was of the opinion that Win exaggerated her cat allergy.

"I'll be fine," Win said. "I'll just take some Benadryl. But, Poppy . . . does he really have to stay here for the whole summer?"

"*Yes,* Win. He really does," Poppy said, feeling hurt all over again. "And I've already told you, I'll stay on top of his shedding. I mean it. Girl Scout's honor," she added, raising her hand.

"You were never a Girl Scout, Poppy."

"No, but you were. And you totally rocked that green sash with all the badges on it," Poppy said, pulling her down the hallway so that they were standing outside the door to Win's bedroom. "Now go to sleep," she added, giving her sister an affectionate push in the direction of her bed. But as she was doing this, something in Win's room caught her eye.

"Win, you're not still doing this, are you?" she asked, walking over to her sister's dresser. She frowned as she examined the objects arranged on top of it. There was a photograph of Win and Kyle, taken at a Fourth of July parade, a set of ticket stubs from the Minnesota State Fair, and a paper coaster from Kieran's, the little Irish pub down the street from the apartment they'd lived in after they'd gotten married. *So she was still doing this,* Poppy thought. Still arranging these little shrines to her marriage. A marriage that had now been over for longer than it had lasted.

But Win, as if knowing how short it would be, had saved everything from it—every photograph, every postcard, every memento—and put them all in neatly labeled cardboard boxes that Poppy referred to, privately, as "the marriage files." Periodically, Win would take things out of the boxes and arrange them on her dresser top. Sometimes, they would be random things. But most of the time, they would all be part of a larger theme. Like now, for instance, the theme was obviously summer, or more specifically, the last summer Win and Kyle had spent together. And this would have been sweet, too, Poppy thought, fingering the ticket stubs to the state fair, if it wasn't also, at the same time, a little . . . well, *morbid.* She looked at Win now and shook her head.

"*What?* What's wrong with my doing this?" Win asked, defensively. "These are just some memories, that's all."

"There's nothing *wrong* with it," Poppy said. "It's just . . ." She paused, trying to find the right way—the kindest way—to put this into words. "Look, don't get me wrong," she said, finally. "I *loved* Kyle. You know that. And I *loved* the two of you together. And by all means, Win, keep a picture of him out, or a picture of the two of you out. But this stuff"—she indicated the dresser top—"put this stuff away. Otherwise you're going to be like that character in the Dickens novel we had to read in high school. Remember her? What was her name? The woman who used to wear her old wedding dress all the time and—"

"Miss Havisham," Win said, impatiently. "Her name was Miss Havisham. And the novel was *Great Expectations*. And I doubt, very much, that you read the whole thing."

"I *definitely* did not read the whole thing," Poppy said, laughing, and her laughter seemed, miraculously, to break the tension that had been building between them. "But I still remember her character. And I don't want you to be like her."

"I'm not like her," Win insisted. "I just like to keep things. And organize things. And . . . and remember things. Remember *him*. And I know you think that it shouldn't be that hard. That I should be able to just hang a picture of him on the wall and be done with it. But it's not like that. It's more . . . *complicated* than that."

"Even now? I mean, Win, he died three years ago," Poppy said, softly.

"Three years is *not* a long time. Not in the general scheme of things."

Poppy was ready to argue this point, but then she changed her mind. After all, who was she to be giving Win advice? Who was she, in her current position, to be giving *anyone* advice? So she hugged her sister instead and said, "You know what? You're right. Three years isn't a long time. Pay no attention to me. If it weren't for you, I'd be homeless right now. Seriously, I'd be sleeping in a bus shelter in Minneapolis."

Later, back in the bedroom she'd spent so many summers in, Poppy puzzled over its dimensions. Had she gotten bigger or had the room gotten smaller? Neither one, she decided. She hadn't grown so much as a centimeter since she'd last stayed here, and the room, well, the room hadn't shrunk, obviously; not when everything in it—except for Sasquatch, on one of the beds, and her boxes, piled unceremoniously in one of the corners—was exactly the same as it had been before. There was the twin bed and dresser set, made of a honeyed pine with decorative acorns carved into them, there were the blue-and-white-checked curtains and bedspreads and window seat cover, and there was the funny little bedside table lamp, whose iron base was the figure of a bear climbing a tree.

And suddenly, Poppy was seized, for the second time that night, with the sensation of having entered a time capsule of her childhood. She walked over to the bookshelf now, and randomly pulled out a book. Nancy Drew's *The Secret of the Old Clock*. It had belonged to her grandmother when she was a child. Poppy flipped it open, read the first page, and smiled. She put it back, and continued her tour of the room, opening one of the dresser's top drawers—it still smelled vaguely of mothballs—and running her fingers over the robins-egg blue dish on the dresser top; the very one she and Win had used to keep their beaded bracelets in.

Poppy wandered around the room a little more, and when her curiosity had been satisfied, she went and sat down on the window seat, a favorite girlhood haunt of hers, especially on rainy days. Tonight, though, she felt pensive. And not just about her sudden move, but about what she'd said to Win, too, about keeping all of those reminders of Kyle on display. Had she been too hard on her, she wondered now, too judgmental? After all, if Win had saved everything from her marriage, she at least had a place to *put* it all. Poppy, on the other hand, was essentially homeless. And then there was the question of whether the things she'd brought with her—she looked now at the rather pathetic collection of suitcases, boxes, and bags jumbled in the corner—

were even *worth* keeping. She reached over and flipped open
the lid of one of the cardboard boxes and then poked around in
it a little. She found a waffle iron she'd never used before, an old
high school yearbook, and a tennis racket with broken strings.
Perfect, she thought. Perfect because these useless items seemed
somehow to sum up the absurdity that had become her life.
Almost thirty years on this earth, and she was still dependent
on her sister for such useful things as grilled cheese sandwiches,
clean towels, and the toothpaste she'd brushed her teeth with
that night. And those were just the *little* things she'd needed
from her sister. Because more than once in Poppy's life, Win's
love and support had kept her going when it had seemed that
nothing else would.

Now she pulled her knees up under her chin, and wrapped
her arms around her legs. She watched, idly, as a daddy longlegs
navigated the other side of the window screen, and wondered
how Win had gotten so far ahead of her. But it wasn't only Win,
of course, who was ahead of her. It was other people her age, too.
People who had homes, hobbies, vacation plans, cars, careers,
spouses, children . . . *lives*, she realized. *Real* lives. She'd sat
by and watched as all of her friends, and Win, too, had chosen
careers, or found work that they'd liked, and invested energy in
relationships, or marriages, or families. What was *wrong* with
her? Why wasn't she able to be like them? And an image of her at
sixteen came, unbidden, to her mind. She was sitting on the fire
escape of their old apartment building in Minneapolis, crying,
her hair tangled, the strap on her sundress torn. She tried to push
the image away. She wouldn't think about that now, not if she
could possibly help it.

And Sasquatch, as if on cue, chose this moment to leap from
the bed he was lying on onto the window seat, and to bump his

head against her hand in a signal that he wanted to be petted. He had an uncanny ability to sense when she was feeling down— which, lately, seemed to be most of the time. She smiled and stroked him under his chin. "I don't know why I'm complaining, Sasquatch," she said now, "not when I've got you in my life." He blinked, seeming to take this compliment as his due, which of course it was. Since Poppy had adopted him as a neighborhood stray when she was sixteen, he'd been one of the few constants in her life. The one person—because to her he was more person than animal—whom she'd never disappointed, and who had never disappointed her, either.

Now, with Sasquatch purring contentedly, she felt herself begin to relax for the first time that day. She'd read somewhere that people with dogs or cats had lower blood pressure than people without them, and she believed it. She felt a little more of the tension ebb out of her body. She wouldn't think about . . . well, she wouldn't think about a lot of things right now. But she *especially* wouldn't think about the expression on Win's face when she'd told her she would need to stay with her for the summer. Because for one second—one split second—she'd seen what Win was thinking. And what she was thinking was, *Oh, Poppy, not again. Please tell me you haven't screwed up again.*

She petted Sasquatch behind his ears, and noticed, not for the first time, that his fur had turned whitish around his eyes and mouth. He was still a perfectly beautiful cat, though, his fur a lovely shade of gray with white front paws that made him look as if he were wearing boots, and eyes the color of the Caribbean Sea. She didn't know exactly how old he was. The veterinarian she'd taken him to when she'd adopted him had guessed he'd been around two or three years old, which would make him around fifteen or sixteen now. But this—Sasquatch's aging—was *another* thing she wouldn't think about, for the simple reason that the thought of her life without him was, well, *unthinkable.*

Besides, she decided, he would like it here this summer. At first, he might miss their old apartment in Minneapolis. He was an indoor-outdoor cat, and there he'd had a windowsill in the kitchen he'd liked to sun himself on, and a whole backyard in which to while away the afternoons. It would be different here, of course. In the city, the greatest threat to Sasquatch, from the animal kingdom at least, had been an irritable skunk or a mangy raccoon. Here, he was clearly not at the top of the food chain. There were fox, coyotes, timber wolves, and even mountain lions, though the latter, she knew, were rarely sighted.

Still, he could go outside here, as long as she watched him like a hawk. No, she corrected herself. As long as she watched the *hawks* like a hawk, because for them, Sasquatch might be just another meal, and thinking about this, she suppressed a little shudder. In the next moment, though, she scooped him up, and deposited him on the end of one of the twin beds. It was time for both of them to be getting some sleep. And after she'd dug her nightgown out of a suitcase and changed into it, and gotten into bed and turned off the lights, she did what she always did at night when she was feeling out of sorts. She searched around under the covers with her foot until she found Sasquatch, a warm, solid lump at the end of the bed, and then she wedged her foot beneath him, and sighed, contentedly.

Win didn't understand how important to her he was, she thought, wriggling her foot. She never would. But if she thought Poppy was willing to just stash him away at a friend's house for the summer, she was mistaken. And her final thought before she fell asleep that night was: *Sasquatch is staying.*

After Poppy went to her room, Win washed her face at the bathroom sink and thought about dismantling her "shrine" to her and Kyle. *Maybe,* she thought, cupping water in her hands and splashing it on her face. Maybe she'd put those things away. But then again, maybe she wouldn't. She turned the faucet off, and reached for a hand towel, looking in the mirror as she patted her face dry. The lighting in this bathroom was not flattering. She knew this from experience. Still, as she leaned closer now and scrutinized her reflection in the mirror, she found herself, in almost every way, wanting. What was wrong with her hair, for instance? She picked up a limp strand that had escaped from her ponytail and held it up for inspection. It was a color commonly referred to as dirty blond, but right now, it just looked dirty, though she had washed it that morning. And her eyes, which were an indeterminate shade of blue, were they always this puffy, or were they like this now because of her cat allergy? And what about her skin? She'd thought she had the beginnings of a summer tan, but under the fluorescent light fixture, her complexion had an unhealthy, almost greenish hue to it.

"And so it begins," she muttered. Because it was almost impossible for her to be with her sister without doing this, without subjecting her appearance to this kind of merciless self-appraisal, and cataloguing all of her physical flaws with the same obsessiveness with which she organized her kitchen utensils.

Why did she even care now? she wondered, rubbing her face dry with the hand towel. Why did it even matter what she looked like when the only man she'd ever loved—a man who'd thought she was beautiful even on her worst day—was gone now? What difference did it make? Besides, in her more rational moments, Win knew she wasn't unattractive. She knew, in fact, she was perfectly attractive. And if she hadn't had Poppy for a sister, if she hadn't been born exactly thirteen months after her, and spent her entire childhood linked, inextricably, to her in the minds of all of their friends, and neighbors, and classmates, she would probably have been more than satisfied with the way she looked.

But their parents, who were both attractive people in their own right, had outdone themselves when they'd produced Poppy. It was as if their first daughter had won some kind of genetic lottery, inheriting the very best physical traits either one of them had to offer. By the time Win arrived, a little over a year later, her family's genes had reverted back to type.

It wasn't that she didn't look like Poppy. She did. She looked enough like her for people to know, without being told, that they were sisters. But somehow, this made it worse. As one of Win's high school classmates had once remarked, with the casual cruelty of that age, *It's like Poppy's the designer handbag, Win, and you're the knockoff.*

Win hung up the hand towel and took a box of Benadryl out of the medicine cabinet, then popped one of the capsules out of its foil packet, and washed it down with another scoop of water from the faucet. There, that should head off the sneezing fit she felt coming on. She put the Benadryl back on the shelf, but she was careful this time not to look in the mirror once she'd closed the cabinet. Instead, she left the bathroom, imagining she already felt an over-the-counter drowsiness setting in, and thinking, still, about Poppy's beauty. It wasn't fair of her to resent Poppy for it. She hadn't chosen it and, if she were to be believed, she couldn't even see it herself. Certainly, she was almost completely without vanity. Even in this age of relentless social media, she stood apart. Her Facebook profile was of her cat, and she had never, to Win's knowledge, taken a selfie. Her idea of getting ready for a night out on the town was brushing her teeth, and the only thing she owned that was even close to makeup was a tube of ChapStick.

Win padded down the hallway, turning off lights as she went. No, she wouldn't resent Poppy's beauty, she decided, coming back into her bedroom. But she couldn't *help* resenting her irresponsibility; Poppy's life was, mysteriously enough, always on the verge of unraveling. And tonight, tonight was *classic* Poppy, though even by Poppy's standards it seemed over the top. No warning she was coming. No mention of bringing anyone, either. She'd just shown up, with a cat that shed his weight in fur every day, a "friend" whose last name she didn't know, and several cardboard boxes that contained the sum total of her life.

Win got into bed then pummeled her pillow into a more acceptable shape and snapped off the bedside table lamp, before flopping down with a finality that suggested anger rather than sleep. Was it fair, though, she wondered now, to blame Poppy for her irresponsibility when you considered the way she'd been raised? Win, of course, *responsible* Win, had been raised the same way, but this time, it was *she* who had been the outlier and Poppy who had been true to their family's form.

Their parents had met, gotten married, and produced two children in quick succession, and then, as far as Win could tell, had never done another conventional thing in their lives again. They weren't bad parents. They weren't abusive or neglectful—well, not *technically* neglectful—though Win sometimes thought that between her father's drinking and her mother's self-absorption, they had skirted dangerously close to it. But their attitude toward their children, most of the time, could best be described as one of mild surprise. As if, having brought them into this world, they forever after seemed to be asking, not unkindly, *What is it, exactly, that you two are doing here?*

In fact, Win thought, tossing irritably in her bed, that was what their father had said to them one morning when he'd walked into the apartment and found them eating cereal at the kitchen table. Win couldn't remember how old she and Poppy were at the time, but they were young, young enough so that their feet didn't touch the floor, but dangled off the chipped, wooden chairs they sat in. It was a summer morning, and they were dressed in cotton night-gowns, spooning cornflakes into their mouths when their father let himself in through the front door and walked into the kitchen.

He didn't look too great. His clothes were askew, his hair was standing on end, and his eyes were bloodshot. Now, of course, Win knew this was the result of a night of hard drinking, but then she'd only thought he looked strange and a little wild. He started to walk past them, then stopped, came back, and stared at them. "What are you two doing here?" he asked, rubbing his eyes.

"We live here," Poppy said, not skipping a beat. Win nodded in agreement.

"Right," he said, as if just realizing this, and then he reached out and put a hand on each of their heads and gave them both a slightly unsteady pat. "You live here," he said. "'Course you do." And then he'd walked out of the kitchen. Still, Win thought, as she began to feel the tug of the Benadryl's chemical drowsiness, Poppy was twenty-nine. She was old enough to be responsible for her actions, despite her upbringing. *Wasn't she?*

Win yawned. In recent years, she'd been prone to insomnia, but tonight she knew that wouldn't be a problem. She thought about their houseguest, Everett West. She hadn't had much of a chance to get to know him. He'd been so quiet during dinner, letting her and Poppy do most of the talking. And Poppy, who'd said she was exhausted, had insisted they all go to bed right after dinner. She wondered now if Everett was asleep. And if not, what was he doing? She had no idea. He was still a stranger to her. Could still be, for all she knew, a serial killer. Should she lock her bedroom door? No, if Everett were inclined to murder her and Poppy, he'd had more than ample time to do so already.

Besides, he didn't look like a serial killer. He looked like someone . . . someone with sleepy eyes, she decided, though she was so sleepy herself she could barely follow her own train of thought. *He has such sleepy eyes. Such nice eyes.* Not like her eyes. Her eyes felt itchy right now . . . so itchy. *That cat.* That cat would make her miserable. All summer long. Poppy would have to find someplace else for him, at least while she stayed here. And her last coherent thought, before she fell asleep was, *That's it, Sasquatch is going.*

CHAPTER 4

A couple of nights later, in another cabin on Butternut Lake—this one larger, and more cluttered, than Win's—Sam Boyd sat down at his dining room table and flipped open his laptop. He'd been trying to watch the same YouTube video all night, and every time he started to play it, he'd been interrupted. *"It's about damn time,"* he muttered, as the short commercial before the video finished, but in that same moment he caught sight of something out of the corner of his eye. He pressed "pause" and snapped his laptop shut.

"All right, who's still up?" he called out, glancing over at the stairs that led up to the cabin's second floor.

"It's me," his son Hunter answered, shuffling into view.

"Lights out was fifteen minutes ago."

"I know, but . . ." Hunter hesitated, and then edged down a few more stairs.

"This can't wait until morning?"

Hunter shook his head.

"Okay, let's hear it," Sam said, itching to watch the video, but knowing that no self-respecting father would watch it in front of his nine-year-old son. He waited while Hunter came down the rest of the stairs and then sidled up to him at the dining room table. "Now, what's this about?" Sam asked.

"Um . . ." Hunter scratched a mosquito bite on his arm.

"Stop scratching," Sam said. Hunter stopped.

"It's about . . . the Fourth of July."

Sam sighed. "Is it that time of year already?" he asked. By "that time of year" he meant the weeks leading up to the Fourth of July, during which his sons (Hunter, and Hunter's twin brother, Tim) began a series of tense negotiations with Sam over how many and what kinds of fireworks they could buy to commemorate a holiday which for them had very little to do with American independence and everything to do with blowing things up.

"Let me see that," Sam said to Hunter now, noticing for the first time that his son was holding a notepad. Hunter handed it over and Sam studied the page it was open to, marveling at the unaccustomed neatness of his son's handwriting. Hunter had made two columns. The one on the right listed the names and desired quantities of each firework, and the one on the left listed their prices. At the bottom of the left-hand column was the sum total Hunter and Tim were proposing to spend on this venture.

"Does your math tutor know you can add this well?" Sam asked, looking up from the notepad.

Hunter smiled his familiar half smile.

"Is this all the money you two have saved?" Sam indicated the total in the bottom left corner.

Hunter nodded.

"How many weeks' allowance is that?"

Hunter considered this. "About six," he said, finally.

"And you're sure this is how you want to spend it?"

Hunter nodded again. He wasn't much of a talker, this kid. Now Sam blew out a long breath, dropped the notepad on the table, and tipped his chair back. Hunter waited, and tried not to scratch his mosquito bite. He and his brother, Tim, were identical twins, but for the quarter sized birthmark on Hunter's neck. It had been years since Sam had needed it to tell his sons apart, but he knew that it had been a lifeline to all of the teachers, and coaches, and Scout leaders in his sons' lives. Otherwise, the two boys shared the same reddish-brown hair, the same bright blue eyes, and the same dusting of freckles across their cheeks and the bridges of their noses. Sam reached out now and tried to smooth down Hunter's hair, but it couldn't be done. It was a minefield of cowlicks. Still, it wouldn't hurt to get him and his brother a haircut before they saw their mother next weekend, Sam thought, and while he was at it, he might as well get them some new pajamas, too. The faded Minnesota Twins T-shirt and the tattered gym shorts that served as Hunter's sleepwear tonight barely covered his gangly arms and legs.

He gave his son's head a final rub and looked back down at the notepad. "What's this?" he asked, pointing to a firework Hunter had listed as "killer bee fountain."

"Oh. That looks like a huge swarm of killer bees," Hunter said, pantomiming a swarm. "Plus, it has one of the loudest whistles of any fountain firework."

Sam smiled. Hunter had just said more to him than he ordinarily said to his father in a whole week. "Well, we wouldn't want to miss out on that one," Sam said. "But remember, I'm going to have to run all of this by your mom, okay?"

"Okay," Hunter said.

"Now, get to bed." And then Sam added, in a slightly louder voice, "*Both* of you."

"'Night Dad," Tim called down, from where Sam knew he'd been waiting, just out of sight, at the top of the stairs.

"'Night Tim," Sam called up. "And Hunter?" he said, before his other son could slink away.

"Yeah?"

"It's going to be a miracle if you and your brother reach adulthood with all ten of your fingers intact."

"Probably," Hunter agreed.

"Now, get out of here," Sam said, good-naturedly, easing his laptop open again.

He clicked on play and then rubbed his eyes. He rested his elbows on the table, and leaned closer, squinting at the screen as the video began.

"Dad?"

He jumped. *"Christ,"* he mumbled, slamming his computer shut. "Cassie, you have *got* to stop sneaking up on me like that," he said, turning to his six-year-old daughter, who was standing beside him.

"I'm sorry. I can't help it if I have quiet feet," Cassie said, holding her hands behind her back and looking down at her bare feet. "I'll try to make them louder," she added, marching them up and down in place.

"No, don't do that," Sam said, softening. "If you do that, they'll be just like your brothers' feet, and we have enough people clomping around in this house as it is. What's wrong, sweetie? Are the boys keeping you awake?"

"Not the boys," she said. She stopped marching, and balanced on one small, pale foot. "The girls."

"The girls?"

"The girls in my baton twirling class. The *mean* girls. I told you about them, remember?"

"Riiight," he said, slowly, leaning back in his chair and trying to remember what the latest drama in baton twirling class had entailed. But it didn't matter. Cassie usually provided him with a recap anyway.

"I mean, I know Gia and Riley are ten years old," she said now—pronouncing *ten* with the special reverence that only a six-year-old could give this age—"but they still act like they're so much better than me. And not just me. They're that way with *all* the six- and seven-year-olds. Do you know what Riley said to Tara today?" she asked, balancing on her other foot now.

"No. What did she say?"

"She said that Tara was *so* bad, she should stand in back at the recital, even though she knows six- and seven-year-olds have to stand in front. They *have* to. I mean, they're so short, if they didn't stand in front, nobody would see them."

"That's true," Sam said, reasonably, hoping to head this conversation off at the pass. "But I'm sure Riley didn't mean any harm in saying that."

"But she *did,*" Cassie said, not to be dissuaded. "She *did* mean harm. She *always* means harm. She told Janelle that her knees are fat. I mean, it's not even her *fault* that her knees are fat. She said she got her knees from her mom. And she said that her mom's knees are not even fat. They're just dimpled. Which is a much nicer way of saying fat, don't you think?"

"I do," Sam said, smiling.

"What were you doing on your computer?" Cassie asked, changing the subject.

"I was going to watch something."

"A cat video?" Cassie asked, hopefully.

"No, not a cat video. Thanks to you, I think I've already seen all five million cat videos online," Sam said, and he reached out and tugged on one of the slightly messy pigtails he'd forgotten to take out of her hair before he'd tucked her into bed earlier. She looked so much like her mother right now, he thought, as she stood there, hopping from one foot to the other, the hem of her Cinderella nightgown not quite covering a scab on her right knee. She had her mother's light brown hair, and bluish-grey eyes, and her fair complexion, too, a complexion that was a lovely mingling of pinks and creams. But if there was no question that she was adorable there was also no question that she was exhausting, and when he said, "Cass, we'll watch a cat video tomorrow. But what do you say you get back into bed now?" He attached a small, silent prayer to his words.

Cassie, though, shrugged noncommittally, and Sam knew she didn't want to go to sleep. She could go to sleep *anytime. Now*, she wanted to talk. She *needed* to talk. And Sam had learned, from hard won experience, to let her do it. "All right, come here," he said, patting his lap, and as she scrambled up into it, she began almost immediately to talk again about the mean girls in her baton twirling class, especially Riley, who had done far worse things, apparently, than accusing someone of having fat knees. And Sam listened, a little absently, and thought about Riley's father, whom he'd gone to high school with. He'd been a bully, too, the kind of guy who was always pushing smaller kids into lockers, or flicking wet towels at his teammates in the locker room after basketball practice. Sam considered telling his daughter about him now, but then decided against it. And it was just as well, because Cassie had already moved on to a different topic, which was the amount of money in her piggy bank—seven dollars and forty-seven cents—and how best to spend it. She'd seen some sparkly barrettes in the window at Butternut Drugs, she told Sam, and she really liked them, but Tara had the same barrettes, and the sparkly stuff on them had already rubbed off, so maybe she should buy a glass animal instead. Sam started to comment, but she changed the subject again. She'd lost a flip-flop today, she told him, it was white with blue polka dots, and she hadn't had time to look for it yet. Still, she listed now all the places it might be. Then she talked, for a little while, about the little ballerina that used to twirl around inside her jewelry box whenever she lifted the lid. She'd broken the ballerina off recently because she'd wanted to play with her, she explained, *outside* the jewelry box, but now she was sorry. She'd tried to put her back on her twirly thing, but she wouldn't stay on it, and Cassie was worried she might never be able to dance again.

There was more after this, about other things, but Sam lost the thread of it. He was remembering instead when he and Alicia had separated three years ago and he'd moved from Minneapolis to this cabin on Butternut Lake with Cassie, Hunter, and Tim. He'd grown up on the lake and although college, marriage, and a career had taken him away from it, he'd always imagined that one day he'd come back here to live. So when he and Alicia's marriage had ended, Sam had suggested that he and the kids move to Butternut and Alicia, after much soul searching, had agreed.

That first year after the divorce, though, there had been a lot of challenges for Sam. He'd been completely unnerved, for instance, by Cassie's nighttime monologues. He thought he knew how to parent his sons. He'd grown up in a family full of boys, and he assumed that the rules for raising them were pretty straightforward. They needed to be fed, and kept reasonably clean, and they needed someone—him, in this case—to basically hold a gun to their head every night while they did their homework. But if his sons seemed to him to be like sturdy houseplants, his daughter seemed more like a hothouse flower. And when he'd gone to tuck her in that first night at the cabin, and she'd starting talking, and kept talking, he'd felt completely out of his depth. What if she asked him a question he couldn't answer? Or needed advice he couldn't give? But then he'd realized that it wasn't answers or advice she needed—it was something much simpler. She needed to be listened to, and that, at least, he knew he could do.

Now, though, Cassie's words, which had taken on a new urgency, broke into his thoughts. "Do you think that's true, Daddy?" she asked, looking up at him, intently.

"Oh, absolutely," he said.

"*You do?*" She looked alarmed.

"I'm . . . I'm sorry. What are we talking about?"

"About Janelle. About whether she saw a ghost or not."

"Oh, no. Of course not. Ghosts aren't real, Cassie. You know that."

"I *know*. I know," she said, looking relieved. "I just forgot." She looked thoughtful for a moment. "Do you know what I think?" she asked.

"What?"

"I think Janelle just has a really good imagination."

He smiled, and kissed the top of her head. "I think so, too," he said. "Now, is there any chance that you could put yourself back to bed?"

She shook her head solemnly.

"I didn't think so," he said, with a barely audible sigh of resignation. "Let's go." But he was back a few minutes later, after depositing her, firmly, into her bed, begging off reading another bedtime story, and promising her, once again, that ghosts were not real, and then checking her closet for her just to be sure they weren't, and finally leaving the hall light on in case they really might be. No sooner had he sat down in front of his computer, though, than his cell phone rang. *"Oh, for God's sakes,"* he said under his breath, but when he saw the name on the incoming call he forgot to be irritated and hit the "talk" button instead.

"Are you still awake?" he asked, by way of saying "hello."

"Awake?" she said. "I'm still at work."

"Alicia, it's ten o'clock," he protested.

"I know. But I have opening arguments tomorrow, and I need to go over them."

"I thought you tried to plead your cases out. You know, save the taxpayers' money."

"Usually, we do. But this one's going to trial."

"What's it about?" he asked, interested. Sometimes he thought what he missed most about their marriage were the daily updates she used to give him on her job.

Now he heard her sigh, and he heard her rustling around, and he knew what she was doing. She was doing what she did at the end of any long workday. She was slipping off her low-heeled pumps, running her fingers lightly over her stocking clad feet, and, wheeling her swivel chair back, she was putting those feet—small and delicate—up on her desk, and in so doing, she was exposing a few more inches of her slender legs as her pencil skirt rode demurely up her thighs. There had been a time when any one of those movements would have left him completely undone. But that time was over.

"What's the case about?" he asked again, sensing she'd settled into this more relaxing position.

"It's . . ." She hesitated. "It's pretty depressing, actually," she said, finally. "I'd rather not talk about it. Tell me about the kids instead," she said wistfully. "I want to hear about something good for a change."

Sam smiled. He understood. It was hard sometimes, in her line of work, to remember there was good in the world. So he told her about the kids. He told her about his conversations with Hunter and with Cassie, and he knew, from experience, not to omit a single detail, like the "killer bee fountain" Hunter and Tim wanted for the Fourth of July and the twirling ballerina Cassie had liberated from her jewelry box with somewhat predictable results.

"I can remember wanting to take my jewelry box ballerina out when I was Cassie's age, too," Alicia said, amused.

"Well, that ballerina's danced her last Swan Lake. Cassie will survive, though. What she might *not* survive is the fact that I still can't figure out how to French braid her hair. Apparently, all the girls at day camp are wearing it that way. But I can't do it. I should be able to. I can still tie all those sailing knots my dad taught me. And I can tie flies, too, for fly-fishing. Why can't I do this thing to her hair?"

"I don't know. But don't worry about it," Alicia said. "I'll do it when the kids are staying with me next weekend. She can wear it home and sleep in it Sunday night, and then wear it to camp on Monday."

"Still . . ." he said, looking over at his laptop.

"Sam," Alicia said, her tone changing. "There's something I need to discuss with you."

"Discuss, huh? That sounds serious," he said, only half joking.

"It's not serious, yet. But it could be."

"Oh," he said, sitting up straighter. He'd known this moment would come, eventually, he just hadn't known *when* it would come. "Who, uh . . . who is he?"

"He's an investigator in the DA's office."

"What kind of stuff does he investigate?"

"White collar crime, mostly. It's interesting. Complicated, but interesting. He spends most of his time on computers. And Sam? He's a nice guy. I think you'd like him. And I think, I *hope*, the kids will like him, too."

"They haven't met him yet?"

"No. And they won't, either, until I think it might . . . you know, go the distance."

He didn't say anything. He was still trying out the idea of Alicia dating someone.

"Anyway," she said, when the silence grew too long. "It's still strictly a weeknight relationship. Which is the way I want it to be for now. My weekends are all about the kids."

"I know that," Sam said. And it was true. It was why Alicia worked such brutal hours during the week, so she could have her weekends free for the kids. It was probably why she was dating someone she'd met at work. Where else would she have the opportunity to meet anyone?

"Are you okay with this, Sam?' she asked now.

"I'm okay with it," Sam said, deciding that he was.

"Is there anyone . . . you're interested in?" Alicia asked.

"Not right now."

"But when you do start seeing someone, Sam, could you give me a heads-up?"

"You'll be the first to know," he said. "After me, that is."

She chuckled. "That's fair. I'll see you on Friday, okay?"

"Okay," he said. Typically, on Friday afternoons he drove the kids to Twin Harbors, which was halfway between Butternut Lake and the Twin Cities, and Alicia met them there and drove them the rest of the way back to her house in a suburb of Minneapolis.

"Good night Sam," she said now, with unmistakable affection. "And get some sleep, okay?"

"Yeah, well, that goes for you, too," he said. And after he'd hung up the phone he did think about going to sleep. It was ten thirty by then, and he'd been up since six thirty that morning. But instead he opened his laptop again, reached out a wary finger, and clicked "play" on the video. Then he leaned closer, staring at the two young women on the screen, one of whom was sitting down, facing the camera, and one of whom was standing beside her, holding a tortoiseshell comb.

"The first step in French braiding hair," the woman with the comb said, *"is to part the hair down the middle all the way to the back of the head."* Sam watched as she did this to the model's hair. *"Now,"* she continued, *"put one side of the hair in a pigtail in order to keep it out of the way so you can work on French braiding the other side. After that, take a small section of hair in the front of the head and divide it into three sections as though you were going to do an ordinary braid. But in this case, you will be braiding over the middle section, not under the middle section, as you generally do in an ordinary braid."*

Sam groped around on the table for a pen and paper. He came up with the pad of paper that Hunter had left, the one with his fireworks wish list on it, and a stubby pencil that had gotten loose from one of the kids' board games. He flipped to a blank page in the pad, and started scribbling, furiously, trying to keep up with the woman's instructions. He'd watched this video at least a half dozen times, and this next part always tripped him up.

"After that," the woman on-screen was saying, *"take the front section that you've divided into three strands and take the front part over the middle and then the back part over the middle.*

Once you've done one strand, you will now take another strand of hair from beneath the part you've already braided once and you will weave that strand over the middle section . . ."

"What the hell?" he muttered, already hopelessly confused. But he kept taking notes. He would learn how to do this if it killed him, he vowed. And, when he looked down later at the incomprehensible scribblings he'd left on the pad, he figured it just *might* kill him.

CHAPTER 5

Although Sam Boyd watched, and then re-watched, the You-Tube video on how to French braid hair several times that week, he was still no closer to knowing how to do it himself. But he wasn't thinking about that as he pulled up outside of his store, Birch Tree Bait, Provisions and Rentals, at 8:05 that Thursday morning. He was thinking about all of the things that needed to get done that day, and he was wishing that the sight of his employees, waiting for him on the front porch of the log cabin style building, inspired more confidence in him.

"'Morning," he said to them, as he started up the steps. "Sorry I'm late. Cassie decided she couldn't go to day camp this morning until we found her missing flip-flop. Want to know where it was?"

No answer. Lincoln Post, Linc for short, was lying on one of the porch benches, looking not so much asleep as unconscious, and Justine Demers was leaning on the porch railing, dragging on a cigarette. He frowned at Justine, and she shrugged, apologetically, and dropped the cigarette, grounding it out under the heel of a combat boot.

"Any sign of life from him?" he asked Justine, gesturing at Linc.

She shook her head. Sam walked over to Linc, leaned down, positioned his mouth next his right ear, and quietly asked, "Does your mom know how much you're drinking every night?"

Linc jerked awake, as if Sam had delivered an electric shock to him, then fell back down on the bench with a groan. "Christ, Sam, if my mom knew that, I'd be a dead man."

"Well, look alive then," Sam said, hefting up the bundle of newspapers sitting on the porch, and taking his keys out of his pocket. "We've got a busy day today. And Justine?" he asked, turning to her.

She raised an eyebrow in response.

"In the future, smoke out back."

She raised the other eyebrow in acknowledgment.

But as Sam jiggled the key in the lock, his annoyance at Linc and Justine fell away, and by the time he'd pushed open the front door, and scanned the two large rooms that comprised his business, it had been replaced by another feeling. Pride. There was no other word for it. And it never failed. Every time he opened this door and saw this place, he felt it. And as he moved through the rooms now, turning on lights, opening blinds, restocking newspapers, inspecting bait, and checking the delivery schedule, he remembered what this place looked like when he'd bought it three years earlier. Then, it had been a mom and pop style bait shop whose best days were so far behind it that even Sam, who'd grown up on the lake, couldn't remember them. What it had going for it was location—it was right off Butternut Lake Drive and situated on one of the prettiest bays on the lake. Still, it didn't have much else to recommend it. The first time he had inspected it, for instance, he'd stuck his hand up at one point and it had gone straight through the ceiling. But he'd bought it anyway, gutted it, and doubled its existing square footage. And then he'd turned it into a kind of north woods convenience and outdoor store. He sold basic groceries, and beer and wine, but also guidebooks, maps, fishing tackle, hunting gear, outboards, bait, coffee, and gas. He also rented canoes, kayaks, and pontoon boats, and offered guides for hire for fishing and kayaking on the nearby Kawishiwi River.

Before he'd opened it, Sam had bet on the fact that Butternut Lake needed a business like Birch Tree Bait, a business that would anchor the north end of the lake, which was twelve miles from the south end of the lake and from the town of Butternut. Although this part of the lake wasn't as well populated as the other end in the off-season, in the summertime it attracted day-trippers from both Duluth and Superior, as well as fishermen and their families from the Twin Cities. And all of these people, it turned out, wanted the same thing: a chance to experience the pristine lakes, rivers, and forests of Northern Minnesota without ever having to be inconvenienced while they were experiencing them. And that was where Sam came in. A 5:30 A.M. fishing call on a chilly, mist shrouded lake was a fine thing; but, later in the day, long after the morning's catch had been scaled, cleaned, and fried for breakfast, being a five minute drive from a place that sold gas, cold beer, and more live bait was also a fine thing. So Sam's calculated gamble had paid off. The north side of Butternut Lake *did* need a business like his, needed it enough that the money he earned during the peak season allowed him to coast, reasonably well, through the off-season.

As Sam was putting money in the cash register, Linc breezed by, swigging from a liter bottle of Coke and carrying a large bag of Barbeque Lay's. Sam shook his head, wordlessly.

"What?" Linc said. "You don't want me to skip breakfast, do you?"

"Definitely not." Sam chuckled. "But when you're done with it, maybe you could invest in a comb. We sell them here, you know."

Linc didn't answer, but as he passed a display of Birch Tree Bait baseball caps near the front counter, he grabbed one and shoved it on over his unruly blond hair.

"Those cost money," Sam called after him.

"Put it on my tab," Linc answered, ripping into the Lay's bag as he headed over to the rental side of the business.

"You're such a brat," Sam muttered, but he muttered it affectionately. It was hard for him to get angry at Linc, harder still for him to *stay* angry at Linc. He'd tried to do both, a couple of times, but never with any real success. Besides, he knew he'd never fire him. Never mind that Linc went out carousing every night, barely dragged himself to work every morning, and ate his weight in free junk food every day. If Sam fired him, his sons, Hunter and Tim, would never forgive him. They worshipped Linc. He was good at every single sport they cared about and, more importantly, he tolerated their presence. When the boys were at the store—which they frequently were—they followed Linc around like two puppies, tripping over their own feet and jostling each other for his attention. And he gave it to them, for the most part, unless there was a young woman in the store who needed to be flirted with. Otherwise, he gave the boys little jobs to do and a little money for doing them, or he told them, and retold them, their favorite stories about his adventures in the great outdoors. And Linc had had many such adventures.

He'd spent his childhood summers on Butternut Lake. His family was from back East—they owned a financial services company that Sam had seen commercials for on television—but Butternut Lake was their preferred vacation destination. Even so, they'd been shocked one year when Linc, who'd graduated from college that Spring, had decided to stay on after the summer ended, and the rest of his family had returned to the East Coast. That had been three years ago. The whole thing had created a huge rift between him and his parents. He was supposed to be back home, being groomed to run the family company, but instead he was in Butternut, being what his father referred to as a "north woods slacker." By night, he drank beer and played pool or darts at any number of little dive bars in the area. By day, depending on the season, he mountain biked, or snowmobiled or kayaked. Two years ago, his parents had cut him off financially, hoping he would come to his senses. He hadn't. Instead, he'd moved out of their palatial lake house and into an old fishing lodge where the rooms were cheap, and he'd gotten a job working for Sam at Birch Tree Bait.

For the most part, Linc managed the boat rental business, but he was also available for hire as a guide, and it was this part of his job, Sam knew, that Linc really lived for. Sam had heard a local remark once that Linc couldn't know this area as well as someone who'd lived here their whole life. He was wrong. He knew it better than anyone Sam had ever met and, what was more, he had a respect for it that bordered on reverence. Sam figured he was lucky to have him, but he didn't know how long he'd last. His parents had been out over Memorial Day weekend, and they'd put the screws on him. Told him it was time to get back to his "real life." And eventually, Sam thought, he would. His parents would wear him down. They were rich, after all, and rich people, in Sam's experience, didn't like the word *no*. Maybe because they didn't hear it often enough to get comfortable with it.

Sam finished filling the register, slid the drawer shut, and looked up in time to see Justine standing at the coffee counter, finishing her twice daily ritual of pouring herself a cup of coffee from one of the industrial sized urns and then stirring five packets of sugar into it. He sighed, and wondered if he should require his employees to attend a nutrition seminar. Certainty Justine looked as if she could use one. She was thin—so thin Sam could see the outline of her shoulder blades through her T-shirt—and her skin was so white it looked nearly translucent. Her thinness and paleness were both set off by her wardrobe, which today consisted of a tiny, white, belly skimming T-shirt that had a black rose on it, and a pair of black denim shorts whose pocket liners peaked out beneath their hems. Completing this look was her peroxided blond hair, which had a half an inch of black roots showing (it had taken Sam forever to figure out that the roots were *supposed* to show), her heavy black eye makeup, and her chipped black nail polish.

For all this, though, there was a delicacy about her that her combat boots couldn't hide, and a prettiness that no amount of black eyeliner could disguise. Sam felt oddly protective over her, but he was careful not to let it show. Partly this was because he didn't want to be anything less than professional in his relationship with her, and partly it was because he figured she could take care of herself. Despite her thinness, she was incredibly strong—she was just as apt to do the heavy lifting around here as he and Linc. And she was also more than competent at her job. Alone, she could stock faster than two people together and, when she worked the register, more often than not she balanced it perfectly.

Now she finished stirring the sugar into her coffee and looked over at him. "Sam, do you think it would be okay if I left early today? I have to take my mom to the doctor."

"Oh, sure. Of course," Sam said, surprised. Justine had never mentioned her mother before. "I hope . . . is she . . . is your mom okay?"

She shrugged. "The doctors just need to run some tests. Just to, you know, rule out this disease she might have. But otherwise, she's fine."

"Oh," Sam said, "that's . . . that's good." Actually, he was not at all sure that it *was* good, but since this was the closest thing to a personal conversation he and Justine had ever had, he didn't know what else to say. He knew almost nothing about her or her life outside the store, other than the fact that she lived in a trailer park north of Butternut. Like Linc, she was in her mid-twenties. *Unlike* Linc, she obviously avoided the outdoors at any cost.

"What time do you need to leave?" Sam asked, trading places with her as she came around behind the counter.

"Four o'clock."

"That's fine," Sam said. "I can cover the register. Or I'll ask Byron to do it for me," he added, since Byron Boughton was even now making his way over to them.

"What am I going to do for you?" Byron asked, arriving at the coffee counter, setting down his briefcase, and pouring himself a cup of coffee.

"You're going to cover the register for me," Sam said, noting that Byron was his usual dapper self that morning. A man of seventy, he dressed neatly in crisp button-down shirts and creased khaki trousers, as though he were dressing for a day at the office. And, in a sense, he was. He reported here every day at 9:00 A.M. and stayed until 5:00 P.M. no matter the season or the weather. But he didn't work at Birch Tree Bait; he was just part and parcel of it.

"Sam, I'll always help you out in a pinch, you know that," Byron said now, adjusting the seersucker hat he wore at all times in the summer. (In the winter he replaced it with a tweed cap.) "And that goes for this lovely young lady as well," he added, gesturing at Justine, who was sipping her coffee behind the register. Justine, in response, graced Byron with one of her rare smiles. She was fond of him, as was Linc, who referred to him, affectionately, as "old man."

Byron went to select a *Minneapolis Star Tribune* from the newspaper rack, and left money for that and his coffee on the counter. Unlike Linc and Justine, Byron actually paid for the things he took from the store. And that was a good thing, too, because occasionally, he came close to outwearing his welcome. The first time Sam had met him, it had been at the old Birch Tree Bait, when Sam was still in discussions with the owner over buying it. Byron, already retired and newly widowed, was a fixture there, too, and Sam had wondered what he would do with himself once his friend sold the business. He'd actually felt bad about displacing him. He shouldn't have. Once Sam reopened, Byron was back again, acting as if he'd never left in the first place. And most of the time, Sam didn't mind. Not really. It was only when Byron dabbled in a little side business of his own that Sam minded. Like now, for instance. After Byron settled himself on a stool at the coffee counter and shook out his *Star Tribune*, Mac Hansen came over to him, and the two of them had a quick conversation during which some money changed hands.

"What was that?" Sam asked, coming over to him.

"What was what?" Byron asked, innocently, going back to his newspaper.

"What was that transaction?"

"That was nothing," he said, not looking up from the paper.

"Byron, I thought we agreed you would conduct your business elsewhere."

"That wasn't business," Byron said, thumbing through the paper to the sports section. "That was just a little . . . *housekeeping*."

"Well, whatever it was, it was illegal," Sam said, exasperated.

"Sam," Byron said, finally putting his newspaper down and giving him his full attention. "I wish you would stop seeing me as someone who breaks the law, and start seeing me instead as someone who provides a valuable community service."

"Ah, so *that's* what you're doing," Sam said.

"That's what I'm doing," Byron agreed, and the two of them would no doubt have continued in this vein if it hadn't been time for Sam to meet with Linc about the day's rentals. Still, Sam thought, as he headed over to the other side of the store, while he would never have admitted it to Byron, he was sometimes inclined to agree with him about his providing a "community service"; he just wished he wouldn't provide it here, at Birch Tree Bait.

The fact was that Byron was a bookie. He took bets on the big four professional sports and, occasionally, started betting pools about local events in Butternut. But he did have his own set of standards and, for someone who'd developed a very lucrative sideline breaking the law, he was still nonetheless deeply principled about the way in which he did it. He never took bets from anyone under twenty-one, or from anyone who already owed him money, or was having financial problems in his life. And he'd told Sam that, on more than one occasion, when someone had gotten in too deep, he'd simply written off their debt.

Sam was thinking about this as he and Linc inspected the canoes and kayaks for the day's rentals, and as he went over the reservation schedule with Jordy, the retired vet who drove the van that took passengers and towed kayaks and canoes to the Kawishiwi River, ten miles away.

"Oh, and don't forget," Linc said, as they finished up and Sam flipped the book shut on the day's reservations. "I'll be out all afternoon tomorrow. Remember those college girls who were in here the other day, the ones who rented a cabin up here for a week?"

Sam nodded. There'd been six of them, each one prettier than the last.

"Well, they want a kayaking guide."

"But not just *any* kayaking guide," Sam said, amused. He was the first to admit that Linc's good looks were good for business.

"No, of course not, Sam. They wanted the best," Linc said, washing down the last of the barbeque potato chips with the final inch of his Coke. And Sam had to admit, his breakfast seemed to have done wonders for him. Whereas forty-five minutes ago he'd been crippled by a hangover, he was now positively exuding good health.

"Hey, Sam," Linc said, craning his neck to see what was happening in the next room. "Margot's here."

"*And?*" Sam said, instantly annoyed. His relationship with Margot, or more accurately, his *lack* of a relationship with Margot, was a constant source of amusement for Linc and Byron.

"*And*, I think it would be rude of you not to say hello to her when she's driven ten miles out of her way to see you," Linc said, taking his baseball cap off and running his fingers through his disheveled hair.

"Linc, she's here for the coffee," Sam said, already exasperated.

"Sorry, Sam. Our coffee's not *that* good," Linc said. "Now go put her out of her misery. She probably spent fifteen minutes this morning deciding which pair of socks to wear with her Tevas."

Sam gave Linc a dirty look, and went to say hello to Margot Hoffman. It was best, he'd learned, to get their daily conversation over with quickly. If he stalled, she stalled, too, finding excuses to wait around the store, and sending Linc and Byron into new fits of amusement. Besides, he told himself, *he liked her.* He really did. He just didn't like her in the same way she appeared to like him.

"Hi Sam," she said, brightly, when he intercepted her at the coffee counter. "I have a big day planned for the kids," she added, her brown eyes shining, and her brown ponytail bobbing with enthusiasm. Margot, an attractive woman in her mid-thirties, always looked to Sam as if she'd stepped out of the pages of an Eddie Bauer catalogue. Clearly, the woman was ready for a hike at any time of the day or night, with her quick-dry khaki clothing, her water bottle clipped to her belt loop, and her backpack slung expectantly over one shoulder. And then, of course, there were the sandals she insisted on wearing with socks, in all but the hottest or coldest weather. Sam had never understood this fashion statement, but perhaps it went with the territory, since Margot was the educator/naturalist at the small natural history museum in Butternut.

When Sam was a kid this "museum" had housed a collection of old birds' nests and taxidermied animals, but in recent years it had expanded to include new exhibits, and it had begun offering a summer program for "junior naturalists." Sam's children were "junior naturalists," as were most of the children in Butternut who were between the ages of five and twelve and whose parents needed a convenient and mildly stimulating place to park them during their summer vacations.

"What's the theme for the day?" Sam asked Margot, who, along with the counselors she oversaw, was very theme oriented.

"It's 'Raptor Rapture,'" she said. "We have a ranger visiting with a tame falcon and several other birds of prey." She beamed. "They've all been injured and can't be released back into the wild, but they should make for a very exciting program. By the way, Sam," she added, "did you get the email on our family programs for summer? We have one coming up called 'What a Hoot.' It's a nighttime walk where we learn about owls and then try to spot them in their natural habitat."

"That sounds really . . . interesting," Sam said. "I'll have to check our calendar."

"Hopefully, you'll be free," she said, smiling up at him. But their conversation ended there, when the first of the day's deliveries arrived, and Sam had to say a hurried good-bye. Later, though, in a rare moment of calm, he felt guilty about her. The expression on her face when she'd told him about the family program had been so . . . *so hopeful*. He hated to disappoint her, but at the same time, he didn't want to lead her on. There'd been times, over the last year, when he'd tried to care about her, tried, even, to be attracted to her; she was so obviously interested in him. In a practical sense, being involved with Margot could have eased the weekday burdens of his single parenthood. She was great with kids, and he could see her taking the boys on informative hikes in the woods near their cabin, or doing age appropriate craft activities with Cassie at their kitchen table. But he wasn't someone who could date a woman for purely practical reasons. Besides, Sam knew you couldn't always choose whom to fall in love with. Sometimes, they chose you.

CHAPTER 6

Poppy's eyes were closed, and she was lying perfectly still. She was in her bikini, on a beach towel at the end of the dock, the sun warm on her skin, the lake water slapping gently against the dock's pilings, and the air redolent with dried pine needles, the not unpleasant tang of algae, and her own coconut scented sunscreen. She wasn't awake, and she wasn't asleep. She was suspended somewhere between the two. And it was perfect. *She* was perfect. And she would continue to be perfect, as long as she didn't open her eyes, didn't move, and, above all, didn't think.

"Poppy?" Win called from the cabin's back door. Poppy ignored her and tried to return to her previously blissful state. But Win was not to be deterred.

"*Poppy,*" she said again, and this time she was standing over her.

Poppy sighed, raised herself up on her elbows, and lifted her sunglasses up onto her head.

"Yes?" she said, squinting up at her.

"Are you going to lie here all day?"

"That was the plan," she said, lying back down. She closed her eyes, already drowsy again, and listened to the distant hum of a motorboat entering the bay, a sound that had provided the backdrop for so many childhood summer afternoons on the lake.

"*Poppy.*"

"What?" Poppy said, slightly startled. She raised herself up again.

"Aren't you worried . . ."

"That I'll get sunburned?" Poppy said. "No. I'm wearing SPF 100. I found it in your medicine cabinet. I didn't even know sunscreen went that high."

"No, I mean, aren't you worried that you won't accomplish anything today?"

"Accomplish anything?" Poppy said, sitting all the way up this time. "Win, it's summertime. It's a time of year when people go on vacation. When they relax. So, that's what I'm doing. I'm relaxing. *That's* what I'm accomplishing." But even with the sun in Poppy's eyes, she could see that Win was unimpressed by her logic.

"Okay, well, in the time you've been relaxing," Win said, "I've paid my bills, had my oil checked, refilled the prescription for my allergy medication, gone grocery shopping, and made lasagna."

Poppy sighed, louder this time, and lay back down again. This conversation was *not* going to end well, she reflected. She was not completely surprised, though, that they were going to have it now. She'd been waiting for it, in fact, for a couple of days.

Still, she had to admit, her and Win's first several days as housemates had gotten off to a good start. No, a *great* start. They'd had fun, just as Poppy had promised they would. They'd made their favorite brownies, from a *Barefoot Contessa* recipe, and when they'd gotten impatient over how long it was taking them to bake, they'd taken them out of the oven before they were done and eaten them, with spoons, directly out of the pan.

They'd spent a day in their pajamas, binge-watching an entire season of *Scandal*. They'd played Monopoly. Or they'd *tried* to play Monopoly, only to discover that too many of the pieces were missing to play it successfully. But they'd had fun figuring that out, anyway. They'd taken their grandfather's ancient motorboat out on the lake—Poppy having miraculously coaxed its engine back to life—and they'd coasted around the little islets, and beaches, and coves in their bay, waiting for the engine to give out again. And when it had, finally, given out, they'd flagged down a couple of fishermen and gotten a tow back to their dock. And they'd sat on that dock, one sultry afternoon, and watched a thunderstorm approach from across the lake, and then ran back up to the cabin just seconds before the sky opened up above them, unleashing a torrential downpour.

But most of all, those first couple of days, they'd talked. They'd talked, and they'd talked, and they'd talked. They'd talked about their parents, they'd talked about their childhood, they'd talked about old friends, and some newer friends, and about one of Win's colleagues at the middle school who drove her crazy with her passive aggressive remarks. They'd talked about whether Poppy should get bangs—they'd decided against it—and whether Win should get a kayak—they'd decided she should, but when they'd looked at the prices of kayaks online they'd changed their minds.

They'd talked the way only sisters and best friends could talk, starting a new subject before they were done with the old, and then coming back to the old one later and picking up right where they'd left off. They talked like this because they knew they would never exhaust their topics of conversation. Each re-examination of a subject could offer new insights. And it could always—always—be talked about some more. Now, of course, Poppy fretted, they wouldn't be *talking* to each other—they'd be having *a talk* with each other. And nothing could be more different than these two things. *The talking* was about anything, anything at all. *The talk* was about Poppy, and about her need to find direction in her life.

But again, Poppy had seen this coming, because as perfect as things had seemed between them those first several days, there had still been warning signs. Win, for instance, had expressed displeasure over the way Poppy had loaded the dishwasher. Apparently, there was a "right" way to do it and a "wrong" way to do it, something that struck Poppy as absurd. Everyone knew the whole point of loading a dishwasher was to get as many dishes into it as possible, as quickly as possible. Who cared where the glasses went, or the plates or the bowls? There'd been a couple of other sticking points, too. Win had come into her room yesterday to find Sasquatch lying on her bed—a definite breach of protocol. She'd shooed him away, but apparently he'd left some fur behind—a miniscule amount in Poppy's opinion, but Win had still made a big deal out of having to wash all of her bedding. And then there'd been the matter of the wet towel Poppy had left on the bathroom floor that morning; Win had delivered it to her room with no words, but with a foreboding expression on her face. Poppy had promised to do better, but honestly, she thought, what was the point of Win *giving* her all of those towels to use if she couldn't leave the occasional one on the floor?

But the biggest problem between them right now was also the oldest problem between them: money. Or, more specifically, *lack* of money, at least on Poppy's part. Because while they'd agreed, the morning after Poppy's arrival, that they would split everything fifty-fifty this summer, it was fast becoming clear to Win that Poppy was already running out of money. Poppy hadn't told her this; not in so many words. But Win had figured it out. The night Win had shopped for and cooked their dinner, for instance, they'd had chicken picatta. The night Poppy had shopped for it and cooked it they'd had frozen pizza.

"Poppy," Win said again now, not even bothering to conceal her annoyance.

"All right," Poppy said, sitting up. "I'm done. No more sunbathing." She stood up, feeling slightly dazed, and began to gather up her belongings. "Let's have the talk."

"The talk?"

"The talk you want us to have," Poppy said, starting up the dock.

"I don't want us to have a talk," Win said.

"You don't?"

"Okay, I do. But not right now. I thought we could have it over dinner. That's why I made the lasagna. And why I thought you could buy us a bottle of wine to go with it."

"All right, I'll drive into town," Poppy said, starting up the steps that led to the cabin. She was already calculating what was the least amount of money she could spend on a drinkable bottle of wine.

"Oh, you don't have to drive into town for it," Win said, following her. "Why don't you just go to Birch Tree Bait."

"That old place where they sell worms?"

"Well, yeah, they still sell those there. But it's been totally redone. It's not just bait and tackle anymore. They actually have a grocery section now, too, and you can get a surprisingly decent bottle of wine there."

Decent as in cheap? Poppy wanted to ask, but didn't.

"Okay, I'll get the wine," Poppy said, breezing in through the cabin's back door, and then pausing for a moment to enjoy the dimness and coolness inside after her marathon sunbathing session. What she really would have liked to do right then was to take a long shower and wash off all of that sunscreen, but she knew Win well enough to know that the sooner she left, the better. Win had that set to her jaw now that Poppy had learned to be wary of. Maybe if she could get a few glasses of wine into her before their talk, it would go better, she thought. Maybe, if she played her cards right, they wouldn't have to have the talk at all.

Poppy hurried into her room now, and gave Sasquatch, who was lying on one of the beds, a quick pat, then rummaged around in her dresser for something to wear. She ended up pulling on a T-shirt and a pair of blue jean cutoffs, and then glanced in the mirror with the thought of doing something about her hair. In the end, though, she left it in a messy bun and instead groped around in the closet for her flip-flops.

"All right, I'll be back soon," she called as she headed for the front door. She grabbed her handbag and was on her way out when Win came after her. "Aren't you forgetting something, Pops?" she asked.

"What?"

"My car keys?"

"Oh, right," Poppy said, a little sheepishly, as Win went to get them for her. And here was *another* source of tension between them: Poppy was completely dependent on Win for transportation.

But once Poppy was out on the road, the windows rolled down and the radio cranked up, she forgot about all of this. It was impossible not to; this stretch of Butternut Lake Drive, the stretch that led away from town, was even prettier than the stretch that came before it. It hewed more closely to the lake, so that on a sun-drenched day like today, you never lost sight of the shimmer of water through the trees. And the trees! Their leaves were still the pale green of early summer, but they were so profuse that the light filtering through them was itself a faint green, and the effect was as if Poppy was driving not on a back road, but on an underwater byway.

She was so entranced by the scenery that she shot right past Birch Tree Bait, and had to slam on the brakes and back up to it. "*Wow*," she said, softly, turning into the graveled parking lot. She would never have guessed this was the same place her grandfather used to take her and Win to when they were children, he to put fresh bait in a Styrofoam cooler, and she and Win to choose ice cream bars from a rusted-out freezer in back. This place was *nice*, she thought, parking the car. Its fishing dock had been shored up and repainted and the beach, which had once been filled with tall weeds and discarded cans, was now a small crescent of golden sand. As she headed up the front steps of the building, she noticed that the old dilapidated porch had been completely renovated, too. Several Adirondack chairs were scattered in the shade and a charming porch swing swayed in the breeze. Over the front door hung a green painted sign with a trout emerging from the water and the words BIRCH TREE BAIT painted under it. She paused for a moment, on her way in, to watch a little girl playing with a baton. *Were girls still doing that?* she wondered. But of course they were. It was only Poppy who'd relegated it to ancient history.

Once inside, Poppy found the beer and wine aisle. She was disappointed by the wine selection, though. It's not that it wasn't good. It was *too* good. *Jeez*, she thought, as she scanned the shelves for an inexpensive bottle, since when did fishermen spend sixteen ninety-nine on a bottle of wine? Still, by searching carefully, she found a few cheaper bottles, including a red wine, tucked way in the back, and covered with dust, whose price tag said $2.89. She picked it up and examined its label carefully. It looked fine, just a little . . . dusty. But she could wipe that off before she got home. Besides, wine was wine. She'd never understood all of those adjectives people threw around about it. Dry, oaky, fruity. What difference did it make, as long as it was drinkable?

She glanced around now, found the front counter, and headed over to it, feeling pleased with her choice. Not only could she afford this bottle of wine, she'd have a little money left over after she paid for it. But as soon as she got to the counter an old anxiety crept up on her. There were three men standing there—one younger, probably in his mid-twenties, and wearing a baseball cap, another about ten years older, probably in his mid to late thirties, standing behind the counter, and another one, an older white haired man wearing a seersucker hat—and when they saw her waiting there, they immediately stopped talking to each other and stared at her. *Just . . . stared at her.* And she did this thing she did whenever people stared at her like that. She just kind of . . . went inside of herself. It was hard to explain. It was like she was there, but at the same time, she wasn't there. She couldn't remember exactly when she'd started doing this, probably in adolescence, but it had become practically second nature to her. Like right now, for instance, she put the bottle of wine on the counter and slid her wallet out of her handbag, and the whole time she was doing this, she was staring at a flyer someone had pinned up on a bulletin board behind the counter. It had to do with a bluegrass music festival—which was something she had no interest in—but she pretended to read it with total concentration.

She was staring at it so hard, in fact, that she was only vaguely conscious that the man behind the counter was speaking to her.

"I'm sorry, what did you say?" she asked, tearing her eyes away from the flyer.

"I said, 'It's at the fairgrounds on Sunday.' Are you interested? Because I've heard some of the bands, and they're pretty good."

Was he asking her out? She felt her face flush with irritation. She *hated* it when guys did this. And she never understood it, either. Why would they think she'd be willing to go out with a stranger? And, in this man's case, since when did buying a bottle of wine from someone constitute an introduction to him? Now, though, she took a five-dollar bill out of her wallet and placed it on the counter, and, as she did so, she leveled her gaze at him. "I don't date people I don't know," she said.

"Excuse me?" he said, picking up her five-dollar bill. Now, apparently, it was his turn to be confused.

"I said, 'I don't go out on dates with people I've never met before.'"

"Did you . . . did you think I was asking you out?" he asked, counting out her change and putting it on the counter.

"Well . . . weren't you?" She picked up her change and put it back in her wallet.

"No, I wasn't," he said, and she saw a flash of irritation in his blue eyes as he put her bottle of wine in a paper bag. "I was just making conversation. This is my business," he added. "I'm not in the habit of using it as a place to try to pick up women."

"Okay," she said, apologetically, her face warm again, though this time only with embarrassment. "I'm sorry. I obviously misunderstood you."

She heard a laugh, a laugh that was quickly disguised as a cough, and she looked over to see the man in the seersucker hat covering his mouth with mock politeness. He looked like he was enjoying himself immensely. So did the guy in the baseball cap, who, even now, was leaning against the counter with a lackadaisical smile on his face. So this was what passed for entertainment around here? Being rude to customers?

"Thank you very much," she said, insincerely, as the proprietor handed her the paper bag.

She turned to go then, but before she'd even taken a step she heard the man behind the counter say, almost as if to himself, "That's a really nice bottle of wine."

She spun around, too irritated to feel self-conscious. "You're the one who sold it to me," she objected. "If it's so bad, why do you even carry it?"

"Actually," he said, "that bottle was already here when I bought this business."

"So, why'd you keep it?" she shot back.

"Because there's no accounting for some people's tastes," he said, with an amused glance at his companions. Poppy turned on her heels and headed for the door, determined not to give him, or his friends, anything else to be amused about. But by the time she reached the front porch, where the little girl was still playing with her baton, she had a new preoccupation: peeling the price tag off the bottle before she got home with it. When she looked up, though, she saw the little girl throw the baton, awkwardly, and saw it come down again, narrowly missing her.

"*Whoa,* hey, careful there," Poppy said, hurrying over to her and picking it up. "You don't want to bop yourself on the head, do you?" she asked the little girl.

She shook her head at Poppy, and there was something so serious and, at the same time, so sweet about her expression that Poppy couldn't help but smile at her. "Here you go," she said, handing her the baton.

She took it from Poppy, then blinked her wide bluish-gray eyes and said, "You're pretty."

"Thank you. So are you," Poppy said, smiling. "What's your name?"

"Cassie," the little girl said, still not taking her eyes off her.

"Is that short for Cassandra?"

"No. It's short for Cassidy. My dad named me after *Butch* Cassidy. Do you know who he was?"

Poppy started to say that she did, but Cassie didn't give her time to. "He was an outlaw," she said. "There's a *movie* about him. But I haven't seen it yet, 'cause it's rated PG, and it's the *old* PG, when they weren't as strict as they are now, so it's *really* rated PG13. My mom says we can see it when I'm thirteen, though, and she said my friend Janelle can watch it with us." She stopped, a little out of breath.

"That's interesting," Poppy said, wondering if all children were this forthcoming about themselves. "It's not every day that I meet a baton twirling outlaw," she said.

"What's your name?" Cassie asked, with a shy smile.

"My name is Poppy, after the flower, which my mom loved, and which my dad probably didn't have any real opinion about. But I should probably get going, Cassie," she said, picturing Win's lasagna, already baking in the oven. "Someone's expecting me. And your mom, or dad, is probably wondering where you are, too," she added, gesturing at the store. "They must be almost done by now."

"Oh, no, my dad's here all the time," Cassie said, swinging her baton. "I can stay out here for as long as I want."

And Poppy fully intended to leave, but the expression on Cassie's face was so sweet, and the sight of the baton was so tempting, that instead Poppy held out her hand. "May I?" she

asked Cassie, indicating the baton, and setting down her handbag and grocery bag.

Cassie nodded, and handed it to her.

"I used to twirl a long time ago. Let's see if I can still remember how," Poppy explained, doing a few basic figure eights, an
arm roll, and a thumb toss.

Cassie clapped, excitedly. "Where'd you learn that?" she
asked.

"In high school. I was a majorette in the marching band,"
Poppy said, handing the baton back to her.

"You're even better than Miss Suzette."

"Who's Miss Suzette?"

"She's our instructor," Cassie said. "She was in the Miss Minnesota pageant once, and for her talent, she twirled. But that was,
like, a long time ago," Cassie said, lowering her voice. "Now she's
kind of old. And she can't always show us everything because she
has bursitis in her elbow." She frowned. "Do you have bursitis?"
she asked Poppy.

Poppy tried not to smile. "No. I'm not even sure I know what it
is," she said, while making way for a family coming up the steps.

"Me neither," Cassie said. And then she thought of something
else. "Poppy?"

"Yes?"

"When you did baton twirling, were you mean to the other
girls who did it with you? The ones who weren't as good as you?"

Poppy considered this question and then shook her head. "No,
I don't think I was mean to them. But then, they were all really
good. You had to be, if you wanted to be in my high school's
marching band."

"Oh," Cassie said, her face falling. "Well, I'll never be good enough to be in a marching band. And the girls in my class—the ten-year-olds, at least—are mean. They say if I make mistakes at our show I'll make everyone look bad."

"I don't believe that," Poppy said. "I don't believe you could make *anyone* look bad, and that includes yourself."

But Cassie looked fretful.

"Do you want to show me your twirl, Cassie?" Poppy asked.

"Okay," she said, a little reluctantly, and then, screwing her face up with concentration, she began to twirl. And Poppy nodded encouragingly, but thought, as she watched her, *No technique. No natural ability, either.*

"That was good," Poppy said brightly, when she was finished. "But, Cassie, why . . . why baton twirling? I mean, there's nothing *wrong* with doing it. But there must be other things to do around here, right? Other sports to play or classes to take?"

"*Wrong*," Cassie said, with an upward roll of her eyes. "There's almost *nothing* to do here. And besides, I *like* baton twirling. I mean, I don't like the part where you twirl the baton, but I like everything else about it. You know, like when we have recitals, we get to have our hair and makeup done by the moms, and we get to wear these twirler outfits. And they are so pretty, and so sparkly and so . . . girlie."

"Oh, they are *definitely* girlie," Poppy agreed.

"And I *like* that," Cassie said, earnestly. "Especially since I live in an all-boy house."

"So, no sisters?"

Cassie shook her head. "Only brothers," she said. "But I *wish* I had a sister. Do you have one?"

"I do," Poppy said. "A younger sister. But do you want to know a secret?"

Cassie nodded emphatically.

"She *acts* like the older sister. She's much more responsible than me."

"Really?" Cassie's eyes widened. "Does she ever get into trouble?"

"No, she leaves that to me," Poppy said wryly. "And she's waiting for me right now," she said, reaching for her things. "We're going to have dinner together, and she's going to tell me how I can be more responsible. But keep twirling, Cassie," she said, heading down the steps. Before she opened the car door, though, she made the mistake of looking back at her. Cassie was still twirling, with predictable results. Poppy hesitated. *I could teach her,* she thought. True, she'd never spent much time with kids before. She'd never really felt like she had anything to offer them. Win had been the one to babysit. And Win had been the one to teach. But this, this was different. She hadn't twirled a baton in forever, and it had still come right back to her. She could still do it. And she could teach someone else to do it, too. She walked back to the porch.

"Cassie," she called up. "How would you like me to help you with your twirling?"

Cassie stopped twirling. "You mean, like, be my tutor?" she asked. "My brother Hunter has a math tutor."

"Sure, I could do that," Poppy said, coming up the steps.

Cassie beamed at her, but then her face fell a little.

"You can't tutor me," she said, ruefully. "Tutors cost money. And I haven't got any. Well, no. I have got *some.* But only seven dollars and forty-seven cents."

That's more than I have, Poppy thought, but what she said was, "Cassie, you're in luck, because I'm not going to charge you anything. It'll be free. But we're going to have to ask your parents, okay?"

"Okay. Let's go ask my dad right now," Cassie said, excitedly, and she took Poppy's hand and started pulling her toward the business's front door.

Poppy laughed. "What's your dad doing here?" she asked, as Cassie led her inside and down one of the aisles. "Grocery shopping?"

"No, silly. He *owns* this place," Cassie said. She kept pulling on Poppy's hand.

"Um, you know what, sweetie?" Poppy said, digging in her heels as she thought about her recent misunderstanding with the owner. "Maybe you and I are getting ahead of ourselves here. Maybe your dad won't think this is such a great idea after all."

"He *has* to," Cassie said, looking up at her, and pulling again with a new strength. "*He* can't help me. He can't twirl a baton. And he can't French braid hair. And he can't *even* put toenail polish on me, even though everyone knows that is a *really* easy thing to do."

"But . . ."

"Come on," Cassie said, giving her hand another tug, but at that moment, Cassie's dad came around the corner of the aisle they were standing in, and, seeing him, Poppy felt an odd little jolt. There was something magnetic about him that she'd been too preoccupied to notice when he was behind the counter. She quickly brushed this thought away, though. And, just then, he saw her and Cassie together. He looked surprised, and not altogether happy.

"What's going on here?" he asked, and Poppy almost cringed with embarrassment. She hadn't thought she'd be seeing him again so soon.

"Daddy, this is Poppy!" Cassie said, breathlessly. "I want you to meet her."

"I think we've already met," he said, coming over to them. He eyed Poppy warily. "Honey, let go of her hand," he said to Cassie. "She's a customer."

"But she's *not* a customer," Cassie said, not letting go of Poppy's hand. "That's what I'm *trying* to explain, Dad. She was a majorette. She was in a marching band. *And* she twirled my baton, and she twirled it *so good.*"

"*Well.* She twirled it so *well*," he corrected.

"She twirled it so *well*," Cassie repeated. "Better even than Miss Suzette. *Plus* she doesn't even have bursitis."

He looked at Poppy questioningly, but Poppy only shrugged.

"Please, Daddy. Can she tutor me for free? The recital's coming up, and I'm *still* dropping my baton."

He looked uncomfortable. "Honey, we . . . we don't really know Poppy," he said, putting a hand on Cassie's head.

"But *I* know her," Cassie said, squeezing Poppy's hand tighter. "I know she's named after a flower that her mom liked. And I know her dad didn't really care what she was named. And—"

"Look," Poppy interrupted. "Why don't we start over again, okay? I'm Poppy Robbins. I'm staying with my sister for the summer. You might know her. Her name is Win? Win Robbins? She teaches at the middle school here." She held out her hand for him to shake.

He shook it, a little stiffly. *Jeez. The man knows how to hold a grudge.* "I'm Sam Boyd," he said. "And yes, of course, I know Win. She's the teacher rep for the PTA."

Of course she is, Poppy thought. "Well then, you know I'm not dangerous," she joked. Because to be Win's sister was to always have a character reference of sorts, whether Poppy deserved it or not.

Sam looked unmoved, though, and this would have been the

time to extract herself from this whole awkward situation, if only Cassie would have relaxed her grip on her hand.

"*Please,*" Cassie said now, shifting her focus away from her dad and onto Poppy. "Would you please tutor me?" And Poppy sighed inwardly. How could anyone say no to someone this adorable?

So she tried again. "Do you think it would be okay, Sam, if I coached Cassie once or twice a week?" she asked him. "I wouldn't charge anything, obviously, and we could work around her schedule." *Especially since I don't have a schedule of my own.*

He looked uneasy. "I'm pretty busy here in the summertime. Cassie knows that. I can't be driving her around all day."

"You won't have to," Poppy assured him. "I can come here."

"*Please, Daddy,*" Cassie said, looking up at him beseechingly. "We won't get in the way. We can go out back. Or in the storage room. *Please.*"

"We could just try it and see how it goes," Poppy interjected.

Sam wavered, and Cassie, sensing victory, began jumping up and down.

"All right," Sam said, looking like a man who'd been beat. "But Poppy and I are going to have to set up a day and a time."

"Okay," Cassie said, still jumping. "But can I borrow your cell phone, Daddy?"

"What for?"

"So I can call Janelle and tell her I have a tutor," she said, beaming at Cassie. "A *pretty* tutor."

CHAPTER 7

Win was taking the lasagna out of the oven when Poppy breezed into the kitchen. "What took you so long?" she asked her.

"I got a job," Poppy said.

"That was fast," Win said skeptically. She set the pan of lasagna down on the stovetop, and reached for the bottle of wine Poppy was holding.

"Well, it doesn't actually pay," Poppy admitted. "But it comes with some fringe benefits."

"Like . . . ?" Win asked, examining the bottle. Why was it so dusty? she wondered. She looked, surreptitiously, for a price tag, but she couldn't find one.

"Like spending time with an adorable six-year-old. Do you know Cassie? Cassie whose dad owns Birch Tree Bait?"

"I know Cassie," Win said.

"I'm going to tutor her in baton twirling."

"Really?" Win said. And now Poppy had her attention. "You haven't twirled since high school."

"Well, it all came right back to me," Poppy said blithely. "But what's up with Cassie's dad?"

"Sam? What do you mean?" Win asked, putting the suspect bottle of wine down and reaching for a knife to cut the lasagna with.

"He was kind of rude to me."

"He was?" Win said, surprised. She sliced into the browned and bubbly lasagna. "Maybe he was having a bad day," she mused.

"Yeah, okay," Poppy said. "But what's his glitch?"

"He doesn't have one," Win said, with a slight frown. She was trying to ensure that all eight slices of lasagna were exactly the same size. "He's divorced. Three kids. And he's a nice guy. A nice guy who half the single teachers I work with have a crush on."

Poppy made a face as if to say, *Him?*

"What? You don't think he's good-looking?" Win said, looking up.

"If you like that type," Poppy said, breaking off a piece of the lasagna's browned crust and nibbling on it.

Win was amused. "You mean the good-looking type?" she said, as she reached up to the cupboard for two plates.

"Oh, let's not use plates," Poppy objected. "Let's just take the whole pan and a couple of forks down to the dock and watch the sunset."

But Win shook her head. "No, I already set the dining room table," she said.

Poppy was aghast. "Win, nobody *eats* at the dining room table. You know that. It's like . . . the first rule of cabin living. The dining room table is for jigsaw puzzles, not *food*." And Win laughed, because Poppy had a point. Even in their grandparents' day, the cabin's dining room had rarely, if ever, been used for dining. Their grandparents had preferred to eat at the cozier kitchen table. But tonight was different. Tonight, Win had set this little-used table—complete with cloth napkins and just-bought flowers—because she wanted to drive home to Poppy the seriousness of the conversation they were going to have over dinner. It was time, once again, for Poppy to make a plan. A plan she would stick to. A plan that was more ambitious than her current plan of spending the summer sunbathing on the dock.

"Look, it'll be fine," Win said, using a spatula to place a generous wedge of lasagna on each of the plates. "It'll be very civilized. We can talk about your new non-paying job, and we can talk about some other things, too. Now, take these to the table," she said, handing the plates to Poppy. "I already put out the salad and the bread." Poppy left with them and when she came back Win was struggling with the corkscrew.

"Here, let me do that," Poppy said, reaching for it, but at that moment they heard a car drive up outside. Win went to the kitchen window, pulled back the curtain, and let it fall closed again.

"It's Everett," she said, turning to Poppy.

"*Everett?*"

"Did you know he was coming tonight?" she asked.

"*No,*" Poppy said. "I had no idea. Maybe . . . maybe that's why he called this afternoon, though. I let it go to voice mail, and I haven't listened to his message yet. He texted me, too, but I . . ."

"But you didn't read it?"

She shook her head, guiltily.

"*Poppy.* How could you be so rude? He *drove* you here."

"I know. *I know.* But I thought that was *it.* I thought that was the end of it. Then, today, when he tried to get in touch, I thought maybe I'd been wrong. And he wanted it to be, you know, something more."

"And you were surprised?"

"*Yes.*"

There was a knock on the front door, but neither of them moved. Finally, Win said, "Well, don't just stand there. Let him in and ask him if he likes lasagna."

"Win, no. I can't," Poppy said, helplessly. "It'll be awkward. I'll have to give him the speech."

"What speech?"

"You know, the one where you tell someone you just want to be friends with them?"

Win sighed, exasperated. *She* didn't know. She'd never had to give anyone that speech before. But for Poppy, obviously, it was different. She probably had it memorized by now. Everett knocked again.

"Poppy, you can't just ignore him," Win said, lowering her voice. "He knows somebody's home. I mean, my car is in the driveway."

"He knows *you're* home," Poppy said. "He doesn't know *I* am. You can—"

"No, I can't. *I won't.* I've been doing that for you my whole life, and I—"

"Shhh," Poppy said, holding a finger to her lips. They listened to the sound of Everett's footsteps going back down the steps. "He's going," she whispered, with obvious relief.

"No, he's not. Not yet," Win said. She started to leave the kitchen, then turned and said to Poppy, in a tone that brokered no compromise, "*You,* go to your room. *Now.* And don't come out until I give you the all clear." They left the kitchen together, Poppy scurrying down the hallway to her room and Win going to open the front door.

"Everett!" she called out, right as he was getting into his car.

"Oh, hey," he said, getting out again. "You're home."

"I'm home," Win said, coming down the steps. "But Poppy's not."

She steeled herself for his disappointment, but Everett seemed to take this news in stride. "Oh, that's fine. I didn't need to see her. It's just, I left her a voice mail and a text—"

"She's really bad at checking her cell phone," Win interrupted. "I've tried to get after her about it, but . . ."

He shrugged. "That's all right. I just wanted to tell her she left a box in my car." He pointed to a shoebox beside the front door that Win hadn't noticed. "I don't know how we missed it that night. It was dark out, I guess. And the next morning . . ."

"The next morning you left in a hurry," Win finished for him. He'd been gone when she and Poppy had woken up. He'd left a note on top of his neatly folded bedding, thanking Win for the grilled cheese sandwich and wishing Poppy good luck with her move.

"Oh, no, I wasn't in a hurry," Everett said now. "I'm just an early riser. Force of habit, I guess." He pushed his hair out of his eyes, in a gesture that Win only now remembered.

"Everett," she said, almost gently. "You didn't . . . you didn't come all the way up here just to deliver that box, did you?"

"No," he said. "I'm on my way up to Birch Lake. It's about an hour north of here."

"I've never been there," Win said. "But I've heard about it. It's supposed to be very pretty."

"It is. My cousin's got a cabin there he's letting me use for the rest of the summer. He and his wife have six-week-old twins, and

I think all that rusticness isn't as appealing as it used to be." He smiled, a little shyly. "Anyway, it's nice to get out of the city in the summertime."

"That's true," Win said, and then surprised herself by asking, "Have you had dinner yet?"

"No," Everett said. "I was going to get something up there."

"Have something here. I just took a lasagna out of the oven, and Poppy had to go out at the last minute. I'd hate for it to go to waste," she said, one corner of her mouth quirking up mischievously at the thought of Poppy having to hide in her bedroom while she and Everett ate in the dining room.

"Are you sure?" Everett said. "Because I'm starving. I'd love some lasagna."

"Good," Win said. And after letting Everett into the cabin and pointing him in the direction of the dining room, she went into the kitchen, and texted Poppy, who texted her right back.

Win: *So, guess what? I invited your sleepy-eyed friend to dinner.*
Poppy: *Whatttttt?*
Win: *Don't worry. I told him you were out. He won't stay long.*
Poppy: *So I have to stay in my room while you two eat??!!*
Win: *Exactly. Check your voice mails next time.*
Poppy: *But I'm hungry.*
Win: *You'll survive.*
Poppy: ☹

Win put her cell phone back in her pocket, and started to open the bottle of wine that Poppy had bought, then changed her mind. She actually had another bottle of red wine—a nicer bottle, she was sure—in the cupboard. She took that out, and after a brief skirmish with the corkscrew, managed to get it open. When she came into the dining room, Everett was standing there, looking as if he didn't know quite what to do with himself.

"Thanks," he said, again. He sat down, a little hesitantly, at the table.

But his hesitancy vanished once he'd tried the food. "This is *so* good," he said, of the lasagna. Win smiled and fiddled with her wineglass. She tried to think of something they could talk about. "So, how did you get into the web design business?" she asked him, finally, when the silence between them threatened to get awkward.

"I grew up in rural Nebraska," he said, "where my family owned a feed store. I started working there, part-time, when I was in high school. But I was never really interested in the feed side of the business. I was more interested in the advertising side of it. You know, the signage and the flyers and the circulars we used to design and print. I started doing those, at first, and then my senior year I designed a website for the business. A very *basic* website," he added.

"Still, your parents must have appreciated that," Win said as she poured wine into his glass.

"They did," he said. He went on to tell her that his parents were thrilled when he chose to major in computer science at the University of Minnesota, but they were *less* thrilled when, after graduation, he opted not to find a job as a programmer but to get a second degree, this one in graphic design. Still, when he'd gone to work for a website design firm after graduation, and his first pro bono job had been for the family business—he'd completely redesigned and updated the feed store's website—they'd stopped complaining. He'd liked his job, he told Win, but he liked his independence, too, and a couple of years ago, he'd struck out on his own. "There were some slow months in the beginning, months when I lived mainly on Kraft macaroni and cheese," he admitted. "But lately, things have started to take off. I've gotten so busy I've had to turn down a couple of projects. Everyone keeps telling me to hire people and expand, but I like working for myself. It gives me the freedom to take on the smaller, quirkier projects I might not consider if I was trying to make payroll for anyone but myself. What about you?" he asked after Win served him a second helping of lasagna. "You're a social studies teacher, aren't you?"

"Uh-huh. I teach seventh and eighth graders at the K-8 school here," she said, watching with pleasure as he helped himself to more salad and garlic bread. It was fun to be cooking for someone other than herself.

"That must be challenging sometimes," Everett said. "Teaching twelve- and thirteen-year-olds. I mean, I remember being that age, and what I was thinking about in class most of the time wasn't in my textbook."

"It can be challenging," Win agreed, "but I love it. And, believe it or not, I've found ways to keep even thirteen-year-olds interested," she said. She told Everett then about how, the winter before, she'd been teaching her seventh grade class about the American Revolution and she'd given her students a list of extra credit options they could choose from if they wanted to improve their grades. A group of boys in her class—none of whom were particularly good students—had chosen to make a movie for their project, and they'd worked exhaustively on it, writing the script, casting the actors, and scouting locations in Butternut that they hoped would resemble Valley Forge, Pennsylvania. The only problem, she told Everett, was that on the freezing cold day of filming, which she was present for, the student director insisted that the actors depicting the ragged, blanket draped colonial sol-

diers, actually go barefoot in the snow, as their historical coun-
terparts had done.

"I was dead set against it," Win said. "I had visions of parents
of frostbitten children suing the school district. But I did some
quick research on how long it took to get frostbite at the current
temperature, and I gave the director three minutes to film the
barefoot scenes."

"Did that authenticity pay off?"

"It did." She smiled and sipped her wine. "The movie was a
huge success. So many people wanted to see it, in fact, that we
had to have a screening at the Butternut Community Center.
The only fallout from it came from one of the mothers of a boy
who'd played a soldier: the "blanket" he'd brought from home
and gotten wet in the snow had actually been a valuable antique
quilt."

"Did *that* lead to a lawsuit?" Everett asked, an amused expression on his face.

"No. The school principal came to my rescue. He's a big sup-
porter of mine, and he calmed the mother down. He told her
that 'all great art comes at a price.'"

"He's right, you know," Everett said. "I once went two days
without sleep designing a website for a pest control company."

Win laughed and reached for the bottle of wine. It was
almost empty. "We drank the whole bottle?" she asked him in
amazement.

"We did," Everett said, with a seriousness that made her laugh
again. "Actually," he amended, "you drank most of it."

"That's not like me *at all*," she said.

"Well, if it's any consolation, I ate most of the lasagna. But that
is like me."

Outside the dining room windows the sun had set, and the

sky had shaded from pale pink to deep lavender. It was dusk, Win's favorite time of day in the summer and, as far as she was concerned, there was only one place to be as evening turned into night at the cabin. "Are you afraid of heights?" she asked Everett.

This is so cool," he murmured. They were sitting on the edge of the boathouse roof, their feet dangling over the lake, which was twelve feet below them. In another half an hour, the sky and the water would be dark, but for now they both held the last vestiges of daylight within them, the sky a dark purple, the water a cobalt blue. A breeze blew then. It had the first hint of the night's coolness in it, and it stirred the branches of the great northern pines, and sent diamond points of light dancing over the water.

"It *is* pretty cool," Win agreed. "You're not nervous about being up here, are you?"

"No. Should I be?"

She shook her head. "The water's deep enough here to jump into. I used to do it, too, when I was little, but only when my grandmother wasn't watching." She'd had to jump alone, though; Poppy was afraid of heights.

And, as if on cue, her cell phone buzzed in her pocket. She slid it out. It was a text from Poppy.

Poppy: *What's going on???*

Win: *Everett and I are on the boathouse roof.*

Poppy: *He's been here forever. What have you been doing?*

Win: *Eating. And talking.*

Poppy: *I hope you saved me some lasagna.*

Win: *Yep. It's on the kitchen counter.*

Poppy: *Good. I'm going to take some of it to my room. I'm so hungry I almost ate my slipper!!!*

Win: *Maybe you still should.*

Poppy: *???*

Win: *For being such a jerk to Everett, who, btw, is a really nice guy.*

Win put her phone back in her pocket. "Poppy," she said, by way of explanation.

Everett nodded, but he didn't ask her when Poppy would be home, and she felt relieved. She hated lying. She hated playing games. And, right now, she hated Poppy, *just a little,* for putting her in a position tonight where she'd felt compelled to do both of these things. She didn't know Everett very well, obviously, but she couldn't help but feel he deserved better than being treated like this. She tried to think, now, of a tactful way of warning him off, or of giving him her own version of Poppy's "speech," but she decided against it. They were having too nice of an evening. Besides, he didn't seem like an unintelligent person. He seemed, in fact, quite the opposite. He'd figure it out. To know Poppy, after all, was to know that, in some very fundamental way, she was unavailable. Out of reach. And not just out of reach to Everett, but to most of the people in her life. Even, sometimes, to Win.

"How well do you know my sister?" she asked, casually.

He shrugged. "Not that well. I used to see her every morning, though, at this coffeehouse in our neighborhood. She'd be there to get a latte; I'd be there to work. On my laptop, I mean. It was great. For the price of a cup of coffee, and all of the ones I could stuff in the tip jar, I'd have an office for the day."

She smiled. "I worked at a coffeehouse once, near the university. We used to call customers like you 'squatters' or, sometimes, 'campers.'"

He laughed. "That sounds about right. Did we drive you crazy?"

"No, I didn't mind people who stayed all day. In fact, on a slow day, it was nice to have them around. What I minded were those people who took their coffee so seriously you wanted to grab them and shake them and say, 'It's coffee. It's hot and brown and caffeinated. Just drink it!' But no, I had to answer questions like 'Is this coffee shade grown?' Or 'Is it small batch roasted?' Or, my personal favorite, 'Were these beans harvested by indigenous peoples?' I told them, honestly, 'I have no idea; being a barista is not my calling in life. I'm just trying to earn enough money to get through school.'

"Then there were those customers who were absolutely obsessive about the way you made their drinks," she said, shaking her head at the memory. "And you knew, no matter how perfectly you made it, they were never going to be satisfied. This one guy, for instance . . ." But she caught herself, stopped, and looked away.

"Was he a jerk?" he asked her.

"He *was* a jerk. But he was also . . . he was also how I met my husband. My *late* husband," she amended. "I'd just started working at this place, and this man—this jerk—came in and . . ." She stopped, suddenly self-conscious. "Do you really . . . want to hear this story?" she asked, unsure of herself.

"I really do," he said, with an easy smile.

"Okay, well, as I said, I'd just started working at this place, and I'd had, like, fifteen minutes of training, and this guy comes in and orders something very complicated. You know, something with at least five qualifying adjectives, like 'a decaf nonfat double vanilla latte with extra foam.' Something like that. But when I make it for him, he's not happy. The foam is wrong. It's not . . . *foamy* enough. So I make it again. But now there's something *else* wrong with it. So I make it one more time. And the line is getting longer, and he's getting angrier, and I'm getting more flustered, and *no one* is helping me. It's like everyone else who

worked there has simultaneously gone on break. Finally, this guy
says to me, 'You know what? Forget it. You're obviously incom-
petent. Just give me a cup of coffee. And I'm *not* paying for it.' I
give him the coffee, even though by now I'm practically crying,
and he takes it and sits down at a table and starts having this
really loud, really obnoxious cell phone conversation about what
an idiot this woman who just served him a cup of coffee is. In the
meantime, the guy who was in line *behind* him orders a drink,
and I can tell he feels sorry for me. He orders something really
easy to make, and he puts a five-dollar bill in the tip jar.

"On his way out, though," Win continued, "he trips, and he
spills his drink all over the jerk, and all over the jerk's designer
suit and five-hundred-dollar shoes. How do I know they were
five-hundred-dollar shoes? Because he starts screaming about
them being ruined and, honestly, I thought he was going to throt-
tle the guy who spilled the coffee on them. That guy keeps his
cool, though. He apologizes, he offers to buy him a new cup of
coffee, he offers to pay to have his suit dry-cleaned. But the other
guy, the jerk, isn't having any of it, and finally he just storms out
of there. And the nice guy watches him go, and then he turns to
me, and he winks at me, and he leaves. Just like that. So, the next
day, when he comes back to see me, you know what I did?"

"You married him?" Everett offered.

She laughed. "Well, yes, *eventually*, but not that day. *That
day*, I gave him my phone number. I mean, wouldn't you have
done the same thing?"

"Um, no. Not as myself, but as you? Yeah. Probably."

She smiled, a little, and swung her dangling feet. "The thing
I like so much about that story," she said, softly, "is that when
I got to know Kyle—that was his name, Kyle—I realized that
what he'd done that day was totally out of character for him. He

wasn't some guy who went around spilling coffee on strangers. He wasn't some . . . hothead. He was the opposite of that. He was logical. Rational. But he told me, later, that even though he didn't know me yet that day, he couldn't stand watching me be bullied."

They lapsed into a comfortable silence, until Everett said, quietly, "I'm guessing it was a happy marriage."

Win had been looking out over the dark water, but she turned to him and said, a little wistfully, "It was. It really was. There were a few skeptics, though, when we first got engaged. My sister was one of them."

He raised his eyebrows in a silent question.

She shrugged. "Poppy thought that, at twenty-two, I was too young to get married. And even though she liked Kyle, a lot, she thought he was too serious. Too . . . *settled.* He was only twenty-seven when I met him, but he was already a certified public accountant. He already owned his own condominium. Already had a 401K plan, and life insurance, and a diversified stock portfolio. But Poppy, Poppy was not impressed. I remember once, she said, 'Win, he's such a *grown-up,*' as if that was a bad thing. Which to her, it was. I mean, he was probably one of the first real grown-ups she'd ever met. God knows our parents didn't act like grown-ups. They acted like a couple of kids." *A couple of spoiled, badly behaved kids,* she almost added. "When we were growing up, they had no concept of how to provide stability, or anything even *close* to it. And for me, I think, that was part of the attraction of Kyle. When Poppy asked me, right before the wedding, 'Aren't you afraid you're going to be bored?' I said, 'Poppy, don't you get it? I *want* to be bored. I want to be bored *out of my mind.*'" She smiled now, remembering this conversation.

"But you weren't bored, were you?" Everett asked, bringing her back to herself.

She smiled and shook her head. "No, of course not. Kyle wasn't boring. He was just . . . stable. Steady." Her voice trailed off and, in the silence, she felt it, that ache deep in her chest, somewhere behind her breastbone. It was a dull, empty, endless ache, an ache that was her missing Kyle, and everything that they had had together.

"You know the rest of the story," she said, when she felt like she couldn't stand the ache anymore; when she felt like it was actually taking up the space she needed to breathe.

He nodded. "Poppy told me. I hope that was all right."

She didn't answer. She looked back out over the lake, and tried to pick out the lights from the cabins she knew were on the opposite shore.

"It was . . . cancer, right?" he asked, gently.

"Right. One spring—we'd just celebrated our second anniversary—he got this cough he just couldn't shake, even after a couple of rounds of antibiotics. But we thought . . . well, it was tax season. He was overworked. He needed a vacation. His doctor, though, thought he needed a chest X-ray. And that was it. Well, that wasn't *it*. There was a lot more after that. But that set everything in motion. That X-ray. And almost a year later . . ." She shook her head, still amazed by how fast, and at the same time how slowly, that year had gone. "It was lung cancer. He was only thirty. He'd never smoked a cigarette in his life. Go figure, huh?" She said this as an attempt at a bleak kind of humor she used sometimes to relieve the tension after she told people.

Everett, though, didn't say anything. Not even the two words people invariably said when she told them about her husband's death. Instead, he looked at her, with his sleepy eyes, and shook his head, almost imperceptibly. And something moved across his face then, a shadow that might have been pain.

"Have you ever . . . lost someone?" she asked him.

But before he could answer her, her cell phone vibrated in her pocket. She sighed, pulled it out, and resisted the urge to throw it into the lake. Instead she read the text from Poppy.

Poppy: *Is he ever leaving???*

"I should probably get going," Everett said, as if in response to the text, though there was no way he could have read it.

"Okay. Come on. I'll walk you to your car."

When she knocked on Poppy's bedroom door, five minutes later, she heard a tentative "Come in."

"The coast is clear," Win said, opening the door. Poppy was curled up on her bed with Sasquatch, eating lasagna.

"Second piece," Poppy said, indicating the plate. "I swear, Win, this is even better cold than it is hot."

Win came into the room holding the box Everett had left and stepped over the clothes that littered the floor.

"Poppy, you didn't need to barricade yourself in here," she said, reaching her bed and sitting down on the edge of it. "Really. You would have had a nice time with us tonight. He's . . . he's easy to talk to."

Poppy eyed the box warily.

"He brought this," Win said, holding it out to her. "You left it in his car."

Poppy put her plate down and reached for it. She opened it up and poked around in it a little.

"Love letters?" Win asked wryly.

Poppy shook her head. "Unpaid bills," she said with a sigh. And it was only then that Win remembered the talk they were supposed to have had that night.

CHAPTER 8

P oppy?"

"Yes, Cassie?"

"Can we take a break?"

"Of course," Poppy said, though their last "break" had ended only five minutes before. Being Cassie's baton twirling tutor, she was quickly learning, involved remarkably little twirling. Mainly, their sessions were spent talking. Or, rather, *Cassie* spent them talking; Poppy spent them listening to Cassie talk.

She didn't mind, though. In fact, this was the third afternoon this week she'd driven over to Birch Tree Bait and spent a pleasant hour with Cassie on its wide, well shaded front porch, practicing arm rolls, chin rolls, and figure eights, and watching the activity ebb and flow around them. There was a mother buying a Fudgesicle for an already sticky toddler, a cranky older man coming in to replace a lost fishing license, and two boy scouts, in uniform, stocking up on flashlight batteries for an overnight camping trip. And now, in the lead up to the Fourth of July weekend, there was a change in tempo. Suddenly, it seemed as if everyone on the lake had their own list of urgently needed supplies: marshmallows, safety matches, paper cups, sparklers, fishing line, insect repellant, and, for one disappointed woman, a beach umbrella. (She was sent to the Butternut Variety Store for this.) Poppy couldn't help but get caught up in the excitement, especially since everyone was talking about the upcoming fireworks display at the fairgrounds. This year, they claimed, would be the best year ever.

Being here was a nice break from being at the cabin, Poppy thought, sitting down on the porch swing with Cassie. At the cabin, she was growing bored with her sunbathing regimen, and Win was increasingly irritated by her sloppiness. Well, *that* and something else. Win had finally figured out that Poppy was broke. *Flat* broke. And she'd reacted to this discovery with something less than sisterly understanding. And *Poppy* had reacted to *Win's* reaction with a defensiveness that quickly gave way to contrition; all in all, a familiar cycle in their relationship.

"I'm exhausted," Cassie said now, with an exaggerated sigh, coming to sit on the porch swing beside Poppy. "I mean, my *wrist* is exhausted," she corrected herself, and she held this pale, slender wrist out to Poppy for inspection.

"It looks very tired," Poppy said seriously. "Remember, Cassie, before you go to bed tonight, do the wrist exercises I showed you." She did one of them now for Cassie's benefit. "They'll help with flexibility and strength."

"Uh-huh," Cassie said, but she wasn't really paying attention to her. She was using her small, sandaled feet to push off from the porch floor and set the swing in motion. Poppy lifted her feet up and held on to one of its chains, and when Cassie was satisfied that they were swinging high enough, she looked up at Poppy and said, with only a trace of her old shyness, "Guess what Janelle said yesterday?"

"What?" Poppy asked, with genuine interest.

And they were off. Or *Cassie*, rather, was off, since Poppy was only occasionally called upon to ask a question, or offer an opinion, or give advice. Cassie talked a little bit about her parents, and a little bit more about her brothers, but mainly, she talked about Janelle, her best friend, about Gia and Riley, the mean girls in her baton twirling class, and about Jackson, a boy in her kindergarten class who used to throw little rolled up bits of paper at her head during circle time. Janelle, especially, was a subject of unending fascination to Cassie. She *might* have seen a real ghost, her father kept tortoises for pets, and her mother had once thrown her bra on stage at a Trace Adkins concert. This last piece of information, Poppy thought, was not entirely appropriate for a six-year-old to know, but Cassie didn't invest it with any lascivious intention, she merely presented it as a statement of fact.

Today, though, Cassie skipped quickly over Janelle, Riley, and Gia, and wanted to talk, instead, about Jackson. "Why does he throw paper balls at me? Does he hate me?" she asked Poppy.

"No, he doesn't hate you," Poppy said, neutrally. She was trying not to overstep any boundaries here. "It's . . . more complicated than that."

Poppy waited for her to reject an answer that was really no answer at all, but instead she asked another question. "Why do grown-ups always use the word *complicated*?"

Poppy laughed. This time, though, Cassie didn't wait for an answer. "I'm thirsty," she said, hopping off the swing and jogging over to the business's front doors. "I'm going to get a Snapple. Do you want one, too?"

"No, thank you," Poppy said. Cassie ran into the store and Poppy gave the swing a little push of her own. She was surprised, once again, by how much she enjoyed spending time with Cassie.

She was adorable, of course, but it was more than that. She had an innocence about her, a sweetness, and a quality of being almost entirely unencumbered by the problems of the adult world. Whereas Poppy, at her age, was already worried about whether her parents would be able to pay the rent. Cassie's dad, of course, was not even remotely like either of Poppy's parents. And as she was thinking this, Birch Tree Bait's front door swung open and Sam came out onto the porch.

"That is one enthusiastic pupil you have there," he said to Poppy.

She smiled. She'd been wrong about Sam. He didn't hold a grudge, and the initial iciness between them had thawed out nicely. In fact, the brief conversations they had before and after these tutoring sessions were the other reason why she liked coming here. "Actually, I think I'm having just as much fun as she is," she told Sam now. "And her thumb toss is really progressing."

He looked at her blankly.

"You have no idea what that is, do you?"

"No."

"Well, you don't need to know. But the thumb toss is one of the building blocks of twirling."

"I'll take your word for it," he said, with another smile, and Poppy had to admit that Win was right. Sam *was* good-looking; good-looking in a flannel shirt, blue jeans, and work boots kind of way. Oh, hell, whom was she kidding? He was good-looking in *every* kind of way. Tall and athletically built, he had a tan that, unlike hers, was not the kind you got from sunbathing, but from just being outside. It suited him, too. It made his eyes look bluer, and brought out the glints of copper in his brown hair.

"I hope you know that you don't have to come here this often," he said, sitting down on the front porch's railing. "Because as much as Cassie loves bragging to all of her friends about her new tutor, she'll understand if you have other commitments."

"But I don't," Poppy said. "At least, not right now. That . . . that could change, though," she added. *No, that has to change,* she reminded herself, *because yesterday you had to borrow money from Win to buy hair elastics.* "I think, actually, I'm going to start looking for a job," she said, with more confidence than she actually felt. "Something just for the summer," she added, quickly. "Something just to tide me over until . . ." *Until what?* She had no idea.

Sam looked at her, speculatively. He seemed to be considering saying something, but then he changed his mind and looked away.

"What?" Poppy asked, sitting up straighter on the swing.

"Well, I might . . . I might have something here."

"Really?" And then, with a raised eyebrow, Poppy asked, "It doesn't have anything to do with the worms, does it?"

He laughed. "No, but it's not much better. I need someone to help on the grocery side of the store. Justine—do you know who she is?"

"The goth?"

"Yes, that's her. She usually covers the register, and when she has time, she does the stocking, too. But when we're this busy, she can't handle both. So this is the point in the summer when I hire someone else. It's usually a college student, or even a responsible high school student, but it could be . . ." His voice trailed off. He seemed embarrassed.

"Are you . . . are you offering me a job?"

"Sort of. I mean, I don't think it's what you're looking for," he said, almost apologetically. "For one thing, it pays minimum wage."

"I'll take it," she said.

He looked surprised. "There are no benefits," he warned.

"I'm your girl."

"There's no security, either. As soon as things slow down, I'll have to let you go."

"Don't look any further than right here," she said, pointing to herself.

He seemed to consider this, then shrugged. "Yeah, okay. Why don't you come in when we open tomorrow and we can take care of the paperwork, and then Justine can get you started before things get too crazy."

"Great," she said brightly, giving the swing another little push. "One quick question, though."

"Yes?" Sam said, standing up to go.

"I noticed you sell Red Vines."

"The licorice?"

She nodded. "Do I get a discount on it?"

"Well, that depends. How much of it are you planning on eating?" He looked amused.

"Oh, only one package a day, at the most."

"Well, you can have that for free, then."

"And you said this job didn't have any benefits," Poppy said. But to herself, she wondered about taking a job that paid less than half what her last job had. This would seem to suggest her life was *not* moving in the right direction. On the other hand, she reasoned, she didn't exactly have a lot of other options; a sad, but true fact of her life at the moment.

Cassie reappeared now, sipping her Snapple. "Daddy, we're practicing," she said pointedly, sitting down on the swing beside Poppy.

Sam smiled. "I'll let you get to it then," he said, and with a quick nod to Poppy, he left them on the porch.

"Are you ready?" Poppy asked Cassie, indicating her baton.

"I'm *almost* ready," Cassie said, with the leisurely air of some-one who still had another fourteen ounces of Snapple to con-sume. She smiled then, an impish smile. "Did I tell you that Janelle's grandmother wears a wig?" she asked, leaning on the swing.

"You did not," Poppy said.

"Well, do you know what happened to it the last time she visited Janelle's family?"

"No. I can't wait to find out, though," Poppy said. And she meant it.

A ll right, Linc, back to work," Sam said, stopping by the coffee counter where Linc was talking to Byron. "And Byron, back to doing whatever it is you do here all day."

"But there's a lull now," Linc protested lazily.

"There won't be for long," Sam said, pouring himself an iced coffee. "In fact," he said, "I just hired someone else to help out around here."

"Who?" Linc asked.

"Poppy," he said, casually, sloshing milk into his coffee. "You know who she is, right? The woman who's been helping Cassie with her baton twirling." He concentrated on stirring his coffee, but he still felt the look Byron and Linc exchanged with each other.

"Uh, we know who she is, Sam," Linc said, obviously amused.

Sam looked at him sharply. "*What?* She needs a job, and we have one here."

"And you couldn't find anyone less attractive to fill it?" Byron said, obviously working hard to keep a straight face.

"Look, the point is not her attractiveness. The point is whether or not she can do the work, and I think she can."

There was another look between Linc and Byron.

"Come on, there's nothing happening here," Sam said.

"Well then," Byron said, settling back on his stool and shaking out his newspaper. "We'll have a front row seat to nothing happening, won't we, Linc?"

CHAPTER 9

On the Fourth of July, Win invited her friend Mary Jane Carpenter to spend the day at the cabin with her and Poppy. Partly, she did this because she hadn't seen that much of Mary Jane lately and she missed her. Mary Jane was a third grade teacher at the K–8 school in Butternut, and when Win had started teaching there two years ago, the two of them had bonded, almost immediately, over bad coffee and Girl Scout cookies in the teachers' lounge. But partly, she'd invited Mary Jane over because two weeks into Poppy's visit Win's patience with her had already begun to fray, and she was hoping that Mary Jane would serve as a buffer between them. And Mary Jane, who was direct, friendly, and, above all else, cheerful, had done just that. Not only had the two sisters gotten along, they'd had fun together. The three of them had spent the whole day—which was warm and sunny, with just the right amount of breeziness—down at the dock, reading magazines, munching on egg salad sandwiches, and floating in the big red-white-and-blue inner tubes Mary Jane had bought at a Fourth of July sale at the Butternut Variety Store.

Now, with the late afternoon sunlight making pleasant, watery reflections on the knotted pine walls of her bedroom, Win was sitting on her bed, freshly showered, and wearing a cotton sundress that she hoped would be kind to her slightly sunburned back and shoulders.

"Do you think I have chipmunk cheeks?" Mary Jane asked, turning to her. She was standing in front of Win's dresser, studying herself, critically, in the mirror that hung above it. Looking in the mirror was what everyone did, eventually, if they spent enough time with Poppy, and the fact that Mary Jane, with her sturdy self-confidence, was not immune to this was strangely comforting to Win.

"No," Win said, though Mary Jane *did*, in fact, have chipmunk cheeks. Still, they were *adorable. She* was adorable. And Win told her she was adorable.

Mary Jane smiled, a faintly preoccupied smile, and sat down, *bounced* down, really, on the bed beside Win. "I think I might be gay," she announced without preamble.

"Well, you better tell that to Bret," Win said. Bret was the man Mary Jane was going to marry in a month.

"No, I don't really think that," Mary Jane said. "It's just that all day today I couldn't stop staring at your sister."

"*Nobody* can stop staring at her," Win said, suddenly irritable.

"Now they can stare at her at Birch Tree Bait," Mary Jane pointed out.

"Right," Win said, rolling her eyes. "Where she'll be taking bags of Cheetos out of boxes and placing them on shelves."

"A job is a job," Mary Jane said. "Plenty of people would be happy to have one like that."

"I know." Win sighed. "But is it wrong of me to want more for her?"

"No," Mary Jane said, frowning slightly. "I know what I would be doing, though, if I were her. I'd be modeling. Honestly, Win, she looks better than the models in the magazines we were read- ing today. Should I . . . suggest it to her?"

"And you think you'd be the first person to ever do that?"

"Probably not."

"Mary Jane, people have been suggesting that to her her *whole life*. And she's always said the same thing. She doesn't think she'd be good at it. Which is possible, I suppose. Apparently, there's more to modeling than just sitting there and looking beautiful."

"It's true," Mary Jane said. "I watched the first nine seasons of *America's Next Top Model*."

"Still, don't you think it's strange that she's never even *tried* to do it before?" Win asked.

"Yeah, kind of," Mary Jane said. "Especially with her natural beauty." She paused. "It *is* natural, isn't it?"

"What do you mean?"

"Does she dye her hair?"

"Nope. That's hers. Roots to tips," Win said of Poppy's glori- ously blond hair.

"What about her eyes?"

"Those are hers, too," Win joked, though she knew what Mary Jane meant. When they were in high school, there'd been a rumor circulating that Poppy's brilliant blue eyes came to her courtesy of tinted contact lenses. It was, alas, not true.

"What about . . . ?" Mary Jane asked, pointing down at the neckline of her own floral print sundress, where, even in a push- up bra, her breasts were still too small to create an impression of cleavage.

"Oh, *those* are definitely real," Win said. "I mean, if Poppy can't even go to the trouble of wearing mascara, she's not about to go to the trouble of getting breast implants." Mary Jane nodded, thoughtfully, but Win was still preoccupied with the modeling question, and she told Mary Jane something about Poppy now that she'd never told anyone but Kyle before. "Do you want to know something weird?" she asked, and then she lowered her voice, even though she knew it wasn't necessary. She could still hear the water from Poppy's shower running.

"What?"

"I think the real reason Poppy's never tried modeling," Win said, "is because she doesn't like having her picture taken. As in, dislikes it intensely."

Mary Jane's eyes widened. "Why?"

"I don't know. I used to tease her about it, but I stopped. It only irritated her, and she wouldn't admit it, anyway."

Mary Jane considered this. "Are there *any* pictures of her?"

"From childhood, yes. But later, starting from when we were teenagers, very few. And most of those were taken at my wedding." Even those, Win remembered, hadn't come easily. She'd insisted that Poppy be in some of the group photos, and Poppy had submitted, though she'd submitted with the determined stoicism of someone who was about to have a root canal.

"She must have pictures of herself with boyfriends, though," Mary Jane said. "I mean, not all of them. But the serious ones, right?"

"The *serious* ones? There haven't *been* any serious ones."

"Okay, *that* really is weird," Mary Jane said. "She's older than we are. And she's never had anyone special in her life?"

"I'm not sure what you mean by special," Win said, in a whisper, because she could hear that Poppy's shower was over now. "She's had boyfriends before, of course, but it's like . . . it's like even before a relationship has really begun, she's already

looking for a way out of it. And then she's just"—she shrugged—
"she's just moving on to someone else." She paused then, worried
about how that sounded. "I don't mean she sleeps around," she
clarified. "She doesn't. She doesn't have one-night stands, but she
also doesn't have long-term relationships. It's a fear of intimacy,
I think, of *both* kinds of intimacy. The emotional kind, and the
other kind, too." The truth, though, was she wasn't even sure if
she was right about all of this or not. Sex was one thing she and
Poppy never discussed. Well, no, that wasn't true. Win had discussed it with Poppy, especially when she was falling in love with
Kyle. Poppy, though, had never returned her confidences. It was a
subject about which she'd always been deliberately vague.

She could tell Mary Jane wanted to pursue this further, but
Win decided to change the subject, and asked Mary Jane instead
for an update on her wedding planning. And then, while Mary
Jane discussed, in great detail, the relative merits of salmon
versus halibut for one of the main course options, Win stopped
paying attention and thought about her sister. No, *worried* about
her sister. If she'd been from a normal family, a *functional* family,
she could have let her parents worry about Poppy. But, as it was,
she had to worry about Poppy, *and* worry about her parents, too.
There wasn't a lot she could do for her mom and dad at this point,
though. For better or for worse—mostly for worse—they were
already following a path that neither one of them seemed capable of diverging from. Poppy was different. She *had* no path. She
had no direction. Most people, Win thought, moved forwards, a
few unlucky ones moved backwards, but Poppy, Poppy seemed
to move sideways.

Had she always been like that? Win wondered, picking at a
loose thread on the patchwork quilt on her bed. No, she hadn't.
There'd been a time, in high school, when she'd been committed

to something. She'd been a majorette in their high school marching band and she'd loved it. She'd been obsessed with it, in fact, obsessed to the point where the hours she'd spent practicing twirling at home in their cramped bedroom had driven Win crazy. But Poppy hadn't just been twirling then, Win recalled. She'd been studying, too. Her grade point average had been high enough for her to apply to Penn State, which was famous for its marching band. And she'd had other interests, too, friends, and fashion, and drawing. But what had happened? Win tried to remember, but it was hard. She'd been so caught up in her own life then: school, babysitting, homework. At some point, though, Poppy had quit marching band, quit studying, quit . . . everything, it seemed, and had just started to drift. There was no other word for it. Except for a few instances—a short-lived relationship with a boyfriend everyone liked, a semester long stint at a community college—she'd been drifting ever since.

Poppy had changed jobs more times than Win could remember. And it wasn't that she got fired—she had a natural intelligence and picked things up quickly—it was that she got "bored" or "restless," or decided it was "time to move on." And the same thing happened with roommates and apartments. Win had lost track of all of the places Poppy had lived over the years, although she always stayed in the same general area of Minneapolis, the area they'd grown up in. Win had talked to her, tactfully, and then not so tactfully, over the years about all of these things. But Poppy, it seemed, was masterful at changing the subject, and equally masterful at avoiding any real introspection.

"Do you agree?" Mary Jane asked now, breaking into Win's thoughts.

"About what?"

"About the grilled asparagus?"

"Oh, definitely," Win said, and she was saved from having to say any more about this when Poppy tapped, lightly, on her half-open door.

"Hey," she said. She was wrapped in one towel, and her hair was wrapped in another one. "Can I borrow your mascara?" she asked Win.

"Since when do you wear mascara?"

"Since now." Poppy shrugged. "Unless you'd rather I not—"

"Top drawer," Win interrupted, pointing at her bureau.

Poppy opened it and rummaged around in it, oblivious to the fact that Win's makeup drawer's classification system was as precise as her utensil drawers'. Finally, though, she pulled out the tube of mascara, unscrewed the wand, and, leaning closer to the mirror, brushed it on her eyelashes.

Mary Jane looked meaningfully at Win.

"Are you sure you don't want to come with us, Win?" Poppy asked, standing back to study the effect.

"I'm sure." She'd told Poppy and Mary Jane that she wouldn't be going with them tonight to the fairgrounds in Butternut for the annual Fourth of July picnic and fireworks. "I'm looking forward to a quiet night at home," she reminded them.

"Okay," Poppy said. She leaned closer to the mirror and applied more mascara to her lashes, and Win felt a flicker of irritation at the way she brushed casually against an old postcard from Kyle that Win had recently propped up on the dresser top.

"Sam's driving Cassie and the twins down to his ex-wife's this afternoon," Poppy said nonchalantly, screwing the wand back into the tube, and putting the mascara back into the dresser drawer. "But he said he still might stop by the fairgrounds later."

Win sat up straighter on the bed. "Poppy, *no*," she said, shaking her head.

"No, what?" her sister asked, innocently.

Win ignored the question. "Don't even think about it. Really. I *like* Sam. He's a nice guy. Just . . . just *don't*."

"Win, calm down. It's a harmless flirtation. That's all."

"Well, it won't be harmless for him. Trust me."

"God, you make it sound like I'm some black widow or something," Poppy said, looking hurt.

"You're not. You just have a long history of skipping out on people." *Not to mention jobs.* "And another thing, Pops," Win said—using the nickname that, for some reason, she only used when she was feeling either affectionate or irritated with her sister—"this is a small town. Long after you've left here, I'll still have to live with all of these people." She looked at Mary Jane, hoping she would back her up on this, but her friend obviously considered herself a spectator here, and she was looking with fascination, from one of them to the other, as if she were watching a tennis match.

"Look, I think you're blowing this out of proportion," Poppy said. "I just like flirting with him, that's all. You're the one who told me that half the single teachers at your school have a crush on him."

Mary Jane finally got involved now, nodding her head vigorously. "Actually, some of the *married* teachers have a crush on him, too," she told Poppy.

"Okay," Win said, throwing up her hands, because now she was exasperated with both of them. "Do what you want, Pops. For the record, though, if things go south with you and Sam, and I have to find someplace other than Birch Tree Bait to make my emergency Ben & Jerry's runs, I will never forgive you. Understood?"

"Understood," Poppy said breezily.

Later, as Win said good-bye to the two of them on the cabin's front porch—Mary Jane and Poppy were driving to the fairgrounds, where they'd meet up with Bret and some of his friends—Poppy pulled Win aside and said, firmly, "I want you to promise me that you won't be reorganizing the linen closet or anything else like that tonight."

"I wasn't planning on it," Win said, though now that Poppy had mentioned the linen closet, she was tempted. The last time she'd gotten a towel out of it she'd noticed that the pale yellow towels were beginning to mix in with the pale green ones.

"Well, even if you were, you might not have time to do it," Poppy said with a sly smile.

"What do you mean?" Win asked.

"I got a text from Everett this afternoon. He's at his cousin's cabin on Birch Lake and he wanted to come by and drop something off."

"Poppy, how many more boxes did you leave in his car?"

"None. It's not a box. It's a bottle of wine. He says he owes it to you from the last time he was here."

Win shook her head. "Poppy, he's using that as an excuse to see you."

"I already told him I'm not going to be here."

"But I am?"

Poppy nodded.

Win frowned, feeling pensive. "What if he wants to wait for you to come back?"

"Win, don't overthink things. He's bringing you a bottle of wine. Just take it and say 'thank you.' And, if you want bonus points for being polite . . ."

"Yes?"

"Ask him if he'd like to stay and drink it with you."

CHAPTER 10

Win, it turned out, did Poppy one better: she invited Everett to stay and drink the bottle of wine with her, and, when they'd finished it, she invited him to stay a little longer and drink *another* bottle of wine with her. Of course, *that* bottle was the same one Poppy had bought at Birch Tree Bait and, as Win sat beside Everett on the boathouse roof, watching him open it, she felt compelled to say, "I can't vouch for this one. I mean, look at it. It's all dusty."

"That means it's aged," he pointed out.

"Maybe," Win said. "But I think there's a difference between aged and old." She didn't really care whether the wine was any good or not, though. She was having too nice of a time.

Everett finished uncorking the bottle, and Win held out the wineglasses for him. "You go first," he said, after he'd filled them.

"I don't think so."

He shrugged good-naturedly, and took a drink from his. "Oh, my God," he said, wincing. "This is *really* bad."

Win laughed. "Should we just . . . pour it out?" she asked, gesturing at the water beneath them.

"That is *the last* thing we should do. I mean, this is obviously toxic," he said, holding up the bottle. "If we pour it in the lake, we could upset the entire ecosystem. I think we're just going to have to do the responsible thing and . . . drink it."

Win smiled and took a tentative sip from her own glass. She shuddered. "I thought I'd had bad wine before," she said. "But I can see now it was just a lead-up to this."

"Sometimes, if you keep drinking it, it starts to taste better," Everett said, taking a fairly decent sized slug from his glass.

"Any better?" she asked.

He shook his head. "Actually, no. I think it's getting worse."

They laughed, and set their glasses aside. They didn't need more wine, anyway. Nature promised to provide the entertainment tonight, since the sky, even by Butternut standards, was spectacular. Why did the stars look so much closer here than they did in the city? Win wondered, idly. There was less light pollution, of course, less air pollution, too. But still, their apparent closeness seemed to defy logic. Each star seemed so distinct against the inky blackness of the night that Win could remember, as a very young child, reaching her hand up to touch one and being disappointed to discover that she couldn't reach it.

"If we'd stayed up here for another hour the last time I came, is this what we would have seen?" Everett asked now, gesturing at the sky.

Win nodded.

"Why would anyone ever come down from here?"

"I don't know," Win murmured, and she smiled as she remembered that during one childhood summer she'd told her grandfather, whom she'd adored, that she was going to move up onto the boathouse roof. And her grandfather, never one to discourage her dreams, had found just the right words to dissuade her, gently, from doing this. But he'd understood the desire behind it, and so, apparently, did Everett.

She watched Everett, in profile, as he brushed his hair out of his eyes in what Win now knew was a habitual gesture. She wondered why he didn't just get it cut but decided she was glad that he didn't. She liked it when he did this, liked it when he pushed aside his longish light brown hair and his sleepy light brown eyes came into view. Did his eyes always look so sleepy? she mused. Or did she only see him when he was tired? She almost asked him, but then she lost her nerve.

Still, looking at him, she had to admit that her first assessment of him as "geeky-cute" hadn't done him justice. He was just plain cute. No, he wasn't cute, he was handsome, handsome in a low-key, pleasant, unobtrusive way that perfectly suited his personality. So why didn't Poppy find him attractive? And, more than that, why didn't she find him kind—which Win, intuitively, knew that he was—and funny, and easy to be with? God knows, Poppy could do worse. Poppy *had* done worse, she was sure of it. Like right now, for instance, with Sam. He was a great guy, as far as Win was concerned, but he was Poppy's *boss*. She *worked* for him. And if that didn't complicate things enough, he was divorced, with a very attractive ex-wife (Win had seen her at school functions) and three children who obviously demanded a lot of time and attention.

She sighed softly, still awed by the crystalline beauty of the night. No more worrying about Poppy, she decided. She'd done enough of that for one day. And besides, if Poppy couldn't see everything Everett had to offer, well, that was too bad for her. But what about . . . what about Everett? Was he waiting, even now, for Poppy to come home, waiting for her to give him some sign that she might be interested in him? She frowned, slightly, think-

ing about this. Poppy wouldn't lead him on, but she wouldn't necessarily give it to him straight, either. After all, she'd already told
Win how much she hated giving the "let's just be friends" speech,
though by now she must surely have had the thing copyrighted.
And, stealing another sideways glance at Everett, Win decided
that he deserved better.

"Everett?"

"Yes?' he said, turning to her.

She bit her lip and tried to think of a way of saying this that
would take the sting out of it, before deciding that there probably wasn't one. "Everett," she said, "this thing, with you and my
sister, it's . . . it's probably not going to work. I don't think she likes
you that way."

She waited for the disappointment to register with him, but he
only shrugged. "I know that."

"And you're . . . okay with it?"

"Yeah, I'm fine. I mean, I'm not going to throw myself off this
roof or anything," he added, feinting a movement towards the lake.

She laughed. "You'd only get wet if you did."

"I'm still not going to do it," he said, smiling.

He was taking it well, she thought, with relief. But still, it
couldn't be easy on his ego. "It's nothing personal, really," she
said. "It has nothing to do with you. It has *everything* to do with
Poppy. She . . ." Win struggled here. "She's not a bad person . . ."

"I never thought that she was. Honestly, when I used to see
her at the coffeehouse, I used to feel sorry for her."

"You did?" Win said, looking at him sharply.

He nodded.

"That's a first," she said, shaking her head. "I mean, of all the
feelings she's inspired in people, I don't think pity has ever been
one of them."

"*Pity's* too strong a word. It's more like . . ." Everett paused. "It's more like I've seen the downside, for her, of the way she looks. It gets her a lot of attention, yes. But I don't think it's necessarily the kind of attention she wants, do you?"

Win hesitated. Everett was right, in a way. Poppy could feel self-conscious about attracting attention, and she could get tired, too, of having to deflect that attention. At the same time, though, Win had never felt *sorry* for her because of this. She'd assumed it just came with the territory. It was an inconvenience, yes, but an inconvenience that Win, when she was younger, would gladly have tolerated if she could have been as beautiful as Poppy.

Now, the breeze that had been blowing off the lake all day strengthened, sending little waves scudding over the dark water and breaking against the sandy shore. Win shivered, a little, though the wind was keeping the mosquitos away, and its coolness felt good on her sunburned skin.

"Do you want to go inside?" Everett asked.

"Not yet," Win said, glad that the subject of Poppy seemed to be closed for now. "Let's stay here a little longer."

He pointed at the opposite shore, where there were flashes of light and muted crackling sounds. "I guess you're going to see some fireworks after all," he said, as a small-scale rocket shot up above the tree line, leaving a trail of sparks behind it.

"It looks like it," Win agreed, over a distant volley of firecrackers.

"You don't mind?" Everett asked.

She looked at him quizzically.

"When your sister texted me back today," he explained, "she said you were staying home tonight because you hate fireworks."

"Oh, no. Not these do-it-yourself ones. I don't mind them. And I *love* sparklers," she added. "But the professional fireworks display they have at the fairgrounds every year? Yeah, I straight up hate that. I haven't been to it in years."

"Is it the noise?"

"No, it's not that. It's . . . it's complicated," she said.

"In what way?"

"In *every* way." She chuckled. But then she turned serious. "When I was kid, we used to come up here for the Fourth of July. I mean, my *parents* used to come up here. Poppy and I were already up here. We spent the whole summer with my grandparents, who were both, just . . . salt of the earth kind of people. I still think, to this day, that whatever is good in my life and Poppy's life, we have them to thank for it. Anyway, my grandparents took the Fourth of July very seriously. If they could have wrapped this entire cabin in red-white-and-blue bunting, they would have. So when my parents would come for the holiday it was understood they would both be on their best behavior. Whatever else my grandparents tolerated from them for the rest of the year, there was an unspoken understanding that they wouldn't tolerate any of it over the Fourth. This meant my dad was sober, or *reasonably* sober, anyway, and my mom was . . . well, my mom was still my mom, but she tried, at least, to put a good face on their marriage, even if it was only for a couple of days.

"The night of the Fourth," she continued, "We'd go to the fairgrounds, and my grandfather would spread blankets out on the grass, and my grandmother would unpack this amazing picnic, and my dad would light sparkers for Poppy and me, and . . . and there we were, the six of us, like any ordinary family, any *happy* family. And just when I thought it couldn't get any better, the fireworks would start. For the first five minutes, I'd enjoy them, I'd think how wonderful they were, how wonderful *we* were, and then I'd start thinking about them ending, and all of us going back to our real lives. You know, with my dad drinking, and disappearing for weeks at a time, and fighting with my mom when he came home, and my mom . . . well, again, just being my mom: flighty, self-absorbed, and generally unreliable. And watching those fireworks, I started to get anxious, *very* anxious. I wanted them to last longer, so we could all stay the way we were right then, but that's the problem with fireworks, they last, what, fifteen or twenty minutes? They never last long enough. And that's why I stopped going to see them. As soon as they start, I think 'Oh, they're so pretty,' and 'This is so much fun.' And then, it never fails, a few minutes later I start getting anxious about them ending. In the end, it just isn't worth it."

She looked down at the dark water and felt her face get warm, but not from her sunburn. What was it about Everett that made her reveal so much about herself, and her life, when she knew so little about him? "Okay," she said, looking up again. "It's your turn. Tell me something about you."

"Like what?"

"Like . . . why do you look tired all the time?"

"Oh. You mean, why are my eyes like this?" He shook his head. "I don't know. They just came that way. Ever since I can remember, people have been asking me if I'm tired. Or worse. In high school . . . well, you can imagine what my teachers thought. My locker was always being subjected to 'random' drug searches."

"But . . . it didn't have drugs in it, did it?" Win asked, not sure why it was suddenly so important to her that it didn't.

"No." He smiled. "I think the worst they ever found was a moldy ham sandwich."

"Well, that's good. At the high school in Minneapolis I was a student teacher at, they used to bring drug-sniffing dogs in, but that doesn't happen here, not at the K–8, anyway."

"That must have been a big change, to go from teaching in a city to a small town."

"It was. *It is.* I didn't plan it, though. I didn't plan on moving up here, either, at least not year-round. My dad, of all people, was the one who gave me the idea for it." And she told Everett another story, a story that began the day of Kyle's memorial service. She hadn't seen her father at the first part of the service—the part that took place in the church. He'd probably sat in the back. He'd never been comfortable with organized religion. But she'd seen him afterwards, at a reception friends of hers had hosted at their house, and she'd been both touched and surprised by his appearance. He was clean-shaven, and he'd bought (or maybe borrowed) a jacket and a tie. What was more, he wasn't drinking anything stronger than coffee. As things were winding down that afternoon, and the other guests were leaving, he'd asked Win if he could speak to her alone.

They'd gone into another room, and he'd taken an envelope out of his pocket and handed it to her. She hadn't wanted to read it then, but he'd insisted that she at least look at it, and when she did, she realized that it was a quitclaim signing her grandparents' cabin over to her. He father had inherited it a year earlier when Win's grandmother had died. She'd tried to argue with him, she'd told him that his parents had left it to him, that *he* should keep it. But he'd said no. That he'd only sell it, or lose it. That he couldn't hold on to anything. Not his wife, not his daughters, not even his guitar. And when Win had pointed out that if he was going to leave it to her, he should leave it to her *and* Poppy, he'd disagreed again. Poppy, he'd told her, was like him. She wouldn't know the value of something until it was too late, until it was already gone.

He'd said some other things, too. Things like he knew he'd

never been a good father, but this was one thing he could do for her. He could give her the cabin and maybe, sometime, she'd go up there, to visit or to live. And maybe it would help her. Help her find some peace again.

"He was right," Everett said, quietly, when she finished telling him this.

"Right about what?"

"Right about your living here one day."

She nodded. "It didn't happen right away, though," she said. *Nothing*, it turned out, had happened right away. She'd been so overwhelmed by loss then that there were times when just leaving her apartment felt like a major accomplishment. Poppy had been wonderful, coming over every day, bullying her into eating, dragging her out to the movies, and just generally insisting that she not give up on her life. It was during this same time that Win first met with Kyle's lawyer, and first saw a copy of Kyle's will. She wasn't surprised he'd left her money. He'd told her he was going to do this. She was only surprised at how much it was: two hundred and fifty thousand dollars, or a small fortune to Win. At the time, she'd felt so desperate in her grief that she'd considered doing something crazy with it. Giving it all, in cash, to a homeless man in her neighborhood, or leaving on a trip around the world and not coming home until the money was gone. In the end, though, she'd done what Kyle would have wanted her to do: she'd made a generous donation to a cancer research organization, and another one to a hospice where Kyle had stayed before he died, and then she'd invested the rest of it in a conservative portfolio of stocks and bonds, and left it there, untouched, for some future day she could never quite imagine.

But she didn't tell any of this to Everett. She told him instead about how, a year after Kyle had died, she was still living in the same apartment they'd lived in together, still going to all the same places they'd gone to together, and still seeing all the same friends they'd seen together. And she'd thought, *This is crazy. No wonder I'm depressed all the time.* So she'd made some calls, found out that there was an opening for a middle school social studies teacher in Butternut, and came up to interview for the job. "I got it, obviously," she said now, "and that fall, two years ago, right before school started, I moved up here. And the rest, I guess, is history."

"Your subject," Everett pointed out, and she smiled. He had an easy way about him, she thought, a way of lightening even the heaviest moments. It was a gift that not many people had.

She looked out over at the water now in time to see another rocket shoot into the air and explode in a shower of multi-colored sparks. "That must be the finale," she said, glancing at her watch. It was getting late, late enough for Everett to be leaving. Except for one thing . . .

"Everett," she said. "You shouldn't drive. We split that first bottle of wine."

"I know."

"You're welcome to sleep on the couch. If it's not too uncomfortable."

"Thank you," he said, his eyes looking especially sleepy. "And I've met your couch before. It's very comfortable."

CHAPTER 11

A few weeks after the Fourth of July, Sam was shut up in his office—a converted, windowless storage room barely large enough to hold a desk, two chairs, and a file cabinet—and was trying to get some work done. He hated being in here. It reminded him of why he'd bought Birch Tree Bait in the first place; he hadn't wanted to work in an office. But business was good now, so good that the only way Sam could get anything done was to hole up in here for a couple of hours every morning before things got too busy. The only trouble was that his employees, his friends, and his regular customers insisted on interrupting him at regular intervals. Like right now, for instance.

"Come in," Sam said, in response to the light but insistent tapping on the door. But he kept his eyes focused on the purchase order on his laptop screen in the hopes of discouraging his visitor from staying any longer than was absolutely necessary.

"Sam?"

"Yes, Justine?" he answered, not looking up.

"Can I ask you a favor?"

He sighed. He looked up. "What?"

"Can you cover the register? Just for a minute? I have to make a phone call."

"Can Byron do it?"

"No. He's . . ."

"Taking a bet?" Sam said, exasperated. "He knows he's not supposed to be doing that here."

"I know, but there's a big game tonight. Plus, Haley Grey is getting her ultrasound today, and a lot of people are betting on whether it's going to be a boy or a girl."

Sam closed his eyes and blew out a long, slow breath. He tried to ignore the sensation of a metal band tightening around his head, the hallmark of the tension headache that had been coming on all morning. When he opened his eyes, though, Justine's expression was so plaintive that he stood up, immediately, and said, "All right. I'll take over. Make it quick, though, okay?"

"Okay. And Sam? Thanks. I wouldn't ask you to do this if it wasn't an emergency."

"It's not . . . it's not your mom, is it?" Sam asked, thinking that, even by her own standards, Justine looked pale today.

"My mom?"

"Weren't you worried that she had some kind of . . . disease?" he reminded her, coming around to the front of his desk and leaning on its edge.

"Oh, *that*. No. That was nothing. She's fine. This time it's my dad."

"Is he okay?"

"He will be," Justine said. "It's just, right now, he's going through a divorce."

"So, he and your mom . . . ?"

"No. Not them. They got divorced a long time ago. This is, let me see, his fifth divorce."

"*Fifth?*" Sam said.

"I'm pretty sure," she said, looking a little less than sure.

Still, he shook his head in disbelief. "Justine, I got divorced *once*. And I can tell you, it was a very time consuming process. I've never understood this. Where does someone find the time to get married and divorced multiple times?"

Justine considered her chipped black finger nail polish. "He just made it a priority, I guess," she said finally, looking up. Her eyes, ringed with their usual heavy black makeup, were completely serious.

"Riiight," Sam said, reaching up to massage his temples. *Yes*, there was definitely going to be a headache, and sooner rather than later.

Justine started to leave his office, but Sam called her back. "Hey, um, how's Poppy doing? I mean, is everything working out there? Is she . . . catching on quickly?"

"She's fine." Justine shrugged. "I have her setting up the s'mores display now."

"Good," Sam said, casually. "That's . . . that's good." And he was glad, for once, that Justine was so obtuse. "If you want some privacy, you can make your phone call in here," he told her, and he left her in his office to console her father, the serial divorcer. There was more aggravation, though, waiting for him at the front counter, where several customers were already milling around impatiently. But as Sam ducked behind the register he still found time to scan the two rooms of the business, taking stock of where everyone was, and what everyone was doing.

There was Byron, sitting at the coffee counter, and writing in the notebook in which he kept meticulous track of all the bets he took. There was Linc, in the next room, supervising a group of vacationers filling out kayak rental forms. And there, at the end of aisle three, was Poppy, her brilliant blond hair seeming to generate its own light as she patiently stacked boxes of graham crackers, bags of marshmallows, and slabs of Hershey's chocolate bars. His eyes lingered on her for a moment, and he was reminded of the other reason he'd sequestered himself in his office. His newest employee was proving to be a distraction, a *major* distraction. She was beautiful, it turned out, but at the same time, she wore her beauty as casually as she might wear a pair of favorite blue jeans. Sam found this captivating. More captivating still was the way she seemed to flirt with him, though he wasn't always sure about this. He could have been misreading her. Either way, though, it added up to the same thing: more distraction.

"Is that it?" Sam asked, reaching for the six-pack of beer a customer had placed on the counter in front of him.

"That's it," a young man's voice said, and something about that voice, its highness, perhaps, made Sam look up at him skeptically. He didn't look old enough to shave, Sam thought, of the short, skinny, curly haired kid in front of him. He didn't even look old enough to grow peach fuzz.

"Can I see your ID?" he asked him.

The kid sighed, as if he had more important things to do, and extracted his license from his wallet. He slid it across the counter to Sam.

Sam glanced at it. "Hawaii, huh? You're a long way from home." "I like to travel," he mumbled.

"It says here you're thirty," Sam said, almost conversationally.

"I am. I look young for my age," he said, careful not to meet Sam's eyes.

"Nobody looks that young for their age," Sam said, reaching for the scissors he kept in a nearby drawer.

"Hey!" the kid yelped, when he realized what Sam was doing.

"Stop!" But it was too late. Sam was already cutting up the fake ID.

"That cost me a lot of money," he said, accusingly, to Sam.

"Well, then you got ripped off," Sam said, sweeping the shards into the trash. "Now get out of here, before I figure out which of the rental cabins you're staying in and I tell your parents."

He glared at Sam, but then something inside him seemed to waver and then break. "Look," he said quietly, glancing nervously back at the line and then leaning closer to Sam. "I got invited to a party tonight. And there are going to be girls there. Actual girls." Sam took a closer look at him. Judging from his concave chest, and his acne-riddled face, he probably didn't see a lot of action, unless of course it was video game action.

"Here, take these to the party," Sam said, coming around to the front of the counter and handing him a couple of bags of Doritos. "Seriously, girls love this Zesty Ranch flavor." He faced him toward the door then and gave him a little push. He didn't say thank you as he left, but Sam hadn't expected him to.

When he went back to ringing up customers, Sam wondered if he'd ever been that young, or that stupid, and decided that he had been both. He'd had an easier time getting beer, though. His friend John had had an uncle who used to buy it for them. His nickname was Seven Fingered Freddie, Sam remembered, due to the fact that he was missing three fingers. He wouldn't tell them how he'd lost those fingers, but Sam and John and their friends had spent hours sitting in the hayloft of an old abandoned barn, drinking beer and speculating on what might have happened to them.

His mind wandered on like this for some time, or at least until he'd handed a customer change for a cup of coffee and a familiar voice said, "Sam! Aren't you even going to say good morning?"

It was Margot Hoffman, her bright green polo shirt emblazoned with the Butternut Nature Museum insignia across her left breast and a matching green visor perched on her head.

"Yes, of course. Good morning, Margot. I'm sorry, I didn't mean to be rude."

"That's all right," Margot said, cheerful as ever. "I still can't believe you missed the fireworks."

"Yeah, I ended up staying at home and trying to get some work done."

"Well, you missed a great show. But you're forgiven, on one condition."

"What's that?"

"You buy tickets to the hoedown."

"Is it . . . that time of year already?" Sam said, of the annual fund-raiser and silent auction for the Butternut Nature Museum. This was held on a farm outside of town, and came complete with a country and western band, strategically placed bales of hay, and enough checked shirts, string-ties, and cowboy boots to convince the denizens of the town that they'd been picked up and transported a thousand miles due west for the evening.

"Yes, Sam, it's that time," Margot said, her brown eyes shining. "And we have a special addition to the festivities this year."

"What's that?" Sam said, trying to muster the requisite enthusiasm.

"A professional square-dance caller."

"No kidding."

"Swear to God. He's the real deal. He makes a living doing it, Sam. Can you believe it?"

"I really can't," Sam said. The thought of square dancing inspired in him a dread so acute that it was very close to panic.

"Well, he'll be there, and I wanted to give you a heads-up

about something else, too," she said. She leaned in and added, in a conspiratorial tone, "This is supposed to be a surprise, but one of the silent auction items is a naturalist-led pontoon boat tour of Butternut Lake. And honestly, Sam, I think your kids would love it."

"Are you by any chance the naturalist?"

She blushed. "Yes, that would be me," she said, fidgeting with a lanyard that hung from the strap of her backpack. "And I can personally guarantee that if you bid on the tour and win, I'll show the twins every single bald eagle's nest on the lake."

"Wow. That's . . . quite an offer," Sam said, and he felt a flicker of irritation then, not at her but at Byron, who'd closed his notebook and was watching his and Margot's exchange with a sly amusement.

"Okay, well, I'll let you get back to work," Margot said. "If it's okay with you, though, I'd love to post these around the store," she added, holding up a sheaf of flyers for the hoedown.

"Of course," Sam said. "Go right ahead."

Margot left then, and Byron drifted over, adjusted his seersucker hat, and leaned on the counter. "You said it yourself, Sam, that was quite an offer from Margot. And I'm not talking about the boat ride, either."

"Byron, come on. Give me a break."

But now Linc sidled up to the counter, a gleeful expression on his face.

"Did you, uh, tell Margot she could plaster those flyers all over the place?" he asked.

"Yes, I did, Linc. It's a worthy cause," Sam said, feeling an ominous thud at his right temple. He came out from behind the counter and grabbed a travel size bottle of Advil from a display and a bottle of water from the refrigerated case.

"You know what else is a worthy cause, Sam?" Linc said. "Margot."

Sam, twisting the cap off the Advil, finally lost his patience. "Cut it out, both of you. She'll hear you," he muttered.

"Oh, Sam," Byron said good-naturedly. "Just ask her out already. The woman is spending a small fortune here just to see you every day."

"I'm not asking her out," Sam said, keeping his voice low. "Just . . . give it a rest, okay?"

He spilled a couple of Advils into his palm, unscrewed the lid on his water bottle, and washed them down. "Byron, do you want to take the register?" he asked, looking over at Byron. But Byron wasn't listening to him. He was still leaning against the counter, but now, instead of joking with Linc, he was gazing off into the middle distance, watching something with rapt attention. Linc, standing next to him, was watching the same thing, his mouth slightly ajar. Sam knew what they were looking at without having to look himself, but he sighed and followed their gaze anyway.

Poppy was done with the s'mores display, and she was down at the other end of the aisle, standing on a stepladder, arranging bottles of barbeque sauce on the top shelf. She was wearing a floral print cotton blouse, faded blue jeans, and Converse sneakers, and her hair was pulled back in a simple ponytail. But it didn't matter, she was still a sight to behold, and God knew how long they would have gone on beholding her if Sam hadn't suddenly said, under his breath, *"This is pathetic."* And, as irritated with himself as he was with them, he knocked Linc's baseball cap off his head, and gave Byron a gentle punch in the arm.

"Knock it off, you two. Really, you look like a couple of puppy dogs. Linc, I think you got some drool on the floor. You should probably wipe it up. And Byron? Come on, you're old enough to be her father. Her *grandfather*."

Sam grumbled a little more about this, but neither one of them seemed particularly penitent. Linc put his baseball cap back on and continued to stare, and Bryon sighed and said, "A man can dream, can't he?" So Sam went back behind the counter and ignored them as he rang up a woman buying enough Popsicles to feed a small army, but by the time he was done with this transaction, he'd made a decision.

"Is Margot still here?" he asked, looking around.

"Why?" Linc asked.

"Because . . . you're right. I should ask her out. I don't know why I haven't done it before."

"*Yes,*" Linc said, pumping his fist in the air. "I told you, old man," he said to Byron.

"You got lucky this time," Byron admitted.

"What are you two talking about?" Sam asked, but he realized, with a sinking feeling, that he already knew. "Byron, this isn't one of your bets, is it?"

Byron looked a little sheepish. "It's a pool, Sam. But it's all in good fun," he insisted. "Just something to keep things interesting around here."

"Unbelievable," Sam said, shaking his head. "You are unbelievable." And then, because he couldn't help being curious, he asked, "What's the bet?"

"Whether you two will go on a date."

"One date?"

Byron nodded.

Sam pulled his wallet out of his pocket and took out a twenty-dollar bill. "I want in," he said, holding it out to Byron.

"You can't get in on your own bet," Byron said, appalled.

"Then pull the whole thing," he said.

Byron looked unhappy, but he took the twenty. "This is not how it's done, Sam."

"It is this time."

"Ah, Byron," Linc said, his mouth twitching in a barely repressed smile. "Tell Sam what else you wanted to bet on."

Byron gave him a dirty look.

"Let's have it, Byron," Sam said.

"Well, I thought about another bet. This would have just been between Linc and me."

"And what would that have been?"

"It would have concerned whether or not you"—here Byron lowered his voice—"whether or not you and Margot closed the deal."

"Closed the deal?" Sam repeated.

Byron cleared his throat, and because he was normally so proper, he looked embarrassed as he explained, "You know, had sexual relations."

"And how were you going to know whether this happened or not, Byron? Did you honestly think I was going to tell you?"

"No." Byron shook his head. "We just assumed that if it happened, you'd be in a better mood than you usually are."

"Never mind," Sam said, snatching the twenty-dollar bill out of Byron's hand. "Just pull the whole thing. And don't ever bet on my personal life again, is that clear?" he added, though he was less angry than amazed. Amazed that his life, so consistently uninteresting to him, could be interesting enough for anyone else to actually bet on.

He hurried out the front door and found Margot putting flyers under the windshield wipers of cars in the parking lot.

"Sam?" she said, looking up. "You don't mind that I'm doing this, do you?"

"No, it's fine."

"Who doesn't love a hoedown, right?" she said.

"Right. Uh, Margot," he said, leaning on the car. "Would you like to go out with me sometime, maybe get dinner or something?"

"I'd love to," she said, her face lighting up.

"When's good for you?"

"Tonight," she said, without hesitation.

"Oh, all right. I'll have to see if I can get a babysitter. It shouldn't be a problem, though. Do you want to grab something at the Corner Bar?" Sam asked, of a place in town where you could get good beer on tap and a decent hamburger.

"That sounds great."

"I'll pick you up at seven."

"I'll see you then," she said.

He turned and started to go back inside, but she called after him. "Sam?"

"Yes?" he said, turning around.

She smiled again. "I thought you'd never ask."

Finding a babysitter, though, was easier said than done. Sam didn't need one very often—he usually saved his socializing for the weekends, when his kids were with their mom—so he only had a short list of people he could call on. He worked his way through it pretty quickly. Lonnie Hagan, his children's favorite babysitter, was on vacation, and Miss Suzette, Cassie's baton twirling teacher, already had a commitment. That left Justine or Linc. They'd both pitched in during emergencies before, with mixed success. (Justine had given his children elaborate henna tattoos of skulls that he'd found somewhat morbid, and Linc had helped them build a near professional blanket fort that had taken Sam days to dismantle.) Still, he trusted them both, and when he found out they were busy, too, he realized he'd reached the bottom of the barrel, otherwise known as Byron. Byron loved the kids, and they loved him, but at night he was apt to be watching whatever televised games he'd taken bets on that day, and Sam suspected that his boys would see this as an opening to slip away and do what it was they most wanted to do, which was to find different ways of blowing things up. Nonetheless, Sam was on the verge of asking Byron to babysit when he walked by Poppy, who was arranging condiments on a shelf.

"Sam!" she said, waylaying him. "Can you answer a question for me?"

"Of course."

"Why would you sell this here?" she asked, holding up a jar of light mayonnaise. "It's an abomination. I mean, taking the fat out of mayonnaise? That's just wrong."

He looked at her quizzically.

"I'm kidding," she said, putting the jar on the shelf.

"Oh, right," he said, feeling the not unpleasant confusion he often felt when he was with her.

"I did need to talk to you about the Red Vines, though," she said, as she continued stacking jars on the shelf. "I know we agreed on one package per day, but I've been having two and sometimes even three. I'm not used to this all-access approach to them. Maybe you should put them behind the counter, just to be safe," she suggested, gracing him with another one of her lovely smiles.

He nodded. *Yes, she was definitely flirting with him.* Even Sam, who'd been out of the game for a while, could tell this.

"I'm kidding, again," she said, when he didn't say anything.

"I know," he said. I'm just . . ." *I'm just distracted by you, by everything about you. But most of all, for some reason, right this second, by the little hollow at the base of your neck. How did you get it so tan? And what would it taste like if I kissed it?*

"I should get going," he said, abruptly, moving on. "I'm trying to find a babysitter for tonight."

"Sam," she called after him. "I'll babysit for you."

He stopped. "You will?"

"Why not?" she said. "Cassie and I can work on her twirling. Her performance is only two weeks away now."

"Well, there are the boys, too."

"I can handle them."

He hesitated.

"Oh, come on. It's the least I can do," she said. "You gave me a job, didn't you? And, by the way, I wouldn't charge you for tonight. It's on the house."

"That's not necessary," he said. "I'll pay you the going rate."

She shrugged, unconcernedly. "What time do you want me to come?"

"Six thirty?"

"Okay," she said. "Is there, uh, anything going on in Butternut tonight that I should know about?" she asked. "Anything . . . exciting?"

"There's nothing exciting going on in Butternut. You should know that by now," he said, and then he made himself say something more, something he hoped would put them back on the professional footing they belonged on. "I'm going on a date."

"Oh . . . that's nice," she said, and she smiled politely, and went back to stocking the condiments. But he'd seen it anyway. Just for a second, when he'd told her, he'd seen the expression on her face. And when he went back to his office it wasn't Margot he thought about, but Poppy. Poppy who'd been disappointed when he'd told her he was going on a date.

CHAPTER 12

When Sam got back to the cabin that night after his date with Margot, he found Poppy on the living room floor, scooping Legos into a plastic bin.

"You don't need to do that," he objected. "We're used to stepping on them. It probably wouldn't feel like home if we didn't."

She smiled but kept picking them up. "I don't mind. How was your night?" she asked, casually, looking not at him but at the Lego strewn rug.

"It was . . . fine," Sam said, and because it felt wrong to watch her pick up his childrens' toys alone, he knelt down and started to pick them up with her. Had it been fine? he wondered of the night. He hoped, for Margot's part, it had been. But for his part, it had been a mixture of tedium and tension. Tedium because, other than the town they lived in and the people they knew, they had almost nothing in common. And tension because, while Margot was careful to broaden her conversation to include topics other than the nature museum, there was always the possibility, Sam felt, that she would suddenly start lecturing him on the environmental hazards of sulfide mining in Northern Minnesota, or on the reasons why the northern long-eared bat should be put on the endangered species list.

On the drive home, they'd finally lapsed into silence, Margot humming along, a little self-consciously, to a song on the radio, and Sam puzzling, silently, over the night's central mystery. Here was an attractive woman whom he wasn't attracted to, an interesting woman whom he wasn't interested in, and a nice woman whose niceness only served to make him feel guilty for not appreciating her niceness more. Maybe it was that guilt that made him kiss her a little more enthusiastically than he'd intended to when he left her at her front door. He'd have to answer for that kiss tomorrow, he thought, when Margot came into Birch Tree Bait, first thing, to get her coffee.

"How'd things go here?" Sam asked, throwing the last Legos into the bin.

"Well, let's see," Poppy said, sitting back on her heels. "From what I could tell, the boys were on their best behavior. And everyone seemed to like dinner, which was chicken nuggets, French fries, and Popsicles. Should there have been a vegetable in there somewhere?" she asked, frowning slightly, her blond hair shining in the lamplight.

"In a perfect world," Sam said. "But, you know, it's not."

She smiled. "Right. Then, after dinner, we tried to play the Game of Life, but it didn't really get off the ground."

Sam nodded. "Cassie just likes to fill up her car with the little pink pegs"—the little pink pegs signified that a player had had daughters—"and drive it around the board."

"Yeah, I figured that out pretty quickly." Poppy laughed. "After that, the boys went up to their room to play, and Cassie practiced twirling a little, and then we tried out some new hairstyles on her, and then . . . oh, and then she showed me her dolls. Did you know that one of them is in a coma, Sam?"

"I did. Cassie got sunscreen in its eyes, and now they won't open, so she decided she was in a coma."

"Well, we talked to her a little, anyway. Your daughter heard somewhere that's what you do with people who are in a coma. You know, in case they can still hear you."

"Exactly," Sam said, standing up, and Poppy stood up, too, brushing her blue jeans off. They were faded and worn at the hems, and her pale blue wool sweater—it was a chilly night—had a hole in one of the elbows. But it didn't matter, Sam thought. She would have looked beautiful in a brown burlap sack.

"Then, after that," Poppy said, "they all got ready for bed, and Cassie went right to sleep, after I'd checked all the places in her room a ghost could be hiding, but the boys"—she shook her head—"I'd leave them in their room, and they'd be in their beds, and then I'd come back, and they would have just popped right back out of them again."

"They do that."

"Eventually, though, they went to sleep," she said. "And that was our night. Until, just now, I started to pick up the toys and you came home."

They stood there for a moment, smiling at each other, and Sam realized that neither one of them wanted her to leave.

"Would you like something to drink?" he asked.

"I'd love something," she said. "What have you got?"

"Coffee, tea, soda, beer, wine."

"I'd love a glass of wine," she said. "Just one. But only if you're having one, too."

"Sure," he said, heading into the kitchen, and wondering,

vaguely, if he was breaking some unwritten rule of parenting. Something like, *Don't drink with your children's babysitter.* But he was pretty sure he'd already broken the rule that came before that: *Don't lust after your children's babysitter.*

Sam took a bottle of white wine out of the refrigerator, opened it, and filled two wineglasses, while Poppy sat down at the scuffed pine table, which, in this cabin, served as the unofficial center of family life. "Sorry about this," he said, setting the wineglasses on the table and trying to clear away some of the clutter that had accumulated there over the course of the day—a pile of half-finished drawings, several dog-eared children's books, and the cereal boxes that no one had bothered to put back in the cupboard after breakfast that morning.

"Oh, no, don't do that," Poppy objected, as Sam tried to shuffle the drawings into a neat stack. "Leave everything where it is. It's nice. I like a little chaos. My sister, on the other hand . . ." She shrugged, picked up her wineglass, and took a sip. "Wow, this is really good," she said.

He drank some, too.

"Do you know a lot about wine?" she asked.

He nodded, a little distractedly. "When we lived in Minneapolis, I was a partner in a wine distributorship." He wasn't thinking about that, though. He was thinking about her eyes. They were so blue. *Cornflower blue,* Sam thought.

"Is that why you carry so many different kinds of wine at Birch Tree Bait?" she asked.

"Uh-huh. The expensive ones don't always sell that well, but every once in a while someone comes in who really appreciates a good bottle, so I keep ordering them."

They were quiet for a moment, and Sam, looking at Poppy, was glad they were sitting at the kitchen table. It seemed less intimate, somehow, than the couch, more . . . *appropriate*. So why, then, did he suddenly imagine himself tugging on one of her ear-lobes with his teeth? He rubbed his eyes, and drank some more wine, and said, apropos of nothing, "I had a long night tonight."

"Did you?"

"It was a first date."

"Oh, well, that explains it. Some of the longest nights of my life have been first dates."

"Have they?"

She nodded. "Honestly, I've had first dates that were so excru-ciating the only thing that saved me was knowing that if I could get back to my apartment by 10:55, I could be in my pajamas, watching a *Seinfeld* rerun by 11:00."

"That bad, huh?"

"That bad. I mean, have you ever been on a really *amazing* first date?"

"Yes," he said, honestly. "I have. My first date with my ex-wife was amazing. I knew, by the end of it, that I was in love with her."

"*You did?* Wow. That must have been one hell of a date." She sipped her wine.

"Actually, on paper, it was a disaster," Sam said. "My car was in the shop so we had to take the bus. We were just kids—both of us were still in college—but even then we knew it was not an auspicious beginning for a date. Then, while we're on the bus, it starts to rain. No, I don't mean rain. I mean *pour*. So we got off the bus and ran to this Chinese restaurant, which was just a couple of blocks away, but by the time we got there we were soaked. And there was a long wait for a table, and we had to just stand there, dripping, until they seated us, like, an hour later. And then, when the waiter came over, Alicia asked him if we could order the fried rice without the shrimp. And she explained to him that she was allergic to shellfish and that if she had even the smallest amount of it, she'd go into anaphylactic shock. And he said 'no problem,' but I think there may have been a language barrier there, or something, because when he came back with our order, there they were, right on top of the fried rice, five *huge* shrimp, staring straight up at us. And the two of us started laughing, laughing so hard that we just had to leave some money on the table and get out of there.

"And when we got outside, it was still raining, so we got soaked all over again, only now, in addition to being wet, we absolutely reeked of Chinese food. It could have been a nightmare. But instead, while we're standing there on the street corner, all I could think of was that Alicia looked beautiful. The raindrops on her hair looked like little glass beads, and her complexion was so perfect, it made her look like she belonged in a soap commercial or something. Then she smiled at me. She just . . . smiled. And I remember it so well, because I could feel it happening. It was like everything in my life just . . . clicked into place. And I thought, 'This is it. She's the one.'"

Poppy toyed with her wineglass, a little pensively. "That's a nice story," she said, finally. "But . . ."

"Yes?"

"It doesn't have a happy ending."

"You mean . . . because we got divorced?"

She nodded.

"Well, that was still years away. Before that, there was a lot of happiness. There still is. I mean, we have three beautiful children together whom we love, I think about as much as it's possible to love anyone. So, in that sense, there are no regrets."

"No, of course not," Poppy said quickly. "I didn't mean that. I meant . . . what happened between the time you stood on that street corner and the time you got divorced? How do you fall out of love with someone? Or is that too personal?" she added.

"No, it's not too personal. It's hard to explain, though, without resorting to an old cliché. We drifted apart."

Poppy frowned. "But here's the thing about 'drifting apart' that I've never understood. Can't you *feel* yourselves drifting apart? Don't you know it's happening *while* it's happening? And isn't there anything you can *do* about it?"

He thought about that for a moment. "It seems like it should be that way, doesn't it? But for us, no, it wasn't like that. Later, looking back on it, I could see it happening. But at the time . . ." He shook his head. "Think about it. Between the two of us, we had, eventually, two jobs, one house, three kids, two cars, and, as I remember it, several goldfish with incredibly short life spans. We were so caught up in the day-to-day of our lives that we couldn't see the big picture anymore. For all of that, though, our marriage might have survived. If I hadn't been . . . unfaithful."

Sam saw it again in her expression: disappointment. And this time, she didn't try to hide it. "You cheated on her?" she asked, and Sam felt her lean, almost imperceptibly, away from him.

"In a sense, I did. But not in the way you're thinking. There wasn't anyone else. It turns out there are other ways you can be disloyal in a marriage, and, in my case, it wasn't with a person. It was with a place."

She looked at him, puzzled.

"I was married to her," he explained, "and I was raising our children with her in suburban Minneapolis, but in my mind, I never left this place. There was always a part of me that was here. Maybe the biggest part of me."

"By 'here' you mean Butternut?"

He nodded. "I grew up here. About three miles away from

where we're sitting right now, actually. And I loved it. When you're a kid, of course, you're not necessarily aware of something like that. You don't wake up every morning and say, 'God, I love this place. To me, it was just home. All of it: the cabin we lived in, the lake, the woods. I don't think I ever thought I would leave it. Not really. Not *permanently*. My parents, though, had other ideas."

He stopped, drank some more of his wine. "They loved it up here, too," he continued. "But it's hard to make a living this far north, and, like a lot of people who live up here year-round, they learned how to do a little bit of everything to make ends meet. They wanted more for my brothers and me, though. There was no question we were going to go to college, and no question, either, that if we came back here, it was only going to be to visit, not to live."

"You had other plans, though," Poppy remarked.

"I did, but I didn't know it until Alicia and I had children of our own. That's when I realized how much I missed it up here. And how much I wanted them to grow up in a place like this. Already, I could see how it was going to be, raising them in the suburbs. I knew they'd be like a lot of kids today. The outdoors would be a destination for them; a place you make little forays into, preferably armed with things like insect repellant, and bottled water, and UV protective clothing. I wanted them to just . . . *grow up* outside, the way I did, so that it wasn't a separate place, it was just where you were. How you lived. And I wanted to teach them all the things my parents taught me, how to hunt and fish and canoe."

"You couldn't just have come up here on the weekends?" Poppy asked, gently.

"I tried that. When Alicia first started working for the DA's office, she was drowning in work. She still is, actually, but then she was so worried about doing a good job that she started not just staying late at the office but bringing work home on weekends, too. And I thought, to help her out, and to give her some peace and quiet around the house, I'd bring the kids up here, and we'd stay with my parents at their cabin—this was before they'd retired and moved to South Carolina. At first, it was just a few weekends here and there, but then it was every other weekend, and then it was every weekend. I told myself it was just temporary, just until Alicia got settled in at work, but the truth was, every time I packed up the car to make the drive back to Minneapolis, I dreaded it. And then one day, I remember—it had been several weeks since we'd been able to get up here—and I drove the kids up on this beautiful fall day, and we went for a walk down by the lake, and I thought, 'For the first time in weeks I feel alive, really alive.' At home, I realized, I was just phoning it in."

"Was that the turning point?"

"No, that came a few months later. It was a winter morning, and things were quiet at work, and I found myself going online to the twenty-four hour webcam at the White Pines Resort and just watching this shot of snow falling on the frozen lake for about fifteen minutes. That's when I knew things had to change."

"Did your wife ever consider moving up here with you?"

"No, it turns out I married someone who really loves being near a city. And who really loves her job, too. Living up here would have been a dead end for her career. There is one prosecutor in this whole county, an elected official who's called the county attorney. And while I'm sure it's a great job, if you can get it, it was never going to satisfy Alicia's ambition."

"So, that was it?" Poppy asked.

"No, not quite. We tried counseling. But in the end, this is what we came up with. We sold our house, and I found a cabin, and a business, both for sale up here, and she found a smaller house outside Minneapolis and we've been making it up as we go along ever since. It's not perfect. Alicia misses the kids. And they miss her. Sometimes the weekends aren't enough. The guilt, I know, can eat her up. But this makes the most sense. I have more time and more flexibility than she does, especially during the off-season, when business is slow. And even when it is busy, I can bring the kids into work if I need to, or, if they're sick, it's easy for me to stay home with them and get someone to cover for me there." He shrugged. "I make it work. Most of the time."

"I can see that," she said, drinking the last of her wine. "I can see it in your kids. They seem happy. They really do."

"I hope they're happy," he said, and he smiled at her. *God, this is so easy,* he thought. Sitting here with her. Talking to her. Why couldn't his date have been this easy? He and Margot would still be there now, still sitting at their little table at the Corner Bar, still talking, if it had been this easy. Hell, they would have closed the place down tonight. Marty, the longtime bartender, would have had to kick them out of there.

"I'd offer you another glass of wine," he said, gesturing to her empty glass, "but you're driving."

"I am," she said, standing up. "And you're working, first thing tomorrow."

"So are you," he reminded her.

"That's true," she said, putting her wineglass on the counter. He re-corked the wine bottle, and she wandered over to the refrigerator and studied the things he'd stuck up on its door—emergency phone numbers, the children's school pictures, and day camp activity schedules.

"I always wished our refrigerator door looked like this when I was a kid," she said, moving aside as he opened it and put the wine bottle back in. "But my parents were too disorganized. And then there was our family life. It wasn't very . . . wholesome. If they'd put things up on the refrigerator, they probably would have been things like eviction notices, or summonses to appear in court."

He looked at her carefully, to see if she was joking, but she wasn't. He wondered what her childhood had been like, and he was about to ask her, but she leaned back against the closed refrigerator door now, and she smiled at him, and tipped her chin up, fractionally. *Okay,* he thought. *Either she wants me to kiss her, or she is doing a very good imitation of someone who wants me to kiss her. The first one,* he decided, but just to be sure, he reached out a finger and ran it gently down the side of her face, from her temple to her jaw. She kept smiling. *Her skin is so soft, and she smells so good,* he thought, leaning closer. He bent, slowly, to kiss her, and she kissed him back, her lips smooth and pliant beneath his. But he pulled back, before the kiss really got started. "I'm sorry," he said. "I can't do this. I *want* to, very much. But it feels wrong to start the night with one woman, and end it with another."

"I . . . I see what you mean. I should go," she said, and he could see that she felt awkward.

He walked her out to her car and said good night. Then he watched until her taillights reached the main road, and eventually disappeared out of sight.

He went back inside and closed the door, stepping on a Lego that had escaped the cleanup. *You're an idiot,* he thought. *If it's not enough that she was the babysitter tonight, she's also your employee.* But truthfully, he'd been an idiot long before tonight. Ever since she'd first walked into Birch Tree Bait, and bought that cheap bottle of wine, he'd been attracted to her. And then he'd hired her, less for her qualifications than because he thought he'd like having her around all day. And he had liked it; he'd liked it a lot, especially when the attraction seemed to be reciprocated. But he would have to stop this tomorrow. Because if he was going to be the kind of boss who got involved with an employee . . . well, then he had no business owning a business.

He went to check on his kids. He got to Tim and Hunter's room first. They were both sprawled out on their beds, Tim's head where his feet should have been, and Hunter's right arm dangling over the side of the mattress. Sam knew better than to try to rearrange either of them into something resembling an orderly night's sleep. He just tousled their heads, in turn, and went to Cassie's room. She was tucked neatly into her bed, the covers barely disturbed, her left cheek resting on the pillow. And her hair, he saw, was braided into a perfect French braid.

A couple of hours later, Poppy was lying in bed, on the verge of sleep, when she saw an image of Sam from that night in his kitchen. And what was startling about it was the clarity with which it came to her. It was less an image than a sense memory, an exact re-creation of the moment before he kissed her. (And damn it, she had *wanted* him to kiss her.) Now, she could see, hear, smell, and feel every detail of it. The way the blue check in Sam's shirt brought out the blue in his eyes, the way the trees outside, tossed in a blustery wind, tapped and creaked against the kitchen windows, the way the cabin had a pleasant wood smoke smell to it, as if there had been a fire in the fireplace recently, the way her face felt warm, as if she'd come into a heated house on a cold day. And thinking about that moment now, she could actually *feel* things clicking into place, just as Sam had said they had for him on his first date with Alicia . . .

She sat up in bed, abruptly. She was awake now. She was *five cups of coffee* awake. She leaned over and snapped on the bed-side table lamp, and Sasquatch, who was curled up at the end of the bed, lifted his head and blinked at her sardonically, as if to say, *Some of us, at least, are trying to sleep here.*

Oh, my God, am I falling in love with him? she wondered. *That's crazy.* She got out of bed, and went to sit on the window seat, using the old-fashioned crank handle to open the window, and resting her forehead against the screen. And then she looked out into the night, as if there she might find the answer to her question: *Was* she falling in love with Sam? And, if she was, why him? And why now?

The *now* was especially perplexing. Here she was, almost thirty, a refugee from the city who'd dated countless men, none of whom had ever inspired anything even close to love in her before, and what had she done this summer? She'd fallen, hard, for the first man she'd met up here.

And it wasn't that there was anything *wrong* with Sam, she thought, as she wrapped her arms around her legs and rested her chin on her knees. There was, in fact, *plenty* right with him. But what about all the other guys she'd met over the years? Some of them had been jerks, of course, but just as many of them had been nice guys who'd seemed intent on connecting with her. In the end, though, she hadn't wanted to get close to any of them, a fact that she suspected, in some cases, had more to do with an unwillingness on her part than with a deficiency on theirs.

As she was puzzling over this, Sasquatch made the leap from the bed to the window seat, and she watched as he batted, half-heartedly, at a moth on the other side of the screen. If she were honest with herself, she knew why she'd shied away from closeness in the past. But she was averse to examining things too closely. She'd worked too hard to lock painful things away. And what was more, she'd gotten too good at it. Still, it was there, now, if only for a second: a memory of herself at sixteen, curled up in her bed, shivering violently, though the night was not cold. *Oh, Poppy, don't dredge that up now,* she told herself, impatiently. She cranked the window shut again—it was getting chilly in the room—and concentrated instead on thinking about something pleasant. Sam.

She saw him every day, at Birch Tree Bait, and she never got tired of it. She loved watching him, she realized, especially with his kids. Cassie and Hunter and Tim were always at the store, and Sam was so great with them. With the twins, he was tough, but fair. With Cassie, he tried to be tough, but he just *melted* when it came to her, and it broke Poppy's heart. But it wasn't just the way he was with his kids that was appealing; it was the way he was with everyone. He was the kind of man who didn't just take care of things; he took care of people, too. Justine, Linc, Byron, locals and tourists alike, he managed them all, through the course of every busy day, with the same patience and ease and unwavering humor. He was the glue that held them all together. And in Birch Tree Bait, he'd given people not just a place to buy ice, or fishing hooks, or postcards, he'd given them a place—a comfortable, relaxed, easy place—to touch base, connect with their friends, or just hang out. Poppy had heard it said, in fact, more than once, that people couldn't remember what they'd done before Sam had reopened the new, improved Birch Tree Bait.

And there was more about Sam . . . he loved Butternut Lake, loved it as much as anyone she'd ever known, and he loved being outdoors, loved being physical. And as for his *physicality* . . .

well, he was sexy. He was *incredibly* sexy. Sexy enough so that Poppy found herself fantasizing about him. How would it feel, she wondered, to touch him, to hold him, to run her fingers over his bare skin, and equally important, how would it feel to have him run *his* fingers over *her* bare skin. *Oh, God,* she thought, *I want him. I just* want *him.* There was no other word for it.

She looked at Sasquatch, who was lying down now, licking one of his paws. "What do you think, Sasquatch?" she asked, seriously. He stopped licking and seemed to consider her question, but no answer was forthcoming. If anything, though, his blue-green eyes seemed faintly critical. And who could blame him? She'd woken him up out of a sound sleep. "I'm sorry," she said, petting him. "And I know, it's ridiculous. Who falls in love for the first time at twenty-nine?"

CHAPTER 13

S o, no boathouse roof tonight," Everett remarked, facing Win from the other side of the couch.

"Not tonight," she agreed. There had been a sudden cold snap earlier in the week, and then, this morning, it had begun to rain, a gray, leaden rain that had brought to Win's mind images of forgotten beach towels dripping on laundry lines, and forlorn plastic bailing jugs floating in the bottoms of canoes. But tonight, the rain had seemingly transformed itself; it no longer felt melancholy but comforting and familiar as it dripped from the cabin's eaves and ran in rivulets down its dark windows.

"I think I'm going to go to bed early," Poppy said, appearing in the living room doorway. "You two"—*please don't say "have fun,"* Win prayed—"have a good night," she said. "I'll see you in the morning, Win," she added, and then she was gone, and Win and Everett were alone again. A log popped in the fireplace, all the louder for the silence in the room, and Everett shifted on the couch. Win, for her part, tried to think of something to say. She didn't mind the not talking; she didn't think *he* minded it, either. But seeing him this time felt different; it wasn't just him stopping by to bring a forgotten box or a "thank you" bottle of wine. Tonight was planned.

The morning after their Fourth of July on the boathouse roof, he'd waited until she'd woken up before he'd left. He was heading back down to Minneapolis later that day to work on a project. *I have your sister's cell phone number, but I don't have yours,* he'd said, as he'd folded up the bedding on the couch. *Could I . . . ?*

Oh, of course, Win had replied, giving him her number. She'd wondered how soon she would hear from him, but, as it turned out, it was only the next day that he'd called to say that he was thinking of going back up to his cousin's cabin in a couple of weeks, and he was hoping he could see her again then. She'd said yes, and invited him for dinner that night.

It had been a success. She'd made a beef stew, and, at the last minute, she'd dug up her grandmother's Irish soda bread recipe and made that, too. She hadn't wanted it to seem like she and Everett were on a date—they weren't, were they?—but having Poppy there with them had helped, even if she hadn't been particularly conversational. (Ever since Poppy had babysat for Sam's kids a couple of days earlier, she'd been floating around the cabin in a state of dreamy preoccupation.)

After dinner, Poppy had offered to wash the dishes—which was a breakthrough, of sorts—and Everett had offered to build a fire in the living room, and then they'd sat down on the couch, where they were now, alone, and, for the time being, silent. *What are we doing?* Win thought. *Are we friends, or are we more than friends?* The night's clues, so far, at least, seemed elusive. After all, if they were friends, why couldn't they think of anything to say to each other? And if they were more than friends, why were they sitting so far apart on the couch?

"Do you, uh, want me to go?" Everett asked now. "It's getting late. If you're tired . . ."

"I'm not tired," Win said. "And even if I were, I wouldn't necessarily be able to sleep. I'm an insomniac."

"So am I," Everett said. "What kind are you?"

"What kind?"

"There are three main kinds of insomnia," he said. "And the reason I know this is because one of the things I've done when I've had insomnia is research insomnia. That's when I found out you can have sleep-onset insomnia, sleep-maintaining insomnia, or early morning awakening. They're all pretty self-explanatory," he said, brushing his hair out of his eyes. "Which kind do you have?"

"The first one. The 'sleep-onset insomnia.'"

He nodded. "I'm more of a sleep-maintaining insomniac myself."

"Were you always an insomniac?"

"Always. When I was a kid, it drove my parents crazy. They'd wake up at 3:00 A.M. to the sound of the *Mighty Morphin Power Rangers* theme song on TV. What about you? Is this a lifelong thing?"

She shook her head. "No, just in the last few years." *Just since Kyle was diagnosed with cancer.*

"What have you tried to fall asleep?"

"Everything," she said, simply. "Everything short of narcotics."

"So . . . warm milk?"

She wrinkled her nose. "Have you ever tasted warm milk? It's disgusting. But yes, I've tried it. I've tried warm baths, too, and cool temperatures in my bedroom at night, and white noise machines set to a rainforest setting, and . . ."

"And watching infomercials?"

She frowned. "No, not those. I mean, people don't watch them on purpose, do they?"

"I do. When I can't sleep."

"Does it work?"

"Better than anything else I've tried."

"And you don't find it annoying watching someone chop vegetables with a Ginsu knife?"

"A Ginsu knife? When's the last time you watched an infomercial?"

"When I was a kid, probably."

"Win, there's a whole brave new world of infomercials out there now," he said, reaching for the television remote on the coffee table. "May I?" he asked, aiming it at the TV.

"Go right ahead."

He turned the TV on, pressed "guide," and scrolled through the channels. "It used to be that you had to wait until late at night to watch these," he explained. "They were sort of like the graveyard of television programming. But not anymore. Now there's a whole channel devoted to them." He clicked on it, and sat back on the couch, closer to Win now than he had been before.

"Oh, this one is a *classic*," he said, gesturing at the screen. And Win, amused by his enthusiasm, turned her attention to it, and she had to admit, it *was* strangely compelling. The infomercial was for a spray on powder which, when matched correctly to the color of someone's hair, could be used to cover his or her thinning hair or bald spot. There were endless shots of someone spraying what looked like fuzzy brown spray paint over shiny bald spots, and endless testimonials from customers who swore the product had changed their lives. When it was over, Win turned to Everett and asked, incredulously, "But how do you take it off? Does it wash off in the shower? And what if someone touches it? Does the color come off on their hand? And wouldn't someone notice, up close, that you don't have a full head of hair but just some kind of spray powder on your bald spot?"

"Those are all good questions, Win," Everett said, "but unfortunately, I can't answer them. I've never used this product before."

"But you've used other products you've seen on this channel?"

"I've ordered a couple of them," he said, a little sheepishly. "But I don't recommend it."

"It's not going to be a problem for me."

"You say that now, but after a few more hours of watching these, you'll want to order something. And I'll be the only thing standing between your credit card and that 1-800 number at the bottom of the screen."

"We're not going to watch more of these, are we?" Win asked. But they did. Win, at first, was understandably critical of the products for sale. She didn't see the need, for instance, for the wearable towel. (Was it really that difficult to just *hold* a towel around yourself?) But gradually, she began to see the logic in the products advertised. Because while she *personally* would not want to practice putting in the bathroom, for avid golfers who spent a lot of time in this room, why not put a miniature putting green in there? And what about the food chopper that promised to transform the way you cooked, ate, and, of course, chopped food? Win suddenly had no idea how she'd lived without it for so many years, though part of this product's appeal might have been the host. He was somewhat hyper, but at the same time, he was so maniacally persuasive that Win could only shake her head admiringly.

"I know," Everett agreed. "If he ever quits his day job, he would make a fantastic cult leader."

But Win's greatest moment of weakness came during an info-mercial for a blanket with sleeves. All the people wearing them looked so cozy, *so warm.* "I need one of those," she said, sud-denly.

"No, you don't."

"*I do.*"

"Where would you wear it, though, other than your bedroom? Because, honestly, Win, if I were you I wouldn't even be seen in it in the living room."

"Why not? Didn't you see that whole family wearing them to some sporting event?" she asked, gesturing at the TV. "I go to the high school football games up here sometimes. I could wear it to one of those."

Everett shook his head. "Not if you wanted to keep your job."

Win was soon distracted by another infomercial, though, this one featuring a piece of material that could be attached to your bra to prevent your cleavage from showing. There were other in-fomercials, too. But she started to lose track of them. It was get-ting late, and, even with what she now knew was her "sleep-onset insomnia" she was getting drowsy. Everett, too, looked sleepier than usual. It seemed suddenly too bright in the room, and Win got up to turn off the overhead light, leaving just the lamps on the end tables on. Then, as the fire died down it got chillier in the room, and she left to turn up the thermostat, and ended up bringing a couple of throw blankets back with her.

She didn't remember falling asleep, but when she woke up, in the gray light of dawn, she was touched to see that Everett had given her the couch to sleep on, and had covered her with a throw. *But where is he?* She propped herself up on one elbow and drowsily looked around. She saw his outline in one of the armchairs.

"Everett," she said, softly, testing to see if he was awake.

"I'm here," he said, and something about his choice of words made her smile.

"I fell asleep," she said, stating the obvious.

"You did. You missed some real winners, too," he said, of the TV's now dark screen.

"Did I?" She smiled. "Like what?"

"Well, let's see. There was one for a vacuum-cleaner-like attachment for cutting hair."

"Oh, right," she said. "I think I went to high school with someone who used one of those. Or maybe," she said, trying to suppress a yawn, "maybe he just had a really bad haircut."

She sensed rather than saw him smile. Outside, the rain had stopped, and the sky was pale gray, shot through with the pale pink of early dawn. Inside, the fire had been reduced to a few glowing embers.

She pulled the throw closer around her. "What time is it?"

She saw him look at his watch. "Depending on your perspective, it's either really early or really late."

"Did you get any sleep?"

He shook his head. "No. I wasn't tired, though. I was thinking."

"What about?" she asked, and when he didn't answer right way, she said, "Everett, that's not fair. You know *way* more about me than I know about you. It's your turn to talk now." And then, with uncharacteristic boldness, she slid over on the couch, and patted the space next to her. "Come on. This is practically your couch by now, anyway," she teased. "You've spent more nights on it than I have. The least I can do is share it with you." He got up, came over, and lay down beside her, careful to leave a space between them. And she studied him in the pale light filtering in from the windows. He looked different. There was the same fair skin, the same light brown hair falling in the same light brown eyes. But there was something else, too, a sadness she'd never seen in him before.

"Everett, what's wrong?"

"Nothing's wrong," he said. "Nothing new, anyway. But . . . do you remember when you asked me, that first night on the boathouse roof, if I'd ever lost anyone I'd loved?"

She nodded. "I remember. You didn't answer me."

"Well, I have lost someone," he said. "I was thinking about her."

"Who was she?" she asked, softly.

"My sister."

"You had a sister?"

"I did. Her name was Flora, after my grandmother, but everybody called her Birdy. She was only four when she died." And when he saw the expression on her face he answered her unasked question. "Cancer," he said, simply.

She drew in a breath. *At four years old?* It was almost too awful to imagine.

"I was twelve when she was born," he said. "My younger brother was ten. She was a surprise for us. She was a surprise for my parents, too, I think. They were both in their late forties already. But she was the best surprise," he said, and his expression was suddenly animated with the memory of her. "She was . . . she was *fascinated* by birds," he said, with a smile. "That's how she got her nickname. My mom noticed one morning, when Birdy was about a year old, that if she positioned her high chair so she could see the bird feeder outside the kitchen window, she would sit there for an hour. Maybe more. Just chasing Cheerios around her little tray table and watching the birds outside."

"By the time she was three," he continued, "she wanted to be an ornithologist. She couldn't *pronounce* the word, of course, but that didn't stop her from wanting to be one." He shook his head in wonder. "I mean, how many three-year-olds even *know* what an ornithologist is?"

"Very few, I imagine," Win said. But she felt a tightening in her chest. She knew what was coming next.

"She got sick the winter after she turned three," Everett said. "I won't tell you all the details, because, in a way, you already know them. Your husband and Birdy were different ages, and they had different kinds of cancer, and different treatments, too, but the experience we had, you and I, the experience of loving them, and of watching them go through that, the sheer terror of it, and the incredible unfairness of it . . ." He stopped for a moment, took a breath, went on. "I can't tell you anything about that you don't already know."

She knew what he meant. She watched Everett, carefully. She got the feeling that he was trying, hard, to compose himself. She didn't press him. But a moment later, he said, "At first, we liked her chances. She had a rare form of childhood lymphoma, its survival rate was only 50 percent, but we thought, why not? Why shouldn't Birdy survive? And what kind of world would it be if she didn't? It looked good, too, for a little while. She was in remission, for several months, and then . . ." He shrugged. "When my parents found out, they didn't know what to do. They were afraid to tell her. But she already knew. She was so brave. She was comforting *them*. She said, 'It'll be all right,' and 'Don't worry about me.'" He stopped again, and it was only then that Win realized she was holding her breath. She exhaled.

"We brought her home from the hospital," he said. "And had a little hospital bed set up in the living room, right in front of the picture window. And then my dad and my brother and I went out and bought every single bird feeder we could find and we hung them there, in a row, outside that window. There were *a lot* of birds there," he said. "We still hang a new one up there, every year, on what would have been her birthday."

He leaned back against the couch, as if exhausted from the effort of telling her all of this.

"Oh, Everett," she said, and she almost—*almost*—said *I'm sorry,* but she caught herself. How many times had people said that to her after Kyle died? Too many times to count. And how many times had hearing it made her feel better? That was easier to answer. None. So instead she reached out and gently, very gently, brushed his hair out of his eyes, and then she leaned over and kissed his smooth, cool forehead.

Had she overstepped some boundary? she wondered. A moment later, though, Everett put his arms around her, and drew her to him. She put her head on his chest, and closed her eyes, and he tightened his arms around her. And they lay that way, without saying anything, as the light grew brighter outside the windows, and the birds started stirring in the trees. *Birdy,* Win thought to herself, listening to their songs, and for a moment she felt unbearably sad. But Everett was solid and warm beside her. She could feel him breathing slow, rhythmic breaths, and she could feel his heart beating, reassuringly, just inches from her ear. They had both seen death, she thought, but they were also both, at this moment, very much alive.

CHAPTER 14

Sam leaned against the front porch railing at Birch Tree Bait and looked out over the lake. It was early evening; the color was slowly draining out of the sky, the feathery clouds were back-lit by the coppery glow of the lowering sun, and the pine trees seemed to be gathering their cool, green shadows within them. And everything—the sky, the clouds, and the trees—was re-flected in the glass smooth surface of the lake. This was Sam's favorite time of day. There was a sense of time slowing down, of the day unwinding itself, of evening setting in at its own relaxed, unhurried pace. Across the bay, a lone canoe glided, sedately, over the water, and, above the tree line, an osprey flew in a lazy circle.

Linc and Jordy had finished loading the kayaks onto the stor-age racks, their laidback conversation drifting over to Sam on the porch, and Justine was gathering up the stray life vests from the dock in an absentminded way that suggested she'd already left work, in spirit if not in actual fact. Poppy was inside closing up the store; Sam could feel the allure of her even from out here on the porch. He resisted the urge to go back inside, though. He needed to think. It was almost a week since he'd kissed Poppy in his kitchen, almost a week since he'd told her, the next morning, that they couldn't have a physical relationship with each other. But Sam understood now that that conversation had closed one door, only to open another one instead.

And now, looking out over the lake, he replayed that morning in his mind. The first thing he'd done after opening Birch Tree Bait was waylay Margot at the coffee counter and ask her if he could speak to her in his office. What followed were five excruciating minutes during which Sam explained to her, as gently as he could, that he valued her much more as a friend than as a girlfriend. This was true. But it left out some crucial information, like the fact that he wasn't attracted to her and the fact that the high point of his night with her had been coming home and kissing Poppy. Still, he hoped that she would take it well, and she did. She left his office with her head held high. She was a class act, as far as Sam was concerned, but, as it turned out, she was also human. She hadn't been back to Birch Tree Bait since then, more proof that it had never been the coffee she'd come for in the first place.

The second thing he'd done that morning was ask Poppy if he could speak to her. "Sure," she said, almost shyly. She was standing on a step stool, arranging boxes of cereal on a top shelf, but she jumped down lightly and brushed the dust off her hands. "What's up?"

"Let's talk in my office," he said. But by the time he was settled in behind his desk, and she was sitting in the only other chair in the room, he felt as stymied as he had by his conversation with Margot. This would be difficult, too, though for totally different reasons. For one thing, the room seemed too small for both of them, especially after that kiss. He could still smell her hair, and still feel the softness of her lips beneath his.

"Is everything okay?" she asked, finally, looking a little worried.

Spit it out, Sam. Just spit it out. "Everything's fine. But . . . what happened last night, that can't happen again."

"*Why?*" She had definitely not seen this coming.

"Because it's not right," he said, leaning his elbows on his desk. "You're my employee. I'm your boss. This is a small business, in a small town."

She nodded, thoughtfully. "Okay. I understand. But . . . what if I wasn't your employee? What if I quit?"

"I don't think that's a good idea," he said, leaning back in his chair. "For one thing, you need this job. You told me that yourself when I hired you."

"I need *a* job, Sam," she pointed out. "If I quit this one, I'll get another one. It shouldn't be that difficult. It's summertime, in a resort community."

"There's more to it than that, though. What if . . . this thing," he said, making a gesture that included both of them, "what if it doesn't work out? Then you've given up your job, and . . ."

She smiled at him. "That's a chance I'm willing to take. And why . . . why do we have to think that far ahead anyway?"

"You don't have to," he said. "But I do." *I have to.* And that was why this conversation was so important. He didn't have the freedom that she had. He couldn't afford to take the chances that she could take. His life was inextricably linked to his children's lives, and to the business that paid their bills. And there was something else, too, something that had been bothering him. What did he *really* know about Poppy? She was beautiful, yes. But what else? Well, she loved Red Vines and loathed low fat mayonnaise. She was the fastest shelf stocker he'd ever had, and that included Justine. She could execute a perfect chin roll with her baton, at least according to Cassie, who adored her. And, once or twice, he'd seen something in her, a fragility maybe, or a vulnerability, that seemed to belie her usually carefree demeanor. It wasn't a lot to know about someone, he conceded, though it was enough to make him want to know more.

"Poppy," he said. "What if . . . what if we took some time to get to know each other?"

"You mean, what if we 'dated'?" she asked, brightening.

"It wouldn't be dating per se," he said, carefully. "It would be more like spending time together. You know, hanging out," he added.

"Yeah, okay," she said, a little hesitantly. "But what would we do?"

He smiled. "We'd talk."

And over the last week, that was exactly what they'd done. They'd talked. Their timing, actually, was perfect. The days continued to be hectic, but the evenings, for Sam at least, were unusually relaxed; the kids had been with Alicia in Grand Rapids, Michigan, where she took them every summer to visit her family for a week at the end of July. So, instead of leaving Birch Tree Bait at closing every evening, Sam was free to stay late, ostensibly to work on those projects he rarely had time for during the busy season, but in reality, to be with Poppy. And Poppy, who'd perfected the art of hanging back at the end of the workday, always found something that needed doing five minutes before her shift was over. Did the other employees notice this? Did they know that she and Sam conspired to be alone after work? Probably. They didn't try that hard to hide it. But if this lent an illicit quality to their time together, there was, in actuality, nothing illicit about it. Sam didn't cross that line again, and Poppy didn't encourage him to cross it, either.

They couldn't control *everything*. They couldn't control their attraction to each other. That was there, between them, in everything they did. It was the reason why Sam didn't invite her over to his cabin for dinner. He didn't trust himself. And it was why he didn't ask her out to dinner, either. Anything that felt too much like a date was bound to end in trouble. Instead, they hung out at Birch Tree Bait for a couple of hours, until it got late and Sam walked Poppy to her car. Usually, during this time, they sat on the front porch, or down at the dock, or, if the evening was cool, inside at the coffee counter.

Poppy told him about her childhood summers on Butternut Lake, and about how those days were among the happiest of her life. She told Sam stories—some funny, and some not so funny—about her flaky mom and her irresponsible, fun loving, but hard drinking dad. She talked a lot about Win, too, whom she loved like crazy, but whom she worried about. Her sister was definitely a little OCD, she explained to Sam, and, despite a new flirtation with a guy named Everett, she still spent too much of her time organizing the things she'd saved from her marriage to her late husband. Poppy's relationship with her cat, Sasquatch, was much less complicated, she explained to Sam. It, and he, were both perfect.

She also told Sam about the string of unrewarding jobs she'd had. She tried to make some of these sound amusing, but it was clear that they'd invariably left her feeling empty. One thing she was not forthcoming about, though, was her past relationships. On this subject she was vague, and Sam didn't feel he had the right to press for any more information.

He told Poppy about his life, too. About his own stalwart and responsible parents, and about his two brothers, who had both settled out west and who he didn't see nearly enough of anymore, but who he stayed in touch with through email and

Skype. He told her about college, about opening Birch Tree Bait, and about some of the adventures, and misadventures, he and Linc had shared in the outdoors. He told her his favorite stories about Cassie and Tim and Hunter, and he talked about his own childhood on Butternut Lake. He said that he and Poppy must have crossed paths at some point during the summers she'd spent here as a kid, maybe at Pearl's, or at the American Legion's Friday night fish fries. But Poppy pointed out that when she was ten, Sam was eighteen; he wouldn't have noticed her if they had crossed paths. He didn't tell her everything, though. He didn't tell her that the more time they spent together, the more attracted to her he was, and the less likely it seemed to him that the two of them could exist in this kind of limbo much longer . . .

"See you tomorrow, Sam," Linc called out now, from the parking lot, as he straddled his motorcycle and started the engine. Sam waved to him, thinking that Linc looked like a kid with a new toy, which in fact he was. He turned to go back inside the store to help Poppy close up, but no sooner had he crossed its threshold than he changed his mind. It was too beautiful outside for either of them to be in here.

"Poppy?" he said, finding her near the sunscreen display. She was finishing up some last minute stocking.

"Hey Sam," she said, "I'm almost done. I haven't closed out the register, though. Justine hasn't showed me how to do it yet."

"Don't worry about it. I'll do it after you leave," he said, opening the refrigerated case behind him. "Do you want something to drink? We can take it down to the lake."

"Sure. I'll have a lemonade," Poppy said. Sam grabbed one for her and an iced tea for himself, and they headed out the back door and down to the water.

"Your kids are due back tonight, aren't they?" Poppy asked, as she sat down at the end of the dock. She kicked her sandals off, rolled up her jeans, and dipped her feet in the water.

"Uh-huh. They'll be here in . . . another couple of hours," he said, checking his watch. He sat down next to her, leaving a few feet of space between them. It didn't matter, though. They didn't have to be touching each other for Sam to feel the incredible charge between them.

"Did they have a good time?" Poppy asked, her eyes following a family of loons swimming along the shoreline.

"They did. I mean, Hunter got poison ivy and Cassie cut her foot on a bottle cap at the beach, but no vacation with children would be complete without a couple of minor disasters. Otherwise, they loved being with their cousins. I mean, you know what that's like, don't you?"

"I don't, actually. I don't have any cousins. Both of my parents were only children."

"Well, it's like siblings, only in some ways, it's better, because there's no . . . baggage. You haven't spent your whole life competing with each other for your parents' attention."

She considered this. "That does sound nice. But in Win's case and mine, our baggage isn't from competing for our parents' attention. They ignored both of us equally," she said wryly.

Sam looked over at her but she smiled and splashed her feet, as though she were kicking the idea away. He'd never had a thing for feet before, he thought, watching her suntanned toes dip in and out of the water, but he decided he could probably develop one for hers. They were so pretty, though, in truth, no prettier than any other part of her, her earlobes, for instance, or her knees, or her wrists. And he suddenly felt a kind of erotic energy between them, a pull that had been there all week, whenever they were physically close to each other, and sometimes, even when they weren't.

She swayed slightly towards him now, as if in response to his thoughts.

"Sam?" she said.

"Yes?"

"I quit."

"You quit?"

"Uh-huh. I'm resigning from Birch Tree Bait. Effective immediately."

"Are you sure about that?" he asked.

"Positive," she said, a smile playing around her lips.

And he leaned over and kissed her, kissed her the way he'd wanted to kiss her the first time he'd seen her, holding that dusty bottle of wine. And she slipped her arms around him and kissed him back. *Poppy*. She was so sweet. She *tasted* so sweet. She tasted like . . . *like Red Vines*, the licorice candy she was always eating. And she felt so soft, he thought, folding her into his arms. He ran a hand through her hair. He'd wanted to do this, too; he'd felt as if it had been almost begging him to touch it.

The kiss changed now. It was still sweet, but harder to contain. He held her closer, and kissed her more deeply. He ran his hand up from her waist, and it brushed, gently, against the side of her breast. She flinched, and pulled away.

"What's wrong?" Sam asked, instantly concerned.

"Nothing. Nothing's wrong," she said, catching her breath.

"Did I . . . ?" *Did I do something I shouldn't have?* Sam wanted to say.

"No," she said, looking away from him and pulling her hair back in a ponytail. "No, you didn't do anything wrong."

But at that moment, Sam's cell phone vibrated in his back pocket. He pulled it out, checking to make sure it wasn't Alicia or one of the kids. "It's Linc," he said, apologetically. "I should take it."

"What's up?" Sam asked, still watching Poppy.

"Nothing's up," Linc said. "I just swerved to avoid a deer, and I ended up running my bike off the road."

"Are you hurt?"

"Just a little scraped up," Linc said, which Sam knew could mean anything. Linc had a tremendous gift for understatement.

"You're sure you're not hurt?" he pressed him.

"No, But my bike won't start. Could you . . . ?"

"Yeah. I'll come and get you. Just tell me where you are."

When Sam hung up, he explained the situation to Poppy.

"Poor guy," she said. "You better get going, Sam." She walked him to his truck.

"Can you lock up for me?" he asked, handing her the keys to Birch Tree Bait.

"Of course. I don't know how to close out the register, though."

"Don't worry about it. I'll do it in the morning before we open. And, uh, come in tomorrow," he said, sorry that he had to leave her like this. "You can pick up your last paycheck and we can figure out a time to have dinner or something." He gave her a quick kiss before he opened the door to his pickup. But something about her expression made him hesitate before he got in. "Are you sure you're okay?" he asked her.

"*Yes,* I'm fine," she said, smiling. "Go." But there was a tremulous quality about her smile that Sam remembered long after he'd driven away.

CHAPTER 15

When Poppy went back inside Birch Tree Bait, the setting sun was filtering in through the shutters, turning the light in the room pink, and casting horizontal shadows onto the walls. It was quiet inside; quiet enough to hear the breeze from the overhead fan ruffling a newspaper someone had left on the coffee counter, quiet enough to hear the alternating buzz and hum of the freezer cases. She'd never been here alone after hours, and she might have enjoyed it—it was strangely soothing—if she hadn't been so full of anger. Not at Sam, at herself. *What is wrong with me?* she thought, resisting the urge to kick the stepladder that was parked at the end of one of the aisles, and instead dragging it over to a window and sitting down on it. *What happened to me down at the dock?* She twisted her hands in the hem of her T-shirt, her body taut with frustration. *Why did I panic like that? I wanted Sam to kiss me, and to touch me. I've wanted it since that night in his kitchen. No, since before that night. So why did I pull away from him?* But the answer came back to her almost immediately: *For the same reason you've always pulled away from everyone.*

But Sam was different, wasn't he? And, more importantly, *she* was different with Sam. She chewed, impatiently, on her lower lip, and felt her anger recede, a little, only to be replaced by disappointment. She wanted to be close to Sam, in more ways than one. So why couldn't she just let herself be? Just . . . turn off the part of her that had flinched when he'd touched—no, grazed— the side of her breast. *Because it's not that simple, Poppy. And you know it.*

She blew out a long, slow breath, and, bathed in the pink light from the windows, she forced herself to think about all of this. It wasn't easy. She'd been careful to compartmentalize her life, and her past. And while she might not have Win's organization skills when it came to kitchen utensils, she had them when it came to her memories. She was good at separating out the ones that were painful, and of relegating them to their own little-used drawer. Of course, they hadn't always *stayed* where she'd put them. And sometimes, after she'd cracked the drawer open on them, it was hard to slam it shut again. But tonight was different. Tonight, she would *let* herself remember, *really remember,* something she'd spent half a lifetime trying to forget . . .

And, just like that, she was back there again. She was sixteen years old, a junior in high school, and it was the first day of spring. No, not the *actual* first day of spring, that had come weeks before. But the first day that felt truly spring-*like* in its mildness and its sunniness, and, to celebrate, Poppy had worn a sundress and a pair of flip-flops to school that morning. It was possible that this had been just a tiny bit premature on her part. It wasn't *that* warm outside, and she was shivering a little as she walked home from school that afternoon. Fortunately for Poppy, though, she was in a state of such pleasant preoccupation that she was barely conscious of being cold. She had a decision to make, an *important* decision, maybe the *most* important decision of her life to date. Certainly, its implications would reach far beyond the present, she reflected, as she shifted her backpack from one shoulder to the other. After all, there could only be *one* first kiss in her lifetime, and only *one* person to share that first kiss with. In all likelihood, she thought, turning onto the street she lived on, she would never forget that person, or that kiss. She might even tell her own daughter about it one day.

And herein lay the problem. Whom should that first kiss be with? Poppy had whittled the list of candidates down to two. The first, Matty Lumner, a senior and co-captain of the basketball team, was the obvious choice. But was it *too* obvious, she wondered, too . . . unimaginative? Which brought her to Taylor Montgomery. Like Poppy, he was only a junior, not a highly coveted senior. And unlike Matty, he was not an athlete; in fact, he was sort of the *opposite* of an athlete, he played the saxophone in the school orchestra. Still, he had soulful brown eyes, and an attractive slouch, and the fact that he played a woodwind instrument seemed to suggest that he was probably pretty good with his lips.

Poppy sighed, dreamily, as she reached the door to her apartment building. She tugged it open, and walked through its somewhat cramped lobby, not bothering to glance at the bank of mailboxes on her left. Her family almost never got any personal mail, except for the occasional birthday card or holiday card from her grandparents. Mostly, what they got were bills, the threatening kind of bills that had words like *final notice* printed on their envelopes. But Poppy wasn't thinking about this today as she boarded the slightly creaky elevator and pressed the button for her floor. She was thinking about the kiss. Or what she and

Win jokingly referred to, in their late night conversations, as "operation first kiss."

When the elevator stopped, and the door slid open, though, reality intruded again. Poppy got off reluctantly. She was sorry now that marching band practice had been canceled today. She hated coming home to an empty apartment. She'd be alone, of course. Her parents were never there, not if they could possibly help it. And Win was only home after six, when the myriad extracurricular activities she participated in had all ended. She let her backpack slide off her shoulder now, and dragged it down the hall after her, thereby allowing it to slow down, if only incrementally, her arrival at the too quiet apartment.

"Hey," she heard someone say.

She jumped. She hadn't even noticed that one of her neighbors was standing in his apartment doorway.

"Hi," she said, offering a neutral smile. Poppy's family didn't really know any of the people on their floor. They'd lived in so many different apartments over the years that they no longer bothered to introduce themselves to anyone. Instead, Poppy and Win gave their own names to the few neighbors who caught their interest, or inspired their dislike. "The mean lady," for instance, lived at the end of their hallway, "the tired couple with the crying baby" lived across the hall, and "the woman with the facial piercings" lived directly to the right of the elevator. This man, the one who'd just said hello, they referred to simply as "the photographer." They'd never spoken to him before, but they'd seen him carrying his equipment in and out of the building, and they'd seen, too, the girls that occasionally came and went from his apartment.

"I'm Rich, by the way," he said, holding out his hand for her to shake. And when he saw her hesitate, he laughed. "It's all right," he said. "I don't bite."

She came closer and shook his hand. "I'm Poppy," she said, studying him, shyly. It was hard to tell how old he was, but he was pretty old, she decided. Thirty-five, at least, and maybe even forty. He was tall and rangy, with dark hair worn longer than the boys at her high school wore it, and with a little patch of a beard worn under his mouth that only later would Poppy learn was referred to as a "soul patch." Add to that his outfit—a vintage rock concert tee, tight jeans, and pair of leather boots—and Poppy supposed he looked pretty cool. Or at least *he* seemed to think he did.

"Ah, *Poppy,*" he said of her name. "Just like poppies in the springtime. You must be enjoying this beautiful weather then?" he asked, giving her sundress a frankly appraising look that made her feel instantly self-conscious.

She blushed, and fidgeted with the dress's neckline. "It's okay," she said, noncommittally, hoisting her backpack back up onto her shoulder again and twisting it around so she could unzip the front compartment and get her keys out.

"*It's okay?*" he said, imitating her nonchalant tone. "Are you kidding? This weather is *gorgeous*. I did a bikini shoot outside today. It's probably the first day I could have done it this spring without the models getting frostbite. Even so, we had to have bathrobes and hot chocolate waiting for them when it was over."

"You did?" she said, interested in spite of herself. "That sounds like fun." She meant the part about the bathrobes and the hot chocolate. She didn't know whether posing for a photographer would be fun or not.

"I don't know if the *models* would have called it fun," he said.

"It's a lot of hard work. But it pays. Each of those girls made five hundred dollars today."

Poppy's eyes widened. "They made that just . . . standing around?" she asked, fascinated.

"Well, in fairness to them, they weren't *just* standing around. There's a lot more to modeling than that. But you know that, don't you? You must have already tested the waters a little."

She stared, blankly, at him.

"You know. Done a little modeling?"

She shook her head.

"None at all?"

"No."

"How is that even possible? A beautiful girl like you? You must have been approached by agents, though."

She hesitated, and then gave her head a tiny shake. This was a lie, though. Twice—once at the Mall of America and once at the Minnesota State Fair—people who'd said they were agents had approached her and given her their cards. But both times, her mom had said no. She was too young to model, she'd told her, and besides, she was too busy to spend her time driving Poppy around to any appointments, anyway.

"*Unbelievable,*" Rich was saying now. "You must know how beautiful you are, though, right? I mean, people must tell you that all the time."

Again, Poppy shook her head. This was another lie. People *did* tell her that all the time. Her feelings about the way she looked, though, were complicated. She knew, objectively, that she was pretty. But she also knew that it shouldn't be the most important thing about her. Her grandparents, whom Poppy adored, often reminded her of this. *Pretty girls are a dime a dozen,* her grandfather would say. *It's what's in here that counts,* he'd add, using two fingers to thump on his chest, over the place where his heart was. And Poppy knew he was right. She knew because the one person she admired more than anyone else in the world, her younger sister, Win, was so much more than just pretty. She was smart and responsible and kind, all the things Poppy worked hard to be, even if they didn't come as naturally to her as they did to Win.

"Well, you are prettier, by far, than any of the models whose pictures I took today," Rich said, leaning on his doorframe. "You should give it a try. I mean, if nothing else, it would be a great way to pick up some easy money."

Easy money, Poppy thought. That sounded appealing. In her family, there was nothing easy about money. Her parents never had any—whether because they didn't like working very much, or they just weren't very good at it, Poppy couldn't be sure—and Win only had a little, and only because she babysat on weekend nights. More often than not, Poppy was left scrambling to pay for her majorette uniforms and her band fees.

"Of course, you'd have to get some head shots done," Rich said, casually. "You need those to call on agents with. They're expensive, though."

"Are they?" Poppy said, feeling disappointed. They were out of the question, then. She smiled a polite smile that she hoped indicated their conversation was over, and she started moving down the hallway to her apartment.

"Hey, sorry about Mr. McKinley," he called after her. She stopped. Mr. McKinley was the building's manager. He didn't like her parents, and they didn't like him.

"What about Mr. McKinley?" she asked, turning around.

He shrugged. "He was up here the other day, talking to your parents. Well, not *talking to*. More like *yelling at*. I could hear him through this," he said, indicating his front door. "I guess there was some problem with the rent," he added, and Poppy's face burned. There was *always* some problem with the rent. It was why they moved so much.

She nodded, and started to move down the hall again. But he came after her. "Hey, don't feel bad about it," he said, when she stopped and turned to him. "I'm friendly with Mr. McKinley. He listens to me. Maybe I could put a good word in for your parents. I mean, if they haven't got the money, they haven't got the money, right?"

Poppy didn't answer him. It was possible, though, that her parents *did* have the money and just didn't feel like spending it on rent. It was also possible they didn't have the money, and were broke, or what her dad liked to call *flat* broke. Sometimes, when they were this, her grandparents sent them money. But they couldn't always afford to help. They lived on her grandfather's military pension, and that wasn't always enough to pay their bills and their son's bills, too. And now, they had rented out their cabin on Butternut Lake so they could afford to live in a retirement community in Florida, where their grandfather said the weather was kinder to old people. (How their grandparents—calm, dependable, steadfast people—had produced Poppy and Win's father was a subject of endless fascination to the sisters.)

"Look, I didn't mean to embarrass you," Rich said. "We all have problems, right?"

Poppy nodded, not sure what else he wanted her to say.

"And you're lucky, in a way, that your problems are financial. Those problems are the easiest to fix. At least for a pretty girl like you."

Poppy looked at him, not understanding.

"I'm going to take your pictures," he explained now. "Your head shots. And I'm going to waive my fee, which, by the way, is *very* high. And then you can take my pictures—*our* pictures—to a modeling agency and start landing some jobs. After that, you should be able to start earning some spending money. And who knows? You might even earn enough to be able to pay the rent one day. What do you say?"

"Maybe," Poppy said, though she didn't like the idea of taking anything for free.

"Maybe?" he teased her. "I think that sounds like a pretty good offer, don't you?"

"I'll have to ask my mom."

"Your mom?" he said, and there was something slightly mocking in his tone. "Is she in charge, then?" he asked. Poppy shrugged, a tiny shrug, because the truth was that in her family, no one was in charge. Unless it was Win, practical Win, who, at fifteen, seemed to have more common sense than both of her parents put together.

"Well, is your mom home now?" Rich asked.

Poppy shook her head.

"Do you know how to reach her?"

She gave another shake of her head.

Rich looked at his watch. "Because I have exactly one hour to do this in."

"Now? You're going to take my pictures now?"

"Why not?"

"I thought you meant . . . you know, you could do it later."

"But I have time *now*. And I don't know when I'll have time again. My schedule's pretty full."

Poppy wavered.

"Come on. I'll leave the front door open, if that'll make you feel better," he said, with an amused roll of his eyes, as if they both knew she was being silly. And maybe she was, Poppy thought then. He was her *neighbor*, wasn't he? He lived on her *floor*. He wasn't going to *do* anything to her. Except take her pictures. For free. She was still nervous as she followed him into his apartment, though, and she made sure that he left the door open, just as he'd said he would.

Once inside, Poppy was surprised to see that his living room was almost empty, except for a narrow blue velvet couch—he called it a *settee*—and his photography equipment. This was his studio, he explained to Poppy. This was where he worked most of the time, unless he was on location, the way he'd been today. He showed her his camera, and his lights, and explained what the umbrella was for, and he even turned on a big fan and had her stand in front of it so that it blew her hair and her dress around. He was trying to make this fun, she saw, but she was too nervous to have fun. Finally, he said they should do some test shots, and he had her sit on the couch. He spent a long time then, fiddling with lenses, and lights, but when he finally started to take pictures of her, he seemed disappointed. He said she looked too tense, and that she needed to relax.

"Would you, uh, like something to drink?" he asked, setting his camera down. "I could offer you a glass of wine, or a cocktail. That might help you unwind a little." But Poppy didn't drink, even at high school parties, and she knew this wasn't the place to start.

"I'm sixteen," she said to him, by way of refusal.

"So?"

"So . . . I'm underage."

"All that means is that you can't *buy* alcohol. But I've already bought it *for* you. Come on. It'll be fun. I'll make you something. A mojito. Do you know what that is? It's made with rum and limes. All the girls are drinking them at the clubs now."

"No, thank you," Poppy said, stiffly.

He looked impatient. "You're kind of uptight for a sixteen-year-old, aren't you?"

She frowned.

"I mean, do you always follow the rules?" he amended, quickly, and this time, when he spoke to her, he smiled, as if he weren't really annoyed at her but only just kind of amused by her.

"Usually," she said, looking down at her hands on her lap. "I think maybe I should leave now," she said.

But he persuaded her to stay. He told her that he'd bring her a glass of ice water, and then he'd put on some music to help her get into the right mood. She waited, on the edge of the couch, while he went into the kitchen. It was only later that she realized he hadn't just gotten her a glass of water. He'd also closed the front door to his apartment.

When he came back, he put on music. The music wasn't the kind that Poppy liked, though, and it was turned up too loud. And Rich kept asking her to do things like lie down on the couch, or pull down the straps on her sundress so that her shoulders looked bare. But Poppy was too uncomfortable to do any of these things.

Finally, he got exasperated. "Look," he said, coming over to her. "I've done everything I can to make this work, but you're not even trying."

Poppy didn't disagree. She *wanted* to try, she just didn't know *how* to. This whole modeling thing, she decided, was harder than it looked. "I have to go now," she said, suddenly anxious. "My sister's going to be home soon."

"You're not wasting all the time I just put into this," he said. He was furious, she saw, and it scared her. She stood up to leave then, but he blocked her way. Only then did she realize how much taller he was than her. "You're not going," he said, pushing her back down onto the couch, and there was something in his expression now that scared her even more. She hadn't seen this thing in him before, whatever it was. He'd been trying to hide it, she understood now. It was angry, though, and mean. And it made him strong. Incredibly strong. She would never have believed such a skinny guy could be so strong.

She was only in his apartment for another five minutes. Maybe less. But it felt like an eternity. Before he let her leave, he warned her that if she told anyone, anyone at all, he'd make sure Mr. McKinley kicked her family out of the building.

Later that night, when Poppy came into her and Win's bedroom, wrapped in a bath towel and still dripping wet from the shower, Win looked up from the book she was reading on her bed. "Are you all right?" she asked, studying Poppy.

"I'm fine," Poppy said. But her voice sounded strange, even to her. She tightened the towel around her and walked over to her dresser, but, once she got there, she felt at a loss. She opened a drawer, randomly, and started to go through it.

"Pops, you're being weird," Win said, from her bed.

"No, I'm not," Poppy said. She listened, again, to her own voice. It sounded completely detached from her. As if it were coming from the bottom of a well.

"Well, that's the third shower you've taken tonight," Win pointed out. "I mean, how dirty can one person be?"

Poppy didn't answer. She was afraid if she did, the panic would flood into her body again. The same panic she'd felt when she'd first gotten back to the apartment and gotten into the shower. Then, it was all she could do to hold her violently shaking body still beneath the too hot water.

She pulled a nightgown out of one of the drawers, and held it up. It was white cotton, with lace edging, and a pattern of pink roses on it. She stared at it, as if she'd never seen it before. And, in a way, she hadn't. Not in the way she was seeing it now. It looked like it belonged to a child, she decided, and staring at it, she felt a wave of something—of fatigue, or sadness, or maybe just plain *oldness*—come over her. The oldness part was strange, of course. She wasn't old. But she felt old now, too old to wear a nightgown that looked like this. She crumpled it up, violently, and stuffed it into a nearby wastebasket. That got Win to close her book, and to get up off her bed, too.

"Why are you throwing that away?" she objected. "Grandma gave it to you." Grandma had given one to Win, too. It was from the Butternut Variety Store and it was identical to this one except that the roses on it were yellow instead of pink.

"I don't want it anymore," Poppy said, indifferently. "It's for a little girl."

"Pops," Win said, coming over to her. "What's wrong? Tell me."

"Nothing's wrong. I just don't feel well," Poppy said, using all of her self-control to not break down and tell Win everything. She remembered Rich's threat. Her whole family could end up on the street. And worse, if she told Win, she would confront him or want to tell the police, and then he might hurt Win, too.

Poppy, moving mechanically, went back to her dresser and put on a pair of underwear and an oversized T-shirt. Win still looked worried. "Do you want me to brush your hair, Pops?" she asked. "It's all tangled up."

Poppy looked at herself in the mirror above the dresser. Her wet hair was impossibly knotted. But she looked away before she could see her face. For some reason, the thought of seeing it scared her. Maybe it was because she was afraid it would look as empty as she felt inside.

"Come on," Win said, gently, leading her over to her bed. Poppy sat down on it and Win sat beside her and started brushing her hair, being careful not to pull too hard, and to work through the knots patiently.

After a few minutes of this, the brush began to move more easily, and Poppy started to relax a little. It felt nice, in a way, especially when Win had settled into a rhythm, running the brush over and over again through Poppy's now smooth hair.

"Win?" Poppy said, finally. "Do you know that man who lives down the hall? The photographer?"

"Uh-huh," Win said, after a moment. Her voice sounded almost sleepy now. As if brushing her sister's hair was having the same sedating effect on her as it was having on Poppy.

"Have you ever talked to him?"

"What? No," Win said.

Poppy took a steadying breath and tried to sound casual. "I mean, did he ever ask you if he could photograph you?"

"Uh-uh. And if he ever did, I'd say no."

"Why?" Poppy asked, softly, trying to emulate Win's almost dreamy tone.

Win skimmed the brush through Poppy's hair, which hung down her back now like a straight, blond curtain.

"Well . . . I don't know him. He's a stranger."

Practical Win, Poppy thought, with a feeling that was part pride, part envy. She would never have gotten herself into the position Poppy had been in today. And there and then was born the idea, long held and not easily let go of, that this had all somehow been Poppy's fault. That she had *let* it happen.

Win brushed her hair for a little while longer, before yawning, sleepily. "My arm's getting tired, Pops. Mind if I stop now?"

"No," Poppy said, feeling it again, that strange sense of being removed. As if she'd somehow become detached from her body. "No, that's okay."

Win went to put the brush on the dresser, and then turned off the lights and got into bed.

"Poppy, are you going to go to sleep?" she asked, after a little while. Poppy was still sitting on her bed where Win had left her.

"Uh-huh," Poppy said, crawling under the covers. But she couldn't get comfortable. She was still scared. And she was cold, too, even though it was warm in their bedroom. She shivered, violently, and curled herself into a ball. In the bed next to her, Win stirred, sighed, and settled into sleep. Poppy listened to the steady rhythm of her breathing, and found that, for a little while, anyway, it soothed her. But then it got harder to stop her body from shaking. She curled it into a tighter ball, and screwed her eyes shut. She wouldn't think about what had happened in that apartment, she told herself. She wouldn't think about anything. She'd keep her mind a perfect blank.

And she was able to do this, but only for a little while. It was hard to shut out the knowledge of what had happened, harder still to shut out the feelings it provoked in her. She was terrified of those feelings, though. They were so overwhelming to her that she was afraid they would be like an enormous wave crashing over her, pushing her under and, ultimately, drowning her. She had to *try* to feel less. *She had to.* And it seemed to her the only way to do this was to forget, to forget as completely as possible, what had happened to her. To bury it. And to never tell anyone, not even Win. That would make it easier to forget, she reasoned, easier to pretend it had never happened.

And now, sitting on the stepladder at Birch Tree Bait, Poppy thought about how the not remembering, the not feeling had seemed like a good strategy that night, curled up under the covers. And in some ways, it had served her well. After all, she had survived those years. Hadn't she? Of course, it had come at a price. Not telling anyone, forgetting—or trying to forget—feeling less, caring less, all of these things had required her, in a sense, to drop out of her own life. She'd perfected the art of not putting too much of herself into any one thing, of not staying in any one place for too long, of not getting too attached to any one person. "Keep moving" had been her mantra. Avoid commitment, don't get too close to anyone, don't get hurt, and, above all, don't take life too seriously. She'd quit marching band, lost interest in going to college, and then moved on to a string of failed relationships—if you could even call them that—lousy jobs, and vacated apartments.

But here was the thing: what had worked for her once wasn't going to work for her anymore. She understood, finally, that she couldn't undo what had happened by simply not thinking about it. In fact, by burying the rape—*Yes*, Poppy thought, *call it by its real name*—by keeping it a secret, she hadn't kept it at bay, she had let it take over her life. Maybe, just maybe, she thought now, the only way to take that life back, and to stop making the same mistakes over and over again, was to bring her secret out of the darkness, and into the light. Where she could see it, and perhaps even let those closest to her see it, too.

The crazy thing was, until the night Sam had kissed her, she'd been content, or she'd *thought* she'd been content, to continue on as she had been. But being on Butternut Lake with Win this summer, and, well . . . being with Sam, had changed her. It had stirred something inside her, something she hadn't felt in a long time. In fact, she had to go back to that spring afternoon, walking home from school, to find it. It was a sense of excitement, of hope and of possibility. It was a feeling that good things were going to happen, and happen sooner rather than later.

She looked around now, surprised that night had fallen outside the windows of Birch Tree Bait. It was time to be closing up. She got up off the stepladder and moved around the room. She was still intensely preoccupied by her thoughts, so much so that everything she did—closing the shutters, turning off the fans and the few remaining lights—had an almost dream-like quality to it. But when she shut the front door behind her, absentmindedly, and turned the key in the lock, she thought, *It's okay. I'll figure this out. I'll see Sam tomorrow. We can talk some more then.* And then she headed down the steps to Win's car, the last one left in the parking lot.

CHAPTER 16

Less than twelve hours later, Poppy was pulling back into that same parking lot. She felt completely different, though, than she had the night before. If she'd gone to sleep weighed down by her new self-knowledge, she'd woken up feeling freer and lighter than she had in a long time. Everything suddenly seemed clear to her. It was as if, while she was sleeping, her priorities—or, more aptly—her *lack* of priorities—had magically rearranged themselves. It wasn't going to be that easy, she knew. People didn't change overnight, did they?

But as she was thinking about this, she noticed a police car parked, haphazardly, as if whoever was in it had gotten out in a hurry. She felt a tightening in her stomach, which she tried to ignore. *So what?* she told herself, getting out of her car. So a policeman is getting a cup of coffee here, or just stopping in to talk to Sam. It wasn't a big deal. She'd seen cops here before. It wasn't like it was off limits to them.

Still, her uneasiness persisted, especially since, when she went inside, Sam was nowhere to be seen, and Linc and Justine, who'd always been friendly to her in the past, now seemed reluctant to meet her eyes. Her stomach tightened a little more.

"Where's Sam?" she asked Justine, who was working the register.

"He's in his office with Roy," Justine said, not looking at her.

"Roy?"

"Roy's a cop," Justine said, and because it was obvious to Poppy that no more information would be forthcoming, she went to get a cup of coffee.

"'Morning Byron," she said, as she filled her cup. He was, as usual, sitting on a stool at the coffee counter, reading the *Minneapolis Star Tribune*.

"'Morning," he said, keeping his eyes trained on the paper. Poppy stared at him, uncomprehendingly. Under ordinary circumstances, Byron was courteous to the point of being chivalrous. Now he was bordering on rudeness. As Poppy poured half-and-half in her coffee, her face burned with indignation. What had she done? And why was everyone giving her the cold shoulder? Did they . . . did they know about her and Sam? And even if they did, why would they all be so angry with her? It wasn't as if Sam was giving her special treatment at work. After work, of course, it was a different story.

She'd just made up her mind to ask Byron what was going on when the door to Sam's office opened and he and a policemen came out. Sam glanced at Poppy, then glanced away. This time her stomach twisted, almost painfully. "Thanks for getting here so fast, Roy," Sam was saying to the cop as he shook his hand.

"'Course. I'll be in touch. But don't, uh, don't get your hopes up."

"No, I'm not going to," Sam said. He walked Roy to the door, opened it for him, and waited until he'd cleared the porch. Then, with another quick glance in her direction, he said, "Poppy, can I see you in my office?"

She nodded, wordlessly, and hurried over. Linc and Justine and Byron, who'd been so unwilling to look at her before, were all looking at her now. She knew they were because she could practically feel their eyes boring into her back.

"Is something wrong?" she asked, trying, and failing, to read Sam's expression. He didn't answer her, though. Once they were in his office with the door closed, he sat down at his desk and gestured for her to sit down, too.

The office was so small that her knees touched his desk. He hated this room, she knew. He only came in here during the busy season when it was absolutely necessary. She waited for him to say something, but instead he leaned back in his swivel chair, sighed, and massaged his eyes.

"Sam, what's going on?" she blurted out. "Why was that policeman here?"

He paused, then answered her question with another question. "Do you remember what you did with the keys I gave you last night?"

"The keys?" she said, reaching instinctively for her handbag, which was sitting on her lap. She opened it and rummaged through it. They weren't in there. Had they fallen out onto the car floor? Had she taken them out last night and left them on her dresser? "I . . . I don't have them," she said, looking helplessly at Sam.

"You don't have them," he said, patiently, "because you left them in the door when you locked up last night."

"How . . ."

"How do I know that?" he asked, his tone still patient. "I know that because they were still in the door when I got to work this morning."

"Oh, thank God," she said, relief welling up in her. "So nobody stole them?"

"No, they didn't need to steal them," he said, and now, in addition to patience, she thought she detected weariness in his tone. "They only needed to borrow them."

"Borrow them?" she repeated, not understanding.

"That's right. They let themselves in with them, and then they cleaned out the cash register."

Poppy sucked in a little breath of surprise. *"You were robbed?"*

"Burglarized. Roy—the police officer who was just here—said it was a crime of opportunity. Someone came by after the store had closed, saw the keys in the door and . . ." He shrugged.

"Does . . . does Roy have any leads?"

He shook his head. "No. He'll keep his ear to the ground, though. If it was a young person, or young people, they might tell their friends about it and word might get out."

"Oh, Sam, I'm so sorry," Poppy said, and she was stunned to feel tears burning in her eyes. She was *not* a crier. "I don't know what happened last night," she said, trying to piece it together. "After you left, I was thinking . . . and I was so preoccupied I didn't realize . . . Oh, God, I feel terrible."

He tipped his chair back again, but otherwise said nothing.

Poppy blinked. A tear ran down her cheek. She was mortified. Beyond mortified, really. And she was something else, too. She was disoriented. She felt like . . . she felt like she didn't know this Sam. He was so different from the man she'd been with yesterday evening. That man had been affectionate, and flirtatious, and funny. He'd always maintained a sense of professionalism during the workday, of course, but still, he'd never been like *this* before. He'd never been so detached, and so, so *impersonal*.

She was seized with a sense of panic. She needed to put things right. She needed to put things back to the way they'd been before. "I'll reimburse you," she said, suddenly. Decisively. "For all of the money you lost."

"Poppy, you can't. It's too much," he said, rubbing his eyes again.

"How much?" she asked, impatiently, as she wiped away a tear with the back of her hand.

"It's doesn't matter," he said.

"It does."

He sighed. "It was around seven hundred and fifty dollars, more than we usually have in cash." She sagged a little in her chair. She didn't have that much money. She didn't have even *close* to that much money. She knew it, and he knew it, too.

"What about insurance?" she asked. "You're covered for this kind of thing, aren't you?"

"No. Not if the theft is due to . . . negligence," he said, and she got the impression that he was somehow trying to soften the sound of that word. It didn't work. It still cut her to the quick. It was such an ugly word, though to her it should at least have been a familiar word. After all, this wasn't the first time in her life she'd been negligent.

A silent sob shook her now, and Sam, looking mildly alarmed, opened one of his desk drawers, looked around in it, and took out a packet of tissue. He handed it to her across the desk. "Look, I don't want you to cry, okay? It could have been worse, it could have been a lot worse," he said, his concern for her registering in his voice. "As far as I can tell, all they took was what was in the till. They could have cleaned this whole place out."

Poppy swallowed back another sob, and ripped into the tissue packet. It was hard to imagine it being any worse than it already was. She extracted a tissue now and mopped her eyes with it.

"Hey, take it easy," he said, and his voice was gentle again. "In the general scheme of things, it's not that big a deal. It was a day's cash earnings. That's it. If we're lucky, we'll make it back today."

She forced herself to take a deep breath and tried to smile. "I guess my quitting last night at least saves you from having to fire me now."

Sam didn't answer. He reached back into his top desk drawer, took out an envelope, and handed it to her. It was her paycheck. He tipped forward in his chair. "Well, yes," he said. "Under the circumstance, I think your leaving is for the best. Don't you?"

She brushed away those words with the sweep of her hand. She didn't *care* about this job. She *cared*, very much, about him. *About them. Together.* She waited for him to say something about this, but when he didn't, she said, uncertainly, "Sam, what about us?"

He hesitated. "Honestly, Poppy, I'm not sure about us right now."

It was so quiet in the small room then that she could hear the clock on Sam's desk ticking. Outside his office, someone called out to someone else, a screen door slammed, a car engine started up. Inside the office, the seconds ticked by.

"Are you saying . . . you don't want to see me anymore?" Poppy asked, in an almost whisper, and she felt as if she had put whatever remained of her pride on the desk between them. It didn't matter, though. Her pride didn't seem important right now.

Her words seemed to galvanize Sam into action, though. He got up, came around to the other side of the desk, and sat on its edge. They were so close now they were almost touching, but what he said now didn't close what little space remained between them.

"Look, Poppy, don't get me wrong," he said. "I'm incredibly attracted to you, and I've really liked getting to know you better this last week. But we're at completely different places in our lives. You're free to come and go as you please. When the summer is over . . . you'll move on. In fact, part of me is surprised you haven't already." She shook her head wordlessly; leaving here was the last thing she wanted to do. "I, on the other hand," Sam continued, "I'm tied to this place. I have three children, a business, a mortgage, *two* mortgages, actually—one on the cabin and one on the store—and a whole lot of other responsibilities I won't bore you with now." Again, she shook her head in protest. She knew what he was doing. He was saying, in the nicest way possible, *You're not like me, you're not a grown-up, and we're done here.*

He looked away from her now. They'd reached an impasse. But it didn't matter. It was still over. Poppy couldn't force him to be in a relationship with her. But he wasn't the only one she was going to miss, she realized, and she was surprised at how much this new knowledge hurt.

"Sam, what about Cassie?" she asked. She was still tutoring her on the front porch of Birch Tree Bait whenever they both had a free afternoon. "Her twirling has improved so much. But we're still working on her routine and her performance is next week."

Sam looked uncomfortable. "I think, right now, it might be better if you gave Cassie some space."

She nodded, miserably. So that would be gone, too. Those pleasant afternoons sitting on the porch swing, watching Cassie twirl, a little, and listening to her talk, a lot.

"I'm sorry," Sam said. "I want you to know how much I appreciate the time you've spent with her. She's loved it. She talks about you all the time. But . . . she's confused about you, too. She's confused about *us*."

Poppy looked at him questioningly.

Sam sighed. "She talked to Alicia about you this last week. And she told her . . . she told her she wants you to move in with us. I'm not clear exactly what she thinks your role would be. I don't know whether she thinks you'd be a sister to her or whether you and me would . . . give her a sister." He looked suddenly embarrassed.

That sounds good, Poppy thought. And it did. The part about giving Cassie a sister.

"Can you understand the position I'm in here, Poppy?" Sam asked her now. And all the humor was gone from his eyes. "I don't want Cassie to hope for something that's not going to happen. She'll be disappointed when you two stop spending time together, but hopefully, it will save her from more disappointment down the road."

"But . . . I promised her I'd go to her performance," she said softly.

"I know you did. She wants you to sit in the front row with her mom and me. I think you can see, though, that that would be . . . inappropriate."

Inappropriate. There was another word Poppy hated. It belonged to the province of guidance counselors, school principals, and people who taught workplace seminars. And now, apparently, it belonged to the idea of her coming to Cassie's twirling performance. She'd already been negligent, God forbid she add inappropriate to the list. Sam stood up. This was her cue to stand up, too. She did.

"Are you okay?" he asked. She nodded. He watched as she

tried to wipe the last traces of tears off her face. He felt bad, she saw. And she was sorry for him now.

He opened the door to his office and she saw him hesitate, wondering how to say good-bye to her. Should he shake her hand? Give her a hug? Kiss her on the cheek? In the end, he settled for a kiss on the cheek. It was a nice guy's kiss, she decided. A nice guy's way of saying, *I don't hate you. I just don't want you in my life anymore.* And in the end, it was that kiss that hurt the most of all.

The following week, Poppy drove down Butternut's Main Street. The charm of its striped awnings, brightly painted wooden benches, and window boxes filled with flowers was lost on her. She was a woman on a mission. She checked her watch as she turned into the Butternut Community Center parking lot. Today, timing was everything. And, as planned, she was exactly five minutes late for the baton twirling performance. If she'd timed it right, and she thought she had, she could slip into a seat in back, unseen, before Cassie went on stage. This was important, because while Cassie had invited her, Sam had *un*invited her during the meeting in his office. But she'd be damned if she was going to miss her star pupil's—her only pupil's—performance. She parked and hurried over to the building, but as she pushed open the lobby doors, she saw a woman sitting at a card table locking up a cash box.

"Hi, I'm here for the show," Poppy said, breathlessly.

"Oh, it's already started," the woman said, officiously. She was older, and wore her glasses on a chain around her neck, and she had blue hair, though it was not, Poppy noted, blue in a fun way.

"I can still go in, though, can't I?" Poppy said, reaching for her wallet. "I'm happy to pay," she added, noting that the hand-lettered sign on the table suggested a five-dollar donation.

"I'm not sure I can let you in now," the woman said. "I mean, I wouldn't want you to disturb the performers. Or the audience, for that matter."

Poppy stared at her, nonplused. Was she serious? This wasn't a Broadway play, this was a bunch of kids twirling batons.

"Look, I'll just slip right in," Poppy said, giving the woman her most charming smile. "Really, they won't even know I'm there," she added, pulling a five out of her wallet and putting it on the table.

She half expected the woman to follow her, but when she didn't Poppy cracked the auditorium door open. The house lights were down, and the group before Cassie's was still on. She choose an aisle seat in the empty back row, then slid down in it as far as she could, and adjusted the visor on her baseball cap until she was satisfied that she was as incognito as she could be in a town the size of Butternut. She searched the room until she found what she was looking for. Sam. There he was, fifth row center. On one side of him were the twins, and on the other side was a woman she assumed was Alicia. Poppy stared at her. There wasn't a lot you could tell from the back of someone's head, of course, but she sensed Alicia was attractive, with long, sleek, light brown hair, loosely knotted at the back of her neck, and a slender back and shoulders visible through a white cotton blouse.

As the performance ended, and the audience applauded, Poppy saw Sam turn to Alicia and say something. She nodded, and smiled up at him, and Poppy was seized by a jealousy so intense it shocked her. She could feel it everywhere in her body. But mostly, she could feel it in her stomach. It was the raw, burning feeling you might get if you drank a too strong cup of coffee on an empty stomach. Or if you drank a can of paint thinner.

Ridiculous, she thought to herself. Because that was what she was being. She had no right to be jealous. None whatsoever. Whatever Poppy and Sam had had, it was over now. And besides, Sam and Alicia were divorced. They weren't in love with each other anymore, he'd said as much to Poppy the night she'd babysat. But they *had been* in love, a voice inside her said. And she realized why she was jealous. She was jealous of everything they'd shared together, the big moments, and the little ones. *There was a lot of happiness there,* Sam had said about their marriage the night they'd sat at his kitchen table. Well, Poppy wanted a piece of that happiness with Sam, wanted it so badly that for a moment she felt light-headed from wanting it. She closed her eyes and waited for the feeling to pass. There would be no fainting here today. If she was going to stalk Sam, and Cassie, too, she could at least do it with a modicum of dignity.

Fortunately, it was time for the six- and seven-year-olds to perform, and as soon as Poppy saw Cassie come out on stage she had to smile. She looked adorable in her costume, a one-piece aquamarine number with tiny sequins sewn onto the bodice and skirt, and a pair of lace up white leather twirler shoes. Her hair and her makeup, Poppy saw with relief, were both blessedly subtle. Still, the overall effect must have more than satisfied Cassie's desire for all things girlie, because she was so excited she could barely contain herself. Poppy watched as she found her parents and brothers in their row, and then beamed at them as she and her four fellow twirlers formed a circle, and waited for the musical cue to start their routine.

Poppy knew this routine by heart. The last time Cassie had rehearsed it with her, she'd done it almost perfectly, and that had been over a week ago. She probably had it down cold by now. Just to be safe, though, Poppy crossed her fingers. The music, "Puttin' on the Ritz," started, and Poppy found herself keeping time with it. *"There you go,"* she murmured, as Cassie did a series of perfect figure eights. But the arm roll was coming up, and Cassie had had a little trouble with this. *"Come on, you can do it,"* she urged her, and when she did do it, again perfectly, it was all Poppy could do not to clap. Then, at last, came the chin roll, which Poppy could not have done better herself. *"Good girl,"* she whispered, and, as the routine ended, she wiped a single, hot tear off her cheek. *"You did it, kid,"* she said, and, knowing that the audience's applause and the performer's bowing would cover her exit, she slipped out of the auditorium and was halfway to her car before Cassie was even off the stage.

CHAPTER 17

On August 8, the Saturday of Mary Jane's wedding, Win stood, slack-jawed, in front of the full-length mirror in her bedroom. "Oh, my God," she said. "What was Mary Jane *thinking*?"

Poppy didn't answer. She was lying on Win's bed, propped up by pillows, and holding Sasquatch in her arms. Win had asked her, repeatedly, not to bring this living, breathing ball of fur into her bedroom—she could practically see him shedding, even from where she stood, across the room—but Poppy had been so miserable the last few weeks that she'd decided to let it slide today.

"I said, 'What was Mary Jane thinking?'" Win repeated, loudly, turning to Poppy and gesturing at her dress.

But Poppy only shrugged. "It looks fine," she said, petting Sasquatch.

"It *doesn't* look fine," Win said, turning to stare into the mirror again. "It looks like what it is, which is a *nightmare*." The dress in question was the bridesmaid's dress that Win would be wearing to Bret and Mary Jane's wedding at the White Pines Resort that evening. It was dark purple, or eggplant, as Win now thought of it, and it had an enormous bow on its right shoulder. The whole thing would have looked comical to her, if it didn't look so hideously ugly.

"That's it. I'm not wearing it," she said, turning her back to the mirror.

"So don't," Poppy said, not even pretending to be interested.

"Oh, right. Like I'm going to be the only one of six bridesmaids not wearing this dress," Win said, and she shot Poppy an irritated look.

Poppy, sensing the look, bestirred herself. "Look, Win, don't worry about it. People *expect* bridesmaid's dresses to be ugly. They'd be disappointed if they weren't. And don't say anything to Mary Jane about it, either," she added. "She can't help it. She probably didn't know how to choose a dress. I mean, who went with her to do it?"

"That . . . that would be me," Win said sheepishly. And even Poppy had to smile.

"*What?*" Win said, coming over to the bed and flopping down on it beside Poppy. "The day we went shopping for it in Duluth last winter it was twenty degrees below zero. We were probably suffering from brain freeze, or something. All I know is, at the time, it seemed like a good idea." She wagged the bow playfully at Poppy. She was trying to get another smile out of her, but this time it didn't work.

"Pops," she said, "come on. Cheer up. It can't be that bad, can it?" But it *was* that bad, if Poppy's demeanor was any indication. Win sighed. She'd tried, she thought, she really had. When Poppy had come back from Sam's office in tears the day after the store had been burglarized, for instance, Win had assured her, repeatedly, that it was a mistake anybody could have made, even though Win knew she herself would never, in a million years, have made it. And not once, during the days that followed, had Win so much as hinted at the fact that now that Poppy had lost her job, it was once again up to Win to pay for gas and groceries and whatever other expenses arose in their lives.

Win hadn't stopped there, though; she'd used every weapon in her sisterly arsenal to make Poppy feel better. She might not be able to cure her sister's broken heart, she'd reasoned, but she could at least make her forget about it for a while. To that end, she'd made her Rice Krispies Treats with M&M's, bought her a stack of paperback mysteries at the drugstore, and forced her to watch a *Real Housewives of Beverley Hills* marathon with her.

But Poppy refused to be consoled, or even, it turned out, to be distracted, and Win was starting to get a little impatient with her. "Pops," she said now, trying out a new tone of firmness, "I know you're sad, but for today, at least, you're going to have to make an effort."

"You mean for the wedding?"

"Yes," Win said. *Especially since I worked so hard to finagle an invitation for you.*

"I was going to talk to you about that," Poppy said, rubbing Sasquatch under his chin, and eliciting a purr from him that was probably audible in the kitchen. "I was thinking, maybe, I'd stay here," she said, stealing a look at Win.

"Absolutely not," Win said. "They're only inviting sixty people, and you're one of them."

"Look, I appreciate them inviting me, I really do," Poppy said. "But I don't want to leave Sasquatch alone for the whole night." After the wedding, Win and Poppy, like most of the other guests, would be spending the night at the White Pines Resort. Win had booked a room with two queen beds and a lake view, and she was personally looking forward to spending the night in relative luxury, and waking up to the resort's famous champagne breakfast the next morning.

Now, she raised an accusatory eyebrow at Poppy. "*Seriously?* That's the best you can do? You don't want to leave Sasquatch alone for the night? Poppy, he's *a cat.* I'm pretty sure he can take care of himself for twelve hours."

"Of course he can. But I'm worried about him. He hasn't been himself lately."

"Poppy, he's purring so much right now he's practically making the bed vibrate," Win pointed out.

"Right *now* he's okay. But lately . . . he's been so lethargic."

Maybe he caught it from you, Win thought. But what she said, not unkindly, was, "He's not lethargic, Pops, he's old."

Poppy shook her head. "This is something else. He doesn't eat that much anymore, and I think he might be losing weight."

"Well, next week you can take him to the vet. Today, you're going to the wedding."

Poppy considered this. "Is there . . . is there any chance Sam will be there?" she asked, finally.

"No," Win said, flatly. "I've seen the guest list, and he's not on it." Poppy sighed, softly, and seemed to disappear back inside herself again. "Okay, look, I wasn't going to tell you this," Win said, hurrying on. "I wanted to surprise you when we got to the wedding. But you've left me with no choice. Bret's cousin John is one of the groomsmen, and he's our age, single, good-looking, *and,* it gets better . . . he's in the Navy. All the other groomsmen are going to be wearing tuxedos, but he's going to be wearing his uniform. I mean, come on, how hot is that?"

Poppy shrugged, indifferently.

"Oh, come on, Pops. Would it kill you to flirt with him?"

"Why don't you flirt with him?" Poppy asked. "If you think he's so great."

"I . . . I haven't actually met him before," Win admitted, but now it was her turn to be irritated. Poppy knew she had feelings for Everett, didn't she? It was true, of course, that Win hadn't told her anything about the last time he'd spent the night, but that was only because Win didn't know *how* to tell her. She couldn't explain it to herself, let alone to another person. All she knew is that something had happened between them that night on the couch when he told her about Birdy, something that had left her feeling closer to him than she had felt to anyone in a long time. Partly, it had been a physical closeness, of course. But more than that, it had been an emotional closeness. A closeness Win had been craving, without knowing, until then, how much she had been craving it.

But where did that leave her and Everett now? she wondered. Were they friends, or were they becoming more than friends? And then there was the thought that nagged at her, occasionally, when she remembered that he had, at first, been interested in Poppy. Was it possible that she was his consolation prize for not having her sister? Not consciously, maybe—he didn't seem capable of making that kind of cold calculation—but unconsciously?

When she looked for answers to these questions, though, she couldn't find them. The morning after their night on the couch together there had been some initial awkwardness between them, and, further complicating matters, when Everett had said goodbye, he'd kissed her on the cheek. Was that him being polite, or something more? She hadn't seen him since, and that had been a couple of weeks ago. He'd been visiting his family in Nebraska, and after that, working on a deadline for a website design. Now, he was back up at his cousin's cabin for the weekend, but she'd told him she'd be busy with the wedding. Still, they'd exchanged texts with each other. Not flirty texts, just . . . funny texts. Casual texts. Though casual was one thing Win had never been very good at when it came to matters of the heart.

"Pops," she said now, turning to her sister with determined cheerfulness. "What's wrong with having a little fun with Bret's cousin? I mean, it wouldn't be a wedding if everyone went back to their own room at the end of the night, would it?"

Poppy looked askance at her. "Is my very proper, very responsible younger sister suggesting that I have a one-night stand?" she asked.

"Why not?" Win said, a little defensively. "If you like him, why not?"

"Because Win," she said, pointedly, "I'm already in love with someone."

"*Sam?*"

"You don't have to sound so surprised," Poppy said. She looked hurt.

"Poppy, I *am* surprised."

"Why? What's wrong with Sam?"

"Nothing. It's not Sam. It's . . . the two of you. You never even *dated* each other, Pops."

"What difference does it make? You don't have to date someone to fall in love with them."

"That's true," Win acknowledged. But she had another theory about why Poppy was so upset. Now she thought about how best to phrase it. "Pops," she said, carefully, "do you think you could be reacting this way, you know, taking this breakup so hard because . . . because it's never happened to you before?"

"You think this is about my ego?"

"No," Win said, quickly, and then, "Well, yeah, sort of. *I do.* I mean, let's face it. Most people don't get to be your age without having someone break up with them. You're in a pretty unique position in that sense. And I think if you'd had more . . . *practice* with rejection, you might be better at handling it now."

Poppy's sat up straighter on the bed, her face flushed. "You're *wrong*, Win. Trust me, the last thing I care about right now is my pride. What I care about is Sam. I thought . . ." She shook her head. "Never mind what I thought," she muttered.

"No, tell me. You thought what?"

"I thought he was the one," she said, softly. She settled back against the pillows and kept her eyes fixed on Sasquatch. Neither of them said anything for a moment. The late afternoon breeze stirred the window curtains, and sent the wind chimes on the front porch tinkling together.

"Oh, Pops," Win said, and because Poppy suddenly seemed so wistful to her, she reached over and hugged her, hard. "Don't give up, okay? Maybe everything will work out with Sam after all."

"I don't think so," Poppy said, hugging her back. "I blew it, Win. I just . . . blew it."

Win didn't say anything, but she patted Poppy on the back, and tried not to think about the fact that Sasquatch, and his offending fur, were only inches away from her nose. *My allergy medication must be working overtime,* she thought, catching sight of the clock on her bedside table.

"Poppy, we have to go," she said. "I have to be at Mary Jane's room at the White Pines in half an hour to help her get ready. And shouldn't you get ready, too?"

"I am ready," Poppy said, with surprise.

"You're wearing that?" Win said, of the simple, maybe *too* simple dress that Poppy had on.

"That was the plan," Poppy said. "Why? What's wrong with it?"

"Nothing's *wrong* with it," Win said. And nothing was. It just didn't look as if Poppy had made any effort in choosing it, or any effort with the rest of her appearance, either. Her hair was brushed, it was true, but it was also pulled back into a ponytail, and she wasn't wearing any jewelry or makeup. Then again, Win had to admit that Poppy didn't really need any more adornment than her natural beauty had already given her. "You know what, Pops?" she said, climbing off the bed. "You look perfect. Really, you do. *I*, on the other hand, need a little more help." She walked over to her dresser and started to put on her makeup. And Poppy finally dragged herself, and Sasquatch, off the bed.

"That's a new picture you've put out," she commented, glancing at the dresser top on her way out of the room.

"Oh, this one. Haven't you seen it before?" Win asked. She paused, her makeup brush in mid-air.

"I don't think so," Poppy said. The picture was one of Win and Kyle at a friend's backyard barbeque. In it, they both looked suntanned, happy, and incredibly, almost ridiculously young. "Do you still have that dress?" Poppy asked, of the pale lilac sundress Win was wearing.

"Somewhere." Win shrugged, brushing powder on her face. "I haven't worn it, though, since . . ." She didn't finish the sentence, but Poppy understood.

She leaned over and kissed Win on the cheek. "Now *that*," she said, pointing at the picture "is a pretty dress."

As they were leaving the cabin fifteen minutes later, Win saw a car coming up the driveway. "I hope Mary Jane's not getting cold feet," she joked to Poppy. But it wasn't Mary Jane's car. It was Everett's.

"That's strange," she murmured. "He knows I'm going to the wedding tonight." But she felt a tremor of excitement as he pulled up in front of the cabin.

"Hey," he said, getting out of his car. "It looks like I just caught you." He was looking directly at Win.

"We're on our way now," she said, her face feeling warm. "I'm sorry. I didn't know you were planning on stopping by."

"Neither did I," he said, smiling at her as he climbed up the steps. And Poppy, who was watching the two of them, sighed resignedly. "I'll wait inside," she said, going back into the cabin and closing the screen door behind her.

But when Win and Everett were left alone on the porch, they both seemed to revert back to their old shyness. "I'm sorry I didn't call," he said, pushing his hair out of his eyes. "I just found out I have to go back to the city tomorrow for some work and I won't be up here again until late next week."

"That's fine," Win said. "But is everything ok?"

He nodded. He looked a little embarrassed. "I just . . . wanted to see you. I'm sorry, I know you hate surprises."

"I *used* to hate surprises. Now, I think, I might actually be starting to like them." She smiled at him. She felt both nervous and flattered at the same time. Here was a cute guy she really liked, and he was pursuing her. *Wasn't he?*

He reached out and touched the bow on her dress, carefully, gingerly, as if it were a potentially deadly spider.

"I know," Win groaned. "It's a hideous dress."

"No, it's not."

"Everett, it's the color of an *eggplant*," she objected.

"I *like* eggplant," he said, coming closer. "It's my favorite vegetable."

"It is?"

"Well, it is *now*," he said. She laughed. "Win, I know you need to go, but I wanted to ask you a question: Can I see you on Thursday? I'll be back up here then."

She smiled. "You drove here to ask me that?" He nodded, seriously. And she didn't know if she moved closer to him or if he moved closer to her, but they kissed. A funny, awkward, *lovely* kiss. A kiss that was like Everett; it took nothing for granted, and it conveyed a shy tenderness.

"You better go," Everett said, when it was over.

"Come with me," Win said, suddenly. Delightedly. "Come to the wedding. You can be my plus one."

"Dressed like this?" he asked, amused. He gestured at the T-shirt and blue jeans he was wearing.

She shrugged. "Mary Jane won't mind."

"I think she might." He smiled.

"No, you're right," she said. "If she's freaked out about the baby scallops not being baby enough she might freak out about what you're wearing."

"Go. Have fun," he said, kissing her quickly this time. "I'll see you soon." He started down the porch steps.

"Everett?"

"Yes?" He turned around.

"Did I answer your question?"

He smiled. "I think you did."

CHAPTER 18

The week after Mary Jane's wedding, the weather turned hot and muggy, and by Thursday it was unbearable. During the day, the still air was heavy with rain that refused to fall, and, at night, the heat lightning sputtered, uselessly, on the horizon, without ever coming any closer. In the un-air-conditioned cabin, Win and Poppy had trouble sleeping. There was no breeze, and even with fans on in their rooms, the sheets seemed to stick to them like a second skin. The days were no better. By noon the temperature was already in the nineties and the only way to stay cool was to keep jumping into the lake. After a while, though, even this did not bring much relief.

But Win, buoyed by the kiss she and Everett had shared, was at first barely conscious of the heat. As the week wore on, though, she became increasingly irritable. And it wasn't just the weather, either. The weather, in fact, might have been the smallest part of it. It was Poppy, too. Poppy, who now spent her days lying listlessly in the hammock Win had strung up at the beginning of summer, and her nights lying listlessly on her bed. She was like some nineteenth century heroine dying of consumption. And

Win, try as she might, could not understand this lethargy. Except for the weeks following Kyle's death, her life had practically been a case study in productivity. And nothing made her happier— well, *almost* nothing—than putting a satisfying check mark next to every single item on a long to-do list.

But Poppy . . . Poppy had been lying in the hammock now for hours, and Sasquatch had been lying in it with her. Win had gone down there earlier, and had delivered a little pep talk to her. Yes, Poppy's heart had been broken, but the only thing to be done about it now was to try to stay busy while giving it time to heal. The more Poppy did, the better she'd feel, starting with getting out of the hammock that second and doing something, doing *anything*, really, just to get going again.

This pep talk had failed to produce the desired results. Poppy had stayed in the hammock, and Win had gone back up to the cabin, where she was now, listening to the radio, emptying the dishwasher, and trying not to think about how hot she was. She thought instead about Mary Jane's wedding. It had been lovely. The ceremony had been sweet, the food had been amazing, and the DJ had been so good that people danced for hours until finally the manager of the White Pines had had to close the party down. Everyone seemed to be having fun, everyone except Poppy. She never did come out of her funk, not even when Bret's handsome cousin John repeatedly asked her to dance. Win paused as she put the last dish away so that she could hear the weather report. They were calling for a storm that evening. *Thank God,* she thought, putting a plate in the cupboard. *It couldn't come soon enough.* She closed the cupboard door and leaned her forehead, briefly, against it. She blew out a long breath, peeled her damp T-shirt away from her skin, and tried to gather up the strands of her hair that had escaped from her ponytail. But as she was doing this she saw something glinting on the kitchen floor, right beside one of her bare feet. She bent down and picked it up, and, holding it between her thumb and forefinger, examined it. It was a three-inch shard of glass. *"Poppy,"* she murmured, darkly, remembering the juice glass her sister had dropped at breakfast that morning. Win had watched her sweep it up with such lethargy that she'd been tempted to take the broom away from her and do it herself, which, obviously, she should have. But by that point in the morning, Win had already picked up Poppy's wet towels from the bathroom floor, and vacuumed a new layer of cat fur off the living room rug. How was it possible to love someone as much as she loved Poppy, she wondered, and, at the same time, find living with them so endlessly trying?

Now, she got down on her hands and knees and looked for more pieces of broken glass. There were three of them. She gathered them up and started to throw them away, but then changed her mind and, saving the largest one, stormed out the cabin's back door and down the steps to the lakeside hammock that Poppy was lying in.

"Excuse me, Poppy," she said, holding up the glass shard for her to see. "Does this look familiar?"

Poppy barely glanced at it. "It's a piece of glass," she said.

"It's a piece of glass that you missed when you swept up this morning, and that I almost stepped on in my bare feet."

"But you didn't," Poppy observed.

"But I *could* have."

Poppy sighed, an exasperated sigh, as if Win were the one being unreasonable. "What would you like me to do, sweep again?"

"No, Poppy, because I've already found the other two pieces you missed."

"Isn't it amazing how far broken glass can travel," Poppy mused.

"No, it's *not* amazing," Win said, "it's a fact of life. And it's why you can't just pick up the big pieces. You have to sweep the entire area so you get all of the little pieces, too."

But Poppy wasn't listening. She sat up in the hammock, swung her legs over the edge, and set Sasquatch down on the ground. He immediately started lapping, frantically, from a bowl of water. It wasn't just *any* bowl, though, Win saw. It was a soup bowl, a soup bowl with a bird of paradise china pattern on it. One of a set of eight Win and Kyle had gotten as a wedding present.

"*Oh, my God,*" Win said, watching, in horror, as Sasquatch continued to drink from it. "Poppy, please tell me you're not using my wedding china for Sasquatch's water bowl."

"Well, obviously, I am," she said, a little sheepishly. "And I'm sorry. But his cat dishes are too small. He's *so* thirsty. I needed something that would hold a lot of water. Besides, you never . . . you never use this stuff," she added, gesturing at the bowl. "It just sits in the cupboard."

"That's the whole point, Poppy."

"You mean, not to use it?"

"No. I mean to only use it for a special occasion. And *this*," she said, gesturing at Sasquatch, who, amazingly enough, was still drinking from the bowl, "this is not one of them."

"Yeah, okay, but . . . I'm worried about him," Poppy said, changing the subject. "Since yesterday, all he's done is drink water and pee. Pee and drink water."

"Poppy, it's hot. He's thirsty."

"It's not only that, though. He's not even . . ." Poppy hesitated. "He's not even using his litter box to pee in. I mean, at least, not all of the time. And it's not like him. You know how fastidious cats are."

"So . . ." Win reached up to massage her temples. "So if he's not peeing in his litter box, where exactly is he . . . ?"

"Don't worry about it," Poppy said quickly. "I've been cleaning up after him. And there were only a few that—"

"Okay, you know what? Forget it," Win said, holding up a hand to stop her. "I don't need to know. I'll just take my wedding china and go." She slid the bowl out from under Sasquatch and started to carry it back up to the cabin. She had to get away from Poppy now. *Right now.* There was a thrumming in her ears that preceded all of their worst fights, and it was building steadily louder.

Poppy, scrambling after Win with Sasquatch in her arms, called out, "I'm sorry about the bowl. I'll put it in the dishwasher now."

"It doesn't go in the dishwasher, Pops," she said, not slowing down.

"Then I'll hand wash it."

"Why, so you can break it?" she said, over her shoulder. "And then not sweep it up?"

"Win, you're not being fair," Poppy protested, right behind her. "Look, I told you, I wasn't thinking. I'm worried about Sasquatch. I made an appointment for him at the vet this afternoon."

"Good," Win said, impatiently, opening the cabin's screen door. "I'm glad you're taking him to the vet. Because now they can tell you what I've already tried to tell you, which is that the only thing wrong with Sasquatch is that he's old, Poppy. He's just . . . *old.*"

"He's not *that* old," Poppy objected.

"Oh, come on, Pops," Win said, rolling her eyes. "He's been sleeping practically all summer, you just haven't wanted to see it."

There was silence from Poppy, and then she said, testily, as she passed Win, "Excuse me. We need to get ready to see the vet. Someone who, unlike you, does not *hate* animals."

"I don't hate animals," Win muttered, holding the soup bowl and staring after Poppy. All she'd done was hint that Sasquatch wasn't going to live forever. Why was that so awful? She was only stating the obvious. If Poppy couldn't accept it, she was in denial. And how had a conversation that had started out being about Poppy not sweeping up all of the pieces of a broken glass ended up being about what a terrible person Win was?

It was infuriating, Win thought, back in the kitchen. She threw away the glass shard and put the soup bowl in the sink. She had taken Poppy in for the summer, she thought, pacing up and down the room, and Poppy had promised to hold up her end of things. Now, though, she was back to where she'd been when she'd first arrived on Win's doorstep. And Win, of course, had to take care of her. Poppy had no job, no money, no car. No Car.

She went to Poppy's bedroom, and, standing in the doorway, said, "I suppose you're going to need to borrow my car to get to the vet's office."

Poppy ignored her. She'd put Sasquatch down on the bed, and she was searching through her closet for something to wear.

"Because if you're going to borrow my car *again,*" Win said, "I'd appreciate it if you'd ask me first." There was no response from Poppy. She'd taken a sundress out of the closet and laid it on the bed.

"Not that it would ever occur to you that *I* might need it this afternoon, or that you should put gas in it occasionally," she continued. Poppy's silence was stoking her anger.

But right before Poppy peeled her faded cotton T-shirt off over her head she said to Win, "I know you don't need the car now because you said Everett was coming this afternoon."

"That's not the point," Win said. "You treat my car like your car. And you treat my house like your house. But you forget that they both cost me money."

Poppy stepped out of her frayed denim shorts and kicked them, rudely, across the room. She started pulling the sundress over her head, and, as she did so, she said, almost more to herself than to Win, "Well, the house part doesn't cost you any money."

"What did you say?" Win asked, instantly alert.

"Nothing," Poppy said, unconcerned. She walked over to her dresser.

"Yes, you did. You implied that I live here for free. And you actually think that's true, don't you?" Win asked, her voice squeaking with indignation.

"Well, you *own* it, don't you?" Poppy said, sounding bored. She took her hair out of its ponytail and started brushing it. "You don't have a mortgage."

"No, I don't. But have you ever heard of something called 'taxes,' Poppy?" she said, so angry now her voice was practically shaking. "I pay the taxes every year on this cabin. And, let me tell you, they are *a lot* of money. And that's not all it costs me, either. I have lots of bills." She started counting them off on her fingers. "Oil and gas, electricity, snow removal, tree removal, lawn mowing. And there's more," she said, too angry to remember what the "more" was.

"Fascinating," Poppy said, under her breath, as she stepped into her flip-flops.

Win felt her face flush hotly. "I'm glad you find it fascinating, Poppy. Maybe it's because you know so little about adult responsibilities. It must be nice, though, to float through life without having to worry about all of the tedious things other people worry about."

Poppy moved back to the dresser and went through her handbag. Her bored expression was gone, and her face was puckered with emotion. "I've been trying to change this summer, Win," she said suddenly, turning to her. "I really have. I didn't *mean* to end up with no job. And I've been thinking about a lot of stuff, too. And . . . I told you, I've been depressed."

"Uh-huh," Win said, too caught up in her own emotions to feel any sympathy for Poppy. "Well, I think we can both agree it's time for you to snap out of it."

"You're not supposed to tell people who are depressed to snap out of it," Poppy said, looking genuinely hurt. "I read that somewhere."

"Okay, fine, except you're not feeling *depressed,* Poppy. You're feeling sorry for yourself. There's a difference."

"You don't know what you're talking about," Poppy said, raising her voice. "I'm going through stuff you don't even *know* about. And as for Sam, I told you how much I cared about him. And I told you how much it hurts for it to be over. But it didn't count with you, did it? No, because you're the expert on loss, Win. You've cornered the market on grief. No one else can even begin to compete with you, can they?"

Win was shocked. "What is that supposed to mean?"

"Oh, *please.* I've watched you all summer long, arranging and rearranging those little shrines on your dresser."

Win felt tears burning in her eyes. "I was trying to remember Kyle," she said.

"Then *remember* him. But stop using him as an excuse to not live your life."

"I *am* living my life," Win said, furiously swiping at her tears. "I have a job. I have friends. And I might even have someone else I care about."

"Everett?" Poppy said dismissively. "I don't think so. I don't see how you can possibly make room for him when you've still got all of the memories of your marriage to Kyle taking up an entire closet. *An entire life*," she amended. And then she picked Sasquatch up off the bed, and carried him to the front door, where she loaded him into his pet carrier. Win followed her and watched her do this. Why, she didn't know. She didn't know what she expected to gain from her and Poppy being together right now. Her emotions were positively in riot; so many different ones were battling with each other that she couldn't separate them, let alone name them or understand them.

But when Poppy, who looked caught between anger and sadness, had latched Sasquatch's pet carrier closed, and picked it up, and settled her handbag on the other arm, she hesitated at the front door. "If you don't mind," she said, her face coloring a little, "I really do need to borrow your car keys. Sasquatch's appointment is in half an hour."

And Win, savoring the irony of Poppy having to ask her for a favor now, went to get her keys off the front hall table. "Here," she said, handing them to Poppy. "And while you're driving into town maybe you can think about *your* life, Poppy. Because the last time I checked it wasn't going *anywhere*. In fact, it's starting to look a lot like Mom and Dad's lives."

Win stood in the doorway and watched Poppy drive away. She was so angry, but her anger had nowhere to go. *It was so unfair*, she thought. Today, heat aside, was supposed to have been a nice day, a special day. Everett was coming soon and they'd planned on taking a swim and going out for dinner in town. Their first date. Their first *real* date. Now she wasn't even sure she wanted to go on it, and, worse, doubts about Everett were creeping in, mixing dangerously with anger. Then, as if on cue, Everett's car came down the driveway. *He must have passed Poppy,* she realized. *Had he been hoping to see her today, too?* After all, she was the reason he'd come here the first time, and maybe even the second and third times. And suddenly, it seemed preposterous to Win that she'd ever believed Everett had come here to see her.

By the time he got out of his car, Win was already halfway down the front porch steps. "She's not here," she said.

"Who's not here?" he asked, caught off guard.

"Poppy," she said, coming up to him.

"That's okay," he said uncertainly. "I didn't come here to see her."

"Are you sure?"

He looked mystified. "Yes. I'm sure."

"Well, all that means is that you've decided to settle for me," she said, folding her arms across her chest.

"Win, what are you *talking* about? I haven't settled for you. I haven't settled for anyone. I don't . . . settle."

She shook her head impatiently. "So, you're saying it was always me you wanted to be with? Since the first time you came up here? Because that's not how I remember it. You came here for Poppy. And you came *back* here for Poppy. And the only reason you ended up with me, Everett, is because she wasn't interested in you."

He looked at her uncomprehendingly, as if she were speaking a language he didn't understand. But then he pushed his hair out of his eyes and said, with an unfamiliar tightness in his voice, "Look, I don't know where this is coming from, but we need to get one thing straight. I *never* came here because I was interested in your sister. Not even the first time. That time, I gave her a ride because she needed a favor, and I like coming up north. The other times, though, I came here to see you. I mean, why do you think I've been spending so much time at my cousin's cabin this summer—"

"*Oh, please,*" Win said, exasperated.

"No, it's true."

She wouldn't let herself be sidetracked, though. "You didn't come back to see me that second time," she reminded him. "You came back to give Poppy a box she left in your trunk."

"I could just as easily have mailed it to her," he pointed out. "I wanted an excuse to see *you.*"

"But you texted *her,*" she pointed out.

"Only because I didn't have your number."

This stymied Win, but only for a moment. "You came to see her that night," she persisted. "And do you know what she did, Everett? She made me say she was out, and then she hid, in her bedroom, the whole night." Later she would wonder what her motivation for telling him this had been. Had she wanted to hurt his feelings, or had she wanted him to see Poppy in an unflattering light? Probably both, she'd decided.

But he only shrugged. "I don't care what Poppy did that night." He wiped perspiration off his brow. "I really don't. But would you please tell me what's going on? The last time I was here, we could barely keep our hands off each other, and now, now I feel like we're strangers or something."

"Maybe we are," she said, and the anger was back. The doubt, too. And the doubt . . . the doubt was *full-blown.*

He leaned on his open car door. He looked hot, but mainly

he looked disappointed. "Why are you selling us both so short, Win?" he asked, quietly.

She didn't answer him; instead, she left him standing there. She heard, but didn't see him, driving away as she went back inside the cabin, slamming the front door so hard behind her that she knocked the wind chimes off their hook. She threw herself onto the living room couch then and buried herself in its pillows. Their feathery softness sunk beneath her weight, and, like them, she felt suddenly deflated, her anger suddenly gone. She lay there, perfectly still, for a long time, oblivious to the suffocating heat. Finally, though, her thoughts coalesced around a question. A question she desperately wanted to know the answer to. And it was not about how Poppy and Everett had failed her, but rather, about how she had failed *them*. Why had she provoked two fights, with two of the people she cared about the most, all within the space of thirty minutes?

Anger, she decided, still buried in the pillows. Anger and doubt and sadness. Anger at the ups and downs of a summer spent living with Poppy. Anger at being the sister who always had to fix things, to prop up what was falling, to mend what was broken. And doubt. Doubt that a guy—a *nice* guy, a *funny* guy, a *cute* guy—could truly be interested in her if her sister was around at the same time. Doubt that she was lovable in her own right, that she was, as her father always said, "winning Win," doubt born of those crucial high school years when she couldn't shake the feeling that she was always standing in Poppy's lovely shadow. And sadness. Sadness that her marriage was over and that Kyle was gone. Sadness that they'd had so little time together, and sadness that the memory of that time was being whittled away by the intervening years. Didn't Poppy get that? Didn't she understand that the reason Win kept those things on her dresser was less because she wanted to remember and more because she was afraid to forget?

Win didn't know how much time passed before she finally stirred on the couch. She felt a breeze, the first one in days, coming in through the open living room windows that faced the lake. She sat up, and started to rearrange the jumbled pillows. She still felt hot, and sticky, and now, tearstained, but she felt something else, too: a new understanding. Yes, she'd fought with Poppy and Everett today, but she'd also fought with herself. Her childhood self, the one who'd felt responsible for her sister and her parents, who'd felt the weight of the world on her shoulders, and who'd believed Poppy was the beautiful sister and she the pale imitation. But she wasn't a child, or even a teenager, anymore. Her life had changed since then. She had work now, and friends, and a town, and a cabin and a place that she loved.

She got up from the couch and went out to retrieve the wind chimes from the porch floor. She disentangled them and hung them carefully on their nail. She knew now what she *should* have done today. She should have taken Everett at his word. And she should have told Poppy, kindly but firmly, to take charge of her life—to look for another job, to talk to Sam, to get up, and to start to move forward—because otherwise their living together was not going to work.

She was going to need to apologize, she realized. To two people. She sat down on the porch steps, and wondered how long she'd have to wait before Poppy came home.

CHAPTER 19

After a long wait in Dr. Swanson's over-air-conditioned waiting room, Poppy sat in his over-air-conditioned office. The fact that she was shivering now, though, probably had less to do with being cold than with what he had just told her.

"Kidney failure?" she repeated.

He shuffled some papers around on his desk. "In layman's terms, it's kidney failure, yes. In veterinary terms, its end-stage chronic renal failure. It's not uncommon in older cats," he added, gently.

"Are you . . . sure that's what it is?" Poppy pressed. "I mean, could you run some more tests?"

Dr. Swanson hesitated. He was an older man with thick white hair and kind blue eyes, and, at first, Poppy had trusted him. Now, she wasn't so sure. He took off his glasses and polished them on his white coat. "It's not necessary to run more tests," he said. "Your cat's blood and urine tests have already confirmed it."

"Okay," Poppy said, refusing to panic. "So, can we start him on dialysis?" She looked down at Sasquatch. He was lying, limply, in her lap.

"Dialysis wouldn't be appropriate under the circumstances," Dr. Swanson said patiently. "His kidney failure is age-related."

"He was fine, though, until recently," Poppy insisted. "I mean, he's been low energy this summer. He's been sleeping more, and eating less. But these *other* things—the thirstiness, and the peeing, and the not eating anything—these are all new. They only started over the last week."

"I know it seems sudden," Dr. Swanson said. "Partly, it's because in a cat this age, the symptoms of aging can mask the symptoms of other illnesses. But partly, too, it's the nature of the disease. By the time chronic kidney failure is symptomatic in a cat, they may have lost as much as 75 percent of their kidney function."

"If I'd brought him sooner—" Poppy began, feeling a wave of guilt, but Dr. Swanson was already shaking his head.

"I can promise you that even if you had the outcome would still be the same."

"The outcome," Poppy said, looking down at Sasquatch again. "You mean . . . death?" she said, her voice dropping to a whisper.

"Yes," Dr. Swanson said, and Poppy noticed that he was speaking softly, too. "That's what I mean."

She closed her eyes. This was not happening. This was too soon. Too fast. She opened her eyes. Dr. Swanson was still sitting there, a concerned expression on his face. His office's waiting room was full of people and their pets, but he wouldn't rush her, she saw. How many pet owners, she wondered, had he delivered this news to over the years? Too many, she decided. She tried to smile at him then, but she couldn't quite manage it. "I'm sorry," she whispered, a lump hardening in her throat. "I knew Sasquatch wouldn't live forever. But I thought the two of us would have more warning. You know, more time to get ready for it."

He smiled, a little sadly. "Can I tell you something?"

She nodded. A single tear slid down her cheek.

"I've been doing this for forty years. And, trust me, there's never enough time to get ready for it."

"What . . . what happens now?" she asked. She was back to whispering again. It was the best she could do. She didn't trust her voice to speak out loud.

"Well, that depends on you. You have some decisions to make."

"You mean, about putting him down?"

"Yes."

"I can't just let him go . . . naturally?"

"You could," he said.

"But you don't recommend it?" she said, already knowing the answer.

"I don't. I think he'd be in a lot of pain."

"I don't want him to be in pain," she said, shaking her head. "I can't even stand to *think* about him being in pain. Is he . . . I mean, is he already in pain?" she asked, horrified. She pulled Sasquatch closer to her.

"It's very likely," he said.

"Oh, God," she murmured, letting a few tears roll unchecked down her cheeks. Dr. Swanson's words, though, had given her a new courage. She didn't want to say good-bye to Sasquatch, but she didn't want him to suffer, either.

"Let's do it," she said, quickly. "Let's . . . put him down."

"All right, but we can't do it right now. You'll have to schedule it with Valerie, our office manager. We should have an opening tomorrow, and, if we don't, we'll make one. In the meantime, we can give him IV fluids before you leave, and we can also prescribe a liquid painkiller for you to give him. That way you'll have a little more time with him," he said. "And he should be reasonably comfortable during that time, too."

"It won't hurt, will it? The putting him down, I mean?"

"No. And we'll give him an injection of a sedative beforehand."

"And afterwards," she asked, her voice tremulous, "do you have any . . . funeral packages?"

He blinked. "Funeral packages?"

"Yes."

"Um, no, nothing like that. Though there's nothing to stop you, of course, from having one privately."

Poppy nodded, miserably. Because who, other than her, would come to a funeral for Sasquatch? And besides, she'd never been good at planning things, anyway. That was Win's strength.

"Whether or not you decide to have a funeral," Dr. Swanson said, "you could still have him cremated."

"I want to do that," she said, decisively. "And I want an urn, too." *The best, most expensive urn available*, she thought. And then she remembered something. She had no money, and therefore no idea how she was going to pay for any of this.

"Dr. Swanson?" she asked, quickly, since he was starting to stand up. "Does your office have, like, a payment plan or something? You know, for people who can't pay for everything up front?" She was too miserable to be ashamed.

"You can work something out with Valerie," he said, unfazed.

"I promise I'll pay for everything. I just need a little time."

He opened the door to the examining room, and then looked back at her. "I'm not worried," he said. "I know Win. She and my wife, Liz, are on the library board together. Your sister, by the way, has been a wonderful addition to this town."

"I believe that," Poppy said, a little wanly. No need to mention here that she and Win were not even on speaking terms with each other now.

After she left the veterinarian's office, Poppy couldn't bring herself to put Sasquatch back in his pet carrier. Which was just as well, since she couldn't bring herself to drive back to the cabin, either. So instead, she put the pet carrier in the backseat of the car and, holding Sasquatch in her arms, crossed over to the other side of Main Street.

It was still sweltering outside. She stood perfectly still, under the red-and-white-striped awning of Pearl's, hoping that if she conserved energy, she would stay cooler. But it didn't work. Little beads of perspiration broke out on her forehead, and Sasquatch's fur, already matted from the heat, stuck to her bare arms. They needed to take refuge in the air-conditioned car, she thought, and the sooner the better, but she didn't know if she had the energy to cross the street again. Her despondency, like the humidity, was weighing her down, and making even the smallest movements feel like they were taking place at the bottom of a swimming pool.

Still, she was about to make a run for the car, when the front door of Pearl's opened, and Caroline, the woman who owned it—a fortyish strawberry blonde—started flipping the sign on it from Open to Closed.

"Hello," she said, seeing Poppy there. "Everything all right?"

Poppy nodded.

"How's your sister?" she asked.

"Fine," she whispered.

"Good." She smiled. Win and Caroline were friends. Every morning during the school year, Win stopped in at Pearl's for their famous blueberry pancakes, or their slow-cooked oatmeal. "Are *you* okay?" Caroline asked, with a slight frown.

Poppy tried to say yes, but found she couldn't form the word.

No matter. If she looked the way she felt, it would be obvious to even the most casual bystander that she was *not* okay.

"Do you two want to come in?" Caroline asked, her eyes traveling down to a bedraggled looking Sasquatch. "Just to cool off?"

Finally, Poppy roused herself. "You're closed," she pointed out.

"Well, for most people," Caroline said. "But not for Win's sister."

Poppy sighed. Once again, she saw, she would be trading on her sister's good name.

"What about . . . ?" Poppy asked, indicating the NO PETS ALLOWED sign on the door.

"Not to worry," Caroline said, smiling. "At least, not when you both look like you're on the verge of heatstroke." She gestured for Poppy to come inside, and, amazingly, Poppy's limbs cooperated, and she walked through the open door and into the deliciously cool café. "Lucky for you, we have a new air-conditioning system," Caroline said, locking the door from the inside and closing the blinds in the front windows. "It used to go on the fritz in weather like this. Why don't you take one of those," she said, gesturing to the row of red leather booths that lined the back wall of the restaurant. "And I'll bring you something cold to drink."

"Thank you," Poppy said. And there was something about this woman's practical brand of kindness that made her want to cry again. She chose one of the booths, and slid into it, and then she sat there, letting the tears that came now fall freely, and mingle with Sasquatch's fur.

"Here you go," Caroline said, reappearing. She set a glass of iced tea down in front of her. "Anything for your friend?" she asked, looking at Sasquatch. "A dish of cream, maybe? Or some tuna fish?"

"No, thank you. He's . . . he's not really eating right now," Poppy explained, reaching into her purse to pay for her drink.

But Caroline waved the money away. "You take your time," she said. "You can let yourself out when you're done."

"Thanks," Poppy said, more tears coursing down her cheeks.

"You're welcome," Caroline said. "And by the way," she added, kindly, before she left, "you're not the first person who's needed this booth to cry in." Poppy sipped her iced tea, gratefully, and then pulled a napkin out of the napkin dispenser and wiped, ineffectually, at her tears. She'd never cried so much in her life as she had this summer, she thought, putting the crumpled napkin in her purse and rearranging Sasquatch in her arms so that she could see his face. He looked better, she decided. Less stressed. Maybe the pain medication had begun to kick in. She rubbed him under his chin, the way he liked her to, and waited for him to purr, but he only blinked at her. Still, he seemed content.

She took a deep breath, and exhaled, slowly. She leaned back against the booth. This was better. This was much better. She wouldn't think about the fight with Win. Not right now. She would think about that later. She would *have* to think about that later. Right now, she would think about Sasquatch. He'd been with her for almost half her life, and, after Win, he'd been the most important part of that life. He'd come into it at a time when she'd needed him the most. She remembered the week after she'd gone into the photographer's apartment, the week that had, finally, brought her Sasquatch.

The day after "it" had happened—she couldn't then bring herself to call it by its real name—Poppy had stayed home from school. She'd told her mom she didn't feel well and her mom, who'd recently decided she was an artist, stayed home and painted in the corner of their living room she referred to as "her studio," while Poppy stayed in her bedroom most of the day. The truth was, she was terrified of running into Rich. She didn't know how or when she'd ever be able to leave the apartment again. But when Win came home from school that afternoon, she had news for her.

"Pops?" Win said, peeking into their bedroom, where Poppy was lying on her bed.

"Yes?" Poppy said, raising herself on one elbow.

"You don't look so great," Win said, as she sat down on the edge of her bed. And Poppy knew this was true. She'd lied about being sick, but now she felt terrible anyway.

"Remember how you were asking last night about the photographer down the hall?" Win asked.

"Yes," Poppy said, sitting up suddenly. She felt panic rising in her.

"I looked into his apartment just now—" Win began, but Poppy grabbed her arm.

"Win, don't *ever* go in there," Poppy said. *"I mean it."*

"What? No, it's fine," Win said. "He moved out. His door was open. The place was empty except for some junk in a corner."

Poppy lay back down on the pillows, awash in a cold, prickly sweat. "Are you sure he's gone?" she whispered.

"Positive. While I was standing there the woman with the facial piercings came down the hall and said he left this morning. He went back to New York. That's where he's from, I guess."

Poppy nodded, distractedly. So he was gone . . . Of course, there was always the possibility that he'd come back again. Not to live, maybe, but to look for her. Poppy didn't think he would, though. She thought she knew why he'd left. He'd left because of what he'd done to her.

Win looked at her curiously. "Pops, what's up with you? You're acting weird." She put her hand on Poppy's forehead. "I don't *think* you have a fever." She frowned.

"No, I'm fine," she said, taking Win's hand away. "I had . . . a stomachache, but I'm better now."

"You sure?"

Poppy hesitated, and, in the first of what would be many times over the ensuing years, she was tempted to tell Win what had happened to her. She didn't, though. After all, Win would make her *do* something about it—tell her high school counselor, or her parents, or the police—and Poppy didn't want to do any of those things. She was ashamed she had let it happen, and afraid, somehow, that if she told someone it would mean seeing him again. (Here she relied on her limited knowledge of the criminal justice system, most of it gleaned from police procedurals or courtroom dramas she'd seen on TV.) Would she have to pick him out of a lineup? Point to him in court? Or worse, come face-to-face with him in a shadowy hallway of some criminal justice building? And this fear of having to do something, and the possibility that it might mean seeing Rich again, persisted, against all reason, long beyond the point when he could have been held accountable for the crime.

And there was another reason she didn't tell her sister then. Sharing it with Win might make *her* feel better, for a little while, but it would make Win feel *terrible*. And then there was the part about forgetting . . . It would be easier for her to forget by herself than for both of them to forget together, wouldn't it?

"Don't worry about me," Poppy said now to Win, who still looked worried. "I'll get better. I promise."

And, in fact, after Poppy returned to school a few days later, two good things happened to her, one after the other. The first happened while she was sitting in Spanish class. She'd felt a familiar cramping sensation. She'd gotten a hall pass, and, in the third stall to the right in the second floor girl's bathroom, she'd learned that she was not pregnant. She was almost light-headed with relief, since this ended a fear almost too terrifying to consider.

And then, that night, a second good thing happened. She met Sasquatch for the first time. She was at her bedroom window, looking out at the night, and trying, hard, not to think about what had happened, when she saw a gray cat slinking along the fire escape. She wondered if he would come to her.

Three nights later, she stood there again.

"Poppy, what are you doing?" Win asked, irritably, from her bed. "I want to go to sleep."

"I'm waiting for him," she said.

"Waiting for who?"

"The cat."

"You mean the flea-bitten thing that you *call* a cat," Win said, with a groan. "Don't pet him anymore, Pops. I swear, if you do, you'll probably get some disease, and then you'll give it to me."

But Poppy ignored her. She liked the cat. She'd already nick-named him Sasquatch—Big Foot had been one of Poppy and Win's childhood obsessions—and she was of the opinion that while he might look a little matted, he most definitely did not have fleas. She knew because she'd petted him three nights in a row and she hadn't seen any on him. Now she hoped that if she left the lights on and the window open and stayed very still, and waited very patiently, he would come again.

"Pops, I'm tired," Win said now. "I have an algebra test tomorrow. Can you please turn the light off?"

"In a minute," Poppy said softly, because right then she saw Sasquatch edging along the fire escape.

Win huffed, and rolled over, pulling the covers over her head.

"Come here, boy," Poppy whispered, but she knew he couldn't be hurried. He would come in his own good time. And, in fact, after a moment's hesitation, he leapt, gracefully, onto the windowsill. Poppy allowed herself to smile, but otherwise stayed still. Now Sasquatch sauntered, casually, over to her, as if their meeting here was a complete coincidence, and not something that was becoming a nightly ritual. Poppy waited until he stopped in front of her, then reached out, slowly, and began to stroke him, running her fingers lightly down his back, from his neck to his tail.

Where had he come from? she wondered. He didn't have a collar on him. Had he run away? Gotten lost? Been left behind? Or had he always been a stray? Or—and this was a worst-case scenario for Poppy—did he already belong to another person or another family, and was he simply visiting her on his nightly trek around the neighborhood? She didn't know. But she hoped, secretly, she was the only human in his life, or, if not the only one, than at least the most important one.

After Poppy petted Sasquatch for a few minutes, he began to purr. It sounded, at first, like an electrical hum, and then it progressed to a steady drone. Poppy sighed, contentedly.

"Pops," Win mumbled. "The lights. Please."

Poppy frowned, and went to turn off the lights. This was usually the point at which Sasquatch left, but tonight he stayed. Poppy, navigating in the dark, came back to the window. She had an idea. She'd never tried anything like this before, but tonight, for some reason, the timing seemed right. She patted Sasquatch again, and then she picked him up, carefully. She waited for some sign of resistance. None came. She carried him over to her bed and set him down on the end of it. She waited for him to jump off. Instead, he curled up with the air of someone who was settling in for the night. Poppy closed the window, and locked it, and then got into bed, slowly, so as not to disturb him. Chances were, he'd wake her in the night and want to be let out the window so he could go back to wherever it was he'd come from.

When Poppy woke up in the morning, though, he was still there, curled up at the end of her bed, luxuriating in the sunshine streaming in through the window. She was so excited she could barely contain herself. *This is better than Christmas morning at Grandpa and Grandma's,* she thought, reaching down to pet him. He started purring again, almost immediately, and Poppy was so happy she barely paid any attention when Win rolled over in her bed and sat up and said, "Oh, my God. You let him sleep here. *Why,* Poppy?"

"Because he makes me feel safe," Poppy said without thinking.

Later that week, she and her dad took Sasquatch to a veterinarian's office. Poppy was anxious because she was afraid that, for some reason, the veterinarian would tell her she couldn't keep Sasquatch. Poppy's dad was anxious because he knew this appointment would cost a lot of money and he had, as usual, very little of it. And Sasquatch was anxious, Poppy assumed, because this was a new and unfamiliar place for him, and because the staff here had already drawn his blood and given him a vaccine. (Poppy was grateful this part of the exam had been done behind the scenes, out of her sight; the very thought of someone sticking a needle into Sasquatch made her feel queasy.)

"It's okay, Sasquatch," she whispered, near his ear, as she held him in her lap. "Everything's going to be all right." And, in fact, at that moment, the veterinarian came back into the examination room, armed with a file folder and a reassuring smile.

"Thank you for waiting," she said, as she pulled a plastic chair over to them and sat down. Poppy had liked her immediately. She seemed so young to be wearing such a serious white coat, though Poppy was interested to see that she'd paired it with some very *un*serious looking high heels. "I've got some good news for you," she said. "Your cat—Sasquatch," she added, respectfully, "has already been neutered. He's healthy, and he doesn't have parasites or fleas."

"I knew it," Poppy said, loyally.

"Overall," the vet continued, "he's in excellent health. Whoever last took care of him, took very good care of him."

"So he's not a feral cat?" Poppy asked. She'd been doing research on feral cats at her school library.

"No. He's definitely not feral. He's too tame. Which brings me to my only real concern here. Are you sure you've done everything you can to find his former owner?"

Poppy nodded, emphatically. "He never had a collar on," she said. "And my sister and I put up flyers with his picture on them all over the neighborhood. And I called all the local animal shelters and gave them his description." This was true. She had done all of these things. She hadn't wanted him to be found, but, on the other hand, she hadn't wanted to keep him if she couldn't do it with a clear conscience.

"All right then," the vet said, beaming at her and Sasquatch. "I think it's fair to say that you, young lady, have got yourself a cat."

Poppy smiled, enthusiastically, but her dad managed only a halfhearted "How about that." Poppy glanced at him. He looked tired. He'd had a late night last night, he'd told her, though as far as she could tell, *all* of his nights were late nights.

"How old do you think he is?" Poppy asked the vet, ignoring him.

"Based on his muscle tone and his fur, I would say about two or three years old."

"Did you hear that?" Poppy said to Sasquatch. "We're going to have a long time together."

"I hope so," the vet said, smiling, but then she turned serious. "My guess is that Sasquatch was abandoned by someone. It's hard to know why. Sometimes, it's due to an owner's death, or a move to another city. Sometimes a family falls on hard times, or a couple splits up and a pet falls through the cracks. If that's the case with him," she said, giving Sasquatch an expert pat, "then I don't think you need to worry about him leaving. But if he left his old owner voluntarily, despite the fact that they were taking good care of him, he might leave again sometime. There are cats like that. They have something . . . call it wanderlust, that makes them not want to stay in any one place for too long. On a brighter note, though," she said, going to get some pamphlets for Poppy. "Let's go over his care and feeding instructions."

After the appointment, Poppy and her dad stood on the corner outside the veterinarian's office, waiting for the light to change. Poppy was holding Sasquatch in his pet carrier, a new purchase of which she was very proud, and her dad was looking wistfully at a bar across the street. He slid his wallet out of his pocket and opened it up. It only had a few ones left in it.

"Your friend here cleaned me out, kid," he said, gesturing at Sasquatch.

"Sorry, Dad," Poppy said. But she wasn't. She asked so little of him, of both of her parents. Besides, she *needed* Sasquatch. Needed him more than her dad could know. He made her feel safe, something Win found absurd. *How can a twelve-pound ball of fur make you feel safe?* she'd asked Poppy. *He just can,* Poppy had said, without trying to explain.

"You know, sweetheart," her dad said now, as the light changed and they started across the street, "your sister thinks she might be allergic to this cat."

"I'll be very careful he stays on my side of the room and I'll vacuum every day," she said.

"Okay," her dad said, doubtfully. "What about what the vet said, though? About how he could leave again one day?"

"Don't worry. He won't," Poppy said, confidently.

And he didn't. He never left. Not once in all those years. Oh, *he wandered*. He wandered *a lot*. But he always came back. He always came home. And it was because of this that she always had a home for him to come back to, even when that "home" was never anything much to brag about. She'd wanted to take good care of him. And she had, hadn't she? His life had been as comfortable, as safe, and as pleasant as she'd known how to make it. Of all the responsibilities she'd shirked, she hadn't shirked this one. And of all the relationships she'd failed at, she hadn't failed at this one.

She'd wondered, often, what would have happened to her if she hadn't adopted him. As it was, there hadn't been much stability in her life, but what little there had been, she could credit him for, and Win, too, of course. They'd been the two constants in her life, the twin lights by which she'd navigated the years.

She leaned down and kissed the top of his head. She'd done her best by him, and it went without saying that he'd done his best by her. "Thank you, Sasquatch," she whispered, wishing that she were more eloquent, and that she could provide him with the tribute she knew he deserved before tomorrow morning. But words failed her. In the end, all she said to him, sitting in one of the back booths at Pearl's, was, "You were a good cat." As inadequate as those words were, they would have to be enough.

CHAPTER 20

When Poppy returned to the cabin, Win was waiting for her on the front porch. "Dr. Swanson called after you left his office," she said, coming down the steps as Poppy was taking Sasquatch's pet carrier out of the backseat. "He was worried about you."

"I'm fine," Poppy said, not meeting her eyes.

"Poppy, I'm sorry. I'm *really sorry*. And about Sasquatch . . . I had *no* idea he was so sick. Here, let me take that," she said, reaching for the pet carrier, but Poppy shrugged off her help.

"I've got it," she said, heading up the steps. By the time she reached the top step, though, she felt suddenly light-headed. She sat down, and put Sasquatch's pet carrier beside her. "I'm just going to rest here for a second," she said.

Win sat down beside her, and watched as she took Sasquatch out. "*Oh,* poor guy," she said.

"You hate him," Poppy pointed out, still not looking at her.

"I don't *hate* him," Win said. "I just can't look at him without sneezing. Can I . . . ?" she asked, reaching for him. And Poppy, stony-faced, let her take him. In all the years she'd had him, Win had never voluntarily held him, but now, Poppy realized, she did it with surprising naturalness.

"Hey, big guy," Win said, softly, and she rubbed him under his chin, just the way he liked it. "Everything's going to be all right," she murmured, eliciting a faint purr from him.

"He seems to be feeling better," she said to Poppy, looking over at her. "What about you. Are you doing okay?"

Poppy shrugged, trying to maintain her aloofness. "I'm fine," she said.

Win looked at her and shook her head, wordlessly. Her expression said, *You're not fine. You're a wreck. Do you think I've known you my whole life without learning* anything *about you?*

"Oh, Win," Poppy said, her stoicism crumbling. "I'm so scared. What am I going to do? I'm supposed to go back there with him tomorrow, but I can't. I just can't."

"Yes, you can," Win said calmly, still rubbing Sasquatch underneath his chin. "Because you don't have to go there alone. I'm going to go with you. And I'm going to stay with you, both of you, the whole time."

"You are?" Poppy said. She felt her fear recede a little.

"Of course," Win said, and she put an arm around Poppy. Poppy edged closer to her, and put her head on Win's shoulder.

"I don't know what I'd do without you," Poppy said, closing her eyes. "I'm sorry I said those things. I didn't mean to hurt you. You're the *last* person I would ever want to hurt. You're my family. You and Sasquatch." But as she said Sasquatch's name it caught in her throat.

Win pulled Poppy closer. "I love you, Pops. You know that, don't you?"

"I know. I love you, too," she murmured. It was quiet on the porch for a little while, until Poppy, lifting her head, asked, "Where's Everett?"

Win groaned. "You weren't the only one I got into an argument with today."

"Really? You and Everett?"

Win nodded glumly. "I'll tell you about it later. Right now, I think we should focus on our friend here. You take him," she said, handing Sasquatch over to Poppy. "I think he misses you."

Poppy held him. He was still low energy, but he seemed better somehow since he'd gotten the IV fluids and the pain medication. She nuzzled his neck.

"It looks like a storm's coming," Win said, pointing to the darkening sky. And it was. Poppy could feel it. It had been maddeningly still and airless all week but now a breeze was shaking the leaves on the trees, and from nearby came a rumble of thunder.

"Should we go inside?" Win asked, reaching for the pet carrier. Poppy nodded. And just as they were closing the front door there was a flash of lightning. This was soon followed by a violent thunderstorm, the kind that no summer at Butternut Lake was ever complete without. Sasquatch, fortunately, appeared not to care. He was drugged into a state of contentment no amount of thunder seemed capable of penetrating. Poppy sat with him on the couch while Win made chicken salad sandwiches for dinner and later, they tried, without success, to interest Sasquatch in his dinner.

Then Poppy and Win talked late into the night—about Sasquatch, about their parents, and about what Poppy would do now that she once again had no job—and when they fell asleep, on top of the covers of Win's bed, with a throw blanket pulled over them, the rain was coming down steadily outside, and Sasquatch was nestled comfortably between them.

CHAPTER 21

That was Dr. Swanson's office," Poppy said, standing in the doorway to Win's bedroom.

Win looked up from the overnight bag she'd laid on top of her bed. "Are they ready?" she asked. She meant Sasquatch's ashes.

Poppy nodded. "They came today."

"That was quick," Win said, putting a nightgown in her bag.

"I know," Poppy said. It had only been a week since Sasquatch had been put down. "Late August must be the slow season at the pet crematorium," she offered, aiming for dark humor when what she was still feeling was quiet misery.

"Well, you're not going to pick them up today, are you? Are they even open on a Saturday?" Win asked, putting her cosmetic case on top of her nightgown, and zipping up her bag.

"They're open. They don't close until six. I thought I'd go there later this afternoon, if I can . . . borrow your car."

"Of course you can borrow it. I'm not going to need it. We're taking Mary Jane's. But, Pops, don't pick them up alone. I'll come with you on Monday."

"No, it's fine," Poppy said. "The hard part is over. *That* part, I could never have done without you. This part's easy. It's just his ashes. Besides," she added, "it'll give me something to do while you're away."

Win frowned. "Are you sure you don't want to come with us?" she asked. She and Mary Jane were driving to a daylong teaching strategies workshop in Duluth and spending the night at a hotel there afterwards. "You'd be on your own today, but there are fun stores to browse in the waterfront area, and tonight the three of us could go out for dinner."

Poppy hesitated.

"Come on," Win said. "Otherwise, I'll spend whatever time we're not at the workshop listening to Mary Jane discuss the 'adjustment process' she's going through, living with Bret for the first time. Apparently, she's shocked to discover he leaves his dirty socks on the floor beside the laundry hamper, instead of making the extra effort to move them six centimeters to the right and actually put them *into* the laundry hamper. I mean, I could have *told* her he'd do this."

Poppy smiled, though her smile was a little weary. In the last week, she'd become the insomniac in the family. It was hard to fall asleep without Sasquatch's comforting presence at the end of her bed, and when she *did* fall asleep, she was apt to wake up and forget, for a moment, that he was gone now. Barely awake, she'd search for his warm body with her foot, only to find the space where he'd usually slept empty. And then, wide-awake, she'd remember putting him down all over again. No wonder then, that sometimes it seemed easier not to go to sleep at all. Still, she had an idea that having his ashes might bring her a modicum of comfort, and maybe even a good night's sleep. Nonetheless, Win was still looking at her hopefully.

"Thanks for the offer," Poppy said, mustering another smile.

"But I don't want to intrude on your and Mary Jane's time together. And I *really* don't want to hear about Bret's dirty socks."

"Fair enough," Win said. She reached for her car keys, and tossed them to Poppy.

Poppy had imagined that picking up Sasquatch's ashes would be a quick affair, but when she got to the veterinarian's office, it was so busy she ended up having to wait for them, which meant sitting on a plastic chair, flipping through an issue of *Modern Cat* magazine, and trying to ignore all of the other pet owners and pets in the room with her. When she came across a picture in the magazine that reminded her too much of Sasquatch, though, she set it aside and ended up watching a little girl who was holding a calico kitten in her arms.

"Mommy, he's scared to see the vet," she said, turning to the woman beside her.

"Don't worry, he'll be fine," her mother assured her. "The only thing I'm concerned about," she added, smiling down at her daughter, "is that you might be holding him too much."

The little girl noticed that Poppy was staring at them. "Do you want to pet him?" she asked, holding her kitten out. "His name is Butterscotch."

"No. No, thank you," Poppy said, trying to smile. She looked away, quickly, fighting back tears. Who knew she wouldn't even be able to *look* at a cat without wanting to cry? She stared straight ahead, and thought about Cassie. She was about the same age as that little girl with the kitten, and, like her, she loved cats. When Poppy had babysat for her, they'd spent part of the night watching cat videos on the Internet. Poppy had told Cassie that she would introduce her to Sasquatch. But it was too late for that now, too late on both counts. She sank down a few inches in her chair.

"Miss Robbins?" the office manager called, and Poppy, glad
for the distraction, went to collect the urn. It looked nice, she
thought, as she signed for it. She'd chosen the "classic brass cre-
mation urn" from the catalogue, thinking it was the most digni-
fied option. "It's so light," she commented, lifting it up, but the
woman at the desk had already moved on to someone else, so she
left, careful not to look at the little girl and the calico kitten again
on her way out.

Back in the car, with Sasquatch's urn stowed safely on the floor
of the front passenger seat, Poppy felt at a loss. She'd planned on
returning to the cabin, but now, as she pulled out of her parking
spot and drove down Main Street, she found she was dreading
its emptiness. She didn't know anywhere else to go, though. Butternut was not exactly known for its nightlife.

She turned on the radio, then cranked the volume up all the
way. She was determined to keep all of her feelings at bay, but
they crowded in on her anyway. Regret, sadness, loneliness, the
last one most of all. Why hadn't she gone with Win and Mary
Jane? she wondered. Anything, even listening to Mary Jane discuss her new marriage ad nauseam, would be better than the
silent cabin waiting for her now.

And it was as she was thinking this, and cruising along a quiet
stretch of road outside of town, that she saw the Mosquito Inn
ahead on her right. It was an old roadhouse that had been there
for . . . well, probably forever, though it was odd to think that
she'd driven by it at least a dozen times this summer without
ever really noticing it. Now, though, as she approached it, she
slowed down and studied it in the early evening light, and decided there was something appealingly retro about it. This was
most likely due to the blue-and-red blinking neon sign, which not

only spelled out MOSQUITO INN but also included an outline of a mosquito hovering over a martini glass. On a whim, she pulled into the rutted driveway and parked in a mostly empty dirt lot. This would be fun, she decided, unfastening her seat belt and reaching for Sasquatch's ashes. (It seemed rude, somehow, to just leave them in the car.) She'd have one cocktail, something sweet and summery. It would give her an excuse not to be alone, for a little while, anyway, and by the time she got home, she'd be that much closer to the evening being over.

When she pushed open the bar's screen door, though, she was disappointed. If the Mosquito Inn had a certain ramshackle charm from the outside, it didn't translate on the inside. It was dark, for one thing, much darker than it should have been considering that it was only early evening, and it smelled of stale beer, and of something else, too, something she didn't care to investigate too closely. And, except for a few older men hunched over their beers at one end of the bar, and a few younger looking guys playing pool in the back, there was no one around.

She hesitated, and tried to remember what she knew about this place. Not much. Her grandfather had never come here. He hadn't been much of a drinker. And it went without saying that Win wasn't one, either. When her sister did have the occasional drink, though, Poppy was pretty sure she went to the Corner Bar on Main Street, which was much nicer than this. But going there would involve getting back in the car and driving again, and, right at this moment, Poppy didn't have the energy.

One drink, she told herself, heading for the side of the bar that was empty. She chose a stool, settled her handbag beside her, and, after considering what to do with the urn, she placed it, discreetly, on the floor underneath the stool. The bartender, a burly man with a handlebar mustache, was wiping a dirty looking counter with a dirty looking rag. He glanced, disinterestedly, at Poppy, then did a double take. He came over to her.

"What can I get you?" he asked.

"Um . . ." She looked around for a cocktail menu. No such thing here. "How about . . . a cosmopolitan," she said.

"We don't serve those."

"Really?" she said. "They're not that hard to make. At least, I don't think they are. They're pink, and they have vodka—"

"We don't serve pink drinks here," he interrupted.

"Oh, okay. Well, then . . . something else that's sweet."

He stared back at her impassively.

"Oh, I know, a sea breeze," she said, brightly. "It's not pink, it's red, so it won't violate the 'no pink drinks' rule here," she said, venturing a smile. He didn't smile back. "And, let's see, it's got vodka and cranberry juice and . . . I'm not sure what else."

He went to mix it. "Vodka and cranberry juice," he said, setting it down on the counter in front of her.

"Thank you," she said, determined to ignore his unfriendliness.

"That'll be three bucks."

Well, at least it's cheap, she thought as she paid. Though even at this price, frankly, the atmosphere here left a little to be desired. She left a dollar bill on the bar for a tip, and took a sip of her drink. *Whoa,* they were not skimping on the vodka here, or at least not on the *amount* of vodka in their mixed drinks. As for its quality, she doubted very much that something that tasted as if it might take the enamel off her teeth was a top-drawer brand.

Still, she was drinking her drink, slowly, when the bartender came back over to her. He looked uncomfortable. "Are you, uh, meeting someone here?" he asked.

"Nope, it's just going to be me," she said, with false cheerfulness.

"'Cause, uh, it can get a little rowdy here later on," he said.

Good to know, Poppy thought, taking a look around the place. Cute sign notwithstanding, it was a dump. Even so, it was a dump she intended to have a cocktail in. "I'm just going to drink this," she said, indicating her sea breeze, "and then I'll be on my way."

He nodded, curtly, and moved away.

She blew out a long breath. He wasn't exactly the friendliest bartender she'd ever come across. So the Mosquito Inn didn't get high points for customer service, either. But she got his point. The crowd, when they got here, would be a little . . . boisterous, probably. She took a hurried sip of her sea breeze, but then she realized that as soon as her glass was empty, she'd be going back to the cabin. Alone. At least here there were people. And noise; the murmur of a conversation at the other end of the bar; the clack of pool balls from the back room. No, she would take her time, she decided. She would simply send a very clear message that she wasn't interested in socializing with anyone. She reached down and lifted the urn out from under her stool and set it on the bar in front of her. *There.* Nobody would bother someone who was obviously in mourning.

A half an hour later, Poppy was still sitting at the bar. Her drink was unfinished—the melting ice puddling on top of the cranberry juice and vodka—and she'd declined the dubious looking bowl of peanuts the bartender had offered her. Instead, after she'd put the urn on the bar, she'd decided to take stock of her life. On the face of it, at least, it had been a brutal accounting. The present, it turned out, looked a lot like the past. She was broke, unemployed, and dependent on Win. Outwardly, nothing had changed.

But inwardly, she knew that was not the case. She was not the same person who'd showed up on Win's doorstep on the first day of summer. She was different. While she'd been stocking shelves, and flirting with Sam, and chatting with Cassie, and sparring with Win, she'd changed. She'd stopped gliding over the surface of life. She'd stopped looking down on it like a casual observer. She'd stopped pretending that the things that concerned everyone else—work, friendships, relationships—didn't concern her. Instead, she'd fallen in love. She'd formed a bond with a little girl. She'd revisited a traumatic experience and taken a hard look at the years that had followed it. But most of all, she'd let herself feel, *really feel,* even when she hadn't necessarily wanted to, even when it had hurt more than she could have possibly imagined.

It had felt that way when Sam had broken things off, she thought, rattling the ice around in her glass. To have finally found someone she'd wanted to take a risk with, and to not be able to take it, that was heartbreaking. What choice had she had, though? Sam had made his case that morning, almost a month ago, in his office at Birch Tree Bait. But when had she made *her* case? she wondered now. When had she told him *exactly* how she felt, *exactly* how much she cared about him? She hadn't. She'd never told him. And that had been a mistake. Which was not to say that if she *had* told him things would have turned out differently. *But they might have.*

She checked her watch. It was seven o'clock. Sam might still be at Birch Tree Bait closing up, but, more likely, he'd be back at his cabin by now. A tremor moved through her; it was part fear and part hope. She'd go there now, she decided, and say what she should have said the last time they'd spoken.

She picked up her handbag and reached for the urn, but before she could slide off her bar stool, she heard someone say, "You're not leaving already, are you?"

She jumped with surprise. She'd been so deep in thought that she hadn't even noticed the man who'd sat down beside her at the bar. She turned to look at him. He was her age, or there-abouts, and he was tall and lean, with tattoos covering the ropey muscles on his arms. His longish black hair was shoved under a trucker hat, and his eyes were a cold, light blue. They played over her now in a way that was too familiar. "I've been watching you since you came in," he said, "but I had to finish my game." He inclined his head towards the pool tables in the back. "What can I get you?" he asked. "Another sea breeze?"

How does he know what I've been drinking? she wondered, unnerved. But she tried to sound casual as she said, "Actually, I'm done." She gestured at her watery drink. "I was just about to leave." She pulled the urn over to her.

"Are those . . . ashes?" he asked, leaning closer. Close enough for her to smell the scent of whiskey on his breath.

"Uh-huh," she said, gathering the urn against her. "They belong to my closest friend." *Talk about a conversation ender.* But he seemed undeterred.

"How about I buy you a drink, then, and we toast your closest friend?"

"No, thanks. I have to meet someone," she lied, getting down off her stool. He slid off his, too.

"Where are you meeting them?" he asked, standing too close to her.

"At my place," she said. She tried to extricate herself from be-tween the two bar stools, but he moved in and closed off her path.

"Your place, huh? I'd like to see that."

"I don't think so," she said, aiming for firm, but missing it and hitting rude instead. "Now, if you'll excuse me," she added, trying to step around him. Once more, he blocked her way. Her heart, of its own accord, had started beating faster. *Stop it,* she told herself. She took a steadying breath and looked around. Was anybody noticing this? His friends were. A couple of them had followed him over from the pool tables and were watching his exchange with her. Far from disapproving, though, they seemed to be enjoying it. The other customers at the bar—there were at least a dozen of them by now—were looking pointedly away. Poppy searched out the bartender, but he was filling a pint glass from a tap and she couldn't catch his eye.

Okay, stay calm, she told herself. *This man's a bully. He can smell fear a mile away. And he likes fear.* And even as she was thinking this, he was smiling at her. It was an ugly smile. "You need to move right now," she said, meeting his cold eyes head-on. "If you don't, I'll call the police."

"Ooh, the police," he drawled, "I'm scared." He stepped back and held his hands up, as if in surrender. "They might arrest me for . . . talking to a girl." He looked at his friends and they laughed. But he'd created a little space between them when he'd stepped back, and Poppy used it now to slip by him.

"Hey," he called after her. "What about that drink?" His friends laughed again. Poppy kept walking, hoping she'd shaken him off. But damn, the man was fast. Before she'd even reached the door, he'd gotten in front of her again, and was leaning, leisurely, against it as if he'd been there all day.

"How about if I drive you home?" he asked. He smiled, what he probably thought was a winning smile, but it didn't touch his eyes.

She tried to beat back a wave of panic. "Get out of my way," she said. "I mean it." She knew she sounded scared. But she couldn't help it. He smiled his ugly smile, and she tried to push past him. Amazingly, he let her.

"Aw, come on, you're not being any fun," he said, following behind her as she pushed through the screen door. Poppy ignored him, and headed for her car. She wished, fervently, that she'd parked closer to the bar, but she was relieved to see there was more activity in the parking lot now than there'd been when she'd arrived. "You've been drinking," he called after her. "Why don't you let me drive you home?"

She picked up her pace. *Don't look back.* She reached into her purse and felt for her car key, then ran her thumb along its edge. It was hardly a weapon, but, then again, what were the chances of him assaulting her while it was still light outside, in full view of other people?

"Hey, if you won't let me drive you home, at least let me follow you there. Just to make sure you get there safe."

She unlocked the car door and yanked it open. She practically dived inside, but it wasn't until she'd slammed the door, and checked to make sure that all the doors were locked, that she allowed herself to look back at him. He was standing outside the bar. His friends had come out, too, and were hanging around him, some of them with their beers in hand. He saw her watching him, and he pantomimed revving a motorcycle, and then pointed to one parked just a few spaces over from her. Was that his? Would he follow her if she left? She felt suddenly sick, and turned away. She knew what she needed to do. She needed to start her engine. She needed to pull out of the parking lot. She needed to get away from here. But she couldn't. She was too afraid. She tried to think clearly. She tried to assess the situation, but she couldn't. She didn't trust herself to. He'd tapped into a fear that defied rationalization. He might be a harmless jerk, trying to liven up an otherwise dull evening. Then again, he could be truly dangerous, someone who, if she left now, would follow her.

Either way, it didn't matter. She was shaking all over, shaking so badly that she knew she couldn't drive. She actually thought, for a second, she might hyperventilate, or worse, faint. That was when she took her cell phone out of her handbag, scrolled through her contacts, and called one of them. After three rings, he answered.

"Poppy?"

"Sam, I—"

"What's wrong?"

"I might be in trouble," she said, pulling in a little breath.

"Where are you?"

"The parking lot of the Mosquito Inn."

There was a pause. She could almost hear him thinking, *What the hell are you doing there?* But what he said was, "What's happening?"

"Nothing, yet. But this guy's bothering me, and I think, if I leave, he might try to follow me home."

"Are you in your car?"

"Yes."

"Are the doors locked?"

"Uh-huh."

"What's he doing?"

"He's just . . ." She looked over at him, and he grinned back at her. "He's just standing there, watching me. He's got some friends with him."

"Okay," he said, and she could sense movement on his end of

the line. "I'm coming. I'll stay on the phone with you, and if he comes any closer than he is already, I'll call the police."

"Thank you," she said, trying to breathe normally.

"Don't worry about it," he said.

Afterwards, she couldn't remember exactly what Sam talked to her about during the ten or fifteen minutes it took for him to drive there. But he kept up a one-sided conversation the whole way. Occasionally, she would hear a background sound; Sam slamming his pickup door shut, Sam turning on the engine. Mostly, though, it was Sam talking about things. Little things. An obnoxious customer who'd come into the store today, a funny movie he'd seen recently, the tree house he and Linc were building for his kids. Sometimes, he'd ask her a quick question. Was the guy still there? How was she doing? Yes, he was still there. And she was doing okay.

The okay part, of course, was relative. She was still on the edge of panic. But she listened to Sam's words, listened to them without necessarily understanding them, and she took solace in them. As long as he kept talking, she could keep breathing.

"Poppy," Sam said, finally. "I'm about two minutes away. I don't want you to get out of your car yet. But I do want you to tell me where it's parked." She looked out the window and described its position.

"All right, I'm pulling in now," he said, after a wait that felt like an eternity. "I see you." Poppy turned and looked out the window, and, as soon as she saw his truck, she collapsed back against the seat. He parked next to her, and, leaving his engine running, got out and came around to her side. He gestured for her to unlock the door, and, as soon as she did, he opened it for her.

"Let's go," he said, motioning her out. She switched off her cell phone, slipped it back in her handbag, and picked up the urn from the seat beside her. But when she tried to get out of the car, her legs felt rubbery, and Sam, in the end, supported her the few feet to his truck and lifted her into it. Then he walked around to his side and opened the door. Before he got in, though, he turned toward the entrance to the Mosquito Inn and stared at Poppy's harasser. Poppy couldn't see the expression on Sam's face; he was facing away from her. But whatever it was, it was enough to un-nerve the man in the trucker hat. He stared back for a moment, then shrugged, and went back inside the bar. His friends, who looked disappointed that the fun had ended so soon, followed him.

Sam got in then. "Put your seat belt on," he said. She yanked it on, and he pulled out of the parking lot. "Is that what I think it is?" he asked, with a sideways look at the urn she was still clutching.

"They're my cat's ashes," she said, shakily.

"Of course they are," he said, quietly, almost to himself.

She turned to him, questioningly, as his truck sped down the road. But he didn't say anything else. Where was the guy she'd been talking to on the phone? she wondered. That Sam had seemed so kind and reassuring. Now he just seemed distant.

"Are you angry at me?" she asked.

He looked over at her for the first time since she'd gotten into the truck, and then looked away. "Not angry. Just surprised. And, honestly, a little worried."

"About me?"

Sam looked over at her again. *"Yes,* about you. I haven't seen you or spoken to you in a month. And then you call me from a bar that's known to be frequented by ex-cons, where you've been drinking, alone. I'm sorry"—he caught himself—"*not* alone, with your cat's ashes. And then I have to practically pour you into my truck. I mean, what the hell, Poppy? Do you go there often?"

"*No*," she said, indignantly, though his tone had been more puzzled than unkind. "I've never been to that place before. I didn't know anything about it. I don't hang out in bars—if that's what you're implying—alone or with other people, and I don't drink a lot, either. Not tonight, and not any other night. The only reason I was even there was because"—here she stopped to catch her breath—"because I'd gone to pick up Sasquatch's ashes at the vet. Win couldn't come with me because she's away, and I wasn't . . . I wasn't prepared for how hard it would be," she said, her voice cracking. "I really wasn't. He was . . . he was my best friend. I know it sounds crazy, or pathetic, or something. But it's true. I got him when I was in high school, after I'd had a . . . a very bad experience, and he helped me. He got me through it. I knew, objectively, he would die someday, but on some level, I don't . . . I don't think I really believed it." She stopped, and concentrated on not crying.

They drove in silence for a minute, and when Sam spoke again, he voice was gentle. "I wasn't implying that you hang out in bars, or that you're a drinker. But don't . . . don't go there again, okay? It's not a nice place. And, um, I'm sorry about Sasquatch. I never met him, obviously. But I'm sure he was a fine cat."

"He was," Poppy agreed, thinking how close his tribute to Sasquatch—simple, but fitting—had been to her own. She felt her heart start to slow and her breathing return to normal, and then an unexpected drowsiness settled over her. Her fear of the man in the trucker cap was gone. So was her indignation at Sam. She yawned, quietly, but Sam still heard her.

"Tired?" he asked.

She nodded. Actually, she was *exhausted*. She doubted that she'd gotten more than a few consecutive hours of sleep all week.

"Well, we'll be back at your cabin soon."

She said nothing, but she thought about being alone again and she sighed.

"What?" Sam asked.

"Nothing. I just . . . don't want to be by myself tonight."

"Are you still scared?"

"Not exactly. It's more like . . ." *It's more like I'm lonely.* And she was, at the thought of going back there. So lonely that it frightened her a little. "Sam, could I spend the night at your place?" she asked suddenly.

Now she heard him sigh. "I don't think that's a good idea."

"I don't mean spend the night as in 'spend the night.' I mean 'sleep on your couch and be gone by the time you wake up.'"

"I don't know," he murmured, but then, after a short silence, he said. "Yeah, okay. You can stay. Tomorrow I'll take you back to the parking lot first thing to pick up your car. But, Poppy?"

"Yes?"

"This isn't going to be a romantic thing."

"Yeah, I get that," she said, and she was careful to keep the disappointment out of her voice.

They didn't speak again until he'd pulled up in front of his cabin, and by then Poppy was so tired she could barely keep her eyes open. She started to open her door, but Sam rushed around and helped her out, and for this she was grateful.

When they got inside, Sam asked her if she wanted something to eat. She was hungry, but eating sounded like it would require too much effort. "Actually, if you could get me a blanket and a pillow for the couch, I think I'll go to sleep now."

"You don't need to sleep on the couch. I've already got the beds on the sleeping porch made up. The kids like to sleep out there sometimes when it's hot."

She followed him through the living room and kitchen, and onto a small screened in porch off the back of the house. He indicated one of the beds and, leaving her things on the floor beside it, she crawled beneath the covers. "Do you need anything?" Sam asked. "A glass of water?"

"No, thank you," she said, her eyes drooping closed.

He sat down gingerly on the end of the bed. "Are you going to be all right?"

"Uh-huh," she said, drowsily. And then, without thinking, right before she fell asleep, she said, "Sam, I am *so* in love with you."

CHAPTER 22

Sometime during the night the smell of coffee invaded Poppy's sleep. It smelled . . . *it smelled delicious.* Was it morning already? She sat up, groggily. But no, the view through the sleeping porch screen was one of almost impenetrable darkness. Someone was awake, though. Someone was brewing coffee. She got out of bed, and, maneuvering by the pale yellow light spilling in from the kitchen, she made her way there and found Sam sitting at the breakfast table, his laptop and a cup of coffee in front of him.

"Hi," she said, from the doorway.

Sam looked up, an unreadable expression on his face.

"The smell of coffee woke me up," she explained, feeling self-conscious in her rumpled clothes.

"Help yourself," he said, neutrally, gesturing at the coffeepot on the counter.

She found a mug in the cupboard, filled it up, and took a carton of half-and-half out of the refrigerator. She poured some into the cup, and found a spoon for stirring. After a moment's hesitation, she came to sit at the table with him.

"What are you doing?" she asked, tentatively, sipping her coffee.

"Inventory," he said, concentrating on his computer screen.

"Do you always work on inventory"—she glanced at the clock on the stove—"at 2:30 A.M.?"

"Do you always tell people that you're in love with them?" he asked, looking up at her.

Her hand wobbled and she spilled a little coffee on the table. She *had* told him that before she'd fallen asleep. Her cheeks flushed, but she held his gaze. "I meant that," she said, quietly.

He shook his head. "You shouldn't throw words like that around."

"I didn't. *I don't.* I've never said that to anyone before. *Ever,*" she said, but he looked unconvinced.

She shrugged. "You can believe whatever you want," she mumbled, wrapping both of her hands around her mug, and staring down into it. She wouldn't take those words back. They were the only words that meant anything to her right now.

She took another sip of coffee, but her stomach clenched, uneasily. When was the last time she'd eaten? she wondered. Lunchtime. And since then, all she'd had was a sea breeze, and now a cup of coffee. The coffee had smelled wonderful, but now it felt as if it was burning a hole in her stomach.

"What's wrong?" Sam asked, noticing her expression.

"Nothing. I think maybe I should eat something, though."

For the first time that night he looked amused. "What, was the menu at the Mosquito Inn not up to your standards?"

She shuddered, remembering the dirty cloth the bartender had wiped the dirty bar with. "Oh, God, they don't actually serve food there, do they?"

She saw a shadow of a smile cross his face. "No. I don't think the Health Department would allow that." He studied her then, not unsympathetically. "Would you like something to eat?"

"I'd love something," she confessed. But when she got up to get it, he waved her back down again. He opened the refrigerator, rummaged around in it, and took out a bowl covered with Saran Wrap. "There's some leftover pancake batter," he offered.

She nodded, eagerly. She was starving now. He put a pan on the stove, turned the gas on, and melted butter into it. When it started to sizzle, he poured the batter in, forming half a dozen perfect circles with it.

"I didn't know you could cook," she said.

"I can't, really. But if I have a specialty, it's breakfast."

"Those look good," Poppy said as Sam flipped the golden pancakes over.

"Most divorced fathers have a few tricks up their sleeves," he said, sliding them onto a plate.

As soon as he put them down in front of her, she practically pounced on them. "Thank you," she said. And, too impatient to be polite, she doused them with syrup and started sawing into them.

It was quiet at the table as Poppy ate, and then she noticed Sam watching her with interest, a smile playing around the corners of his mouth.

"I'm sorry," she said, and even though her mouth was still full she was already spearing more pancake onto her fork. "I'm being rude, aren't I?"

"No," Sam said, smiling as she put another forkful into her mouth. "Actually, yeah, you kind of are. But it's cute. You remind me of . . . you remind me of a kid, stuffing your face like that."

She swallowed, and put her fork down. Suddenly, she wasn't hungry anymore.

"What's wrong?"

She shrugged. "Is that how you think of me? Like a little kid?"

"Right now, yes."

"Because that's *not* how I want you to think of me."

"How do you want me to think of you?"

"As a woman. Preferably, a desirable woman."

"And you don't think I think of you that way?"

She shook her head.

"Poppy, do you know why I'm sitting in my kitchen, drinking coffee, and working at 2:30 A.M.?"

"No," she said, honestly.

"Because it is taking all of my willpower not to do what I really want to do, which is to take you up to my bedroom . . ."

Poppy gulped. "Really?"

"Yes," he said, staring back at her steadily.

She ran a tongue along her lower lip. It was sticky with syrup. "So why . . . why are we sitting down here?"

"Because I need to spend a night with you like I need a hole in my head."

That broke the mood. She scowled at him. "That's not a very nice thing to say."

"No," he agreed. "It's true, though."

She stood up and started to clear her plate from the table.

"Hey, come on. Don't get mad," he said, and when she passed him on her way to the sink he caught the sleeve of her blouse and tugged on it, playfully. She let him take the plate out of her hands. He set it on the table and pulled her into his lap. He put his arms around her waist and nuzzled her neck. "I said I didn't *need* a hole in my head. I didn't say I wasn't willing to have one. As long as it's small, and it's in a very inconspicuous place."

Poppy laughed. It was impossible for her to stay mad at him

right now. His lips left her neck and found her lips. "Mmmm, you always taste so sweet." He reached across the table for the bottle of syrup. "You know," he said, "we could have some fun with this."

"What do you mean?"

His smiled, mischievously, and, holding up the bottle, he pantomimed pouring it down the front of her blouse.

"Sam!" she said, but she was laughing. Then she turned serious. "Does this mean we're going up to your room?"

"Do you want us to?"

She nodded, her heart pounding. "If you don't . . . don't think it will be a mistake."

"Oh, I *definitely* think it will be a mistake," he said, but he was smiling.

"Will you . . . carry me?" she asked, thinking of all the movies she'd seen this done in. It had always struck her as the height of romance.

"I can probably do that," he said teasingly. "Let's go." He picked her up and carried her through the kitchen, into the living room, and up the stairs. And Poppy savored the feel of his arms around her and of her cheek resting against his chest. He reached the top step, turned down the hallway, and then stopped in the doorway to his room.

"You sure you want to do this?" he asked, looking down at her.

"*Yes,*" she said, her desire mixing with nervousness.

He lay her down on his bed, and lay down beside her. They held each other then, and kissed each other, and Poppy pressed herself against him, and pulled his T-shirt off, and ran her hands over his bare chest. She was waiting for him to undress her, too, but he took his time, and continued at a relaxed, unhurried pace that Poppy found maddening. She wanted him so badly. Didn't he know that?

"Are you going to take my clothes off?" she asked, finally.

"I was getting around to it," he said, smiling.

Well, you could get around to it a little faster, she thought. But at that moment Sam began to unbutton her blouse. He took off everything except her pale blue, lace edged bra and panties. She had fantasized about this moment so many times over the last several weeks, but, as it turned out, even in her fantasies it hadn't been this sweet.

Sam, almost against his will, let his eyes brush over her. She was beautiful, no doubt about it, but he couldn't help but think she didn't belong here, in his already rumpled bed, with its brown-and-white-checked sheets and scratchy brown blanket. No, she belonged somewhere else, on a tropical island, maybe. Frolicking on a powdery white sand beach, with bottle green water licking her ankles, and palm fronds waving above her head.

"Is something wrong?" she asked him.

"*Nothing* is wrong," he assured her. "This is just a little surreal, having you in my bed like this."

"Surreal in a good way?"

"Yes," he said, leaning down to kiss her sweet, syrupy mouth. "In a very good way." He thought now about the box of condoms in his bedside table drawer, tucked under a financial document so boring looking that it would discourage even his most curious child from looking any further.

He kissed her more deeply, hungry for her taste and for the feel of her body against his. Still, he knew he needed to go slowly. He remembered the night on the dock at Birch Tree Bait. His hand had brushed against her breast while they were kissing and it was as if he had delivered an electric shock to her.

There was more kissing now, more touching, and stroking. Sam loved the way she ran her hands over his chest and back and stomach; even with his blue jeans and her panties separating them, he was unbelievably aroused. He dipped his fingers inside her bra and caressed her nipples, then trailed a hand lightly down her stomach, which was silky smooth and perfectly suntanned. But when he reached the waistband of her panties, he felt, or imagined he felt, a little tremor pass through her. He didn't know if it was desire, or something else. Something like fear. Because when he thought about it now, that was what he had seen in her eyes down at the dock. She'd been quick to cover it up, but it had been there nonetheless. He'd frightened her, crossing a line he hadn't even known was there.

He stopped what he was doing. "Poppy," he said, understanding something about her for the first time. "Did . . . did somebody . . . hurt you?"

She hesitated.

"I know we never talked about this," he said, "but that night, the night Linc got in an accident, when we were kissing, something happened. You pulled away from me. Do you remember?"

"Yes," she said. But now she wouldn't meet his eyes.

"Poppy," he said again, turning her face gently towards him. "What happened that night? And . . . before that night?"

She sighed, clearly troubled.

"If you don't want to talk about it . . ."

"No, I do. I want to, Sam. But I'm not sure I know how to. I've never told anyone about it before."

Sam waited. He thought about turning off the bedside table lamp. Would it be easier for her to tell him this in the dark?

Maybe. But he wanted to see her face, especially since he sensed how important this was. So he didn't rush her, but when she bit her lower lip in frustration, he knew how hard she was finding it to put this into words.

Finally, he said, "You know, sometimes how you say something matters less than just . . . saying it."

So she told Sam the story, slowly. Haltingly. Sometimes she looked at him. Sometimes she didn't. It was hard to listen to, partly because he knew what was coming, and partly because he knew it was too late to protect her. He thought of Poppy at sixteen, walking home from school on a spring day, and he wished he could turn back the clock and change the course of that afternoon. He knew now, in the telling of it, how much it had altered her life. And the fact that she'd carried this with her all of these years without ever telling anyone seemed to him to have been a terrible burden. When she was done talking, he pulled the sheet up over them and folded her into his arms, trying to transmit as much warmth to her body as he could.

"I'm so sorry that happened to you," he said. She nestled against him. "Are you okay? Right now, I mean."

She met his eyes. "I'm okay," she said. And she sounded surprised. "I didn't know I could do that. And, by the way Sam, the reason I forgot to take the keys out of the lock when I was closing Birch Tree Bait that night was because I was so preoccupied. I'd let myself think about that, really think about it, for the first time in years."

He stroked her back, and kissed her, tenderly, on her temple. But the conversation wasn't over yet. He had another question for her. "So, the men you've been with since then . . . you've never wanted to tell any of them?"

"No," she said, softly. And then, for the first time since coming up to his bedroom, she smiled. "Believe it or not, Sam, even though I'm in your bed in the middle of the night in my bra and panties, I actually have a problem with intimacy." She propped herself up on her elbow. "Once, I had a boyfriend for six months. That was a personal record for me. Usually, I tried to end things before they got to that point. But I thought he might be different. He was . . . he was a nice guy, a *really* nice guy. And, more importantly, he wasn't in any hurry for us to, you know, be together, or if he was, he didn't let it show. He said he'd wait, until marriage, if necessary. He thought that was the issue for me, and I let him think that. And then one day, I decided, we should try. Just . . . *try*. He didn't know about what had happened to me, but he knew I didn't have a lot of experience, and I thought it would be all right. When the time came, though, I panicked. I just completely . . . panicked. I broke up with him after that. I told him I wasn't ready for a serious relationship."

"And that was it?"

"No." She tucked a strand of hair behind her ear. "Last year, I went to my ten-year high school reunion. And I saw this guy I'd had a crush on my junior year. He used to play the saxophone in the school orchestra."

"So, he's a musician?"

"Now?" She smiled. "No, he's an insurance adjuster. I trusted him, though. I thought, 'This guy's a good guy.' I could just tell. I mean, I didn't want to have a relationship with him. I just wanted to see if it could happen. So I asked him back to my apartment, and I told him this was a one-time thing, and he seemed okay with it. Later I was glad I asked him. Because it . . . it worked."

"It worked?"

"It happened," Poppy amended. "It was all right. It wasn't *great*. But I didn't freak out, either. I didn't want to see him again afterwards—not that way, anyway—but I was okay with what happened. I was kind of testing the waters with him, I guess."

There was a pause. "And me? Are you testing the waters with me?"

"God, no. This isn't some kind of experiment. Can't you tell that, Sam?"

He could tell. He could tell by the way she was looking at him right now. But that didn't mean that this should go any further tonight. "We don't need to do this, Poppy," he said. "You know that, don't you? We can talk. Or sleep."

"No," she said, shaking her head. "No more talking." And, as if to drive this point home, she placed her palms on his chest. She ran them, lightly, up and down. "We've talked enough for one night."

Still, Sam hesitated, thinking about what she'd told him. He couldn't put it away now. It was too . . . too big. Too complicated. And it made him want to fix it, he realized. It made him want to make it right. But he couldn't. Not tonight, maybe not ever.

"Kiss me," she said, softly, and the bedside table light seemed to be glowing all around her blond hair. He leaned in to kiss her. Maybe, he thought, maybe the best thing to do was to concentrate on the present. It was possible, he knew, in love as in life, to overthink things, to overanalyze them. What if all they needed to know right now was that they wanted each other, they cared about each other, and they trusted each other?

"I'll tell you what, Poppy," he said now, savoring the silkiness of her skin against his. "We'll take it slowly. Very slowly. And if you want us to stop, at any time, you just say so. And we'll stop. Okay?"

"Okay," she whispered.

CHAPTER 23

ater, much later, as the morning sunlight began to slide, almost imperceptibly, over the bed they were lying in, Poppy tried to rouse herself. She'd been drowsing in and out of sleep, her cheek resting in the crook of Sam's neck, her arm thrown over his chest, and she had a vague sense of time passing, of seconds ticking by and minutes accumulating. She stirred in his arms, and tried to sit up, but her limbs felt so heavy, *so deliciously heavy,* that she gave up almost immediately and nestled against him instead.

"I can't move," she murmured into his neck. She felt, rather than saw, him smile.

"So don't," he said, tightening his arms around her.

"I'll have to, eventually," she pointed out. She shifted her cheek, fractionally, so that it was now resting against the warm solidity of his chest. "I mean, I'll need to eat, won't I?"

"Hmmm," he said, moving one of his hands to the small of her back. "I'll bring you breakfast in bed."

"But then you'd have to leave me," she objected, running a hand over his chest.

"You're right. I don't want to do that," he said. He left one hand on the small of her back and raised the other hand up and ran it, languorously, through her hair. "Maybe we can get someone to bring us food."

She smiled, stretched, and wondered, idly, how much longer they could reasonably stay here, hungry or not. "What time is it?" she asked, turning her head so that her lips could nuzzle his chest.

He took his hand out of her hair and lifted his watch up. "It's eleven thirty," he said.

"*Eleven thirty?*" She lifted her head up and stared at him in disbelief. "Don't you . . . don't you have to go to work?"

"Nope. I texted Byron early this morning and asked him to cover for me."

"I don't remember you doing that."

"You were sleeping, as I recall."

"And you didn't wake me up?"

"No. Why would I have?"

"So we could have been doing something other than sleeping," she said, raising herself on one elbow.

"We *had* been doing something other than sleeping."

She smiled at his reference to their lovemaking. They had taken it slowly, at first, until Poppy hadn't wanted to take it slowly anymore. Her ardor had surprised her. Where had it come from? Had it been there all along, waiting for Sam? Maybe, she thought, remembering the skill and tenderness with which he had touched, and stroked, and kissed her. And suddenly she was impatient for more. She didn't want them to waste any time, and she told him that now.

He was amused. "Poppy," he said, turning on his side so that they were facing each other, with only a sheet covering them. "We still have four hours before I have to pick up my kids."

"Four hours? *That's it?*"

"Yes, Poppy. Four hours. That's a long time."

She shook her head. "It's not. Not when . . ." *Not when I've never made love like that before.* She tried to think of how to say this, but she didn't know how to. She'd never talked about sex with anyone before, not even Win.

But he was caressing her breasts now and she could feel her nipples hardening and the rest of her body tingling. He leaned down and ran a tongue over one nipple, and Poppy moaned and arched her back reflexively. She felt a rush of warmth spread through her whole body.

"Now, what were we talking about?" he said teasingly.

She smiled, but she didn't want to talk anymore. Still, he seemed to be waiting for some kind of an answer. "What I was *going* to say was that what happened last night was so . . . *so good,*" she said, moving her hands up into his hair and rumpling it. "I knew, of course, that it was *supposed* to be good, fantastic even, but hearing about it, and actually experiencing it? Those are two completely different things."

Sam had been stroking the inside of her thighs, but now his hands stilled and his blue eyes were serious.

"What's wrong?" she asked.

"Nothing's wrong. I'm just . . . so sorry that happened to you," he said, gently brushing hair off her face. "I wish I could make it . . . go away. Undo it."

"I tried that, for a long time. I tried to make it go away. I tried to pretend it never happened. But it didn't work," she said, reaching out to touch his face. "The talking about it, though, the way we did last night, I think that might help." She kissed him, tenderly, and then he ran his fingers through her hair, something she already knew he loved to do. And for a little while, as they held each other, it was as if everything else had dropped away from them. It was just the two of them, and this bed, and they had all the time in the world. Except that they didn't, of course. And as the tempo of their kissing changed, their hunger for each other returned.

"You're right, Poppy, four hours isn't a lot of time," Sam said as he pulled away, and reached to open the bedside table drawer. But as he was doing this, Poppy, wanting him to hurry, made a small, impatient sound. He turned to look at her and smiled. He touched her hair, fanned out on the pillow around her. The noontime sunlight was pouring into the room now, filling it with a bright golden light.

"You are so beautiful. You know that, don't you?" he asked.

"People have told me that. But I've never felt that way before. Until right now."

Later, Sam drove Poppy back to the Mosquito Inn to pick up Win's car. It was a lovely drive. The road was dappled with sunshine, and the warm breeze blowing onto Poppy's face through the open window was fragrant and sweet with the smell of wildflowers growing in the roadside ditches. The best part of the drive, though, was that for its entire duration, Sam kept a hand resting on her knee. It was a gesture that seemed to her to be both intimate and protective, and it had the added advantage, too, of carrying with it a faintly erotic charge. She could have quite happily spent the rest of her life driving down this road with Sam, she decided. The only caveat, of course, would be that they would need to make frequent stops, pulling onto the abandoned logging roads that dotted the forest around them, and making love in the backseat.

Too soon, though, Sam was pulling into the Mosquito Inn's lot. "Well, Win's car is still here," he said, stopping next to it. "That's a good sign." And, with a final squeeze of her knee, he got out to inspect it. "It looks fine," he said, turning to Poppy, who'd joined him. "A friend of mine got his tires slashed when he was parked here once, but it looks like you got lucky last night."

"I certainty did," Poppy said, with a mischievous smile. She faced him and slipped her hands into the back pockets of his blue jeans.

"Are you flirting with me?" Sam asked, raising an eyebrow.

"Definitely," Poppy said.

He laughed and pulled her into his arms. "I miss you already," he said. "Which reminds me . . ."

"Yes?"

"When can I see you again?"

"Soon," she said, resting her cheek on his chest.

"How soon?"

"Very soon."

"Good," he said, pulling her closer. "I want to tell my kids that we'll be seeing each other. And I should give Alicia a heads-up, too. I told her I'd let her know if I had a girlfriend."

"Okay," she said, relishing the idea of being Sam's girlfriend. It was juvenile, perhaps, but she couldn't help it.

"I gotta get going," he said then. "In case I hit traffic." And he kissed her, a long, lingering kiss that felt more like a hello than a good-bye.

Afterwards, he opened the car door for her. "Drive carefully," he said.

"I will," she promised, as she slid behind the wheel.

But as she started to pull out of the parking lot, he called after her, "*Poppy!* You forgot something." She stopped the car, and Sam brought her the urn with Sasquatch's ashes in it.

"Thank you. I can't believe I forgot this," she said.

"What are you going to do with it?" he asked, leaning on the car.

"Well," she said, setting the urn on the floor of the passenger side. "I was going to keep it on my bedside table, but now I'm not so sure. I might sprinkle the ashes near my grandmother's begonia garden out behind the cabin. That's where he used to like sunning himself in the late afternoon. He was happy there, I think."

He smiled. "That sounds like a good place for them, then."

CHAPTER 24

When Poppy pulled up to the cabin Win was sitting on the front porch steps waiting for her.

"Are you home already?" Poppy asked her, getting out of the car.

"I just got back," Win said.

"You didn't need the car, did you?" Poppy asked.

"No-oo," Win said, looking at Poppy a little strangely as she climbed up the steps.

"Well, I hope you weren't worried about me," Poppy said, sitting down next to her. "I would have called you, but I thought . . ." She stopped. "*What?*" she said. "Why are you staring at me that way?"

"No reason."

"*Win.*"

"*Okay.* I'm staring at you because I'm wondering where you were last night. I'm guessing it was in somebody's bed. And I don't think you were sleeping the whole time."

"Is it that obvious?" Poppy asked, astonished.

"To me it is."

"But, I mean, how can you tell?"

"Well, let's see. Your hair looks like you've been in a wind tunnel," Win said, and Poppy immediately reached up to touch it. It was completely disheveled. It hadn't even occurred to her to try to do anything with it before she'd left Sam's house. "*And* you're not wearing a bra," Win continued. Again, true. Poppy's bra was in her handbag. "*And . . .*" Win studied her. "This one's harder," she said. "I can't quite describe it. You look . . . *glowy*. You look totally relaxed, the way you would after a night of, well . . . great sex."

"And a morning, too," Poppy said, laughing. She was surprised by her own openness.

"I want details," Win said, playfully bumping her knee against Poppy's knee. "I mean it."

"Um, all right," she said. "Well, first of all, I was with Sam," she began.

"I *hope* you were with Sam," Win teased.

"And we met up at the Mosquito Inn—"

"What were you doing at that dive?"

"I didn't know it was a dive."

"Poppy, someone got *stabbed* there last spring."

"Oh. *That's* why the bartender wasn't that welcoming. I think he wanted me to leave, and I did, eventually, with a little help from Sam. But before that—"

"You know what?" Win said. "Skip this part. It's taking too long. Just cut to the bedroom. Or the kitchen, or the stairs, or wherever you were."

"Win," Poppy said, laughing. "We were in a bed."

"Okay, so you don't get any points for creativity there. But keep going."

"It was . . . it was amazing," Poppy said, shaking her head.

"*That's it?* That's *all* you're going to give me? You talk to me about your sex life, what, *once* in twenty-eight years, and you're going to use a single adjective to describe it?"

"I'm sorry," Poppy said, tucking a strand of her wayward hair behind one ear. "It's nothing personal. I just don't know *how* to talk about it. You know that."

"I know," Win said. "But can you learn?"

"I'll try." Poppy smiled. And then she yawned. "I promise, Win, I'll tell you more about it later. Right now, though, I'm starving."

"Come on inside, then. There's some leftover pasta in the fridge."

Poppy started to go, but something stopped her. She stood there for a moment, and then she sat back down on the step beside Win. She took a deep breath. She didn't want to do this, especially now. She was exhausted, for one thing. And it would completely dispel her blissful happiness, for another. But she knew it was necessary. Last night, she'd told Sam. And this afternoon, she would tell Win. She'd kept this secret from her sister long enough, and she understood now that in keeping it from her sister, she had somehow kept it from herself as well. But not anymore. Today was a new beginning for her, and she wanted it to start with the truth.

"Win, I need to tell you something," she said now.

"About last night?" Win smiled.

Poppy shook her head. "No. It's about something that happened . . . a long time ago."

"Poppy, you look so serious." Win frowned.

"That's because what I'm going to tell you *is* serious."

"You're scaring me."

"Don't be scared. It's going to be okay," Poppy said, slipping her arm around Win's shoulders, and she wondered, as she did so, if her reassurance was as much for herself as it was for Win.

Fifteen minutes later, Poppy and Win had moved inside the cabin and were sitting together on the living room couch. Poppy was crying. Win was not. Win's reaction, in fact, had been completely unexpected. Poppy had imagined telling her about the incident many times over the years, but it had never occurred to her that Win's response to hearing about it would be anything other than to comfort her and console her. To play, in short, the motherly role she'd always played with Poppy, even though she was a year younger than her. But there was nothing maternal about Win now. There was instead something almost . . . *homicidal* about her. Poppy had never seen her like this before. She was practically incandescent with anger.

"I'm going to kill him," she said, her body shaking all over. "I am. I swear to God, I'm going track him down and kill him."

"Win, calm down," Poppy said, though she was having difficulty getting her own emotions under control. "Just . . . calm down. This is not who you are. And I wouldn't have told you if I thought you were going to do something crazy. You're supposed to be the logical one, remember?"

"I'm not feeling very logical right now," Win said, still shaking. She must have seen the expression of alarm on Poppy's face, though, because she took a deep breath as if to steady herself and reached out to pat Poppy's back. "It's all right," she said, "I'm not going to kill him, obviously. I couldn't even kill the spider I found in the bathroom last night. I had to put it outside. But that doesn't mean I don't want to see that man punished for what he did to you."

Poppy shook her head. "It's too late," she said, wiping at a tear. "What do you mean?"

"He can't be charged with . . . with it," she said, stumbling over the place that word should have gone. "The statute of limitations is nine years in Minnesota. And even if it wasn't, Win, I don't have any evidence. I didn't go to a doctor and I didn't, you know, save my clothes or anything."

Win was silent for a moment, thinking this over, and when she set her jaw, and narrowed her eyes, Poppy knew she'd made a decision. "I know what we'll do," she said, in a voice that was eerily calm. Poppy almost shivered. She'd hate to be the person on the receiving end of that look, and that voice. "We'll track him down, and we'll punish him ourselves. I read an article about this once. A woman couldn't get justice through the legal system, so she took matters into her own hands. She spray painted 'rapist' on this man's car and then she handed out flyers to his neighbors, and—"

"Win, we don't know where he lives," Poppy interrupted. "We don't even know his *last name*."

"We'll hire a detective," Win said.

Poppy swiped, impatiently, at another tear. "And say . . . what? That all we can tell them about this man is his first name and an address where he lived thirteen years ago?"

"*And* we can tell them he's a photographer," Win reminded her. "You know what," she said, suddenly animated, "maybe I'll start looking for him myself, online. After all, how many professional photographers can there be named Rich?"

"Um, I don't know, *thousands*?" Poppy suggested, quirking an eyebrow. "And even if there weren't, Win, how would you be able to recognize him from an online photo? When I first brought him up, you barely remembered him."

"So . . . you'll help me."

Poppy shook her head. "No, I won't. Believe me, Win, I regret not going to the police. I do. And I know that because I didn't, he might have done this to someone else. I wish I had understood that then. *I really do.* I didn't, though, and I have to live with that. But finding him, or confronting him, or whatever, it's not going to change what happened. Besides, I don't want it ruling my life anymore. I'm going to try to get past it, and now, you're going to have to, too."

"I can't," Win said, helplessly, and she sagged back against the sofa cushions as though all of the anger had suddenly drained out of her, leaving nothing in its place. And then, much to Poppy's astonishment, Win began to cry. Not the hot, silent tears Poppy had been crying, but great, gasping sobs that racked her whole body. Poppy hadn't seen her cry this way since Kyle had died.

"Hey, Win. It's okay," Poppy said, gathering her into her arms. "I'm all right. I wasn't always, but I am now. I must be stronger than I seem," she added, patting Win on the back.

Win started to say something, but it was lost in a sob. She took a deep, shuddering breath, and tried again. "I'm sor-sor-sorry," she said, with great effort.

"Win, you don't have anything to be sorry for," Poppy said.

Win nodded an emphatic yes. "I'm sorry for cr-cr-crying," she said, sobbing harder. "This happened to you. Not me. I need to be st-st-strong for you."

"Oh, that," Poppy said, with a teary smile. "That's okay. I don't mind your crying. It's better than your being angry. I mean, you scared me for a minute there. I thought you were going to go all vigilante on me. You know, like Dirty Harry, only if Dirty Harry had been a middle school social studies teacher with no knowledge of firearms."

Win laughed, a little, through her tears, and Poppy took this as a good sign. She got up to get a box of tissues, and Win took it from her, gratefully.

"I'm still angry," Win said, when she was able to. She mopped at her tears with a tissue.

"Not at me, I hope," Poppy said.

"No, of course not. I'm angry at him, mostly. But I'm angry at Mom and Dad, too."

"Oh, God," Poppy said, "leave them out of this."

"Why should we?" Win said, stubbornly. "We always let them off the hook. If they'd been around more, if they'd known what was going on in our lives, this would never have happened. *Or*, if it had, you would have *told* them it had happened." Win paused, and blew her nose. "And I'm angry at myself," she continued, going to throw her tissue away.

Poppy started to protest, but Win, sitting back down on the couch, waved her off. "No, I am. I remember that time. How strange you were acting. You had nightmares, and you started sleeping all the time, after school and on weekends. I thought you were being . . . lazy. I knew something was wrong, though. *I knew it*. Why didn't I put all the pieces together?"

"Because you were a kid, Win," Poppy said, taking a tissue from the box, too. "Because you were fifteen years old, and, like me, you were basically on your own already. It wasn't your responsibility to take care of me. But you know what?" she said, putting her arms around Win again. "You *did* take care of me. In a lot of ways, you did. Afterwards, just having you there helped me, whether you knew it or not. I remember that night, after it happened, I kept taking showers. I was such a wreck. And you asked me if you could brush my hair, and you did. You brushed it, for a long time, and it made me feel better. It was a little thing, maybe, but in a way, it saved me. You did a lot of little things like that over the years, Win. A lot of big things, too."

"I don't know," Win said, doubtfully. "I just wish . . . I just wish you'd told me . . ."

Poppy sighed. She had known this would come. "Are you angry at me?"

"No. I'm not," Win said, shaking her head. "And I don't want you to think that, either. But I *am* trying to understand, Pops. We were so close then. *So close.* I would have done anything for you. I *still* would."

"I know," Poppy said, softly. She felt another tear running down her cheek now, and she caught it with the crumpled tissue in her hand. "I *know* that. The not telling you, though, it's hard to explain. I was ashamed, I guess. I thought it was my fault. First I'd gone into a stranger's apartment, and then, well, I'd done something else, too. I wasn't really sure *what* that something was, but I felt like I'd given him the wrong idea, or sent him the wrong signal. But it wasn't until years later that I realized *I* hadn't done anything wrong. That nothing I'd said or done that day could have given him the permission to do what he did to me.

"And then, then there was another thing, too," Poppy said, looking down at her lap and tearing the sodden piece of tissue in her hands into tiny shreds. "I honestly believed if I never told anyone, and I never thought about it, it would be like it never happened. I could just . . . make it go away. Stupid, I know," she added, crumpling up the slivers of tissue in her hands. "That was the plan, though. It was years before I realized how badly it was working."

"Oh, Pops," Win said, hugging her. "It's okay. You did all right. And things are going to be different for you now, aren't they?"

Poppy considered this. "Yes," she said, "I think so. Twelve hours ago, I hadn't told anybody this, and now I've told two people. And, Win? I feel different already. I do. And not just because of what happened between Sam and me," she added, flashing on an image of Sam in bed that morning. He'd been propped up on one elbow, and smiling at her, his hair tousled, his blue eyes heavy-lidded after their lovemaking.

"Will you promise me something?" Win asked.

"Of course."

"Promise me you'll tell someone else about this, too. Someone who knows more about it than I do, like a therapist or a support group leader or something. Because Pops, as much as I wish it were possible, one night of great sex isn't going to resolve all of this for you."

But it wasn't just *great sex,* Poppy almost said. And she thought about the tenderness with which she and Sam had made love to each other. And she thought about that moment, right before it was over, when they'd held on to each other, and it was as if they were falling, falling together, falling through space, but then they had landed, softly, right back in his bed. And she thought about afterwards, about the way he'd run his fingers down her back, over and over again, until she'd fallen asleep to this sensation. It was much more than just great sex. It was the beginning of something. But she didn't know how to put this into words for Win. Besides, her practical sister had a point.

"You're right, Win," she agreed. "I need to find someone—a professional, or a group—to talk to about what happened. I've put this off long enough. Right now, though, all I want to do is get something to eat and crawl into bed." The combination of sex, and crying, had been cathartic, Poppy thought. Cathartic but exhausting.

Win nodded, seemingly satisfied. But then Poppy saw a tremor go through her again. "You're still angry," she said.

"I am. At him. And I will be, for a long time. Maybe forever. What he did to you, Poppy, he took so much away from you . . ."

"He did," Poppy said simply. "But you know what? He's not taking anything more."

CHAPTER 25

With Labor Day weekend fast approaching, Sam and Linc were working late one night at Birch Tree Bait, inspecting the rental equipment. All of the canoes, kayaks, and life jackets needed to be checked for damage, and, if necessary, repaired before the third-busiest weekend of the summer arrived. Sam didn't mind the work. It was kind of nice, actually, to have a distraction, however small, to take his mind off Poppy. It wasn't that he didn't want to think about her. He did. *All* he wanted to do was think about her and the night they'd spent together that past weekend. But while he was fantasizing about her—the silky little dip at the small of her back, or the slightly sweet, slightly salty taste of her collarbone as he ran his tongue along it, or the sound of her breathing, soft and rhythmic, as she slept beside him— the demands of his life continued unabated. And those demands, which included running a business and raising three children, showed no signs of letting up.

"Look at this, Sam," Linc said in disbelief, holding up a life vest that had an enormous gouge in it. "Did somebody try to . . . *eat* it?" he asked.

Sam looked up from the kayak hull he was inspecting. "We can't repair that," he said. "Throw it away."

Linc sighed with disgust and tossed it aside. "*A little respect, people,*" he mumbled, picking up another life vest. "Oh, guess who I saw last night?" he asked Sam, testing its straps.

"Who?"

"Margot."

Sam grimaced, slightly. She hadn't been back to Birch Tree Bait since he'd told her he thought they should just be friends. "What was she doing?"

"She was at the Moccasin Bar, just . . . *full on* making out with this guy. I asked someone who he was and they said he was Margot's new boyfriend. He's a ranger. He trains injured falcons in his spare time. Apparently, she met him when he brought one of them over to the museum."

"Oh, right. Raptor Rapture," Sam said, moving on to the next kayak on the rack.

"What's that?"

"That's what she called the program the day he visited nature camp."

"Huh. Well, she certainly looked like she was in rapture last night," Linc commented.

"Good for her," Sam said. "I've always liked her. Maybe she'll feel like she can start getting her morning coffee here again."

"Sam, it was never the coffee she wanted," Linc said, looking over at him with a mischievous glint in his eye.

Sam ignored him, but a moment later Linc turned suddenly serious. "Can I talk to you?" he asked, coming over to him.

"Sure. What's up?"

"You know our end of summer fishing trip?"

"Uh-huh." The last two years, Sam and Linc had taken a day

off after Labor Day to fish the Kawishiwi River. They both looked forward to it. It was a full day affair, and afterwards—much to the delight of his kids—Sam invited everyone over to the cabin for a fried walleye dinner. "What about it?" Sam asked, pausing in his work.

"I was wondering if we could make it a little earlier this year," Linc said hesitantly. "Like tomorrow, for instance; we have a slow day."

"Why the hurry?" Sam asked. Linc looked away guiltily.

"You're quitting," Sam said. It was not a question. It was a statement. "So . . . the prodigal son is returning home?"

"Something like that," Linc mumbled. He looked like a kid who had to tell the teacher he hadn't done his homework, as opposed to, say, a young man who was about to return to the East Coast and take his place at the head of his family's financial services company.

"I knew this was coming," Sam said. "I just didn't know it was coming so soon."

"It's not soon enough for my parents," Linc said ruefully. "They think I've wasted the last few years of my life."

"I'll bet they do," Sam said, though, from his perspective, nothing could have been further from the truth. Not all the work Linc had done at Birch Tree Bait had been fascinating, of course, and that included inspecting life vests. And the pay, well, the pay hadn't been great, either, at least not compared to a job on Wall Street. But when Sam thought of all the time Linc had been able to spend outdoors, hunting and fishing, kayaking and mountain biking, snowmobiling and ATVing, he couldn't help but wonder if these last years wouldn't end up being the happiest of Linc's life. The ones he remembered long after he'd forgotten everything else.

"You're going to be hard to replace," Sam said. "You know that, don't you?"

"*Hard* to replace?" Linc objected, and he was back to his grinning, confident self. "I'd say *impossible* is more like it."

"You're probably right. Will you stay through Labor Day, though?"

"'Course. And Sam?"

"Yeah?"

"I'll miss this," he said, making a gesture that Sam knew was meant to include all of Birch Tree Bait, and all of the people who worked there or, like Byron, just spent time there. "But my parents are right. I can't spend the rest of my life living in a fishing lodge and cooking my meals on a hot plate. It's time," he added, though without any real conviction.

"I know," Sam said. "And I understand. Your parents are counting on you, and you don't want to let them down. I'd say that's pretty much the definition of being a good son."

"Maybe," Linc acknowledged. "But I haven't quite thrown in the towel yet. I made a deal with them. I told them I would try it for one year. If I hate it, I'm going to go back to school. Not for business, but for forestry management. And with their blessing, too, or so they say. Anyway, that was the best compromise I could come up with." He smiled, wryly.

"I think that's fair," Sam said, already missing Linc. And then, to lighten the mood, he said, "Let's take a break and grab a couple of beers. The rest of this stuff can wait."

Five minutes later, they were sitting at Birch Tree Bait's coffee counter drinking their beers. "I wonder if they serve Pabst Blue Ribbon at the country club," Linc said, sipping his tallboy. (They'd both agreed that, under the circumstances, a twelve-ouncer probably wasn't going to cut it tonight.)

"I doubt very much that they do," Sam said, taking a long drink from his PBR. "Linc," he said, putting his can down. "How the hell am I going to tell my boys you're leaving?"

"I don't know," Linc said, looking depressed. "I can't believe I'm not going to be seeing them every day. Seriously, they'll probably grow, like, six inches over the next year."

"At least," Sam said. "You're going to come back and visit, aren't you?"

"Oh, yeah. Every summer. I'm going to be able to use the family cabin again."

"Cabin?" Sam snorted, since this particular cabin was at least five thousand square feet.

"Anyway." Linc shrugged. "I'm glad we finished the tree house." The tree house in question was a summer-long project that Sam and Linc had been working on back at Sam's cabin. They'd hammered the last nail in the week before.

"You know," Sam said, "the boys are practically living in that tree now."

"I'm jealous," Linc said. And Sam knew he was only half joking. He asked Linc then whether or not he'd told Bryon and Justine about his leaving. He hadn't. And Linc was worried about how both of them would take it. They sipped their beers in silence for a little while, and Sam's mind drifted back to Poppy. It wasn't enough just to think about her, he realized, he wanted to talk about her, too.

"By the way," he said to Linc, "I've started seeing Poppy. It's still new. Very new."

Linc raised his eyebrows. "We wondered about that. But, after she left . . ."

"Yeah, I know. She gave me a call last weekend, though. She was in a bit of a bind. And then, well, one thing led to another . . ."

"It usually does." Linc grinned. "I think that's great, though, Sam, I really do." He took a slug of his beer. "You think she'll be hanging around here?"

"I hope so."

"'Cause some of the regulars were saying how they missed her," Linc said. "Apparently, when she was working here, some of them were making up excuses to come in so they could just, you know, look at her."

Sam frowned. "Linc, the way she looks . . . that's not all of who she is. That's not even the *biggest* part of who she is. She's . . ." He paused. *What was she?* Well, she was a lot of things, some of them contradictory. She was vulnerable, for instance, but, at the same time, she was tough, too. She'd been hurt, obviously, but she was also a survivor. And despite having had some darkness in her life, she carried with her a brightness, a lightness, and a sunniness that Sam felt irresistibly drawn to.

"Sam, it's okay, I get it," Linc said. "You think she's special. And obviously, she is. You wouldn't be with her if she wasn't. You know what?" he added. "I think this calls for a toast."

"What are we drinking to?"

"To . . . another great summer."

"I'll drink to that," Sam said, raising his can.

CHAPTER 26

When Sam opened the front door for Poppy the next morning, the sun—a smudge of tangerine on the horizon—was just beginning to rise, and a tattered white mist still hung over the lake. "Hey," he said, pulling her into his arms, and nuzzling her neck with his lips. "Thank you for coming so early."

"Mmm, you're welcome," she said, wrapping her arms around him. "Where are the kids?" She looked over his shoulder into the cabin.

"They're still asleep," he said, only letting go of her long enough to close the front door. "Which means I have you all to myself for a few minutes." He kissed her then, a kiss that was made no less pleasurable by the scratchiness of his razor-stubbled chin. She liked this Sam, she decided, this early morning Sam. This sleepy, unshaved, coffee scented Sam. She liked him *a lot*. Then again, she had yet to meet a side of Sam she *didn't* like a lot.

She sighed, happily, her body folded into his. But a moment later, as he was reaching his hands under her sweater and stroking her back, she came to her senses. "We should stop now," she said.

"You're right. We should stop while we still can." But he didn't stop. Instead, he asked, "Will you remind me why we ever got out of bed that day?"

"Because you have other responsibilities?" she suggested.

"Oh, right. Speaking of those . . . I better get going," he said, reluctantly. "Linc's waiting for me outside Birch Tree Bait." He reached for a sweatshirt hanging on one of the hooks beside the front door. He pulled it on and then pulled a fleece vest on over it. "By the way," he said, taking a baseball cap from another hook. "I might be out of network on the river today. I don't always get cell coverage there. And Alicia's in court. But I'll check my messages whenever I can, all right?"

She nodded, suddenly nervous. She hadn't felt this way the first time she'd babysat for him. Then it had seemed fun. Kind of like a lark. Now, it felt . . . weightier, more serious. After all, her role in Sam's children's lives was going to change, wasn't it? Or at least it would as soon as he told them about her. *About them*. She wondered if he'd done that yet, and she asked him now.

"No, I haven't told them yet," he said, as he tugged his baseball cap on. "I haven't had time. I mean, I *have* had time, but the time has never been right. I'm going to do it soon, though. I promise." He studied her more closely. "You're not . . . worried about today, are you? About being with them?"

She nodded, a little sheepishly. "I want them to like me," she admitted.

"Are you kidding? They *already* love you. Well, *Cassie* loves you. The boys will come to love you."

"I hope so," she said, but Sam didn't give her time to think any more about this now.

"I've got to get my gear in the truck," he said, giving her a good-bye kiss and opening the front door. "Make yourself comfortable here. The kids should sleep for a couple more hours, and then it's cereal for breakfast, and hot dogs for lunch. Cassie has some things planned for the two of you, and the boys should be fine with minimal supervision, especially now that I've confiscated the last of their firecrackers. They'll probably want to spend most of their time in the tree house, anyway."

"Can they go up there alone?"

Sam nodded. "You'll be able to see them from the kitchen window." He started to leave, then stopped. "Oh, by the way, I told Cassie she could watch *Frozen* again this morning," he said. "I think she's trying to reach the one-thousandth viewing mark." He started to leave and then came back to kiss her one more time. "You look beautiful in the morning," he said. And then he left.

Poppy closed the door behind him and watched through the window as he went into the garage, got a fishing rod and tackle box out, and put them in his truck. Then, he got into his pickup and, with a wave to her, drove away. She stood there for a moment, staring after him, missing him already. She looked at her watch, did a calculation. She would see him again in six hours, maybe less. So why did it feel like an eternity now? She sighed, amazed that, one by one, all of the clichés she'd ever heard about love were proving true. Had she really thought she would be exempt from all of that? she wondered now. Yes, she had. In some very fundamental way, she had. How wrong she had been. And how glad she was that she had been wrong, she thought with a little smile. It was scary. It was nerve racking. It was frustrating—how long would it be before they got to spend a whole night together again? But most of all, it was wonderful.

She left the window, finally. The house was so quiet that as she padded through the living room, she could hear her Converse sneakers squeaking on the hardwood floor. She went into the kitchen, poured herself a cup of coffee, and, when she opened the refrigerator in search of some half-and-half, ended up lingering there for a moment, curious about its contents. There was very little evidence of Sam in here, she decided. The half-and-half, a bottle of white wine, some spicy brown mustard—everything else in it was for children. Chocolate milk, juice boxes, squeezable tubes of yogurt, strawberry jelly, ketchup. She checked the freezer. More of the same. Chicken nuggets shaped like dinosaurs, Popsicles, frozen peas.

As she left the kitchen for the living room she mused that the whole house was like the refrigerator. The whole house was for children. Wherever she looked, there was evidence of children living here, children having fun here . . . children *being children* here. There, on the dining table, was an unfinished game of Chutes and Ladders. And there, on the couch, was a well worn copy of *The Phantom Tollbooth*. And there, in an open cupboard built into the wall beside the back door, were baseball mitts, bicycle helmets, and soccer balls.

Oddly enough, Poppy thought, settling into an oversized leather chair in the living room, she felt comfortable here. In fact, with the exception of Win's cabin, she felt more comfortable here than she'd ever felt anywhere else before. It was strange. Not only did she not have any children of her own, but, unlike Win, she hadn't spent a lot of time with other people's children, either. Well, unless she counted Cassie. But as she sipped her coffee and looked around the room, she knew she could be happy here. Knew she was, in fact, *already* happy here.

But she caught herself. *One step at a time, Poppy. You and Sam haven't even been on an official first date yet . . . It's a little soon to be moving in with him and his children.* So, to distract herself, she reached into the nearby magazine basket and tried to find something to read. *Ah, here's Sam,* she thought. *In this basket.* She sifted through copies of *Field & Stream, Outdoor Life,* and *Freshwater Fishing.* She ended up flipping through the first one and she was so relaxed as she did so that when she heard someone say, *"Poppy?"* right beside her elbow, she let out a little yelp.

"Cassie, oh my God. You scared me, honey. Where did you come from?"

"From upstairs," Cassie said seriously. "I'm sorry I scared you. My dad says I have quiet feet."

"You have *very* quiet feet," Poppy agreed, laughing. "But why are you up so early, honey?"

Cassie smiled. She still looked sleepy. She was wearing her nightgown, and an imprint of the covers was still on her cheek, but her gray-blue eyes were shining with excitement. "I woke up on purpose. My dad told me you were going to be here this morning, so last night, before I went to sleep, I told my brain to wake me up early, and it *did.* It listened."

"Well, that's because you have a very good brain." Poppy smiled.

"Can I . . . ?" Cassie asked, indicating her lap.

"Of course," Poppy said, and Cassie crawled into her lap and hugged her. Poppy hugged her back, shocked by how much she had missed her. Had she ever missed anyone this much? Only Win, she decided. Win and Sam and now Sasquatch.

"Poppy? I'm glad you're back," Cassie said.

"Thanks, kiddo," Poppy said, cheerfully, but Cassie's choice of words made something catch in her throat. She *was* back. And it felt *so right.* Still, she wondered what Sam had told Cassie, first about why Poppy would be missing from her life, and then about why she would be coming back into it. She made a mental note to ask him. In the meantime, she hoped Cassie didn't ask her any questions she didn't know how to answer.

"Poppy?" Cassie said.

"Uh-huh," Poppy said, suddenly nervous.

"Can we watch *Frozen*?"

The morning passed at a desultory but pleasant pace. When the twins finally came downstairs, looking as sleep-creased and adorable as their sister had looked, they had cereal at the kitchen table. Then, while Hunter and Tim played with their Legos, Cassie dragged Poppy up to her bedroom—a little island of femininity in an otherwise masculine sea—to play with her dolls. This time she introduced Poppy to all of them, except for one, whom she pointedly ignored.

"Is there something wrong with this one?" Poppy asked, finally, going to pick her up.

Cassie frowned, and then gave her head a little shake. But then she leaned over, cupped her hands around Poppy's ear, and whispered, "She doesn't like me."

"Why not?" Poppy whispered back.

"Because I don't play with her as much as the other dolls, and she's mad at me. Look," she whispered, "she's giving me a dirty look."

Poppy looked at the doll. She was smiling, placidly, at no one in particular. Still, Cassie's relationships with her dolls were obviously more complicated than Poppy had imagined.

"Cassie," she whispered back. "Why don't we just put her in a closet if she makes you uncomfortable?"

Cassie shook her head emphatically. "*No.* Then she'd *really* be mad at me."

Poppy, careful not to smile, put the doll back on the shelf.

But as the noon hour approached she insisted that the kids all get dressed, and, by the time they'd done this and Poppy had tried out three different hairstyles on Cassie, they were all hungry again. After lunch, there was a general debate about what to do next. Poppy had brought a bathing suit, fully expecting to take everyone swimming, but the day remained cool and overcast. Cassie wanted to stay inside and draw and the twins wanted to play in the tree house, a ten-foot-by-ten-foot pine structure nestled in the lower branches of a sprawling oak tree in the front yard.

"Your brothers don't talk very much, do they?" Poppy commented, sitting across the kitchen table from Cassie and watching out the window as Hunter climbed the last few rungs of the tree house ladder. She'd hardly been able to get a word out of either of them all morning.

"Mostly they talk to each other," Cassie said, concentrating on her drawing.

Poppy considered this. She knew next to nothing about little boys. "What do they like to do?" she asked. "I mean, other than play with Legos?"

Cassie hesitated. "Can you keep a secret?"

"I think so," Poppy said. God knew she'd kept one of her own long enough.

"Sometimes," Cassie said, "when my dad's not around, my brothers blow things up."

"Blow things up?"

Cassie nodded. "With firecrackers. I've seen them do it. Out in the woods. But I haven't told anyone. I'm not a tattletale," she added, proudly.

"What . . . what kinds of things do they blow up?" Poppy asked.

Cassie shrugged. "Plastic bottles. Apples. Stuff like that. Once they blew up a whole bag of flour. Everything in the forest around it was white afterwards."

"I'll bet it was," Poppy said. She looked out the kitchen window as Tim scrambled up the tree house ladder.

"My dad says my brothers are part monkey," Cassie commented, watching Tim. "I could go up there, too, if I wanted to. But I don't want to. I'm *not* part monkey," she added, seriously.

"Neither am I," Poppy said. "I'm afraid of heights."

"You are?"

Poppy nodded. "When I was younger, my sister used to try to get me to jump off the boathouse roof at my grandparents' cabin. I was too scared, though. But you know what?" she said. "It looked like fun. Sometimes, watching her, I was a little jealous."

"You were jealous of your sister?" Cassie asked, fascinated. She loved it when Poppy talked about her and Win.

"Oh, definitely," Poppy said, smiling.

Cassie smiled back at her, and then, shyly, edged her drawing across the table to her. "Do you think this is good enough to put on the refrigerator, Poppy?"

Poppy looked down at the drawing. It was of her and Cassie, both of them twirling batons. Cassie was wearing the costume she'd worn to the recital, and her hair was in a little bun, and Poppy was wearing the blouse and jeans she had on now, and her long hair was spilling across the page in a tidal wave of bright yellow magic marker.

"This is *definitely* good enough to put on the fridge," she told Cassie. "But do you think I could put it on *my* fridge? Just for a little while?"

"Really?" Cassie said, her eyes wide.

"Really. I mean, if that's all right with you."

"It is."

"Good," Poppy said. "It'll be on loan to me, then. Don't let me forget it when I go home."

Cassie started to say something, but Poppy didn't hear it, because at that moment Tim, who was coming down the tree house ladder, slipped and fell to the ground. He yelped. Poppy was on her feet and out the kitchen door before he could even pick himself up.

"You okay, Tim?" she asked, hurrying over to him. Inwardly she was relieved; he hadn't fallen far and he hadn't hit his head.

But when he stood up, he looked positively ill. His face was chalk white and he was holding his right arm at a funny angle. *Broken,* she thought, with a tremor of fear and the first knife-edge of panic. But she caught herself. *Get it together, now. You're the adult here.* And, miraculously, the fear and panic receded enough for her to take charge.

"Can you move it, honey?" she asked Tim, kneeling down so that she was at his level.

He tried, and winced. A tear slid down his cheek. "It hurts too much," he said. Hunter came down the ladder now and stood beside his brother. He looked scared. And soon Cassie, a little breathless, joined them.

Poppy looked at Tim's arm carefully, but she didn't touch it. She knew a little bit about injuries from all the football games she'd been to when she was a majorette, and she knew that this wasn't an open fracture, which was the most dangerous kind of break. Still, his arm was a little swollen, and he was in pain, probably in more pain than he was letting on. Clearly, he needed to go to the emergency room, but after a quick mental calculation, she decided it would be faster for her to drive him there than to wait for an ambulance. Butternut relied on a volunteer ambulance department, and it wasn't unheard of for people to wait up to half an hour for its members to reach the more remote cabins on the lake. Then, there was still the thirty-minute trip to the hospital.

"Tim," she said, making eye contact with him. "You need to get your arm checked out by a doctor, okay?"

He nodded, a tiny nod, and his freckles stood out dramatically against his chalky skin.

"I'm going to drive you to the hospital, and Cassie and Hunter are going to come with us, okay?"

He nodded again.

"All right, let's go," she said, amazed by how calm she was acting when, in fact, she was so nervous that her palms had started to sweat. "Cassie, put your shoes on," she added, giving the three of them a quick glance and noticing that Cassie was barefoot. "I'll be right back," she said, heading inside into the kitchen where she'd seen the emergency numbers and the kid's health insurance information tacked up on a bulletin board. She took these pieces of paper down. She had Sam's number in her phone, but she'd need to call Alicia, too, she realized. Then, she checked her handbag. Car keys, wallet, cell phone.

When she left the cabin, the three children were waiting on the front lawn, Cassie and Hunter looking serious, and Tim still looking ill. As they all got into the car, she called Sam and Alicia. Both calls went to voice mail, but Poppy left a brief message for each of them, relieved that she'd managed to keep the anxiety out of her voice. After the kids were buckled into the backseat— she managed to fasten Tim's seat belt without touching his arm—she got in and made it as far as the end of the driveway before she realized it was too quiet.

"Hey," she said, glancing back at them. "Do you three know '99 Bottles of Beer'?"

"We know it," Cassie said. "But my mom makes us sing '99 Bottles of Coke.'"

"All right, let's sing that," Poppy said, pulling out onto the main road. And they did. They sang it several times before they reached the hospital. And Poppy was careful to drive at the speed limit, and to come to a full stop at stop signs, and to signal before she changed lanes. She'd been to this hospital only once before, when she was eleven and Win had sprained her ankle, but luckily, she found it now without any difficulty.

She checked the backseat frequently. Cassie and Hunter were belting out the words to the song, and Tim, who sat between them, was singing them more softly. He was resting his head on Hunter's shoulder, and, on the other side of him, the side with the good arm, he was holding Cassie's little hand tightly in his own.

Later, as she sat in the waiting room with Hunter and Cassie, Poppy was relieved to see Win walking through the hospital's sliding glass doors.

"You're here," she said, as Win came over to them.

"Of course I'm here," Win said. "I browbeat Mary Jane into giving me a ride," she explained. "She's parking now."

"Thank God for Mary Jane," Poppy said. "Did you bring change?"

"I brought all the change I could scrounge up," Win said. She took a plastic bag full of quarters out of her purse and held it out to Hunter.

"Wow," he said, taking it from her. "That could buy a lot of stuff at the vending machines."

"It could," Poppy said, with as much sternness as she could muster. "But you and Cassie can only get two items each."

"That's it?" he said, his face falling. "But they have the best stuff here. There are, like, five machines."

Poppy wavered. He'd just said three whole sentences to her and she was so pleased that, for a moment, she considered telling him he could buy as many bags of gummy worms or packets of Goldfish or Oreos as Win's change would allow for. But she caught herself. "That's it, kiddo," she said.

Hunter and Cassie walked off in the direction of the vending machines, and Poppy sank, gratefully, into a chair. "Thanks for coming," she said. "What a time for me not to have any change or small bills."

"Don't mention it," Win said, sitting down beside her. "How're you holding up?"

"Me? I'm fine. I was so worried about Tim, though. Win, you should have seen him after it happened. His face was so white I could have counted every single one of his freckles if I'd wanted to."

"But he's okay now?"

"He's okay," Poppy said. She blew out a long breath. "I mean, the drive here was interminable. It felt like it took at least eight hours. Once we got here, though, everything started to happen really fast. Before I knew it, almost, he'd been admitted, and examined, and x-rayed. And, Win? He was *such* a trooper. Honestly, I would have cried like a baby if I'd broken my arm at his age. But he was absolutely stoic. And Hunter and Cassie," she said, shaking her head, "they were *so* good to him. They really took care of him."

"That's what siblings are for," Win reminded her. "But I take it his dad's with him now?"

"He is. He got here just in time to be with Tim while he's having his cast put on. It's going to be electric green," she added, with amusement. "Because why would anyone want a white cast when they could have an electric green cast?"

Win smiled. "Did you talk to Sam's wife?"

"Her name is Alicia. Yes, she called me back as soon as she got out of court. Fortunately, by then the doctor had told us it was a fractured radius. It helps, I think, if you can put a name to something. It makes it seem less scary." They were quiet for a moment. "Oh, I should have asked Hunter and Cassie to get something for Tim," Poppy said, looking in the direction of the vending machines. "He's going to be hungry by the time he's done here."

"I'm sure they'll have some quarters left when they get back." Win smiled. "And Pops? You're a natural. You're already thinking like a mom."

"I don't know about that," Poppy said. "I just did what anyone else would have done."

"I don't know. I think some people might have freaked out."

"Honestly, Win, I *wanted* to freak out," Poppy admitted. "But I told myself I had to hold it together, for Tim's sake, anyway, and for Cassie's and Hunter's, too. They all kept looking at me like I actually knew what I was doing."

"You *did* know what you were doing."

Poppy shook her head. "No. I was faking it."

Win laughed. "Poppy, *everyone* starts out by faking it. It's the first rule of being an adult. It's only when you've faked it for long enough that you actually start to believe it yourself."

CHAPTER 27

"All right, so, you're probably wondering why I've called this meeting," Sam said that night, looking around the kitchen table at Cassie, Hunter, and Tim. After they'd gotten back from the hospital, Sam had given them their dinner and supervised their showers—Tim with a plastic bag over his cast—and now the three of them were at their cleanest, and, frankly, their most lovable, their wet hair neatly combed, their clean pajamas still smelling faintly of laundry detergent.

"I know what this is about," Cassie said, squirming with excitement. "You want to tell us Poppy's your girlfriend, don't you?"

Sam stared at her. *How did she know that?* "We'll get to Poppy and me in a minute," he said. "Right now, I want you all to know how proud I am of you. Tim, you were very brave this afternoon, and Hunter and Cassie, you were, too. I can't ask any more of the three of you than that you support each other in a crisis, and that you stay strong, together, the way you did today. As a parent, I hope the worst thing that ever happens to any of you is a broken arm, but if that's not the case, if life has more in store for you than that, then at least I know you'll always be there for each other."

Sam looked around the table. The three of them stared back at him, solemnly. They weren't used to him being this serious, Sam knew, and he had to smile when Tim raised his hand—his *left* hand—to ask a question.

"Tim, that's not necessary. What is it?"

"Uh, can I still go in the tree house?"

"Not with that cast on, you can't."

"But . . . after?"

Sam sighed. "I think so. I'll need to talk to your mom about that first. For now, I'd like you to keep both feet on the ground. Do you think that's possible?"

Tim nodded.

"*Now* can we talk about Poppy?" Cassie asked, squirming again.

"Yes," Sam said. "We can." Having said that, though, he was stumped. *Damn it,* why hadn't he bought a book about how to do this? He knew such a book existed. There was a whole cottage industry of books written for divorced parents. The one he needed right now probably had a reassuringly upbeat title like *When Dad's Ready to Date Again*, or something like that. But once more, Cassie got ahead of him.

"Are you and Poppy going to get married?" she asked.

"*Whoa*, Cassie. That is *not* why I called this meeting," he said. "Poppy and I are going to be friends. We're going to be . . . *special* friends. I'm going to be spending time with her. And, because we're a family, I won't be the only one spending time with her. You'll be spending time with her, too. So, I wanted to know what you think of that." He looked around at the three of them. Cassie was pleased, but the twins, as usual, were more circumspect.

"Is she going to be eating dinner here with us?" Hunter asked, finally.

"Sometimes. If she's not too picky, that is," he added, with a smile. "We'll have to explain to her about chicken nuggets being on the menu five nights a week."

"No, but, I mean, are we going to have to chew with our mouths closed and everything?" Hunter pressed.

"Oh, I see," Sam said. "You're asking if she's going to enforce table manners the way your mom does." This was an area of family life in which Sam had been woefully inadequate.

"Uh-huh," Hunter said.

"Well, let's assume, for now, that your mom and I will be responsible for that. And, by the way, Hunter, I am going to be stepping up my game here. Using a napkin at mealtime will no longer be optional. Is that understood?"

Hunter nodded warily.

"Any more questions?" Sam asked, looking around again.

"What about Mom?" Tim asked.

"What about her?" Sam answered, casually, though he felt suddenly tense. He'd heard about children of divorce fantasizing about their parents getting back together again. Was Tim thinking that Sam dating Poppy would rule that out? As it turned out, though, his son was worried about something a little less complicated.

"You'll have someone," Tim said now, "but what about Mom? Won't she be lonely?"

Sam shook his head, then reached out and ruffled Tim's damp hair. He wondered if perhaps his breaking his arm had given him a new sense of empathy. But no, Sam thought. It had always been there. He just didn't keep it in view for everyone to see. "Your mom won't be lonely, Tim," Sam said, "because she has a special friend of her own. I'll let her tell you about him, but I know he must be a really good guy, because your mom wouldn't like him if he wasn't. But you can judge for yourself. I think she'd like you to meet him, sometime soon, so that'll be fun, right?" But Tim looked unsure about whether this would be fun or not.

Sam sighed. He and Alicia had discussed this recently, when he'd told her about Poppy. It had been a strange conversation. How odd to share this happiness with someone else, he thought, when that someone else had been the last person to make you this happy. It was all right, though. They would adjust to this new phase of their relationship, just as they had adjusted to all the other phases. After all, they had a huge incentive to work together: their three amazing children.

"In the meantime, though," Sam said, "even with our new friends, your mom and I are going to keep talking to each other. And we're going to be talking about *everything*. Bedtime. And homework. And tree houses. You name it. That's not going to change. All right, anything else?" He looked around. Now it was Cassie's turn to seem pensive.

"Dad, you know how Mom reads *Mrs. Piggle-Wiggle* to me?" she asked.

"Yes."

"Will Poppy read it to me, too? Because those books are at Mom's, and if I bring them here, I might forget to take them back, and then Mom couldn't read them to me. And, plus, what if we get all mixed about where we are in the book? Mom always keeps a bookmark in it that has a butterfly on it, but what if Poppy doesn't have a bookmark with a butterfly on it, or even any bookmark at all?"

Sam looked longingly at one of the kitchen cupboards. There

was a really good bottle of red wine in it he'd love to open right about now. But instead he explained to Cassie—patiently, he hoped—that reading *Mrs. Piggle-Wiggle* was something she and her mother would do together. She and Poppy, he hoped, would do other things together.

"Like twirling?" Cassie suggested, brightly.

"Like twirling," Sam agreed, and, sensing a general sleepiness setting in around the table, he announced that it was bedtime. "Tim, your mom wants you to call her before you go to sleep," he reminded him. And then he hugged and kissed them all good night. Recently, Hunter and Tim had been something less than active participants in these nightly hugs. They didn't so much hug Sam as allow Sam to hug them. Tonight, though, was different. There was a real hug from Hunter, and a real, though one-armed, hug from Tim.

Cassie, though, found an excuse to linger at the kitchen table even after the boys had gone. "Dad, did you know that the last time I went to Janelle's her mom helped us make friendship bracelets and I made one for Poppy?" she asked, climbing into Sam's lap.

"I didn't know that," Sam said, as she snuggled against him.

"I'm going to give it to her the next time I see her," she said, hugging him. "I like her, Daddy. I like her *so* much."

"Me, too, sweetie," Sam said, hugging her back. "Me, too."

CHAPTER 28

H mm, a little to the left, I think," Poppy said, frowning at the photograph Win had just hung on the wall in the cabin's hallway.

Win nudged the frame, slightly to the left, and then stood back. "How's that?"

Poppy studied it again. "Now just a tiny bit to the right."

Win made an almost infinitesimal adjustment to its frame. "What do you think?" she asked, stepping aside.

"I think it is . . . perfect," Poppy said, with a satisfied smile. "And I'm so glad you chose that picture."

"Are you?" Win said, looking at the photograph in question. It was of Kyle sitting on the living room couch in their old apartment. (She'd already hung two smaller ones of the two of them together on this same wall.) "I don't know," she mused of this larger one of Kyle. "I sort of feel like I should have chosen a picture of him doing something important."

"Important like what?" Poppy asked.

"Important like . . . summiting a mountain or something."

"I wasn't aware that Kyle was a mountain climber," Poppy said, with a trace of amusement.

"No, he wasn't," Win said. "But he isn't *doing* anything in this picture. He's just kind of *being*."

"That's true," Poppy said. "But that's life, isn't it? Most of us aren't doing something important every second of every day. Most of us are just kind of . . . going about our lives. And if you were Kyle, well, then that was a good life, wasn't it?"

Win nodded, thoughtfully, and made another minor adjustment to the frame. And then she smiled, because Poppy had reminded her of what she'd liked about this picture in the first place. She'd taken it of Kyle on a winter afternoon, somewhere between the two of them reading the Sunday paper and the two of them watching the Vikings game. It had been a lazy, slow, relaxed afternoon, an ordinary afternoon. But its ordinariness, she decided, was part of what she'd liked about it. And then there was Kyle's smile. She hadn't told him she was taking his picture. She'd just said, *Kyle,* and he'd looked up and smiled at her. That smile was the other part of what she liked about the picture. Because that smile was for her.

"Are you happy with it?" Poppy asked, taking Win by the hand and leading her into the living room.

"I am. But I'm exhausted, too," she said, flopping down on the couch. "Who knew moving a few boxes could be so much work?"

"It was more than a few," Poppy pointed out, sitting down next to Win. Earlier in the evening, the two of them had carried all of the boxes Win had saved from her marriage to Kyle up to the cabin's attic. They would be fine there, Poppy had assured her. And they weren't going anywhere, either. They'd never be more than an attic hatch and a pull-down stair away. What was impor-

tant, she'd told Win, was to do something—even if that something was only symbolic—to mark the end of that chapter in
her life. When they'd come back downstairs, they'd hung up the
photograph that she'd picked up at the framers yesterday. "See?"
Poppy had said. "You're not putting him away. You're not forgetting about him. He'll still be a part of your life. He'll *always* be a
part of your life. You're just making room for other things to be a
part of your life, too."

But as Win lounged on the couch now, she wondered what
those other things in her life would be. There was work, of course;
school had started and she was already learning the names of new
students, preparing for back-to-school night, and designing lesson
plans. Suddenly, though, it didn't seem like enough. Maybe, in
truth, it had never been enough. It had just taken Everett coming
into her life, and then leaving it again, to make her understand this.

"Win, just call him," Poppy said, with that uncanny ability she
had to read her mind.

Win straightened up, abruptly. "I can't."

"Why not?"

"Because I already left him a voice mail, and he didn't re-
spond."

This was true. A week ago, after much agonizing about what
she would say to Everett, and much consulting with Poppy over
it, Win had finally called him to apologize. When he hadn't answered, though, she'd left a stumbling voice mail instead.

"Look, if this is about your pride, forget it," Poppy said. "It's
not worth it. Pick up the phone and call him. And if he doesn't
answer, call him again. And if he doesn't answer that, we'll drive
up to the city and stake out the coffeehouse he hangs out at."

"You mean we'll stalk him?" Win clarified.

"Yes. But in a totally nonthreatening way."

Win laughed. "Pops, he already thinks I'm crazy. If we do that, he'll think I'm even crazier. I'm just going to let things . . . run their course," she said, with a shrug. She noticed then that Poppy had a smudge on her cheek, probably from their trips up to the attic. "You have a little dirt on your face," she said, reaching over now and rubbing it away with her thumb. "There," she said, when it was gone.

Poppy smiled at her. "You are going to make a good mother someday, Win."

"I don't know about that," Win murmured. "I didn't have a very good role model, did I?"

"Are you kidding? You don't need a role model. You were born to be a mom," Poppy said, loyally. "Look how responsible you feel for everyone in your life."

"Oh, that reminds me," Win said, jumping up. "I have something for you." She went over to the mantelpiece, took down an envelope, and handed it to Poppy. Poppy, curious, opened it up and slid out a sheet of paper.

"What is this?" She frowned.

"It's the deed to the cabin. I've had it put in both of our names. Now, before you say anything—" Win began, but Poppy interrupted her.

"Win, no. It's your cabin. Dad gave it to you—" she started.

"Would you just *listen*?" Win said. "It wasn't Dad's decision to make. And if Grandpa and Grandma had known he was going to do it, they wouldn't have liked it. They would have wanted us both to have it."

"Win, that's really nice but—"

"It's not meant to be *nice*. It's meant to be *fair*."

"It *wouldn't* be fair, though. Because I haven't helped you pay the taxes, or any of the other things you told me about, either. You know, the tree removal and stuff like that."

Win blushed, remembering their argument. "Don't worry about that. After all, I have been living here. I should have been paying for those things."

"And what about the money I already owe you for this summer? For groceries and gas?"

"Let's figure that out later," Win said. "Right now, you need to think about what you want to do next. I mean, do you want to keep living here with me? Or do you want me to buy you out? Or . . . do you need more time to mull things over?"

"I, I think I need more time. But I have figured out a couple of things," Poppy said. "I want to stay in Butternut. I want to be with Sam. And I want to go back to school."

"College?" Win said, surprised. Poppy nodded. Win considered this. She had spent years urging Poppy to get her degree, but now she was more circumspect. Everything she'd thought she'd known about Poppy before she'd had to revisit, and she couldn't pretend anymore that she had all the answers. Still, she could encourage her.

"Pops, all of those things sound good. And the rest of it"—she shrugged—"the rest of it will fall into place."

Poppy looked down at the deed again, and then looked back up at Win. "I've been thinking about something else, actually. About trying to help other women who've been . . ." Her voice trailed off.

Win waited. She hadn't heard Poppy say that word yet.

"Other women who've been raped or sexually assaulted," Poppy finished quietly.

Win felt her eyes glaze over with tears, but she kept her voice steady as she said, "I think you'd be good at that, Pops. I really do."

"You think so?" Poppy said, pleased. She'd been to a support group in Duluth the week before, and while she'd hadn't said much about herself—that, she hoped, would come in time— she'd been impressed by how sensitive and skillful the group's facilitator had been.

"Absolutely," Win said. "I think you could really make a difference in people's lives." And she thought about what her grandfather used to say about Poppy, that she was more than just a pretty face. Yes, she was. Even if some people couldn't see past it, she was still *so* much more than just a pretty face.

Now Poppy folded up the deed, put it back in the envelope, and set it on the coffee table in front of them. "Thank you," she said to Win, indicating the lease. "And thank you for this summer." And now, when Win tried to interrupt her, to wave her thanks away, it was Poppy's turn to shush her.

"No, seriously," she said. "You took me in when my life was falling apart. You gave me a place to live. And you supported me, even when you didn't always want to," she added, with a smile. But then she turned serious. "I never could have gotten through all this stuff—Sasquatch, the breakup with Sam, and dealing with everything else—if it hadn't been for you." She reached to hug Win and Win felt her eyes mist up again. She was determined not to cry, though. There had been enough crying for one summer.

Dusk was falling outside the living room windows now, and a new chilliness, a harbinger of fall, was setting in. It was Win who finally spoke. "Pops, aren't you supposed to meet Sam soon?" she asked, interrupting their hug.

Poppy checked her watch. "Pretty soon." Sam was dropping off his kids with their mom, and afterwards, he'd asked Poppy to come over to his cabin. "Are you okay here by yourself, though?" she asked Win.

"*Yes,* I'm fine. And don't come back here on my account, either. Not when you two could be in bed together."

Poppy's face turned pink.

"You are so cute when you blush," Win said, hugging her again.

After Poppy left, Win found herself in the kitchen, surveying the contents of the top utensil drawer. It was out of order; a nutmeg grinder had, strangely enough, migrated up from the bottom drawer where she'd put it earlier in the summer. "*Poppy,*" she murmured. And then she smiled. *The girl did have a sense of humor.* She started to remove the offending item, and then stopped. *Nope,* she was not going to do this. She dropped it casually back into the drawer. *Life is too short to spend your time rearranging utensil drawers, or linen closets, for that matter.* And here she had to give Poppy credit again. Because among the other things she'd done this summer was to nudge Win away from her too zealous reverence for order.

But what to do on this chilly night? she wondered, closing the drawer. What she *really* wanted to do was text Everett. *But you haven't heard back from him,* her rational voice said. She ignored it, though, and texted him anyway.

Win: *I miss our nights on the boathouse roof.*

And before she had even put her phone down on the kitchen counter, it vibrated.

Everett: *I miss them too.*

She started to text back, then called him instead.

Four hours later, she was sitting on the front porch steps, wrapped in a wooly sweater, when he drove up.

"It's too late to watch the sunset," she said shyly, as he sat down beside her, "but we could watch infomercials."

"Or not," he said, smiling his sleepy-eyed smile at her.

"I thought you hated me when you didn't answer my voice mail," she blurted out. Then, self-consciously, she pulled her sweater closer around her, and pretended to study the branches of the nearby birch trees, which were glowing brightly in the light from the front porch.

"Win, I didn't hate you. I could *never* hate you. I just didn't know what to do."

"But you were mad at me," she said, stealing a look at him.

"No, I wasn't. Okay, I was. But by the time I got home that day, I'd cooled off. I wasn't angry anymore. I was . . . I was sad for you. How could you think I was coming to see you as part of some plot to get closer to your sister? And how could you not know what an amazing person you are in your own right?" She felt her heart tighten in her chest.

"I don't know . . ." she said. "I lost track of myself, I guess. Does that ever happen to you? Do you ever get caught up in the past, in your childhood, and forget you're not back there anymore? That you're not that person anymore? That you're actually years and miles away from those days?"

"Yes. It happens to me every time I go back to Nebraska. Especially since I sleep in a bedroom there that still has my old model airplanes hanging in it."

He leaned forward and kissed her, putting his hand gently but firmly on her back. This kiss was different from that first awkward kiss on the porch before Mary Jane's wedding. This kiss was more self-assured, *sexy,* even. This was a part of him she didn't yet know. *Hmmm, there was going to be a lot to discover about Everett.*

He pulled away. "I forgot. I brought you something," he said. He brushed his hair out of his eyes. *Oh,* she'd missed that. She'd missed *him,* even more than she'd realized.

"What is it?" she asked as he pulled a narrow rectangular box and a book of matches out of his jacket pocket.

"You said you didn't like fireworks, but you did like sparklers." He took one out of the box and handed it to her and then he held a match to it and it crackled to life, throwing sparks in a small but beautiful frenzy.

"Everett?" she asked him, after she'd watched the sparkler burn down with a childish delight. "Can we start over again, you and me?"

He smiled at her. "I think we just did."

CHAPTER 29

Y ou might want to save some of those for our paying
customers," Sam said, amused, as he glanced over at Poppy.
She smiled and bit into another strand of licorice. She was sitting
on the counter at Birch Tree Bait, her legs dangling over the
side, watching Sam cash out the register. It was a Friday night in
mid-September, and he'd dropped the kids off with Alicia that
evening. And now . . . now he and Poppy had the whole weekend
together. Thinking about this, Sam emptied out the cash drawer
a little faster.

"You should see them together, Sam," Poppy said, returning
to the conversation they'd been having about Win and Everett.
"They're taking it slowly. And it's adorable."

Sam looked up. "So . . . it's happily ever after?"

"I hope so," Poppy said, and, impulsively, she held her arms
out to him. "Come here," she said. Sam stopped what he was
doing and came into her arms. He pulled her against him, and
she wrapped her legs around his waist and kissed him, her mouth
sweet with the taste of Red Vines, a taste he was really beginning
to love.

"Have you given any thought to my offer?" he asked finally, kissing her neck instead of her lips. Poppy was planning on applying for the spring semester at University of Minnesota Duluth, but right now she was looking for a job. And Sam wanted her to work with him at Birch Tree Bait again.

"I've thought about it," she said. "But do you think it's a good idea?"

"Seeing you more? I think it's a *great* idea."

"No, I mean, I thought you didn't want to have a relationship with someone who worked for you."

"This is different. I wouldn't be dating one of my employees. I'd be hiring my girlfriend."

"'Girlfriend,'" she mused. "I like the way that sounds."

"Do you?" he asked, pulling her closer. "I'm glad. But Poppy, what are we still doing here?" He looked at his watch. "We only have . . . forty-three and a half hours left before I pick up the kids."

She laughed, and ran her hands up under his work shirt. "I think you said something about closing out the cash register," she reminded him.

"I did, didn't I?" he said, leaving her reluctantly and going back to his work. But while he was doing this, Poppy was looking around the store, speculatively.

"Sam," she said, hopping down from the counter, "I think I would like to work here, at least until school starts. "In fact"—she grabbed his hand and pulled him out from behind the register—"I think I might have a few suggestions." She led him over to a nearby wall. "What color is this?" she asked, tapping on it.

"It's green."

"It's *dark* green."

"It's Benjamin Moore's 'Balsam' if you want to get technical about it," he said. "And I thought, under the circumstances, it was appropriate." He nodded in the direction of the windows. "You've noticed the pine trees out there, haven't you? All one million acres of them?"

"Yes, I've noticed them. But this color makes it so much darker in here than it needs to be. How about a nice, bright, sunny yellow?"

"Maybe," Sam said, looking around.

"And the coffee counter," she continued, pulling him over to it. "Right now it's just Byron and his cronies who hang out here, but if you painted it a nice color, and put in more comfortable stools, and added a tea selection—herbal would be nice—maybe it wouldn't be only men who wanted to spend time here."

"That's probably true," Sam said, surveying the area. But she was already dragging him down one of the grocery aisles. And Sam laughed, because he could see it in her eyes. The excitement. He knew that feeling. He'd felt it the first time he'd come here as a prospective buyer. He was barely through the door of the old place when, in his mind, he was already knocking down walls, tearing up floors, and putting in windows. Poppy's plans seemed a little less dramatic, but she was no less determined about them.

She stopped in the produce section, if you could actually *call* it a section. It was more of a produce *corner,* and a rather limited one at that.

"I know what you're going to say," Sam said, quickly, trying to preempt her. "But most of the renters stock up on their produce at the IGA in town. If they forget something, like an onion, or they want a few more apples, or a bunch of bananas, then we've got this."

In response, Poppy picked up a shrink-wrapped head of iceberg lettuce, and held it out to him, without comment. There was no denying that it looked sad.

"I know, I know," he said. "But shelf space here will always be limited."

"This from a man who stocks *twelve* different kinds of beer?"

He sighed. Produce was not his forte. If he hadn't promised Alicia that he would feed their children fresh fruits and vegetables daily, everything that they ate would probably have come out of a bag, or a box, or a can.

"We could probably get another kind of lettuce," he conceded to Poppy.

"You think so?" she asked, teasingly, putting the iceberg lettuce back on the shelf. She reached out and slid her fingers into the front waistband of his jeans, and pulled him against her. He groaned a little, deep in his throat. It wouldn't take much more encouragement for him than this to make love to her right here, right now. "Do you think you can get some baby romaine, maybe?" she asked, playfully.

"I think so, but this isn't Whole Foods," he mumbled distractedly. He ran his fingers through her hair, and then buried his face in it, and breathed deeply. It was sweet and fresh, like her.

"So . . . you're never going to have arugula, is that what you're trying to tell me?"

"No arugula," he agreed. "The other things, though, those would be nice," he admitted.

"Sam?" she asked, snuggling closer.

"Yes?"

"Can we go back to your place now?"

CHAPTER 30

By early October the trees on Butternut Lake were already aflame with color, oranges and reds and burnished yellows that on this crisp afternoon contrasted dramatically with the brilliant blue of the water. In another month, these leaves would be gathered in piles in yards or swirling along Butternut Lake drive on windy afternoons. But for now, Poppy thought, her bare feet planted firmly at the edge of the boathouse roof, they were still gloriously beautiful.

"Are you ready?" Win asked, standing beside her. Poppy shivered in the chilly air. An hour ago, in the warmth of the cabin, over a cup of hot chocolate, she'd mentioned to Win that she'd always wanted to jump off the boathouse roof. She'd watched Win do this many times when they were kids, and while it had looked like fun, she'd always been too afraid to join her. That was all the encouragement Win had needed. She'd insisted they change into their bathing suits and then she'd dragged a by-then nervous Poppy out here.

"Okay, Pops, let's do it now, right now," she said, reaching for her hand. "Before the snows come," she added teasingly.

"I'm scared," Poppy admitted, looking down at the water twelve feet below them.

"That's no reason not to do it," Win said.

Poppy gripped her hand tighter and closed her eyes.

"Ready? One, two, three," Win counted down. Right before they jumped, Poppy opened her eyes. And she was so glad she did. Because in that moment, the moment before they hit the water, there was only the rush of air, the thrill of freedom, and the dazzling blue of the sky above them and the water below them.

About the author

2 Meet Mary McNear

About the book

3 Reading Group Discussion
  Questions

Insights,
Interviews
& More . . .

Read on

5 Have You Read?
  More from Mary McNear

Meet Mary McNear

Photo by Amelia Kennedy

MARY McNEAR, *New York Times* and *USA Today* bestselling author of the Butternut Lake series, writes in a local doughnut shop, where she sips Diet Pepsi, observes the hubbub of neighborhood life, and tries to resist the constant temptation of freshly made doughnuts. Mary bases her novels on a lifetime of summers spent in a small town on a lake in the northern Midwest. She lives in San Francisco with her family. ◠

Reading Group Discussion Questions

1. Poppy returns to Butternut Lake because she has nowhere else to go, but also because it's the one place she truly considers home. Is there a place of your heart that you truly consider "home," even if it is somewhere you haven't been in years?

2. Win and Poppy react to their upbringing in very different ways. Poppy is a free spirit. Win tries to control her world. Do you think their coping mechanisms have worked for them? And is it possible that Poppy is also, in her own way, just as much a control freak as her sister?

3. Win protests that three years isn't long enough to get over her husband's death. Do you think it's been long? Is there ever really an expiration date on grief?

4. Do you think Win actually is allergic to Sasquatch? Or is she just upset that his presence is an interruption to her routine?

5. Sam and Alicia seem to have found a very sensible way to deal with their divorce. Do you feel Sam may have been selfish in his desire to move back to Butternut? Was Alicia at all at fault for choosing to stay in the city? Or did they simply grow apart? ▶

Reading Group Discussion Questions
(continued)

6. Justine is a very mysterious character. What do you think is truly going on in her life?

7. Sasquatch was the one constant in Poppy's life. Do you believe animals can sense the pain in their human companions? Is it at all possible that he knew the time had come when he could let go?

8. Sisters are always fascinating as characters in books, movies, and on television. Why do you think the sister-sister relationship is such an intriguing one? Do you know sisters like Win and Poppy—two women raised by the same people who are wildly different individuals?

9. Rich the photographer is not brought to justice, and it's possible he never will be. Have you ever had to face a situation where you needed to accept that a perfect outcome may not be possible?

10. Do you think it was fair that Win and Poppy's grandparents left the cabin solely to Win? ∽

Have You Read?
More from
Mary McNear

For more books by Mary McNear
check out

MOONLIGHT ON BUTTERNUT LAKE

New York Times and *USA Today* bestselling author Mary McNear takes us home to Butternut Lake, where the townspeople are sure to look after anyone they consider their own. . . .

Mila Jones has fled the big city seeking a safe haven on the serene shores of Butternut Lake. Her position looking after Reid Ford is more than a job. It's a chance at a fresh start. And although her sullen patient does everything he can to make her quit, Mila refuses to give up on him.

But Mila isn't the only one needing refuge. Haunted by the car accident that nearly killed him, Reid has hidden himself away. He wants Mila to just leave him alone. And he wishes the whole town would stop looking after his well-being.

Against all odds, Mila slowly draws Reid out. Soon they form a tentative, yet increasingly deeper bond with each other, as well as becoming part of the day-to-day fabric of Butternut Lake itself. But the world has a way of intruding, even in such a serene place . . . and when Mila's violent husband forces his way back into her life, she and Reid are compelled to face down the past.

Have You Read? *(continued)*

**BUTTERNUT LAKE:
THE NIGHT BEFORE CHRISTMAS**

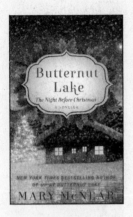

You're invited to Christmas at Butternut Lake! *New York Times* and *USA Today* bestselling author Mary McNear, author of *Up at Butternut Lake* and *Butternut Summer*, takes us home for the holidays in this joyful e-original novella.

Butternut Lake is so beautiful at Christmas—from the delightfully decorated shops to the cozy homes with their twinkling lights outside to the lake itself. And this year so much is happening!

A wedding: Caroline meticulously plans her perfect Christmastime dream wedding to Jack, remarrying him after many years apart.

A baby: Allie and Walker are expecting the best Christmas gift of all—their first baby together.

A reunion: Daisy, Caroline and Jack's daughter, is returning home after a long semester away at college.

But what's Christmas without complications? Walker smothers Allie with worry; Daisy pines for her true love, Will, away in the army. And then the unthinkable happens—and Caroline's wedding plans are ruined.

And just when it seems all is lost, the people of Butternut Lake come together to give their friends the greatest gifts of all. . . .

Every summer on Butternut Lake the
tourists arrive, the shops open, and
the waves lap its tree-lined shores, just
as they have for years. But this season
everything changes for one mother and
daughter who've always called the lake
home. . . .

Caroline's life is turned upside down
the moment her ex-husband, Jack, strides
through the door of her coffee shop. He
seems changed—stronger, steadier, and
determined to make amends with
Caroline and their daughter, Daisy.
Is he really different, or is he the same
irresistibly charming but irresponsible
man he was when he left Butternut Lake
eighteen years ago? Caroline, whose life
is stuck on pause as her finances are
going down the tubes, is tempted to
let him back into her life . . . but would
it be wise?

For Caroline's daughter, Daisy, the
summer is filled with surprises. Home
from college, she's reunited with the
father she adores—but hardly knows—
and swept away by her first true love.
But Will isn't what her mother wants
for her—all Caroline can see is that he's
the kind of sexy "bad boy" Daisy should
stay away from.

As the long, lazy days of summer pass,
Daisy and Caroline come to realize that
even if Butternut Lake doesn't change,
life does. . . .

UP AT BUTTERNUT LAKE

It's summer, and after ten years away, Allie Beckett has returned to the family cabin beside tranquil Butternut Lake, where as a teenager she spent so many carefree days. She's promised her five-year-old son, Wyatt, they will be happy there. She's promised herself this is the place to begin again after the death of her husband in Afghanistan. The cabin holds so many wonderful memories, but from the moment she crosses its threshold Allie is seized with doubts. Has she done the right thing uprooting her little boy from the only home he's ever known?

Allie and her son are embraced by the townsfolk, and her reunions are joyous ones—with her friend Jax, now a young mother of three with one more on the way, and Caroline, the owner of the local coffee shop. And then there are newcomers like Walker Ford, who mostly keeps to himself—until he takes a shine to Wyatt . . . and to Allie.

Everyone knows that moving forward is never easy, and as the long, lazy days of summer take hold, Allie must learn to unlock the hidden longings of her heart, and to accept that in order to face the future we must also confront—and understand—what has come before.